DARK STATE

Christopher J. Lynch

DARK STATE

Copyright © 2022 Christopher J. Lynch

Cover design by PhillipsCovers.com

ISBN: 978-0-9907273-5-4

ACKNOWLEDGEMENTS

I would like to thank the following people without whom this book would not have been possible:

Robert Garde and Richard Landis for their expertise of wastewater treatment.

Mike Wenschlag for his infinite knowledge of refinery co-generation operation.

Eric Koch for his vast experience with diesel production and transportation.

Jim Hone for his expertise of emergency response planning and implementation.

Anonymous sources from the Los Angeles Department of Water and Power and Southern California Edison for confirming my worst fears.

Natalie Coric for her skill in respiratory treatment.

Richard Rudman for his vast knowledge of commercial emergency radio communications.

Daniel Gorton for his expertise of dialysis treatment and facilities.

Zach Pena for helping me understand military operations and procedures.

Robb Mayberry of CAL-OES, for his assistance helping me understand the operation of disaster response and management.

Don Boland of the California Utilities Emergency association for his intimate knowledge of California's utility infrastructure.

Professor Fred Fuld III for his expertise of stock markets, currency supplies, and all things financial.

Lloyd Klefstad for sharing with me his knowledge of airport emergency operations.

Andrea L. Rodgers of the Parent-Sorensen Mortuary and Crematory for her expertise in mortuary practices and processes.

Richard Prior for his know-how of emergency radio operations.

This book is dedicated to the tireless work of the men and women of CAL-OES, the California Office of Emergency Services, who have also provided incredible access and support in my endeavor.

PREFACE

Although DARK STATE is a work of fiction, it could very easily become fact.

The genesis of the book originated several years ago during my previous career as an industrial electrician at a major oil refinery. I was in a meeting to discuss an upcoming large-scale project for the expansion of one of our plants. An engineer inquired about the delivery timeline for a specific piece of specialized electrical equipment—in this case, an electrical sub-station.

"That's nine months to a year out," one of the others in the room replied, and so we went on about our business.

Often, the premise of a novel is sparked by a single utterance, experience, or observation of the writer. And that was the case here.

As off-hand as the statement was about the long lead time of the sub-station, it piqued my curiosity. What if a piece of equipment—critical to the operation of the grid—was destroyed or otherwise rendered useless and, it had a similarly long lead-time? How would its lack of availability impact our society...for nine months...or a year?

And so, I began an earnest quest to learn as much as possible about the grid. I read Phillip F. Schewe's book, THE GRID, which went into great detail about not just the functionality and design of the grid, but also the history of electricity and how we got to point where a large, interconnected system was required. I also read, Ted Koppel's book, LIGHT'S OUT, which further highlighted the vulnerability of our grid as well as the long lead time of some of its vital components.

In both Koppel's and Schewe's books, each postulated that the single most important part of the grid wasn't the wires, the transmission towers, or even the power plants themselves, (there are approximately 1,500 in California), it was the HPTs, or high-power transformers. HPTs are the big links in the chain that make up an electrical grid. They are massive, specially designed pieces of equipment. And, they have lead times of a year or more. Sadly, they are no longer manufactured in the US.

More ominous is the vulnerability of these critical pieces of equipment. Most are remotely located and have marginally effective security. As if to underscore their exposure, an HPT station on Metcalf, California near San Jose was the subject of an attack in 2013, in which snipers disabled several transformers with high powered rifles.

Fortunately, other substations were able to maintain system integrity, and grid disruption was minimal. Security officials admit that we were lucky; if conditions had been different, the results could have been catastrophic. They considered Metcalf to be a 'probing' or practice attack.

That attack initiated the commissioning of a report to Congress in 2014 entitled: Physical Security of the U.S. Power Grid: High-Voltage Transformer Substations. The report was prepared by Paul W. Parfomak a Specialist in Energy and Infrastructure Policy from the Congressional Research Service. https://sgp.fas.org/crs/homesec/R43604.pdf

Mr. Parfomak highlighted the criticality of the HPTs as well as their exposure to attack. The report was also made available to the energy companies. Since then, in my opinion, little has been done to mitigate the risks cited in the document.

In 2017, I traveled to the Devers substation near Palm Springs, California to witness just how defenseless the facility was. I drove right up to the rear yard, and was able to get to within 200 feet of the targets: 5 HPTs (See picture below). The only thing separating me from them was a thin 6-foot-high chain link fence topped with a few limp strands of barbed wire. I took pictures, walked around, and spent approximately 20 minutes examining the facility. No one inquired about my presence there. My dark suspicions were confirmed.

At Devers 500 KVA sub-station, circa 2017

Since my visit, the Devers station and others have 'beefed up' security by installing 10-foot-high block walls and badge operated electric gates. But there are no bollards to protect the gate from a vehicular assault. And as far as the effectiveness of the wall, I recalled an age-old security adage; "Show me a ten-foot-high wall, and I'll show you an eleven-foot ladder." Bottom line; gates, locks, and walls, only keep out honest people. Perimeter security is woefully inadequate considering the value of the equipment!

I followed my visit to Devers with more extensive research: learning about electrical grid layout and design, HPT station locations, grid vulnerabilities, and most importantly, the devastating and debilitating effects if all of 25 stations were destroyed in a coordinated attack. The information was from open sources including many Government websites. One of the most important of these was The Power Outage Incident Annex to the Response and Recovery Federal Interagency Operational Plans. Link: https://www.fema.gov/sites/default/files/2020-07/fema_incident-annex_power-outage.pdf It is an amazing and frightful read. You will find the links to other sources at the end of relevant chapters.

I also spoke to experts within the electrical utilities industry: first responders, communications, fuel delivery, back-up generators, and CAL-OES (California Office of Emergency Services) personnel who allowed me unfettered access to their technical specialists, during a private tour of their facility. Additionally, I toured CAL-ISO, the control hub for California's electrical grid. It was a sobering look at the susceptibility of the grid and the precarious existence of California's residents.

So, if you would like to see how easy it is to take down the California grid, and just how devastating such an attack would be, simply turn the page.

"The enemy will never attack you where you are strongest...He will attack where you are weakest. If you do not know your weakest point, be certain, your enemy will."

—Sun Tzu, on The Art of War

PART I:
LAMBS TO THE SLAUGHTER

CHAPTER ONE
(TEN MONTHS EARLIER)

Chinese Ministry of State Security
Beijing, China

China's Minister of Science stepped into the conference room, along with his country's Ambassador to Iran. The windowless room was considered the most secure in the building, and was built inside another chamber fitted with a mesh of fine copper wire known as a 'Faraday Cage.' Already seated at the table were the Chinese's counterparts; the Iranian Ambassador, and the Iranian Minister of Science.

To enter the room, they had all been screened by no less than three armed guards, all of whom checked for—and then relieved them of—any electronic devices, as well as paper and pen. Each attendee was then required to strip naked, submit to a body scan, and don powder blue Tyvek suits with disposable paper slippers. The uniformity had the effect of making the parties in attendance appear on equal footing, but everyone knew that was not the case.

The room was furnished with four simple chairs, and a small conference table with a glass top to ensure visibility of all movements. No surprises here. A small white board with a marker and eraser sat on the table. CCTV cameras were mounted in every corner of the room, as well as in the ceilings and floors.

Even with all of the countermeasures in place, the Chinese knew that no place could be one hundred percent secure against eavesdropping, and so it was already understood by all parties that they would only communicate by words written on the white board. After the meeting, the board would be triple erased, and incinerated.

The Iranians stood and the four men shook hands wordlessly before sitting down. The Chinese Ambassador reached for the white board and wrote in Chinese characters; *"We are here to discuss our mutual enemy."*

The Iranians looked at each other and then the ambassador wrote; *"The Americans?"*

The two Chinese men nodded their heads gravely.

For decades, the Americans had been exerting their will on the People's Republic in an attempt to keep their great country in the dark ages. Now, after years of toil and sacrifice, China was finally emerging as a world economic power, only to be beaten down by the imperialists with crippling trade sanctions, vilification of their human rights record, and meddling in their rightful claim to Taiwan. As far as the party officials were concerned, the time had come to go on the offensive.

More importantly, the Chinese knew the Iranians had suffered equally, if not more so, from the American aggressors and their Israel-pandering/Islamophobic tendencies, and would be willing to go along with their plan.

The Chinese Ambassador wiped the board clean and then wrote; *"We have an offer, if you are interested."*

The Iranian Ambassador responded noncommittally by scrawling; *"It is possible."*

The Chinese Ambassador smiled and nodded to their guests. Then he picked up the marker, and handed it to his country's Minister of Science.

The Minister of Science leaned over and wrote a single word on the white board; *"Krytrons."*

Both Iranians' eyes went wide with disbelief.

Used as triggers for nuclear weapons, the high voltage, high-speed switching devices were on a short list of items that the United States and the International Atomic Energy Agency (IAEA) kept under extremely tight control. The Chinese knew the Iranians could surreptitiously enrich all the uranium it wanted, but without the triggers to start the fissile reaction, they would have nothing but a mass of radioactive metal to show for their efforts. The Chinese had the devices, and Iran desperately needed them for its secret weapons program. Now the only question was, what would they do to get them?

The Iranian Ambassador turned to his science minister, who swallowed so hard his Adam's apple bobbed in his neck. He nodded his head vigorously.

Although they kept their expressions neutral, inwardly, the two Chinese officials were amused by the Iranian's response. The ancient Persians had always fancied themselves as being among the savviest of traders of everything from camels to their prized hand-woven rugs. Now though, the Chinese were holding the cards, and the Iranians were the suckers at the table.

The Iranian Ambassador picked up the pen and quickly wrote; *"What do you require?"*

The Chinese Ambassador smiled again, and then took his sweet time erasing the board; the Iranians could afford to sweat a little.

Finally, he wrote;

"A favor."

CHAPTER TWO
(PRESENT DAY)

Banning, California
Wednesday, 2:24 p.m.
- 12 hours, 11 minutes

For the fifth time since he and his family had checked into the Pioneer Motel, Muhammad Dujani carefully drew back the curtain and peered into the parking lot. The orange and white U-Haul truck still sat in its parking space and appeared unmolested; no one was taking an interest in it. That was good. When it was dark and guests had settled into their rooms for the evening, it would be even better. Allah had willed it.

His family car, a late model mini-van that his wife and children would escape in when the time was right, was parked next to the truck. No one was interested in it as well. To all appearances, they were simply another family sick of the political climate and high taxes of California, looking to find a better way of life. That was the story Muhammad had given the desk clerk when he checked in, being careful not to overplay his hand and arouse suspicion.

"Kaifa haloka?" his wife, Bana asked him.

"I'm fine," he replied to her in English.

He slowly moved the curtain back to its resting place, and turned toward her. He placed his hands on her shoulders and took stock of the woman he had married a decade ago in Turkey.

They had been among the first to flee from Syria after the Arab Spring had backfired and Assad's government began to crackdown on anyone who did not pledge unconditional support for his brutal and corrupt regimen. They soon made their way to England where they settled, hoping the stay would be temporary and that the Americans and Europeans would come to their rescue and liberate their homeland.

But the young engineer from Damascus and his wife soon learned they were to be left out in the cold. The Europeans could never find consensus on how to handle the situation, and the American President at the time was an impotent coward concerned more about the rights of homosexuals and global warming than genocide. Worse yet was the next administration, who had all but declared war on Islam. Before long, Muhammad Dujani had joined a Mosque in London, and was set forth on the path toward radicalization.

The Americans, he understood now, only cared about the Middle East as far as they could drill an oil well into the ground or to protect their Zionist controllers, the Israelis. They had been in bed with the hedonistic Saudis for eighty years, and they were never going to be part of any solution unless it served their purposes. The Americans were the problem, and they would remain so until something drastic happened to wake them from their comfortable slumber. A plan was soon hatched that would initiate that change.

By arranging for employment in California at a job that would not set off any alarm bells, his handlers at the Mosque in London were able to secure a temporary work visa for him in the United States. Before long, the Dujanis had left England and Muhammad had taken a position at a company that manufactured equipment for food processing, and moved his family to the Los Angeles area where he was instructed to wait patiently for further instruction. Five months later, those instructions came.

It had been a long day. Earlier, he had packed up his family's necessary belongings, along with a bare minimum for himself, loaded them into the mini-van, and driven east out of Los Angeles. He met with his handler in a coffee shop in a busy strip mall in West Covina. The man gave him the keys to the U-Haul truck, a satellite photo (courtesy Google Earth) of the intended target, and a new iPhone.

The phone was set up with GPS directions to his site, although he was still instructed to memorize the photo, especially where he was to park the truck. The phone also had a phony Facebook account established and he was given the login name and password. His instructions were to monitor it for a specific posting from one of his Facebook 'friends.' Muhammad nodded that he understood the instructions, and swore he would not fail Allah.

"Allahu Akbar," his handler had said.

5

Back at the motel, the couple's two children, a boy Ahmad, aged four, and Fabia, a girl, three, were watching a movie on an iPad when Muhammad heard the distinctive chime of a Facebook notification. He unlocked the phone and examined the posting. It was from the Facebook 'friend' he was supposed to be monitoring and contained a picture of an innocuous-looking American family enjoying Disneyland along with the verbiage, "Having a great time at the happiest place on Earth!"

Muhammad knew the Facebook profile was phony, as was his, and that the picture had been pirated from someone else's social media account. But nothing mattered about the posting, other than the time it came in: 2:35 p.m.

He "liked" the posting, which was his way of checking in, and noted that seven others had already done so. Then he looked longingly at his wife and his children, knowing he had only twelve hours to live.

CHAPTER THREE

Standing next to the pallets of bottled water at the front of Johnson's Supermarket, Store Manager Barbara Williams requested the report number from the police officer.

"Four-one-four-seven-two," he recited blandly.

She copied the number into the small notepad she always kept in her pocket and said, "Thanks," as nicely as she could, realizing the altercation—no matter who's fault it was, would create a mountain of paperwork for her to deal with.

Just great, she thought. As if she weren't behind enough already today, she would have to deal with this situation. There would be a report to write up to send to the company's headquarters, endless back and forth emails, and she would have to deal with Dean Timmons, the employee who had gotten into the fracas that left a suspected shoplifter with a bloody nose, possibly even broken.

She started back to her office at the rear of the store, but before she could take two steps, a cashier stopped her.

"I haven't taken my break yet," the young girl said.

"Okay," Barbara said and glanced at the other registers. Three more were open, but one only had a single customer in it. She turned to the next customer in the line for the cashier.

"Ma'am, would you mind moving to register three?'

The woman looked over with an expression of irritation and appeared to be on the verge of protesting. Then, after a moment, she huffed and began pushing her cart to the other register.

"Thank you," Barbara said pleasantly to her.

Just as the woman moved off, another man, who was a transient and a regular at the store, absently took her place in line. He was Caucasian, on the shorter side and compactly built. He appeared to be about thirty years old, but it was difficult to tell as his skin had the dark, leathery appearance of someone who lived in the elements 24/7. Unlike many of the homeless, his hair was kept closely cropped. Several scars were visible on his scalp.

The employees at the store had given him the nickname "Batteries," as this constituted the bulk of his purchases. One of his prized possessions was an old-school type boom-box which he carried with him and listened to constantly, usually tuned to news or talk radio shows.

He never said anything or caused trouble, and always paid in cash—paper and coin—probably from the recycled cans and bottles he collected.

"Sir," Barbara said. "Could you please move over to this other register?"

He looked at her mutely, then shuffled over.

Barbara slipped between the registers and closed the metal gate behind her, preventing any new customers from queuing up.

"Finish here and then take your break," she called out over her shoulder.

"Okay," she heard the cashier respond, followed by the ubiquitous beeps as items were scanned through the bar-code reader.

On her way to her office, she turned to the left and headed toward the canned goods aisle where she knew Timmons was stocking shelves. He was a good kid, really, but he tended to jump into things too aggressively. A standout linebacker at the local high school, he was quick to show off his physical abilities when it came to dealing with shoplifters, derelicts, and other sundry troublemakers a grocery store had to deal with on an almost daily basis. His nickname on the gridiron was "Mean Dean," and Barbara didn't want him to develop the same reputation here at Johnson's.

She was almost to the end of the canned food aisle when her cell phone started buzzing. She pulled out her phone, and saw the call was from her teenage daughter, Olivia.

She slipped the phone back into her pocket and let the call go to voicemail. Employees were forbidden to use their phones any time other than their breaks, and she didn't want to set a bad example by demonstrating a double standard.

She turned the corner into the aisle and saw Timmons standing next to a half-empty box of canned green beans. Next to him was Stephanie Pratt, a head cashier who also served as the union steward for the cashiers, baggers, and stock boys. The two had their heads leaning toward one another and were in a muted conversation. Both of them stopped suddenly and turned to Barbara as she came around the corner. It was well known Stephanie didn't like Barbara, but Barbara didn't care. She was here to run a store, not win a popularity contest with her employees.

She marched up to the two and looked straight at Timmons, who turned his gaze downward. She noticed the knuckles on his right hand still had some blood on them.

"Are you okay?" she asked, hoping to come off as sincere.

"Yeah." The burly kid nodded.

"Good. I'm glad to hear it. When you finish here, you need to come to my office so we can talk about this."

"He can have me present," Stephanie chimed in unnecessarily. Barbara was well versed in the union rules, having been a steward herself before moving into management.

"I understand his rights," Barbara said flatly, not looking at her. "Whenever you're done here, Dean."

She marched away and started again to her office. She turned the corner at the end of the canned food aisle and was stopped by a middle-aged man.

"Excuse me," he said. "Do you carry pine nuts?"

Barbara turned and pointed.

"Aisle thirteen, about midway down. They're right next to the dried fruit."

"Thanks."

She continued on to the rear of the store and started to climb the stairs to her cramped office. On the way up, she pulled out her phone, unlocked it and listened to the voice mail from her daughter.

"Mom it's me," the recording said. "Can you bring home some Tampax? I just started my period, and we're almost out again."

She pushed through the door to her office and sat down at her desk.

Sure, she typed, and hit send.

She set the phone down on her desk, shook the mouse to wake up her computer, logged in, and began typing up her report of the incident.

At least there was some good news today, she thought wryly; her teenaged daughter was still having her periods.

CHAPTER FOUR

Pittsburg, California
Wednesday, 4:47 p.m.
- 9 hours, 48 minutes

Although he was in a hurry to get home, Walter Gronsky still wasn't going to take any chances. He altered his route home as he always did, and before pulling into his apartment, drove his four-wheeled drive Jeep around the block several times looking for any suspicious cars, persons, or things out of place.

He lived in a tiny one-bedroom apartment in Pittsburg, an industrial suburb located in the East Bay region of the San Francisco Bay Area. From a racial and social standpoint, he could not have picked a more incongruent place to live. Pittsburg was, for the most part, a liberal city, homosexual friendly, and with a substantial immigrant population, many of whom were in the US illegally, and probably lived in his building.

Liberals, Walter Gronsky knew, maintained an attitude of *Live and Let Live*—and this would be their downfall.

Seeing nothing out of order, he pulled his vehicle into his assigned space in the apartment building's underground parking lot. He kept the motor running and put the gear selector into reverse just to be on the safe side. With his foot pressed on the brake pedal but ready to punch the accelerator, he looked around carefully. Seeing no one, he finally shifted into park and switched off the motor. He grabbed a gym bag on the seat next to him and unzipped it, inserting his hand into the bag to remove his .45 caliber Glock G-38 pistol. It was like all of his firearms; unregistered, purchased at various gun shows or parking lots throughout the country, and had the serial number ground off and peened to make it untraceable. Screw the God dammed nosey government!

He tucked the gun into a holster in the small of his back, slipped his windbreaker down over it to conceal it, and stepped out of the Jeep. He closed the door as silently as he could and hit the key fob to lock it and set the alarm.

He headed to his apartment on the second story, walking past the piles of trash some of the residents had left for someone else to deal with. In his mind, Walter already had decided who the offenders were.

"Fucking useless spics," he said bitterly under his breath.

He climbed the steps to the second-floor landing and looked around for any strangers lurking about. Seeing none, he walked down the landing toward his apartment, but continued past his door, giving it a furtive glance to see if it had been disturbed.

He stopped at the end of the landing, turned around, and watched and listened for a few more minutes.

No one had followed him and all he could hear was the sound of some crappy Mexican soap opera blaring from one of the apartments. He smelled rancid oil and imagined one of his neighbors' frying stacks of tortillas again.

Don't those greasers eat anything but fucking tortillas and beans? He wondered angrily.

Satisfied, he turned back toward his apartment and unlocked the door. He opened the door and stepped quickly inside, drawing his Glock in the same swift movement. He didn't close or lock the door behind him, lest he need to make a hasty escape, but pushed it so that it was only a few inches open.

He didn't switch on any lights, and instead jumped to the side of the door, eliminating the possibility he would create a silhouette against the outside light, thus making himself an easy target. The windows had aluminum foil on them, and with the room pitch black, any intruders would be at a disadvantage.

He waited silently for a few moments, listening and watching for any movement. He didn't sense any, but before he turned on the lights or closed and locked the door behind him, he switched on the ultra-high intensity flashlight that was mounted to the underside of his Glock.

Instantly the cramped and cluttered room was bathed in a piercing blue-white light of the 600-lumen device. Besides giving him the advantage of sight, if anyone moved out from the shadows, he could easily blind them—before he shot their asses dead of course.

Not detecting any movement, he moved back to the front door and pushed it closed further, so that it was open just a crack. Then he moved off into his bedroom, sweeping the light and the Glock as he went. He checked under the bed, and then turned toward the closet. He had removed the closet door long ago, and aimed the flashlight beam below the bottoms of his clothes. No legs protruded, so he moved on to the windows. They were covered in foil as well, and closed permanently with heavy-duty lag bolts. They were undisturbed.

The last room to check was the bathroom. It also had its door removed and no shower curtain. From outside the bathroom, he could see that no one was standing in the tub, but Walter Gronsky didn't take anything for granted, and so he approached it carefully and peered over the lip carefully to see if anyone was lying in wait. He wondered—and not for the first time, if he shot at someone and missed, how much the slug might ricochet around the porcelain coated cast iron.

With the adjoining rooms cleared, he moved back into the living room and took one final look around. Satisfied, he moved back across the room and closed the door and locked the two double-keyed deadbolts.

Then he switched on the lights.

Walter Gronsky was home.

CHAPTER FIVE

Lakewood, California
Wednesday, 4:50 p.m.
- 9 hours, 45 minutes

As she did every day at around five o'clock, Barbara Williams gave a turnover regarding store issues to her replacement, Second Shift Store Manager, Carla Gonzalez. There was a freezer on aisle six that seemed to be having issues again. Several crates of Brussel sprouts had spoiled and had to be replaced. The women's restroom had a leak in the sink. And of course, she told her the news about the altercation between Dean Timmons and the shoplifter.

Satisfied she had adequately briefed her replacement, she left through the rear exit of the store, and began the trek home. Rather than drive, she walked home almost every day—except for the rare occasions when Southern California experienced rain.

Just as she turned at the first block, she saw the homeless man, Batteries, as he set up a makeshift camp on a bus bench. It was illegal in the city to be in possession of a shopping cart, and so a cast-off baby carrier filled with all of his worldly possessions sat nearby. His radio rejuvenated with fresh C cells; Barbara could just make out the vitriol of a talk radio show emanating from the speakers.

Transients notwithstanding, she didn't mind the walk home. It was only half a mile, and the neighborhoods she passed through were relatively clean and safe. Lakewood was a comfortable bedroom community south and east of Los Angeles, and bordered by the large town of Long Beach to the south. As she walked along the wide boulevards with landscaped medians, she had some time to think and unwind a little bit before getting home.

After discovering her husband, Tom, was having an affair with a coworker a year and half ago, they had split up. A few months of trying to get him into therapy to 'patch things up,' had yielded nothing but painful wounds, and so she came to the realization that he had no desire to reconcile, even though he would take a substantial financial hit. His new girlfriend was half of Barbara's age.

Their divorce was bitter, tumultuous—and costly. She got to keep their four-bedroom house, but even with her alimony, child support, and income from managing the store, she was unable to continue to pay the mortgage on it, and had to sell it back to her ex—a decision she loathed.

Since then, she had done a lot of downsizing and consolidation. She sold off or gave away the bulk of her furniture, and moved her two children and her mom into a tiny three-bedroom apartment they all managed to squeeze into. Her mom functioned as both babysitter and taxi service for her two children while she was at work, and therefore had use of their only car during the day.

It wasn't perfect, but they had a roof over their heads, and they were safe and secure. She often wondered though, if she was doing the best she could for her family.

CHAPTER SIX

Cal ISO Headquarters
Folsom, California
Wednesday, 6:49 p.m.
- 7 hours, 46 minutes

Supervisor Gary Dicey finished reading the turnover report from the previous shift and rose from his desk in the vast control center of Cal-ISO. He had some emails to follow up on, and some new ones to send, but he still liked getting up and talking to his operators before he buried himself in the mundane tasks of his job. After all, even though he could analyze the data displayed on the giant screens as much as anyone else, his team of operators were closer to the action and therefore really had a handle on what was going on with the California grid.

Created following the 1992 passage of the Federal Energy Policy Act, Cal-ISO, or California Independent Service Operators, had assumed control of the bulk of the management of the state's electrical energy. The organization, which was made up of over 500 employees, kept a pulse on the estimated 55,000 megawatts of capacity produced by more than 1,400 far-flung power plants located throughout the state. The incoming power was connected and managed by 25,526 miles of transmission lines, thousands of transformers, and hundreds of switching stations. In short, Cal-ISO's mission was to keep the lights on for nearly 40 million Californians.

Trailing in the race towards deregulation of other industries, the champions of the Cal-ISO project had argued that if electricity was thought of as a commodity—like oil or gasoline, it could become more reliable and cheaper by nature of being traded in a true market place environment. Electricity was bought, sold, traded and managed here by bringing together the various suppliers and consumers.

The modern steel and glass building, which was completed in 1998, served as the nerve center for all of this horse-trading and acted as the traffic controller of electrons on California's enormously complex electrical grid. It was an ultra-secure location with an armed security force, and quadruple redundant remote servers. The location in Folsom had even been selected based on the area's seismic stability, as well as its distance from the California flood plain. Nothing was left to chance when it came to operating the grid.

Gary stepped over to one of the two desks that handled the generation side of the energy equation.

"How are we looking Steve?" he asked.

Steve Ory was one of the senior operators in the room, and had started at about the same time as Gary. The two had trained together, spent many a long shift together, and had ridden out some of the power outages that occurred over the years. A former nuclear sub reactor operator from the US Navy, Steve had the bearing and focus that was required for this type of job.

"Looking good," he said confidently. "We've got three peakers set to come on line in the next couple of hours. That should more than make up for the Backus scheduled outage. And even if one of the peakers dropped, Sally over in market control said that she could find 5 megawatts real fast to make it up."

"Great," Gary said, placing his hand on Steve's shoulder. Even though Gary's star had risen faster than Steve's, and he had made it to the position of shift manager before him, there was no animosity between the two men. Gary expected as much from a military veteran; the men and women who served our country understood the respect for rank better than anyone did.

Gary moved away from Steve's desk and towards the center of the large control room floor, named the Yakout Mansour Control Center after the former president and CEO of Cal-ISO.

There were twelve identical semicircular desks in the room manned by ten operators. Like Gary, all of them worked the same shift as he; twelve hours on for four days in a row, followed by two days off. All of the desks contained an array of LCD displays that provided real time data of the flow of electricity in and out of the grid for the operator. At the front of the room were giant monitors that displayed time and frequency, deviation, actual versus calculated electricity demand curves, P-min or Power Minimum, as well as status and alarm displays.

At the far right of the array of screens, a specialized Google Earth display showed real time thermal as well as visual imaging for the state of California. The operators of Cal-ISO used this to keep tabs on wildfires as well as climate fluctuations. Weather was a huge factor in the power industry and to that end, a TV monitor in the center of the wall ran the Weather Channel 24/7.

Gary made a quick scan of the giant board and knew he should have felt good about what he was seeing. At 59.98 hertz, the frequency—or 'freeks' as the operators referred to them, were well within the required tolerance. They also had no ACE (Area Control Error), or EMS (Energy Management System) alarms. All in all, a smooth-running ship.

But something was nagging at the twenty two-year veteran of the energy industry. He felt as if things were flowing too smoothly, and in a job where 40 million people depended on you to keep the juice flowing, there was always something to fret about. Maybe the peakers wouldn't come on line as scheduled? Or maybe a freak electrical storm in the central valley would spark a wildfire that would bring down some transmission lines?

Maybe this, maybe that. He shook it off and returned to his desk. He knew the best operators in the industry surrounded him, and that they could handle anything that was thrown at them.

Besides that, this was his last shift. He could look forward to his two days off and being able to attend his granddaughter's recital on Friday. He smiled at the thought of seeing her up on the stage performing.

He sat back down at his desk and returned to his emails. In just the short period of time he had walked the floor, five new ones had popped into his in-box.

CHAPTER SEVEN

Shanice Dixon was working late, as was her nature. In front of her on the two computer monitors were the latest stats regarding the golden state's snowpack, predicted stream runoff, and most importantly, vegetation growth. The information was data recently compiled by the California Department of Forestry and Fire Protection, or CAL-FIRE. The agency was comprised of scientists, climatologists, and seasoned firefighting professionals, and was responsible for fire prediction models, as well as helping to coordinate responses for the wildfires that plagued California on a seasonal basis.

So closely did CAL-FIRE work with CAL-OES, it even maintained a permanent office in the main building on the fourteen-acre site. Shanice had just concluded a very long and in-depth meeting regarding the forecast and contingency planning, but as was her nature, she still had to go over the data one more time - just to be sure.

At thirty-eight years old, she was the youngest director of the massive CAL-OES, the epicenter for disaster management in California. After the Covid-19 pandemic faded, the agency's previous director, Alan Brewer, had decided to call it quits and retire. And in the weeks and days before his well-deserved retirement party, he had lobbied the state's governor to make Shanice his replacement.

Brewer had worked closely with Shanice through the years, and saw firsthand her drive and dedication, but as a Chief Deputy Director with only two years in the job, her catapult to the top spot in the states disaster management agency did not come without controversy.

As a woman—*and an African American*, she knew that many around her considered it to be a social promotion based on not just her gender, but her race as well. In PR terms, she was what was known as a 'two-fer.' Not only would she be the first African American in the job, but the first female as well. And for the public image of a high-profile organization such as CAL-OES, it simply didn't get any better than that.

Shanice knew the suspicions that surrounded her elevation to the top spot, but she was no stranger to adversity, and had always felt she had to work twice as hard to measure up in other people's eyes, including her own father.

A social psychologist, he had once given Shanice and her twin sister, Jada, an IQ test when they were ten years old. The purpose of the test was, "just for fun," he had said.

But the results of the test—in which her twin scored seven points higher, left an indelible impression on Shanice that she would have to work harder and smarter to prove herself to her dad, and to everyone around her.

She feverishly worked her way onto the honor roles of both her elementary and high schools, and it paid off. In high school, she was both valedictorian as well as number one in her class with a 4.6 GPA. Scholarship offers flooded in, and she finally settled on dual degrees in Master of Arts in Emergency Management/Homeland Security, as well as an MBA at Arizona State University.

Still with insatiable drive, she doubled down on her studies and graduated Summa Cum Laude from the prestigious university. She was currently working on her PhD in emergency management while also juggling the myriad duties of her position at OES. On average, she got by on four hours of sleep per night.

Her cell phone buzzed that she had a new text. She looked down to see that it was from her husband, George, an accomplished man in his own right as a successful CPA.

The text read: *"Dinner? Or should I just plan on not seeing you until breakfast? LOL"*

Shanice sighed, and tapped out a response.

"Sorry," she wrote. *"Another 20 minutes. I promise."* She followed the verbiage with a couple of red hearts.

She tapped 'SEND' and then went back to the fire season forecast, looking for any gaps in the planning that they needed to get ahead of. Besides wildfires and accompanying mudslides, the only other major disaster California and the OES typically dealt with were the unpredictable and sometimes catastrophic earthquakes that hit them every couple of decades.

Two disasters were plenty to have to deal with in a state as large as this one, Shanice thought wryly. *Thank God we didn't have hurricanes, tornados, or blizzards to contend with as well.*

In a few seconds, her husband replied to her text with an emoticon of a tiny yellow face, its mouth a straight line and one eyebrow cocked skeptically.

Shanice stared at it and smiled thinly at her husband's comical retort. Truthfully though, she felt skeptical herself that she would be out of here in twenty minutes.

CHAPTER EIGHT

Lakewood, California
Wednesday, 9:14 p.m.
- 5 hours, 21 minutes

Jake Sullivan waited as he did every night to make his final move. Lurking in the shadows under some trees by the end of the lot at the fast-food restaurant, he watched and waited as the store served the late-comers.

As a former sniper with the Army Rangers serving in the Afghanistan War, he understood better than most the value of patience. Patience to watch and wait for the enemy, and patience to wait for the best shot. Because of this mettle, he had racked up an impressive number of confirmed kills, was richly decorated, and had risen quickly to the rank of Gunnery Sargent.

He had forgotten about most of the men—and some of the women, that he had killed; they were targets, and no more. Seeing their blood explode from the exit wound, be it head or chest, had little effect on him. It was what was known darkly amongst the troops as 'the Pink Cloud,' and it was the gory confirmation that the target had sucked its last breath and was neutralized. But one target stuck with him, and became his undoing.

His unit was stationed in Kandahar supporting regular Army and Marine units. The area he was in had recently seen a large uptick in IED attacks on vehicles, many using civilians, including children. Tensions were high, and Jake and his spotter, Lance Corporal Ted Green, were set up on a rooftop overlooking one of the busy intersections of the city when a convoy of Humvees moved through. Traffic bogged down, and then came to an abrupt stop as a cart carrying dead chickens for market tipped over in the intersection. The Humvees were trapped, along with the men in them.

"Stand by," Ted had said warily, and scanned the intersection with his binoculars.

Jake pulled the M24 Sniper rifle tighter into his shoulder and waited for Ted's instructions.

"Contact!" Ted said. "Running up to the second Hummer. Shit!! He's got a package. He's got a package!"

Automatically, Jake swung the rifle around to the second Humvee. What he saw gave him pause. It was a young boy, no older than ten, carrying a box. He was heading straight for the driver's side door of the vehicle.

"Kid!" he yelled to Ted, hoping his partner would reassess and call him off.

"Orders Jake!" Ted said. "Orders! We've got to take him. Drop him, drop him!"

Jake knew it was the truth, they had orders to shoot anyone who got within thirty feet of a vehicle. He took a deep breath, lined up the crosshairs on the young boy's back and squeezed the trigger. The 7.62mm round rocketed out of the heavy barrel at over 2,500 feet per second and slammed into the boy's back, exploding his chest as it expanded and passed through.

Blood and organ matter, including parts of the boy's heart, blew out onto the street. A thousand people scattered, and women started to scream. Instantly, the Humvees went on high alert. Troops, called 'dismounts' jumped from the vehicle and set up lines of fire.

Ted slapped Jake on the back and said, "You saved their fucking asses Jake. You saved our guys."

Except he didn't.

A subsequent investigation found that the boy was only carrying loaves of bread to sell to the troops. Jake was exonerated for the incident and was considered to be following the rules of engagement of the combat zone, but it would be the last time he would do so.

He refused to go out on patrols and was written up for being insubordinate and derelict of duty. He was sent to the unit's psychiatrist, who did little for him other than to tell him that he wasn't crazy, and needed to do what he was told. Finally, he snapped and punched a First Lieutenant.

He was put on the first plane back home and dishonorably discharged from the service, a death sentence in what is known in military circles as, "having bad paper."

Back home, he fared no better and was unable to reintegrate with civilian society. His dishonorable discharge prevented him from finding employment at even the most menial of jobs and so, like many other veterans suffering from PTSD, he ended up on the homeless on the streets.

CHAPTER NINE

Lakewood, California
Wednesday, 9:27 p.m.
- 5 hours, 8 minutes

Olivia looked up from the screen on her phone just long enough to lash out at her mother.

"I can't believe you mom!" she bellowed. "I'm the only girl in my class who can't go out!"

Barbara Williams sat looking at her daughter, trying to maintain a sympathetic but firm expression and to defuse the volatile situation, but it was tough. She had always known that sooner or later, she was going to have to deal with the raging hormones of adolescence, but she always thought it would be a team effort of her and Tom's, not flying solo through the storm herself. Besides Olivia, she had a six-year-old son, Freddie, who, although he was a bit of a handful himself, was nothing like dealing with the teenaged angst of a girl on the verge of womanhood.

"I'm sorry Olivia, but fourteen years old is too young to start dating."

Staring at the phone display, Olivia tapped a few keys before looking back up.

"No, it's not!" she shot back. "Lots of my friends do."

"Well, that's their parent's decision, not mine," Barbara replied firmly. "I'm sorry."

Her daughter glared at her. "No, you're not!" she challenged.

Olivia's phone chimed, and she navigated the screen to an incoming message.

"Oh great!" she cried. "Everyone's already talking about Nick and I; about how great we are for each other!"

She turned her gaze back up at her mom and hissed, "I hate you!"

They both stared silently at each other in the cramped living room; two boxers glaring from opposite corners. Witnessing the battle of wills unfold was Barbara's mom, Jane, who thankfully hadn't interjected and generally ignored the barbs being thrown. She continued to work on her word puzzle, as quiet as a church mouse.

Olivia broke the silence first.

"Maybe I should just go to live with dad," she snipped.

Inwardly, Barbara bristled at the mention of her ex—who was currently off frolicking in Hawaii with his little bimbo. But she kept her expression neutral; she had expected such a power play and threat to come sooner or later. And although she was tempted, she fought the urge to fire back and inform her daughter that her father wanted nothing more to do with his children other than to maintain his child support and tolerate having to see them twice a month. He was too busy playing house with his new younger model.

Realizing she wasn't going to get a rise out of her mom, Olivia stood up in a huff and headed toward her bedroom. She stopped midway across the room and turned to Barbara.

"Where are my Tampax?" she demanded.

Barbara groaned, realizing she had forgotten to pick them up before she left the store.

"Ugh!" she groaned. "I'm sorry Olivia, I forgot. It was a craz—"

"I've only got two left!" her daughter interrupted, then added angrily. "You're impossible!"

She stormed off and headed toward her bedroom.

"Don't slam the do—," Barbara started to say.

The request came too late, as the apartment echoed with the loud bang of a door being slammed shut.

Barbara and her mom sat in silence regarding each other for a long time. She always wondered if her mom thought she should have tried harder to patch things up with Tom. Worse yet, did she think her daughter had not been a 'proper' wife and was the impetus for his infidelity. It was a nagging question in her mind and one that she did not want to broach, fearing she might not enjoy the answer. Finally, she got up and headed into the kitchen.

"Do you want a glass of wine mom?" she called out, reaching under the kitchen counter. "I know I need one."

"No thanks," her mom replied. "Remember, I have my dialysis this Friday."

"Oh yeah, that's right," Barbara called out over her shoulder. "Glad I have this schedule this week."

Barbara returned with a glass of white wine and sat back down in her chair. She took a sip and set it on the table next to her. She looked over at her mom and sighed wearily, hoping to garner some sympathy over the feud with Olivia. It didn't work.

"You were the same way," her mom said matter-of-factly.

"What? No, I wasn't."

"Yes, you were. Remember that boy Bobby Thomas?"

"That was different," Barbara protested. "Kids are much more sexually active these days."

"Not that much," her mom replied.

Barbara let it go and took another sip of wine. She stared out blankly towards the walls of the room, realizing that she didn't have it in her to argue with her mom as well.

Before long, she started to drift off and realized she needed to get to bed. Tomorrow would be another day to slay dragons, both at work and now, at home.

CHAPTER TEN

Walter Gronsky had many sources for intel: *The Proud Boys, Boo-galoo, various Q followers, and the Gilded Three-Elevens,* but his most trusted authority was a fellow freedom fighter by the name of *Patriot Man.* As soon as he heard the familiar voice in his earpiece, he turned up the volume.

He was seated at the tiny kitchen table in his apartment next to his Tecsun PL-660 PLL short-wave radio. A single wire leading up to his earphones connected him to the radio's output jack, ensuring that no one could eavesdrop on him. On the table in front of him was a small notepad, a pen, and his loaded Glock. He also had a disposable lighter in case he had to destroy his notes quickly.

A wire with an alligator clip was attached to the radio's small mast antenna and ran across the room. It was strung over the top of his stove and continued on up into the air vent above it. Protruding through the vent and sticking out into the night sky was a thin homemade antenna Walter had fabricated to increase the radio's ability to pull in signals.

The antenna was not a permanent fixture and he had to surreptitiously extend it when he wanted to listen. It was a lot of work to do every time he tuned in, but the sight of an antenna on the apartment roof might draw unneeded attention from the nosy government, and Walter couldn't take the chance. Now, he would be rewarded for all his efforts.

"Good evening my fellow patriots of The Organization," the voice began. *"It is day one hundred twenty-seven of our battle to retake control of our country...our liberties. Liberties fought for and died for by our white ancestors, brave men and women who stood up to the tyranny of a foreign power of unclean heritage. Liberties which are being systematically siphoned away from us each waking day by our corrupt and compromised government;*

*a government made up of liberals and controlled by the bloodsucking glo-
balist kikes, the perverted faggots, the nigger apologists, and the spic loving
cucks! I ask you, my fellow patriots; are you ready to stand up and do what
is needed to fight this new tyranny!"*

Walter took a deep breath and felt the bile rise in his stomach.
He hated liberals and spics and niggers and faggots, but most of all
he hated the Jews because they controlled everything; our government, our banks, even what movies and TV shows we saw. Fucking
globalist mockies!

*"In fact, information about a new government plot has just been uncov-
ered by our organization that I must share with you! But first, I must tell you
sadly that this information was paid for by the blood of some of our fellow
patriots. And even though time is of the essence, we must have a moment of
silence to honor the memories of these brave individuals who made the ultimate sacrifice."*

A few moments of the hiss of empty radio transmission filled
Walter's earpiece. The passing of these fellow patriots reminded
him just how much of a life and death struggle this war had become. He only imagined the poor souls being dumped into one of
the many mass graves the government maintained for those who
did not cower to their globalist Jew handlers and fall into lock step.
Walter Gronsky vowed he would never become one of the lemmings, and would die before he would ever give up.

*"Thank you, my fellow patriots. Before I share with you the details of this
latest effort by our government to subvert our freedoms, I must take the time
to thank some of our fellow patriots for supporting our cause. Our organization, like many others has to rely on the generous support from people like
you, soldiers in our greater cause. A big thank you goes out to MGTOW from
the heartland of America, Rolling fourteen eighty-eight from the Fourth Re-
ich USA, Ghost Skin Hammer of Stars and Bars Forever, Proud Boy from
Hymie Hater USA..."*

Walter had sent some of his American Eagle gold coins to Patriot man in the past. It was easy enough to do if you listened carefully to the coded instructions included in every transmission. He
made a mental note to send in another donation.

*"Thank you again for your generous donations my fellow patriots. I know
that it may seem like a sacrifice now, but just imagine when we are triumphant
in our battle and you no longer have to pay illegal taxes to the blood-sucking
government to support the free-loading illegal immigrants that have invaded*

our country, and to the lazy and shiftless niggers that roam our streets raping and robbing!"

Patriot Man paused dramatically for effect before continuing.

"And now, for some news that you must hear, information that will save your life! Information which our fellow patriots of the organization have only been able to obtain through the ultimate sacrifice!"

Instinctively, Walter leaned closer to the radio even though he was listening through his earpiece. He picked up his pen and put it to his paper notepad.

"For several months now, the United States government has been quietly recruiting legions of kike attorneys to facilitate the release of tens of thousands of spic and nigger inmates from our jails and prisons. Their plan is to use them as a secret army in a race war to target you and your families. As I broadcast this, legions of these barbarians are quietly being transported into neighborhoods like yours and directed by Antifa, to rape and murder our wives and daughters. Even worse, some of the young ones will be spared death in order to be sold as sex slaves by the Clintons and their henchmen. You, my fellow patriots, God's chosen people of the Arian race, are the only thing, the last rampart in our war to prevent this from happening. But if you will not fight, then this will be the dawn of the white genocide!"

Walter Gronsky felt his face get flush with anger as his breath quickened and his pulse raced. He jotted down a "K" on his notepad along with an arrow pointing to the letters, "N" and "S." Over the letters "N" and "S" he drew a series of straight lines to represent the bars of a prison cell.

"But believe me when I say this my fellow patriots; it will not be a fair fight. Oh no, that's not how the Jew boys play. Those Kike attorneys know that we are armed, armed to the teeth and ready to fight to the death if we need to. So, they are also planning an elaborate ruse to allow the government to declare Marshall Law and to take away our defenses. And make no mistake about it, those hymie globalist are very crafty when it comes to creating lies that the rest of the world believes. Remember the fairy tales about the so called 'Jewish Holocaust.' Well, these slippery bastards are going to be pulling the same stunt very, very soon. We still don't know what it will be, but it will be big!"

"Unfortunately, there are plenty of sheep out there my fellow patriots, cucks who will roll over at the first sign and give up their guns, and then watch as their wives and daughters are raped and then killed in front of them. But our puppet government and the Jews that control them also know

that there are individuals out there like you and I who will not willingly give up our guns, our freedoms, and our lives without a fight. My fellow patriots, this is it. This is the beginning of the white genocide! Will you fight with me, or will you roll over? This is our last stand! This, my fellow patriots, is kill, or be killed!"

Walter threw down his pen and grabbed his Glock angrily. It took all of his resolve not to go out and start shooting every nigger, spic, and kike he could find.

CHAPTER ELEVEN

Lakewood, Calif.
Wednesday 11:22 p.m.
- 3 hours, 13 minutes

Jake Sullivan watched silently from the shadows as the last of the trash was taken out and thrown into the dumpster behind the fast-food restaurant. The remaining lights were extinguished, and the employees exited and headed to their cars. The manager was the last to leave. and he locked and checked the doors on the way out. In a few moments, he was in his car and headed out of the parking lot. Then Jake made his move.

He knew that even though restaurants tried to slow down production the closer they got to closing; less burgers grilled, less fries made, and so forth, they typically always had leftover food that had to be tossed out at the end of the night.

Jake threw his rucksack over and quickly scaled the tiny fenced compound surrounding the dumpster. He opened the lid as silently as possible, climbed in, and then went scavenging.

The first couple of bags he found were from the trash bins located inside the store and contained not just the used wrappers, napkins, and drink cups from the day's customers, but half eaten burgers, random chicken nuggets, and soggy fries drenched in ketchup. He had eaten these slim pickings before out of desperation, but the real good stuff was in the restaurant leftovers.

He struck pay-dirt with the third bag, opening it and smelling the aroma of long kept warm burgers and fries straight from under the lights. He re-tied the bag so as to not give himself away, loaded everything he could pack into his rucksack and returned the same way he had come, leaving no trace of his presence less a lock got installed on the dumpster lid.

The weather forecast on his radio had said the temp was going to dip down tonight, but at least no rain was predicted. Armed with this knowledge, he settled on one of his go-to spots to help him keep warm for the evening.

A medium sized electrical transformer that fed the strip mall where the restaurant was located, sat inside a cinder block enclosure at the far end of the lot. It had a locked metal gate on it, but the top was open to allow ventilation and the walls were only about five feet high, child's-play for someone who was used to scaling the hideouts of insurgents in the 'Sand-box.'

He scanned the parking lot for any prying eyes from customers, workers or - worst of all - other homeless. Not finding any, he grabbed his mummy bag and then ditched his baby carrier into the bushes for the night.

Carrying the sleeping bag, rucksack, and his cherished boom box to the transformer, he deftly scaled the low walls and ducked down in the enclosure.

Inside, the transformer hummed as electrons were invisibly induced from one set of copper coils to another, stepping down the voltage coming from the high voltage lines overhead. The monotonous sound was as soothing as a mother's coos are to her baby.

A gap of about two feet separated the transformer from the block walls on all four sides, leaving him just enough room to squeeze in between. Jake cleared out some trash people had tossed into the enclosure, rolled out his sleeping bag in the gap, and climbed in.

The transformer not only produced the tranquil, white noise that soothed his nerves, but the transfer of energy also gave off heat and the metal sides were toasty warm. He turned in his bag and rolled up onto his side in a fetal position, situating his back against the wall of the device.

Before long, former Army Ranger Jake Sullivan began to drift off, hoping that he wouldn't have another nightmare tonight.

CHAPTER TWELVE

Somewhere over Colorado,
Wednesday, 11:44 p.m. (PST)
- 2 Hours, 51 Minutes

The Gates Learjet 35A cruised comfortably at 37,000 feet, easily clearing the peaks of America's largest mountain range. The custom private jet was headed to Los Angeles from Teterboro Airport in New Jersey. Although it was an older model, the 35A had been upgraded with some of the most advanced avionic systems in the world as well as the GX Aviation's high-speed Ka-band Broadband Service System. It was a pricey addition to an already expensive plane, but as more and more business travelers demanded uninterrupted connectivity, the system provided full time cell phone usage, as well as high speed internet to the plane's occupants.

Alan Binder sat in the forward-facing plush leather seat, his cell phone pressed to his ear, and with venom in his voice. In his other hand, he had a scotch on the rocks—his fourth. The veteran actor had two Golden Globes to his credit, and had been nominated three times, but never garnered an Oscar. He had a star on the Hollywood Walk of Fame, was instantly recognizable, and was still considered an 'A-lister' for big budget films. But in a town with a short memory, and an even greater penchant to toss people to the curb, you were only as good as your last picture—and Alan Binder now had two flops in a row.

"God damn it, Joel!" he screamed into the phone. "Why the hell aren't you at Barbara's party yet?"

Besides the pilot, and copilot, Binder's personal assistant, Marianne Corelli was on board and sitting in the rear facing seat across from him. She was in her mid-twenties, attractive, and was a British ex-pat. Raised in a theatre performing family, she nevertheless grew weary of the stage after a few years. She headed to the United States to stake her own claim acting on the big and small screen, thinking naively that her genuine accent would set her apart from the competition. Before long she realized her miscalculation as there weren't many British roles, and, that the accent was one of the most imitable of all to do.

Realizing her predicament, she switched gears and decided to work on the other side of the camera—far on the other side. She enrolled at USC Film School as a feature film writer, and a couple years later graduated near the top of class. She was talented and driven, but by now was battle hardened and had heard enough horror stories about people not wanting to 'pay their dues' to succeed in this town. She knew what she had to do to make it, no matter what the pain.

In her hands was her iPad, always ready to take notes, retrieve emails, or catch the latest industry gossip for her boss.

"I was working on some important paperwork," Joel Birnbaum replied, knowing nothing would satisfy his most difficult, albeit bankable client.

"Fuck your paperwork!" Binder yelled. "You need to be there!"

"I'm on my way there now. But you know what a bitch traffic is in Beverly Hills."

"Well get your ass there and get to Spinder and get him primed. I don't want that no-talent Cleason to get to him first. I happen to know that Spinder just optioned the script, and is looking to start attaching people. That's *my* fucking role Joel! I need it after those last two dogs you talked me into!"

On the other end of the phone, Joel Birnbaum fought back the urge to sigh.

"Alan," he said carefully. "Nobody knew what was going to happen to those scripts in rewrite. Granted, they were shit, but they're not career killers. You're a great actor, and you can recover."

Binder drained the last of his scotch and signaled Marianne to get him another one. His assistant turned and reached for the bottle of Johnny Walker Blue Label in the mini-bar. She took a fresh glass, added some ice and poured.

"Well, I fucking better recover!" she heard her boss say. "And I need that role to do it Joel. You're my fucking manager for Christ's sake...so fucking manage!"

He terminated the call to his agent just as Marianne handed him a fresh drink and took his empty glass. He took a hearty swallow and exhaled.

Then he looked at his glass and said, "Look at this shit," he said. "When I ask for Blue Label, I expect King-Fucking-George!"

Then he looked up at her and said, "Take a note never to fly with these cheap-ass bastards again."

"Yes Mr. Binder," she said, promptly recording it on her tablet.

Binder took another drink from his glass and swirled it around, seemingly mesmerized by the amber liquid. Then he looked at Marianne.

"When did you say my Ferrari payment was due?" He asked her absently.

Marianne consulted her tablet, and said, "Nine days ago, so it's technically *over*due."

"Send them a letter," he said. "Tell them there was a screw-up with my bank account and that I'll get it to them by the end of the month."

"Yes sir."

"And while you're at it, when did my ex-wife's attorney send that fucking letter demanding more alimony?"

Marianne consulted her tablet again, "A week and a half ago."

"Fucking cunt. She never complained when she was walking on the red carpet with me, or shopping on Rodeo. What did my attorney say?"

Marianne tapped a few more soft keys on her tablet and pulled up the email to Binder from his attorney. "Do you want me to read it to you?" she asked.

"No, God damn it! I can fucking read, just give me the gist of it. Can we fight that bitch or not?"

Marianne scanned the letter and said, "Yes, Mr. Almays says they don't have a case, but they're probably going to take us to trial, so he'll have to prepare a counter argument. 'But don't worry' he says, 'you won't have to shell out any more money.'"

"Ha, Alan Binder snorted. "Except to him! Fifteen-hundred per billable hour! He'll work two hours on it and charge me ten! Attorneys; Blood-sucking cocksuckers!"

He took another swallow of his scotch, then laughed.

"Ha, that's kind of funny, isn't it?" he said.

Marianne was confused, "What's funny Mr. Binder?"

"If you're a cocksucker," he explained. "You really wouldn't be sucking blood - unless you were doing something *really wrong*. Ha, ha, ha!"

Marianne smiled faintly and kept her expression neutral. In public, actor Alan Binder was known as a charming, affable, even generous person with his pet charity to raise awareness for autism. But behind closed doors, he was an arrogant, self-absorbed, vulgar asshole. Before she applied and took the job, she knew that he went through personal assistants like water, but he *was* connected and could be the one who could help get her career as a screenwriter jumpstarted. She just had to grin and bear it until that day came.

He started to make a face then and began rubbing the sides of his shoes together.

"Damn it," he said. "My foot itches!"

He lifted his leg and put his foot into Marianne's lap.

She set down her tablet, removed his shoe, and started to scratch his foot.

CHAPTER THIRTEEN

Banning, California
Thursday, 1:50 a.m.
- 0 hours, 45 minutes

"Alhamdulillah rabbil aalamin," Muhammad whispered softly in the dim hotel room. For the past hour, the Syrian had been making his final dua or prayer, asking Allah for both strength to carry out his mission, as well as forgiveness for his past weaknesses and transgressions.

After saying goodbye to his family, before sending them south to Mexico where they would be safe, he had bathed carefully, making sure he was strictly clean before presenting himself to Allah, exactly as the Quran required. Then, with his prayer rug extended, and its niche at the top of the stitching following the qibla, or direction towards Mecca, he began reciting the Durood for the Prophet.

His dua completed, he rose, then bent to roll the rug carefully before tucking it under his arm. He pulled the cell-phone from his pocket and logged into Facebook. Beside his own confirmation, all forty-nine of his other Facebook 'friends' had checked in by 'liking' the posting. The Fatwa was all set to go.

He activated the GPS on the phone and allowed it to begin plotting his route. He had already studied his map and knew how to get there, but when he was close enough to his target to be detected, he was to turn off his headlights and continue by following the instructions of the GPS.

He stepped through the door of the motel room and out into the cool night. A slight breeze was blowing that felt pleasant on his skin. He felt energized and alive. He was serving Allah and making a better world for his family and for all of Islam.

He pulled the door closed behind him, but didn't bother to lock it. He had no valuables in the room and besides, in just a short time, with his service to Allah complete, he would have everything he could ever need.

CHAPTER FOURTEEN

Near Joshua Tree, California
Thursday, 2:22 a.m.
- 13 minutes

The 10 East Freeway was mostly empty except for a few late-night travelers and semi-trucks. Muhammed drove at the speed limit, and stayed over to the right to allow faster cars to pass him by. According to the traffic app on his phone, he was slightly ahead of schedule and had a comfortable couple of minutes to spare.

Next to him in the passenger's seat was an HB-10 Handi Blaster, a device barely larger than a garage door remote. It was the device used to initiate the electrical charge to detonate up to ten blasting caps, and it was widely utilized by demolition firms, construction companies, mining—virtually anyone who wanted to blow something up. A single pair of wires led from the device to the truck's rear cargo container. Muhammed had not inspected the device or even opened the cargo doors. He was told that everything had been taken care of, and that it wasn't his concern.

Besides the blaster, there were also a pair of night vision goggles that would help him see in the darkness when he extinguished his headlights. And finally, there was a semi-automatic rifle. The rifle was a Chinese knockoff of the ubiquitous AK-47 and had a clip with 30 full metal jacketed rounds loaded in it. He had removed it from behind the seat before he left the motel. One round was already chambered in the breech, and the safety was on.

The rifle was there for two purposes—neither of which Muhammed hoped he'd have to resort to. One purpose was to dispatch anyone such as police or security that tried to interfere with the mission. The second was to use in case the explosives he was carrying somehow malfunctioned, and he had to resort to a backup plan of shooting holes into the transformers, before turning the gun on himself.

The GPS announced the turnoff for Highway 62 before he saw the sign. The road headed north up through a pass between the San Bernardino Mountain Range before continuing on through the towns of Yucca Valley, Joshua Tree, and Twenty-Nine Palms.

"Take Exit One-Seventeen for State Route Sixty-Two and veer left north to destination."

Muhammed slowed the truck and turned onto the exit. Soon he was heading north on Hwy 62. He checked the display on the truck's radio; it read 2:30 a.m. Five minutes to go. He was getting close and could begin to feel the goose-pimples on his arms raise up.

In the dark gray sky above the desert landscape, he could make out the silhouettes of windmills turning lazily in the breeze and generating electricity. He laughed inwardly; it was ironic that their silent, autonomous contributions to the grid, would soon be for naught.

"In one quarter mile, turn right onto Dillon Road."

In just a few moments, he came to the intersection of Dillon Road and slowed the truck to turn.

He came out of the turn and with one hand on the wheel reached over and switched on the NVG's. In a few seconds he could see in the darkness of the cab that they had indeed activated, the greenish hued light illuminating the textures of the vinyl seat cover.

Accelerating slightly, he continued on and could just make out the run-down trailers and ramshackle homes of some of the local residents. This was Indian reservation land and it reminded him of America's infidel's history of taking the indigenous people's land and destroying their culture, just like the Zionist pigs of Israel did to Palestine. The time was long overdue to stop them.

"Turn left onto Diablo Road in one eighth mile."

Muhammed could see no other autos in his side mirrors or ahead of him and he pulled the NVG's onto his head while switching off his headlights.

After the goggles adjusted, the view on the road in front of him took on an alien, otherworldly appearance. He attempted to swallow, but found that his mouth was as dry as the desert outside. He saw Diablo Road in the milky image in front of him, and slowed down to turn.

"Turn left onto Diablo Road and continue on for approximately one point one mile to destination."

Muhammed felt his breathing quicken as he moved the truck along in the darkness. In the distance off to the right, he could see the 500 thousand-volt Southern California Edison switching station known as the Devers looming. It many ways it looked like a giant child's construction play-set. It was one of twenty-three similar stations located throughout California which formed the backbone of the energy grid for the most populous state in the US. These stations were the big links in the chain, and without them, no electricity could get through.

He passed more windmills before crossing over Powerline Road which represented the southern border of the giant facility. He drove past the main entrance and continued on to the rear maintenance entrance. He glanced at the clock display on the truck's radio face just as it changed from 2:23 to 2:24 a.m. He was right on time.

"Turn left at destination in approximately one quarter mile."

"Allah!" Muhammed breathed excitedly, and switched off the GPS.

Not far ahead, he could see the short driveway leading up to the maintenance entrance. There was a guard shack located here, but he had been briefed that it was unoccupied unless the plant was experiencing high traffic from maintenance or construction crews doing work at the plant.

Since the attack on the Metcalf station in 2013, when snipers took out several of the HPT, or high-power transformers that made up the backbone of the grid, the utilities had invested in more security to prevent future attacks. Where formerly a simple chain linked fence with barbed wire had ringed the Devers facility, a ten-foot-high concrete wall with spike strips now stood in its place.

But, even the laziest or most uninspired thief or terrorist knew that you didn't attempt to penetrate at a facility's strong point, only at its weakest. And that weakness was the automatic sliding steel gate that allowed personnel in or out of the area.

It was tall and constructed of steel, but it would be no match for a six-thousand-pound vehicle slamming into it at full force. The security measures implemented here and probably at the other facilities Mohammed thought were little more than window dressing designed to satisfy the public and the handful or so of regulators and politicians who had demanded that, "Something needs to be done to protect the grid!"

And, so that's what they got; something.

Rather than install bollards to prevent a vehicle from crashing the gate, or even K-Rails to slow the vehicles, the utilities only went so far as to implement half-baked, 'check the box and save the profit' measures, that they would soon realize were folly.

He veered into the left lane where oncoming traffic would normally have been and slowed to a crawl before turning the truck toward the right in a large arc. It was now lined up, and aimed directly at the sliding gate.

Muhammad Dujani waited patiently and watched until the clock's display switched to 2:35 a.m.

Then he pushed the accelerator all the way to the floor.

CHAPTER FIFTEEN

Devers Transmission Station
Thursday, 2:35 a.m.
0 hours, 0 minutes

The three-ton vehicle picked up speed surprisingly well and covered the short distance of the driveway in just a few seconds. It
slammed into the steel gate, which easily broke loose of its guide
rails and fell flat in front of him. Muhammed drove right over it.

He knew security cameras would have recorded the breach, but
it didn't matter. The plant was normally staffed by only two workers and a security guard and by the time they got to him, it would
be too late.

Once through the entrance, he pushed on the brakes of the truck
and slowed it down to a more sedate speed. He made a quick left
turn on the plant's internal maintenance road, and then a quick
right onto another road.

Off to his right side were his targets; the HPT's. They were the
size of large garden sheds and constructed of metal cases containing miles of copper windings. Inside the housings, special oil acted
as insulation as well as provided cooling.

There were two banks of the units; one with three HPTs and one
with two. He had been given specific instructions as to where to
park his truck based upon the arced shape of the blast wave.

As soon as he was in position, he put the truck into park and
grabbed the electrical blaster on the seat next to him. He depressed
the charge switch. In less than two seconds, the indicator light illuminated, telling him the unit was charged and ready to go.

He took a final deep breath and screamed, "Allahu Akbar!"

Then he depressed the "fire" switch.

Instantly, electricity coursed through the short length or wire
leading from the cab into the cargo compartment. The wire split
into several other wires, and the electrical current easily pushed

through the tiny bridge wires of the blasting caps, melting them in the process.

The blasting caps detonated, and initiated an explosive wave into the main explosives; 460 pounds of ammonium nitrate fuel oil, the same type of explosive used in the Oklahoma City Bombing.

The truck had been packed with over four thousand ½" steel ball bearings embedded in a net on the right side of the explosives, and facing outward toward the targets. On the left side, sandbags had been stacked to keep the blast wave focused outward toward the right-hand side of the truck.

The force blew the fiberglass side of the truck's cargo box away as the projectiles headed to their targets at ten times the speed of sound.

The balls easily tore through the 5/8" thick steel of the outer shells of the transformers, before continuing on into the heart of the unit where they sliced through the high voltage windings of the transformer.

Hundreds of the conductive copper strips were cut through, opening the circuit and instantly terminating the flow of electricity induced into them. Circuit breakers began to open.

And in less than one second, the transformers went from active, pulsing pieces of electrical equipment critical to the function of the electrical grid, to useless hunks of steel and copper.

* * *

All across California, at HPT stations like Del Amo, Santa Clarita, and Vincent, a similar situation played out, hopelessly destroying the transformers, and severing the big links in the chain that were the California electrical grid.

Also targeted and destroyed were HPTs at the Sacramento Municipal Utility District, or SMUD, as well as the Los Angeles Department of Water and Power's receiving stations. These sub-grids either weren't part of the main California grid, or they had the ability to 'island' themselves during an upset. For total annihilation of the grid, they had to be taken out as well.

With every critical link in the grid destroyed, in a matter of seconds, the great state of California would go dark. And in a short time, would also become completely paralyzed.

"Despite their great size and internal complexity [high voltage] transformers can be readily disabled or destroyed." A Mitsubishi Electric Power Products Inc. official was also quoted as saying, "Such a task would be surprisingly simple."

Source: The Independent Congressional Research Service
https://sgp.fas.org/crs/homesec/R43604.pdf

"Penetrating the 5/8 to 3/4-inch steel tank with any device could short-circuit the windings and irreparably destroy the transformer."

Source: https://fas.org/sgp/crs/homesec/R43604.pdf

CHAPTER SIXTEEN

Cal-ISO Headquarters
Folsom, California
Thursday, 2:35 a.m.
0 hours, 0 minutes

They came in like a tsunami, startling even the most unflappable of operators. It was like switching on a stereo receiver when the volume had been left at maximum. Instantly, the Yakout Mansour control room was awash in a flood of alarms of all strata: low level, medium level, high level, and emergency. Each alarm had a different sound and cadence to it, and the cacophony of sounds was nearly deafening.

Several of the giant screens at the front of the control room lit up like the proverbial Christmas tree, with most indicators switching from green to yellow, or worst of all, red.

Throughout the room, bodies stiffened as the operators went into rapid response mode, typing keys or making mouse clicks as fast as they could to acknowledge the thousands of alarms scrolling endlessly across their displays. As soon as they saw them, they called out the issue.

"Forty-one eleven line is down," someone said.

"Pacific Intertie opened," another added.

"We've lost Helms, Oroville and Alamitos," someone else said. "Now... Ivanpah."

"Sixty-six kay-vee in Madera down."

"Western grid is showing oscillations."

The light's flickered momentarily as the building lost power from their own utility, the Sacramento Municipal Utility District, or SMUD, and switched onto emergency back-up power.

"We're on UPS and backup generator A," someone announced. "SMUD just took a hit."

Gary jumped up from his desk and moved to the center of the room, feeling for some reason he was in more control by standing here. The problem he could see was that he really wasn't; no one was in control at this point.

"Ormond Beach tripped out on over-speed."

"La Paloma is down on freeks."

"Diablo Canyon Nuke just pulled the plug."

"All 220 and 66 kay-vee lines are going under-volt."

"Nevada, Oregon and Arizona reporting oscillations in the critical range, they're about ready to island."

Gary knew what the last statement meant. Even though the California grid functioned as one giant entity, it was still connected to the greater Western States grid, which was comprised of eleven US states and two Canadian Provinces. It was officially called the Western States Intertie, but was known casually by the operators as 'The Donut,' due to its infinite connectivity. And when any state's grid experienced an imbalance or loss, the other players in the donut tried to make it up by exporting some of their own power. But in a catastrophic event - such as what appeared to be unfolding before their eyes—the other states experienced violent oscillations of frequency and current. In these cases, they could try to ride it out to help the affected state—putting their own grids at risk. Or they could let circuit breakers open to protect themselves.

Gary was trying desperately to process the situation and understand it, as he knew his operators were, but it was extremely difficult. He was observing a phenomenon known in the energy and petrochemical control industry as 'alarm flooding,' a situation where a human being—no matter how well trained and qualified, could not keep up with the demand of so many emergencies to deal with. Often times, they simply couldn't process all the information and make correct decisions.

Knowing that his operators would soon be overwhelmed, Dicey ran back to his desk and navigated to a screen that would allow him to inhibit low and medium priority alarms, only allowing the high and emergency ones to audibly alarm.

The move cut down the din somewhat, but it was still a scene of pandemonium.

Then, the phones started to ring.

Gary looked at his phone display and saw a call coming in from Lincoln, California. Lincoln was the satellite control center for Folsom, and served as a backup in case Folsom needed help.

"Gary Dicey," he said abruptly, picking up the line.

"Gary, it's me, Phil," the exasperated voice on the other end said. "Are you guys seeing what I'm seeing, or do we have a major instrumentation problem?"

"We're seeing it," Gary said, and could hear redundant alarm bells going off in the background. Gary knew that the Lincoln Control Center didn't have the same staffing as Folsom, and realized that as hectic as it was for him and his crew, his counterpart had it far worse. "And I don't think it's instrumentation Phil."

"Do you think we were hacked, or a solar flare?" Phil asked.

"I don't know," Gary admitted, realizing that a cyber-attack was always the big boogie man of expected threats to the grid. Then one of the Folsom operators called out the worst of all possible scenarios.

"We've lost Devers," he said. "And Serrano and Vincent."

"Freeks going to zero," someone else yelled.

Just then, another operator, who had somehow managed to acknowledge his alarms, answered one of the incoming phone calls and yelled out, "Vincent said they just had a major explosion and lost everything."

"Everything?" Gary asked, but felt in his gut he already knew the answer.

"Yeah, all the HPTs and some other stuff. They think it was a bomb of some sort. The place is destroyed."

Gary looked over at the far lower left-hand display on the control board and saw his worst nightmare; all of the main status alarms for the twenty-three HPT stations that formed the big links of the California grid had changed from green to red. The HPT stations were dead in the water.

Someone else yelled out, "Devers says the same thing. Huge explosion and they've got a fire on their hands."

"Gary," Steve Ory then said gravely. "Look at the sat image."

Everyone in the room turned to look at the real time satellite image. Even with the remaining alarms and the telephones ringing, the room fell strangely quiet as the operators stared in disbelief.

Other than a few pinpoints of light from the handful or so micro-grids that existed in the state, and the bright flashes from the HPT stations as equipment arced and exploded, the once bright state of California, was now completely dark.

PART II:
AND THEN EVERYTHING WAS DIFFERENT
... EVEN THE SKY

CHAPTER SEVENTEEN

Chico, California
Thursday, 2:35 a.m.
0 hours, 0 minutes

Leon Morales felt it at almost the same instant he heard it; a tightening in his chest as his lungs—wracked with severe COPD from a lifetime of smoking, struggled to pull in enough oxygen to breath.

By his bedside was his BiPAP machine, a mechanical device that pushed air and oxygen into his lungs through a mask over his mouth and nose. It was an older machine and had a backup battery, but only for status alarms and display. The machine was in alarm state currently, and a loud screech filled the tiny bedroom.

Morales lived by himself in a modest home on a quiet street that he and his wife had owned and raised their children in for over forty-five years. She had passed away a year and a half ago this May. Shattered by the loss, but fiercely independent, Leon stubbornly refused to be a burden to his children, or worst of all, go into a nursing home and wait to die. At this moment, the wisdom of his decision would be put to the test.

In a matter of just a few lost breaths, his pulse began to race and he struggled to climb out of bed and find his cell phone to call 911. It was nearly impossible as the room was pitch black and he was disoriented.

He tripped on his own shoes by the side of the bed and knocked over his nightstand. A small lamp and the BiPAP tumbled to the floor, the later continuing its unabated wail.

He regained his footing, but with his throat muscles contracting, the CO_2 levels in his blood began to quickly rise. His pulse pounded like a drum in his ears. Instinctively, he tore the mask off of his face and fought to pull in enough air to breath.

His lungs were so weakened, it was an exercise in futility that only caused him to panic further. By now, he was getting dizzy and more disoriented, even to the point of wondering if it was all a bad dream and he would soon wake up.

No such luck.

He staggered and fell forward, hitting his forehead on the edge of the door and opening a huge gash. It was incredibly painful and he wanted to scream, but he had no breath to exhale.

Instead, he fell onto his back on the floor of his bedroom, writhing and struggling to breathe like a fish out of water. His chest felt like an elephant was standing on it.

In just a few moments, the room that was so dark, began to spin and became a beautiful bright light. And along with the light, he saw his beloved wife.

Without realizing it, Leon Morales would become the first of tens of thousands of deaths in what would become the most devastating terrorist attack in U.S. history.

Currently, 175,697 individuals are medically dependent on electricity in the state of California.

Source: US health and Human Services https://empowermap.hhs.gov/

CHAPTER EIGHTEEN

Torrance, California
Thursday, 2:35 a.m.
0 hours, 0 minutes

Jim Miller hated these kinds of nights. It seemed as if as soon as he showed up for his assigned twelve-hour shift at the one hundred sixty thousand barrel per day refinery, he'd been putting out fires. Not in the literal sense mind you—although he was on the refinery's emergency response team and had seen his share of fires and toxic spills, but from an equipment and process standpoint.

In his eleventh year as a plant operator, he had been assigned to the giant facility's FCC unit, a highly dangerous process other employees darkly referred to as, the 'bomb' of the refinery. And tonight, the 'bomb' just wasn't cooperating.

There were over-pressure issues in one of the unit's surge drums, a control valve that seemed to be sticking intermittently, and one of the electrostatic precipitators circuits had blown, slowing down the feed rate of the unit.

He only had enough time to gobble down some leftover pizza in the control house kitchen when another problem cropped up: a level indicator on one of the columns was suspect and he would have to manually climb the hundred or so feet to the third deck to inspect it.

Holding his flashlight on the back side of the visual gauge glass, he pressed the button on his radio and called out the true reading, "I'm showing about thirty percent in the glass. What do you guys show in the house?"

He had barely gotten the words out of his mouth when the plant lighting suddenly flickered and then went completely dark. A split second later, giant electric motors for the feed pumps and gas compressors started to shut down, whining slowly to a stop.

"Shit!" was all he said. A veteran of many crises in the refinery, Miller knew immediately what it all meant: a blackout. And anyone who worked in a refinery long enough could tell you they would take a fire—or even an explosion, over a power outage any day.

The slow rolling of the feed motors and gas compressors instantly created an over pressure in the pipes, vessels, and columns that surrounded him. Giant relief valves, designed to prevent catastrophic ruptures of equipment, violently popped open, the sudden rush of thousands of pounds of pressure causing them to roar with the fury and deafening sound of a rocket taking off.

Some of the valves exhausted straight to the atmosphere, but most shunted the highly flammable gas to the refinery's giant flare stacks to burn off. Just as quickly as it had gone dark, the refinery was bathed in light again as fireballs, stretching hundreds of feet high blasted into the air.

And just as quickly, Jim Miller's night went from bad, to worse.

Only about half of California refineries have enough cogeneration capacity to continue running safely during a power outage.
Source: https://www.eia.gov/outlooks/steo/special/pdf/california.pdf

CHAPTER NINETEEN

San Diego, California
Thursday, 2:35 a.m.
0 hours, 0 minutes

Like most veteran firefighters waiting for the alarm to sound, San Diego Fire Chief Tim Dillon always slept with one ear open.

It didn't take much then to rouse him from his sleep when he heard the station's diesel generator kicking on and the automatic transfer switches activating.

His years of experience and diligent attention to details - especially when it came to planning for and responding to emergencies, told him that the station would be fine, but the cause of the outage perplexed him.

The wind was calm tonight and, being located far enough on the windward side of Soledad Mountain, they weren't in any fire prone areas. The most likely scenarios then were a car crash taking down a pole, or even one of the utilities transformers not having been maintained and blowing up.

Either way, he knew he had to be ready to respond to the source of the outage, as well as the inevitable rescues of people—most likely cleaning crews trapped in the elevators of buildings. And if the outage went on for too long, his team would be responding to house fires started by candles, as well as carbon monoxide poisonings from people using stoves to heat their homes. All and all, it would make for a very busy night.

More than anything though, Dillon learned long ago not to dwell on the 'what–ifs?' and waste precious sleep. When he heard the last of the transfer switches click in, he turned over and buried his face in his pillow. He knew how to fall asleep on command, and was just starting to drift off when the station's lights suddenly came on and the PA system broadcast a 'Long Tone' alarm, typically a medical call as opposed to a fire. Dillon rolled out of his bed and was pulling on his turnouts when he heard the dispatch operator announce:

"Information to all agencies. Information to all agencies: We are currently experiencing a very widespread power outage. Reports are coming in from other call centers and it is presumed that it is statewide. I repeat, outage may be statewide. Standby for updates. Dispatch clear."

"The whole state?" He said to himself incredulously.

In the hallway outside his door, he could hear the shuffle of feet and conversation as the other firefighters went into emergency standby mode. The main front doors would be rolled up, the stations rigs moved out and portable radios would be grabbed out of charging stations.

Dillon continued putting on his turnouts and boots and headed out into the hall. In there, he ran into Jim Kawagoye, one of his Lieutenants.

"Holy shit," Kawagoye uttered over the sound of the trucks being started downstairs. "The whole damn state?"

Chief Dillon didn't respond or speculate and instead asked his second in command, "You got this for a second?"

"Yes sir."

"Okay, I'm going to check something out. I'll be there in two."

The Lieutenant nodded and moved over to the pole opening in the floor to slide down into the truck bays.

Dillon turned in the opposite direction and headed down the hall from his room. He opened a door that led to the roof of the two-story building, climbed the short flight of stairs up, and went outside.

From his vantage point thirty feet up, in every direction he turned, and as far as he could see, the world was utterly dark.

As a veteran of the mutual aid efforts for both the Oklahoma City Bombing and 9-11, Tim Dillon understood terrorist attacks and he suddenly felt a chill rise up on his back. He reached into his pants pocket, pulled out his cell phone and dialed. It rang twice before a sleepy woman's voice answered.

"Hullo?" his wife said.

"It's me," he said. "I think this might be it."

"What?" his wife said, confused and still a little bit drowsy. "What might be it?"

"Power outage," Dillon said. "The whole state, they're saying. And I'm betting it's a terrorist attack."

"Oh my God!"

"And you know what that means," Dillon continued. "And what it's going to be like in a couple of days; we talked about it. You need to follow the plan."

The 'plan,' Dillon spoke of, was a quick escape from the state in the event of a large-scale disaster, natural or manmade. They had rehearsed it several times.

The cars were always kept fueled between ¾ and full, and his wife had a list of items to take as well as 'bug-out' bags for her and their two children. She was to drive one of the cars to the airport in Phoenix, catch the next flight to Kansas City where her folks lived, and stay there until further notice.

"Oh my God," she repeated, now with despair in her voice.

"Honey, you have to do it," Dillon said firmly. "For you and the kids."

"I know." She said sadly.

"All right," Dillon said finally, "I've got to handle things here."

"I love you Tim," his wife said.

"And I love you too. And that's why we're doing this."

CHAPTER TWENTY

Lakewood, California
Thursday, 2:35 a.m.
0 hours, 0 minutes

Jake Sullivan was curled up next to the transformer that supplied the local strip mall with power, his backside warmed by the invisible flow of electricity between the coils within it. His rucksack was tucked up under his head as a pillow and his hand was curled around the grip of the Navy combat knife that he always carried with him.

The warmth and gentle hum of the transformer, and with his weapon at the ready, allowed him the comfort to sleep as well as anyone who lived on the streets could sleep. Presently, he was dreaming of his days growing up; he was climbing a tree, higher and higher. It seemed as if he was in the sky at some point and had left the bounds of earth, the clouds were his friends and he reached out to him. Then, everything went black and time stood still.

He was suddenly awake and alert, his eyes open and searching, his hand gripping the handle of the knife tightly. Was it a threat? A gang member trying to shake him down, a cop rousting him and forcing him to move on? Or, another homeless person creeping up on him to knife him in his sleep?

Conditioned as he was to become instantly aware of his situation, it took only a second or so for him to get his bearings, but when he did, he established that there was no immediate threat that he could detect. But still, something was different. And then he noticed it, the hum of the generator was gone. And all around him it was pitch black, as dark as the darkest nights in Afghanistan. Nights that were so dark you couldn't see your hand in front of your face.

He turned his head, looking skyward. Above him, the billions of stars of the Milky Way galaxy shown with a brilliance he hadn't seen in a long time.

Feeling with his free hand, he switched on his boom box, keeping the volume low so as to not be detected. The announcer was rattling on about what he knew, which was basically nothing.

"...big blackout it seems. We are on generator power here and my engineer says it's as dark outside as far as the eye can see. We don't know what's happening yet, but we'll try to get you some info as soon as we can folks..."

I know what's happening, Jake thought wryly to himself. And it's long overdue.

CHAPTER TWENTY-ONE

Halison, California
Thursday, 2:35 a.m.
0 hours, 0 minutes

When it started life in 2002, the Generac 50-kilowatt back-up generator was an efficient, well-engineered machine designed to provide years of reliable service. The Halison City Council voted to authorize the purchase along with the manufacturer's recommended five-year maintenance contract that included annual load testing, a thirty-point inspection, routine preventative maintenance, and fuel polishing.

After all, they reasoned, their constituents deserved nothing but the best when it came to a reliable municipal water supply.

Then, in 2007, the sub-prime mortgage crisis hit and with it, the subsequent financial collapse. Businesses failed, tourism in the small town took a hit, and real estate prices and property tax revenue plunged.

The town's coffers, once plump from years of steadily rising revenues, soon dried up causing some tough belt tightening decisions to be made. And one of these decisions was to not renew the soon to be expiring generator maintenance service contract.

The reasoning at the time was that the generator had never failed to start and run during its annual testing cycle, and that the town had plenty of capable employees who could pick up the slack. They, the town leadership, would make repairs on an as needed basis to maintain the integrity of their system until things improved economically. The measure passed unanimously and the contract was not renewed.

At first, the in-house program seemed to be off to a good start. Several of the municipal water system employees took the ball and began a regular inspection and testing schedule. But then, over the next several years, these employees began to retire. Their replacements were woefully ill prepared to maintain the inspection and testing of the device and soon a turf war erupted between different departments within the city as to who should 'own the damn thing'.

The water department argued it should be the responsibility of the town's fire department since they relied on the water for extinguishing blazes. The fire department kicked the can over to the public works department, who then went crying to the city's leadership that they were stretched thin as it was, and that it was unfair to 'dump it on them'.

Finally, the town's mayor interceded and made a King Solomon-*esque* decision mandating that all departments would from that point on share in the inspection and testing of the generator. In what was once one department's responsibility, now became everyone's responsibility, which soon translated to: *it was NO ONE'S responsibility*.

And so, the $15,000 Generac 50KW sat, and sat, and sat for years with nary a cursory look-see or a test run. A family of opossums actually found their way in and took up residence inside.

And when the auto-start contact engaged to fire up the Mitsubishi 3300CC diesel engine, there wasn't even enough energy from the decades old battery to pull in the starter solenoid.

The town's water pump, programmed to refill the one hundred-fifty-foot-high water tower during off-peak hours, stopped cold. The landmark, onion shaped tower, with the words, *HALISON: A TOWN TO REMEMBER*, proudly emblazoned on it, was filled to only one third of its normal capacity. Even with rationing, it would run dry within a couple of days.

All across the state, hundreds of similarly neglected generators would fail to start, affecting not just municipalities and utilities, but businesses, schools, and even nursing homes. Those customers who could get through to repair shops soon found they were put into 'the queue,' and just would have to wait. Some shops, overwhelmed by both the sheer volume of calls plus the high numbers of AWOL employees, gave up answering their phones altogether.

"The single most frequent service call for generator failure is related to battery failure."
Source: https://www.ecmweb.com/maintenance-repair-operations/ article/20888304/top-nine-reasons-generators-fail-to-start

CHAPTER TWENTY-TWO

Hanford, California
Thursday, 2:36 a.m.
+ 0 hours, 1 minute

Night manager Dianna Smith-Day grabbed the two pots, regular and decaf, angled her slight body past a waitress who was manning the long counter, and headed toward her self-assigned tables to refill her customer's cups.

The veteran of many years in the restaurant business, Day didn't mind the night shift and in fact, normally volunteered for it. She was divorced, with no interest in a new relationship, and both her children were grown and had moved on with their own lives. Besides, at this hour of the night, the clientele was mostly a mixture of workers coming off of swing shifts, lonely elderly who found it difficult to sleep without their dear departed spouse, as well as a couple revelers who needed coffee and food to sober up before they dared hitting the road. As long as they didn't make trouble, she was fine to serve them.

It was just as she was approaching her first table, a regular that she knew as Max, when the lights went out. Instinctively, she froze in her spot, the coffee pot partially raised. Almost instantly, the normal din of the restaurant: quiet conversations, utensils scraping on plates, even the background music that she had long since forgotten was playing, suddenly went silent.

No stranger to occasional power outages, Day remained frozen, expecting the lights to flicker back to life. But they didn't.

She turned her gaze outside through the giant windows that faced the parking lot. In other blackouts, some of the street lights and ambient light from other nearby business would help to keep at least some illumination available inside. But the world had gone utterly, completely black.

She couldn't see anyone inside the restaurant, but in the darkness, she imagined others doing the same thing.

"What the hell?" someone finally said, breaking the silence.

Another customer turned on the light on his mobile phone. Pretty soon others were following suit and Day removed her own phone from the pocket in her half-apron and switched it on as well.

The restaurant was soon filled with the harsh beams of the mobile devices. Some people went back to eating their meals while others sat with puzzled expressions.

She refilled her customer's coffee cup and then turned and made her way back to the office. There were supposed to be several larger flashlights and spare batteries in the emergency box and she wanted to use those rather than drain her cell battery.

Just then, a loud crash of pots and pans, followed by swearing in Spanish, erupted from the kitchen.

She sighed audibly, realizing it was going to a very long night. To the others, the bodies strangely illuminated by their cell phones, she called out.

"Everybody please stay seated. I'm going to get some flashlights." Thinking as she said it that she hoped that they had not been stolen, and, that the batteries were still somewhat charged. If she was lucky and they weren't dead or lost, she thought that they could at least ride it out until the power came back on.

But within just a couple of hours, Dianna Smith-Day dismissed her crew, locked the doors to the restaurant, and headed home to her own dark apartment, praying all the while that the food in the restaurant's refrigerators wouldn't spoil before the power came back on.

CHAPTER TWENTY-THREE

Los Angeles Department of Water and Power –
Halldale Receiving Station
Carson, California
Thursday, 2:37 a.m.
+ 0 hours, 2 minutes

Deputy Sheriff Steve Bowen was not far from the location when he witnessed it; a loud explosion, followed by a blinding light that lit up the sky over the homes in the neighborhood he was patrolling. Immediately, he grabbed the microphone in his car and reported in.

"Dispatch, from patrol three. I just heard a loud explosion coming from the area around Del Amo and Denker Avenue. I'm going to investigate."

"Roger patrol three. Be advised that we just lost all power here and are going onto backup generators."

Then, Deputy Bowen noticed that everything was dark, the street lights on the poles, the houses that he drove past. He must have been so startled by the explosion and flash of light, he hadn't noticed until then.

"Roger that, same here; power appears to be out. Might have something to do with it."

Several other patrol cars chimed in then from various locations then and reported the same thing: no lights anywhere to be seen.

A veteran of thirteen years in the department, seven in the Los Angeles County jail system and six on street patrol, the deputy thought he had seen it all, until now.

He switched his headlamps onto high beam and turned on his overhead light bar. Even with his high beams on, he still could barely see and so he took it slow, threading his way through the narrow streets toward the source of the explosion.

He passed by some of the small homes that were located in the mostly industrial area known as the Harbor Gateway, and could just make out the silhouettes of several people who had come out of their houses to see what had happened.

As he got closer to the presumed location of the explosion, he switched on his spotlight and trained the beam ahead of him. In the closing distance he could see that it was some sort of an electrical sub-station. A couple small fires were burning, and he could see occasional bright flashes as the equipment arced. At that point he stopped, thinking there could be downed electrical lines.

"Dispatch, this is patrol three again. I'm pulled up at about the fifteen-hundred block of Del Amo Boulevard. It appears that a large electrical substation has exploded. There are some small fires and I'm seeing some of the equipment arcing. I'm not going to proceed any farther until DWP can get out here and make it safe. In the meantime, I'm going to try to establish a perimeter and put up some tape. Request backup."

"Roger patrol three. We'll notify DWP and County Fire as well. All available units, assist patrol three at the fifteen hundred block of Del Amo Boulevard.

A couple of other patrol cars responded that they were en route.

Bowen turned his patrol car hard to the left to block the street, switched on his Mag-Light and then got out to start setting up some crime scene tape.

It was then, when he was stepping out of the car that he almost lost his footing from something under his feet, catching himself from falling by grabbing onto the top of the patrol car door.

Recovered, he turned the beam of his flashlight toward the ground and saw several round shiny metallic objects. He picked one of them up and noticed it was a steel ball bearing about half an inch in diameter.

He swept the beam further along the pavement and noticed more and more of them, dozens in fact. The he saw something else.

Stepping gingerly, he walked the short distance and picked up the object. As someone who had spent his off time restoring old cars, he recognized it immediately for what it was: part of the suspension of a vehicle, possibly a truck of some sort.

His mind flashed back to some of his training and to some of the case studies on terrorism he had read. He thought of the World Trade Center bombing and the pieces of truck parts that they had found in the aftermath.

He depressed the transmit button on the microphone clipped to his lapel. "Dispatch from patrol three. We're gonna need the captain out here as well. I think we have a terrorist incident on our hands."

CHAPTER TWENTY-FOUR

Ontario International Airport
Ontario, California
Thursday, 2:38 a.m.
+ 0 hours, 3 minutes

Lloyd Klefstad saw the lights flicker in his office at the same time his computer went down, then the lights went out completely and the room went dark. As the night superintendent for one of the fastest growing airports in California, he knew that they were well prepared to deal with occasional power outages and so he sat calmly in the dark, waiting for the backup generators to kick in and the auto transfer switches to reroute the power.

His patience was rewarded a few seconds later as the lights came back on. His computer was down though and he would have to re-boot it. He depressed the power switch and soon heard the fans and the hard drive whirling back to life. While he was waiting, he picked up the phone and contacted the air traffic control office on the other side of the runway to see if they knew what was going on.

"Hey Bill," Klefstad said as soon as the phone was answered. "Did you guys go on backup too, or was it just over on our side?"

"Yeah, we did," Bill Franklin, the ATC supervisor replied. In the background, Klefstad heard what sounded like more than the usual amount of chatter from the conversations between the pilots and controllers. But it wasn't just the volume of talk, the tone sounded different as well.

"Do you know what happened?" Klefstad asked.

"No," the supervisor admitted. "But we're hearing from some of the pilots in the air that it's completely black out there, as far as they can see."

"You're kidding?" Klefstad said incredulously, knowing that the visibility was nearly unlimited tonight, and for a pilot, thousands of feet off of the ground not seeing anything …

"Jesus," Klefstad said, "This must be pretty widespread then."

"I was thinking the same thing," Franklin said. "I—"

He paused mid-sentence and then quickly said, "Standby one."

Lloyd Klefstad could hear some muffled conversation in the background and from the tone of it, it didn't sound good. Finally, Bill Franklin got back on.

"Sorry Lloyd," he said. "My lead just told me that all of the other airports are out of power as well."

"All of them?" Klefstad said stunned, knowing that in addition to back-up power, some, like Los Angeles International had three independent power feeds coming in.

"Yeah. Burbank, John Wayne...even LAX."

"Holy cow!" Lloyd exclaimed. "So, we don't even have any relief airports to reroute to if we need them?"

"Nope," Franklin said. "And the other airports are calling *us* for relief."

Just then, another phone began ringing in the background of the ATC building.

"Stand by Lloyd," Franklin said quickly. The line went dead momentarily as Klefstad was put on hold, his mind racing through the protocols for events such as this. Finally, Bill Franklin came back on.

"FAA Lloyd," he said simply. "They're calling for a temporary flight restriction. We have to ground all outbound and get what we have in the air landed ASAP. All inbound airports to us are getting gate-holds as we speak."

"Great," Klefstad said, thinking back to the chaos immediately following the 9-11 attacks. Then he added, "I'm going to start working the phones to see what I can find out. I'm also going to call in the airport manager. You just get those planes on the ground safely and hold the others."

"Got it," Bill Frank said, and then hung up.

Lloyd Klefstad sat back in his chair. His computer had finished booting up, and was asking him if he wanted to 'restore the previous session?'

Restore the previous session? He thought ironically. *What I'd really like is to have some normalcy restored.*

CHAPTER TWENTY-FIVE

On the border of Los Angeles and San Bernardino counties
Elevation 15,200 feet
Thursday, 2:40 a.m.
+ 0 hours, 5 minutes

The pilot of the Lear Jet was instantly catapulted thirty years back in time when the lights of the Los Angeles basin suddenly extinguished. A former Naval Aviator, he had been flying F/A-18 Hornets in the opening moments of the air campaign of Operation Desert Storm when graphite filled or, *black-out bombs*, were dropped over Baghdad, short circuiting the electrical grid. The specialized weapons took down not just the Iraqi air defenses, but also critical infrastructure such as sanitation and water treatment plants. Seeing the instant blackness through his windscreen, the veteran pilot got an ominous feeling. Then his radio headset crackled.

He and his copilot listened carefully to the instructions being given to them by air traffic control, and then the pilot acknowledged by way of repeating back the information. In the meantime, his copilot began working on the route to the new destination given to them.

"We're being told to divert to Long Beach Airport Mr. Binder," the pilot called back through the opening in the bulkhead that separated the cockpit from the main cabin.

"What!" the actor screamed. "Why the fuck are we diverting?"

"Look out your window Mr. Binder," the pilot replied calmly. "The Los Angeles area had just experienced a widespread power outage, and the safest place for us to land is Long Beach."

Alan turned to look out his side window as his personal assistant Marianne Corelli followed suit across the narrow aisle of the private jet. Below them and as far as the eye could see, the world was pure blackness. They might as well have been staring into a black curtain placed over the window.

The copilot tapped the pilot on the shoulder just then and pointed to a display with their new course. The pilot nodded, gave his second in command a thumbs up and got on the radio to inform ATC of their route and to get clearance to land.

"Well fuck that!" Alan Binder bellowed. He got up out of his seat and leaned forward into the cockpit. "My limo is at the Van Nuys Airport and I'm going to miss a very important party if we don't land there. You tell those cocksuckers that we're going to land there. I'm the fucking customer here, and that's an order!"

Between balancing the duties of having to make a change in course, deal with the control tower, and manage the dozens of other tasks required to fly a jet, the pilot had finally had it with his most demanding and abusive customer ever.

"I don't care who you are in Hollywood!" he yelled, turning to Alan with an angry finger pointing into his face. "Up here, you are my passenger and my responsibility! And I am the captain of this airship! Now get out of the cockpit, sit down, and buckle in for God's sake!"

"Fuck!" Alan yelled, turning away from the pilot and returning to his seat. He drained the remainder of his scotch and then turned to Marianne. "Call the fucking limo company and reroute them," he barked at her.

"Yes Mr. Binder," she replied softly.

He turned toward the window and gazed outward to the inky blackness. Then, he had a flash of inspiration.

"Pilot," he yelled out. "Did you say that *all* of LA was without lights?"

"Yes sir," the pilot responded flatly.

Speaking to himself, Alan Binder laid out the logic of a new brilliant plan. "Then that means Barbara's party will be in the dark as well. I'll get candles and bring them to the party!" he said triumphantly. "I'll be a fucking hero!"

He turned to Marianna, who was already on phone talking to limo driver.

"As soon as you get done rerouting the limo," he told her. "Find me a store that carries candles."

"Yes Mr. Binder."

CHAPTER TWENTY-SIX

Los Angeles Communications Center
Glendale, California
Thursday, 2:43 a.m.
+ 0 hours, 8 minutes

"Nine-one-one operator, four-o-two," Francis Donegan spoke into her headset. "What's your emergency?"

"All my power is off," the caller, a male, who sounded inebriated, announced. "Do you know when it will be back on?"

"No sir, we don't," Donegan replied. "Are you having any sort of a medical emergency? Do you have a B-pap machine, or any other medical device that requires power?"

"Well, no, I don't. But it's just, you know, a pain in the ass. So, you don't know when it will be back on?"

"No sir. You'll have to check with your utility company."

She disconnected the call and moved to the next one in the queue.

A veteran dispatcher with over twenty-one years of experience, Donegan had heard it all, responding to the 911 calls through riots, earthquakes, and the crazy calls that inevitably came in from people who couldn't distinguish between a true emergency and routine inconvenience.

"Do you know if the water rates are going up?"

"How can I get tickets to the Bruce Springsteen concert?"

And, *"Do you know if McDonald's still has McRibs?"*

She also knew as soon as she saw the lights flicker in the eighteen-thousand-square-foot facility and they went onto backup power, that she would have to start handling these types of calls as well. Probably another drunk hit a power pole, she thought initially.

As the calls continued to come in however, they weren't just from their immediate area seven miles from downtown Los Angeles, but from all of the far flung reaches of the four-thousand plus square mile area the giant facility served.

In between calls, Francis allowed herself a moment to glance at the giant windows that faced outside. She had never seen a view like it.

There were no lights of any kind: streetlights, businesses. Everything was pitch black, darker than she had ever seen it. It gave her an ominous feeling, rare for someone who had seen and heard so much in her career.

"Nine-one-one operator Four-o-two. What's your emergency?"

"Yeah. My power went out and I raise tropical fish and ..."

There were three displays on her desktop at her work station, similar to the other fifty-four stations on the floor. The two center displays were dedicated to the handling of phone calls. But the outside monitor, the one to her right, was like any other office computer and used to handle emails, IMs, etcetera's.

As the caller was droning on about the temperature requirements for raising Angel fish, Francis noticed a high priority email coming from the department supervisor. She grabbed her computer mouse and clicked to open it.

It said in big bold red letters: POWER OUT IN ENTIRE STATE. POSSIBLE TERRORIST ATTACK. MORE DETAILS TO COME.

She stared at it for a moment, trying to absorb the gravity of the situation. Then, she turned her attention back to the caller, Mr. Angel Fish.

"I'm sorry sir. But we have no idea when the power will come back on. And I'm sorry about your fish. You'll have to contact your utility company."

Then she disconnected the call, and reread the email.

She began to feel lightheaded and nauseous.

CHAPTER TWENTY-SEVEN

El Dorado Hills, California
Thursday, 2:50 a.m.
+ 0 hours, 15 minutes

Nana, Shanice's late grandmother, was reaching out to her. To Shanice, the woman had always been one of the most important parts of her life, and she hoped that she (Shanice) had been one of her Nana's favorites. But her grandmother was frustrated now, reaching out toward her with her hands, her two strong hands, callused from a lifetime of domestic labor, but always gentle in touch.

But Nana couldn't reach her, and Shanice was stuck to the ground, like her feet were glued to it. And then there was the buzzing. Every time her grandmother and her hands would get close, the buzzing would snap them back. Finally, Nana withdrew her hands, looked straight into her granddaughter's eyes and nodded, knowingly, as if she knew it was all going to be okay.

Then, the buzzing got louder, and louder, and Nana faded away. Shanice woke with a start, her eyes searching in the inky darkness, wondering why she couldn't see. What happened to the nightlights plugged into the walls on each side of their beds?

Then, she discovered the source of the buzzing, and with it, the source of the *only* light in the pitch-black room.

Shanice always kept her work cellphone on the nightstand next to their bed. Part of her wanted it to never go off and interrupt what little sleep she could get on a nightly basis. But the other part of her, the part that lived for the adrenaline rush that most—if not all, CAL-OES members, got from jumping headlong into a crisis, was thrilled to hear its call to action.

She fumbled with the phone and after a few attempts, swiped the screen and entered the code to unlock it.

"Hello?"

"Hi Shanice. It's Jerelyn Weber," a woman's voice said.

A 24/7 operation, CAL-OES maintained a skeleton crew in what was known as the 'Warning Center' to constantly monitor for emergencies as they cropped up. Overseeing them was the executive duty officer, which tonight was Weber. Shanice had once held the same position, and knew that you didn't call the CAL-OES director in the middle of the night unless it was very important. In her mind, she ran through all the possible scenarios which might trigger such action: a big plane crash, a fire that might be threatening her own home and neighborhood.

"What's up Jerelyn?" she asked, excited, yet wondering if she would dread the answer.

"Power outage. Huge one. The whole state we're thinking."

"What! The whole state?" Shanice asked a little too loudly, causing her husband to stir in the bed next to her.

"That's what we're hearing from CAL-ISO," Weber confirmed. "They saw the whole thing go down. It might be a terrorist attack."

"I'm on my way in," she said quickly. "Start calling all of the key players. And if CAL-ISO can send someone over or Zoom in, I'd like to hear from them as well."

"Yes, ma'am. Anything else?"

"Yes, he may know already, but contact the governor and tell him what we know so far and that we are going to start mobilizing."

"Got it," she said and then hung up.

Using her phone to find her way through the house, Shanice located the "Go-bag" she kept at home in the utility room. She kept a duplicate bag at work, but you could never be too prepared.

She rooted through the bag and first located her headlamp. She pulled it onto her head, switched it on and grabbed some clothes from inside, pulling them on hurriedly.

Dressed and ready to go in just a few minutes, she headed back into the bedroom to wake up her husband. He surprised her by already being awake, and actually startled her when he called out in the dark.

"You have to go in?" He asked.

"Yes. Big power outage. The whole state they're saying."

"You're kidding!" he said, and even in the darkness of the room she could see him sit up in the bed.

"I wish I was," she said, and then leaned over to kiss him good-bye. "Gotta go," she said, then quickly added. "No idea when I'll be home."

"What's new?" her husband quipped.

Shanice was too busy to fire back a snappy rejoinder, and instead moved around to the other side of the bed to head out.

She was just heading through the door of their bedroom, when something told her to go back. She turned around, went to her nightstand, and picked up one last thing to put in her go-bag.

It was her Nana's bible.

CHAPTER TWENTY-EIGHT

Outside of Barstow, California
Thursday, 2:51 a.m.
+ 0 hours, 16 minutes

Jerry Barnett III sat high up in the cab of his Peterbilt model 579. One of the newest models from the perennial manufacturer, it was considered the most "aerodynamic" conventional truck that they made. Barnett loved it.

A lifelong driver with over three million miles under his belt, Barnett figured that tonight's run south on Interstate 15 towards Los Angeles would be just another routine entry in his driver's logbook—or so he thought.

Down to a quarter of a tank, he was just outside the city of Barstow where he planned to stop to refuel and grab some coffee, when he noticed it: the lights on the highway signs were out.

The first one he thought could be attributed to a bad bulb or some kids shooting it out with twenty-twos, but then he saw a second sign out, and then another and another.

He grabbed the microphone on his CB radio and depressed the transmit button.

"Breaker thirteen. This is Barnyard out here on the boulevard runnin' down south to Barstow. Got my eyes on a bunch of lights out on the signs. Anyone else got their ears on and seeing the same? Over."

He released the button and pretty soon a voice came back.

"That's a big ten-four Barnyard. I'm headn' inta ya and seeing black eyes the whole way. Over."

Another voice, heading westbound on Interstate 40, soon confirmed the same thing.

Black eyes, trucker lingo for lights out, and from every direction coming into Barstow, Barnett thought ominously to himself. Luckily though, he had traveled this same route hundreds of times, and he could still read the signs through the illumination of the Peterbilt's high-beams. The next sign read: *Barstow 8 miles.*

And boy, he thought. *The desert seemed darker than he had ever remembered it.*

Finally, he was able to make out the exit for the truck stop and got off, finding his way through the darkness toward it.

The lights were out on the sign, the building and the fueling islands, but several rigs were parked on the lot running with their lights on, making it easier to navigate in.

He pulled onto an empty island and noticed about a half dozen or so drivers standing by one of the rigs and talking. He walked toward them, hoping they could tell him what was going on.

"No power?' he asked.

"Yup, and that means no fuel as well," one of them said.

"You all know what's goin on?"

Every man shook his head no.

One man spat tobacco juice on the concrete, then said, "Just that it happened is all."

"Is the coffee's still hot at least?" Barnett asked hopefully.

One of the truckers took a sip from a paper cup.

"Sort of," he said. "You might want to get ya some while it's still warm. Could be a long night."

Trucking is the most commonly used mode for California's freight transportation accounting for 70% of freight movement into the state. Trucks transport almost all freight and services during some point within the supply chain.

Source: https://dot.ca.gov/-/media/dot-media/programs/ transportation-planning/documents/freight-cfmp-2019-draft/00- cfmpdraftchapter17final.pdf

CHAPTER TWENTY-NINE

Fitchburg, California
Thursday, 3:11 a.m.
+ 0 hours, 36 minutes

Steven Castro was glad he was up when the power went out, knowing that timing was everything in his line of work, and that he could get the jump on others of a similar ilk.

A career criminal, and a three striker who had had his sentence commuted during the Covid-19 Pandemic, Castro knew a good situation when he saw one.

He had been partying at his homeboy Jayden's crib and enjoying some good weed when all of a sudden, the lights went out. The stereo, which had blasting out some vintage Tupac at nearly full volume, went silent as well, much to the relief of the neighbors.

And so, the parolee bailed out on his 'homey's' tiny Section 8 housing unit as soon as he realized the opportunity in front of him; power failures meant no alarm systems, and no alarms meant that looting the nearby pawn shops, jewelry stores, and cell phone dealers would be child's play.

A few minutes later he had returned home to the apartment he shared with his latest girlfriend, grabbed some tools and the school backpacks some crack-moms had traded him for some dope, and was out the door.

It was time to go to work.

CHAPTER THIRTY

Beijing, China
Thursday, 7:12 p.m. (3:12 a.m. PST)
+ 0 hours, 37 minutes

Sixteen hours ahead of PST in the US, Gao Zemin, the current President of China, his trusted advisors, and high-ranking members of the military, were monitoring the rapidly evolving situation closely. Besides the real time feed from a Yaogan-30 spy satellite high above the western US, CNN, Al Jazeera and the BBC were all starting to report the outage.

Zemin, who had personally greenlighted the operation, was pleased that the Iranians had come through and delivered. As mercurial as they were, he knew from experience that it was often difficult to be able to rely on them.

The Islamic Republic had used their ties to Hezbollah to act as proxies for the attack. And with the terrorist group insulating the Iranians, and the Iranians acting for the Chinese, the People's Republic was three times removed from the attack, and therefore could not easily be connected to it.

One of the president's loyal aides pointed then to a TV monitor showing CNN Money. The crawl at the bottom of the screen catalogued the damage already being done to the financial markets.

The Shanghai Stock exchange had been closed for several hours, but trading on European markets was brisk along with afterhours trading on some exchanges and currency trading on the Forex. Already, the ripple effects of the attack were being felt. Futures on all three of the major US indices were plummeting, and the US dollar was down against almost all other currencies, including the Yuan. Not surprisingly, gold prices were headed into the stratosphere as investors scurried to the perennial economic lifeboat.

Zemin smiled when he read the crawl, but he knew that this was just the knee jerk reaction of investors, who always took a short view of everything. The real damage, the long term one for which

America would take decades—or possibly never, to recover from, was having its precarious supply chains grind to a screeching halt, as well as the sudden unemployment of tens of millions of people.

Everything: manufacturing, high tech, medicine, food production and distribution—all ran on energy in one form or another. Without it, and the efficient manufacture and distribution of goods, the California economy would crumple. And by virtue of being the fifth largest economy in the world and nearly one half of the US economy, America's economy would collapse as well.

Granted, China would lose substantially in the short term as America was also one of its biggest customers and trading partners, and there would be some suffering. But the People's Republic always played the long game, and knew well of sacrifice.

"To abandon self for others; to sacrifice oneself to help the people," Zemin thought, recalling the famous chengyu.

The president also knew that the suffering of the Chinese people would not be painted with a broad brush, nor shared equally by all. From painstaking monitoring of people's social media accounts, those who had not faithfully supported the People's party would rightfully carry the greatest burden. They would receive a smaller number of rations, take the most undesirable of jobs, and work for less than the country's loyal patriots. It was, Zemin felt, only fair.

Most importantly, in a short time, the arrogant imperialists with their trade sanctions and anti-Chinese rhetoric would finally be brought to their knees. The People's Republic would be ready to step in and fill the economic, political—and eventually, military vacuum. Before long, with no other substantial power to stand in their way, the Chinese would rule the world, as was their supreme destiny.

President Gao Zemin smiled broadly at the thought of it.

CHAPTER THIRTY-ONE

Long Beach International Airport
Long Beach, California
Thursday, 3:20 a.m.
+ 0 hours, 45 minutes

The Lear Jet touched down at Long Beach International Airport just after 3:20 a.m. Emergency lights lit up the runways and some of the outer buildings, but beyond them, it was still pitch black.

Marianne had fortunately been able to reroute the limo which was now waiting for them on a small apron off of the main tarmac. As the jet rolled up to a stop, the driver flashed his lights to let them know he was there.

After shutting down the engines and securing the aircraft, the copilot unlatched the inside door and opened it, lowering the stairs in the process.

As soon as the stairs were down, Alan burst out of his seat, grabbing what remained of the blue label scotch in the process. He went down the stairs, refusing the offer of the copilot's hand to help him down, and nearly fell, either from the enveloping darkness or from his blood alcohol level.

'I'm fine," he announced impatiently. "Just late to the party... thanks to you guys!"

The copilot said nothing and waited for Marianne to help her down.

"Thank you," she said graciously, then added. "For everything."

"Not a problem," the copilot replied knowingly. "Comes with the territory."

"So where are you off to now?" she asked, genuinely interested.

"Nowhere," the copilot said. "Were stuck here until further notice. TFR; temporary flight restrictions. No flights going in or out until they figure out what's going on."

"Oh my," she said. "Just like nine-eleven."

"Yep. Drive safe. We'll be here holding down the fort."

Alan was waiting impatiently for Marianne when she walked over to the limo. The uniformed driver, a man, who in the darkness looked to be in his early twenties, was outside and holding the rear door open for them.

"Wow," she said. "Those pilots are grounded and are stuck here until further notice. Just like after nine-eleven."

"Well, that's their fucking problem," Alan said bitterly. "C'mon. We've got to get those candles and get to the party."

"Yes Mr. Binder."

Before he climbed in, Alan took a swig of scotch straight from the bottle and looked up at the sky. Above them, the Milky Way was as bright and brilliant as anyone in the modern world had ever seen.

"I wonder what all that shit is," Alan said before he climbed into the limo.

Inside, he put the cap back onto the bottle and tossed it onto the floor.

"Oh, before I forget, give me my gun back," he said to Marianne.

She reached into her bag, pulled out a Glock 17 Gen 5 handgun, and handed it over to her boss. As a well-known A-list celebrity, Alan Binder had many fans, some of whom couldn't quite keep their distance from him. For several years, he employed the services of a professional bodyguard to travel with him wherever he went to take care of the crazies wherever they might pop up.

But after a costly divorce and with the two recent bombs cutting into his negotiating power to wrangle higher and higher salaries for films, he had to cut back on his expenses and fired the body guard. Still, he was determined not to sacrifice his safety in the process and so he hired an expert firearms instructor, became proficient with all sorts of weapons, and between his connections was able to procure one of the nearly impossible-to-get concealed carry permits in the golden state.

Alan took the gun and holster and put in back on under his jacket.

"Get back on the phone and find those candles," he told Marianne.

"Yes Mr. Binder."

"Driver," Alan barked out, "Three-o-seven, Carolwood Drive, Hombly Hills."

"Yes sir."

Marianne took the phone away from her ear just as the driver started the motor and began to pull out of the airport. "I'm afraid I can't find any stores that are open for the candles Mr. Binder," she informed him. "I think maybe the phones are out too."

"Well keep trying," Alan said impatiently. "I need to make a splash when we get to Barbara's"

"Yes Mr. Binder," she said, and started dialing another number.

"Driver!" Alan practically yelled. "I need you to step on it."

"I can only go so fast with the signals out," the driver responded.

"I don't want your God damned excuses!" Alan snapped. "I need to get to that party."

CHAPTER THIRTY-TWO

San Jose, California
Thursday, 3:21 a.m.
+ 0 hours, 46 minutes

Min Tran drove to his pawn shop, Star Jewelry and Loan, in the downtown section of San Jose as soon as he realized the power was out. The area was one of the most crime-ridden in San Jose, and with a large assortment of jewelry, watches, electronics, and guns, his store would be one of the top targets for looting in the area. He had already suffered enough losses from the rioting and looting sparked by the Black Lives Matter protests, and he vowed to not give up without a fight this time around.

A Vietnamese immigrant, he had survived the communist's 're-education camps' after the fall of Saigon, but unfortunately, his father and older brother did not. Fortune finally smiled on him though in 1989 when his mother, his younger sister, and he were allowed admission to the United States through the Orderly Departure Program.

Seeking the American dream, he settled in the San Jose area with other refugees and worked tirelessly to own his own business, a business that was now under siege.

Armed with a short-barreled pump shotgun and a .38 special revolver, he took up a station behind one of the long glass counters in the back of his store and waited. It was pitch black inside and he had trouble seeing, but enough ambient light was coming from the stars outside to at least allow him to watch for silhouettes of intruders trying to break in.

Not wanting to tip his hand, he watched and waited patiently as looter after looter came and tried unsuccessfully to break through the steel barred gates that covered the entire front of his store, before moving on to softer targets.

Then, he noticed something odd happening. A group of what he assumed was young men had massed outside the store. But they were no longer trying the doors and instead were just waiting.

He briefly considered shouting at them and letting them know he had a gun when all of a sudden, they moved apart from each other, creating a path about eight feet wide. Then he saw why, and he knew it was going to get very bad, very quick.

The light of the headlight beams appeared on the glass at the front of his store, getting larger and more intense with each passing second. The inside of the store was quickly bathed in light and he could no longer hide in the shadows. He raised the shotgun up and aimed toward the window just as a pickup truck came crashing through the front of his store.

Glass shattered and flew everywhere. The metal gate was ripped from its hinges and folded in like a piece of paper. The front of the truck, its lights still on, stopped just inches away from the glass counter he was hiding behind.

Min Tron let loose with a 12-gauge blast from the shotgun at the windshield of the truck and at the driver inside. The buckshot spider-webbed the windshield, but because it was made of laminated safety glass and sloped, did not penetrate through or injure the driver.

Min Tran fired again just as he saw the throng from outside flood into the store, pushing past the limp gate. More and more soon followed, and he soon turned his attention toward the looters instead of trying to shoot through the glass. He aimed at a random man in the charging mob and pulled the trigger just as the driver's door of the truck open and the shot ricocheted off of it.

Then, he saw a flash in the mob and heard another gunshot that wasn't his. The bullet hit his right shoulder squarely and swung his body around like it was body blow. The shotgun fell from his hands and he struggled to pull the .38 special from his waistband to continue to fight.

He was too late as another shot hit him in the chest.

He fell backward against the wall of his store and into the shelves containing tools, antiques, and electronics. The shelves came loose from the wall and along with the items on them, crashed down on top of him. His breathing was choked as he began to drown from the blood gushing into his lungs.

Desperately, he tried to retrieve the revolver to make one last stand, but then he saw the silhouette of another man standing over him and pointing a gun. He had survived the war with the US, the reeducation camps, and the treacherous journey across the ocean to escape Southeast Asia, but he knew now that he wouldn't survive the American dream.

The man fired, and the last thing Min Tran saw in his life was the flash of the barrel.

CHAPTER THIRTY-THREE

CAL-OES
Mather, California
Thursday, 3:27 a.m.
+ 0 hours, 52 minutes

Shanice Dixon stepped into the lobby of the CAL-OES main building and was immediately greeted by Jerelyn Weber, the same executive duty officer who had called her at home. She had to drive slower and more cautiously over the twenty-six-mile trip from El Dorado Hills to Mather as it was more difficult with no lights on the freeway or at the intersections.

The OES campus, consisting of a large main and several smaller buildings totaling 118,000 square feet, was already on generator power and would remain so for fourteen days before running out of fuel. The buildings not only had redundant generators, and backup UPS systems, but was hardened with redundant internet connections, and phone lines. Microwave and satellite antennas and dishes dotted the roofs. Fourteen days of food and fresh water were also kept on site at all times.

Weber informed her that she had already contacted several members of the team as well as Gary Dicey from CAL–ISO.

"Are they all coming in?" she asked, as they stepped quickly into and through the massive State Operations Center, aka, the "SOC". The room was the centerpiece of the main building and the nerve center of emergency operations and response for the enormous state. Filling the 3,800 square foot room was row upon row of computer terminals, several of which were already being manned by other employees. The giant forty-foot-high main wall was arrayed with thirty, 70" TV monitors and several Jumbotrons. The monitors were switched on to various networks such as CNN, FOX and some of the smaller local TV news stations.

All of the news outlets were reporting the outage with some of them having camera crews already on the ground. Shanice knew that it wouldn't be long before they began hounding her team and the governor for updates.

"Some are here, but most are still in transit," Weber replied as they walked up the steps to the main conference room. Just to the right of them and above the main control center wall was a suite reserved for the Governor during times of extreme emergency, such as now.

The door to the conference room was already open and Shanice and Weber stepped inside and took their seats. The room had a large mahogany table in its center with seating for fourteen. Several more chairs were situated against the walls of the room and another large TV monitor was mounted on the far wall. A triangular-shaped conference call base station was located in the center of the table.

Already in the room and seated at the table were some of the heads of departments within OES: Communications, Logistics, and Response and Recovery Ops, as well as representatives from CAL-Fire, STTAC, CHP, FEMA Region 9, and, the governor's office. Several other underlings occupied the chairs against the walls.

Shanice turned first to the representative from the governor's office, a female staffer who looked to be younger than thirty.

"The governor?"

"Already informed. He was in a conference in Denver and is flying back on a military transport as we speak. ETA..."

She looked at her phone. "Six O'clock. Maybe sooner."

"Does he want to conference in right now?"

"No ma'am. I asked him and he said that not unless you need him to. He said he'd rather 'just let you do your job' and will catch up later."

"Sounds good," Shanice said, finding it refreshing that a politician would allow her and her team some breathing room.

"What about an EAS? Does the governor want us to send one out now?"

"Negative," Ms. Dixon. "He wants to wait until at least he touches down and we have more info."

Shanice nodded and then turned to the OES communications head, "Based on what we learn in this meeting, start to put a draft together for the governor's review."

"Yes ma'am," she said and started to get to work composing a message on her tablet.

Shanice swung her chair in the direction of her Acting Deputy Director for Response and Recovery.

"Call the others in transit on their cells or sats and see if we can have them conference in, so we can get started ASAP."

"Yes ma'am."

The conference call unit on the table began to pipe in with the sounds of others calling in: reps from Health and Human Services, EPA, DOE, and Gary Dicey from Cal-ISO.

Figuring she had enough key players to get the ball rolling, Shanice decided to start the meeting. She went around the room quickly and had people state their name and job responsibility, then let those conferencing in follow suit. After that, she asked Gary Dicey to bring everyone up to speed.

"First of all; I apologize for not being able to join you in person," Gary's voice said through the speaker. "But it's still pretty crazy here trying to figure out what's going on."

"Understood Mr. Dicey," Shanice said. "We're just happy to have you call in." She had spoken to the Cal-ISO supervisor a couple of times on the phone before, and they met once or twice at a conference, but besides that, they didn't know each other very well.

"Can you start by telling us exactly what you saw happen tonight?" Shanice continued.

"Sure," Gary said, and then went on to detail in chronological order how the night unfolded; the grid running smooth, no fires, electrical storms or other threats. Then, at approximately 2:35 am, all hell breaking loose. Alarms, losing one segment after another, donut oscillations with the greater western grid and the states of Nevada and Washington. Then we went completely dark."

"Do you now if the other states are down as well?"

"Nevada was able to quickly island from us and save themselves, but Washington got hit pretty hard by our oscillations and went down. Then they cascaded to Montana, and took them down as well. The last I heard, they've each lost about thirty percent of their grid, but are slowly getting it back on line."

Another caller came in on the conference call just then and announced her name and title, "Marie Sheldon from Regional Ops Southern."

Shanice said, "Thanks for calling in Marie. I'm not going to go through all the introductions again, but right now, Gary Dicey from Cal-ISO is bringing us up to speed, so I'll let him continue."

"Understood."

"Gary, did you speak to any of the operators at the affected sites?" a rep from the DOE asked.

"Yes, and they all stated about the same thing; they heard a massive explosion, followed by a complete loss of power. After realizing they had no control, they went outside to do a physical inspection."

"And what did they find when they went out there?" Shanice followed up.

"Pieces of trucks near the scene along with thousands of ball bearings on the ground. The transformers were Swiss-cheesed from the ball bearings, and all the insulating oil leaked out as well. It's a mess."

"All of them saw the same thing?" DOE asked.

"Everyone I spoke to," Gary replied.

"Truck bombs?" The question came from Jay Behnken, the on-duty supervisor of the STTAC, The State Terrorism Threat Assessment Center, which was located nearby in the state's Security Information Center. 'STACK,' as they were referred to, was the agency tasked with analyzing terrorist threats and liaising with the investigative agencies.

"That's what it looks like," Gary said. "And it looks like they were positioned to take out the HPT's, also known as LPT's"

"HPT's?" Shanice asked.

The DOE rep was about to cut in and answer, but then Gary beat him to the punch. As it was, the Cal-ISO supervisor was well versed in the hardware that made up the grid.

"They are the high-power transformers that tie together the grid - essentially from the power plants that generate the power - to the sub-stations that distribute it."

"Are PG&E, DWP, and Edison sending out crews to assess the damage?" Shanice asked the DOE rep.

"Yes, But I'm not sure if they have arrived yet," he said. "As you can imagine, communications are tough."

Shanice turned her attention back to the conference call unit and to Gary. "But it looks to your people on the ground like it was a terrorist attack?"

"Unfortunately. Yes Ma'am."

Shanice turned to Behnken, "What have you guys heard over at stack?" she asked.

"Pretty much the same thing ma'am," the supervisor said. He was a transplant from the Texas Division of Emergency Management and spoke with a slow drawl that belied his intellect and circumspection.

"We're all hear'n pretty much the same thing as y'all from our law enforcement partners throughout the state."

"Has FBI and DHS been notified to make a solid determination?"

"Yes ma'am," He drawled. "In route as we speak."

They all sat there, looking at one another or lost in their own thoughts. Finally, Shanice sighed heavily and stated what they all knew.

"Well, it sounds very much as if we've had a large-scale terrorist attack that has effectively taken down the entire electrical grid of California."

"Are you going to inform the Governor that it was a terrorist attack?" The communications director asked. "Or, should I do it?"

"I'll do it," Shanice said. "As soon as we adjourn here, I'll call him. But I'm not going to say for sure it was – that's not my authority, just that it looks very likely and that STACK, FBI and DHS are all on it."

The CAL–OES Director turned toward the rest of them then.

"Everyone else, start contacting all of the people in your sphere and have them get in here ASAP with their go-bags. We're going to level one, full activation. Also pull up your copy of the Power Outage Incident Annex from DHS and start getting up to speed. I want your mission assignments activated. We are going to need all the help we can get. I want to reconvene here…"

"She looked at her watch, "At o-seven-hundred. Gary, are you still there?"

"Yes I am."

"Any chance you could break away for a face to face at seven? The governor should be here by then, and I think he'll want you present."

"Sure thing. I get relieved at six, and I'll come straight over there."

"Great, and thank you."

She looked around the room at all the people assembled there, people she was in charge of and whom she would now have to depend on more than ever.

"Ladies and gentlemen, I don't think I need to tell you this, but the lives of forty million people are now in our hands."

DHS Power Outage Incident Annex
Source: https://www.fema.gov/sites/default/files/2020-07/fema_ incident-annex_power-outage.pdf

CHAPTER THIRTY-FOUR

San Francisco, California
Thursday, 3:39 a.m.
+ 1 hour, 4 minutes

A little more than an hour ago, the host of the KCBS overnight news program, Tom Calderwood, saw the flicker of the lights in the studio, and then heard the rumble as the backup generator started up. Before long, the ATS had engaged and the broadcast and engineering booths, separated by a thick sheet of soundproof glass, looked no worse for wear. Calderwood and his engineer, Padmini Laghari had been through a couple of blackouts before, and knew that the station was protected.

Deemed part of critical infrastructure after the protests and occasional takeovers of broadcast stations by radical groups in the 1970s, the US government had implemented strict measures designed to keep key radio and TV stations operational during all but the most extreme natural and manmade disasters. Considered primary entry points for the Emergency Alert System, the buildings were newly built or retrofitted to the highest seismic standards and with security as tight as many prisons. The buildings had redundant backup generators and large stocks of fuel, and the transmitters and antenna were redundant and located in separate locations. They had food and water to last up to thirty days and many of the buildings were hardened against EMP, or electro-magnetic pulse.

Within a few minutes after the blackout, the calls to the station had started to come in, typically from chronic night owls or from the older listeners who couldn't sleep at night and had nothing better to do but listen to the same news they had heard broadcast all day long.

But the calls didn't originate from just the immediate surrounding area. At 50,000 watts of power the reach of the historic radio station often stretched as far south as Bakersfield and as far north as Redding, and this was where a representative share of the calls came from.

As disparate and far-flung as they were however, almost all of them said the same thing, 'The lights and everything else suddenly went out, and it was darkness as far as the eye could see.' Some reported hearing explosions as well.

During a commercial break, Calderwood grabbed a rechargeable flashlight and went up to the roof where some of the directional antennas were mounted and looked for himself. Switching off the flashlight, he saw—or rather was enveloped in, the blackness; total, absolute and endless blackness in every direction. A blackness so deep that even the Milky Way Galaxy was clearly visible overhead.

Hastings quickly returned to the broadcast booth and was just adjusting his headset when, Michelle Gillies, the Philippine anchor of the CBS TV Morning News Program entered the engineer's booth.

Nestled between Telegraph Hill and San Francisco's financial district, the building housed not just the CBS Radio affiliate, but its signature TV station as well.

Gillies was petite, attractive and sported a cute figure as well as a thick mane of black hair that didn't quit. Tom could observe, even through the thick glass that separated them, that she hadn't finished applying all of her makeup, and was wearing a disposable makeup bib around her neck to keep the stains off of her snug fitting cream colored blouse.

Gillies knew that the radio station was still on a commercial break and wouldn't be live again for about a minute so she quickly grabbed a headset off of the engineer's console, pulled one side of it up to her ear so as not to muss up her hair and spoke into it.

"Tom, do you know what's going on?" She asked. "It was dark as crap coming in."

"Just that this must be big," he responded. "We're getting calls from all over the place saying the same thing. I'd expect an EAS message any minute to come through the EDIS. I called our station manager, and he's on his way in."

"Got it," she quickly replied, glancing at her watch. "We're going live in less than thirty, but without power, how many people will be watching is the question."

"Right," Calderwood replied, knowing that as long as cars still had radios, and there were still battery powered portables, radio would always reign as the go-to media in an emergency over television.

"If you hear anything, please let me know and I'll do the same," Gillies then added. "Deal?"

"Deal."

The TV anchor dropped her headset onto the engineer's console, blew Calderwood a quick kiss, and then turned and marched out the door as quickly as she had come in.

Just then, Padmini held up her slender brown hand and started counting down. First five fingers...then four...three...two...

"We are back live now here at KCBS, AM Seven-Forty," Calderwood said. "And if you haven't heard—or somehow haven't been affected by it, the greater bay area has just experienced what appears to be a very large-scale power outage. Now, let's get to some more of your calls."

He stared down at the call board in front of him and saw that all of the lights were blinking. He shook his head in astonishment and then pressed one at random.

"Hello, you're on the air..."

EAS: Emergency Alert System
EDIS: Emergency Digital Information System
Source: https://www.caloes.ca.gov/WarningCenterSite/Documents/
StateofCaliforniaEAS-Plan.pdf

CHAPTER THIRTY-FIVE

McNair, California
Thursday, 3:40 a.m.
+ 1 hour, 5 minutes

Newly elected Councilman Wayne Kelly was the first to arrive at the McNair Emergency Operations Center after his phone received an automatic text instructing him to assemble along with the other emergency operations team members.

Truth be told though, the facility wasn't a true, dedicated EOC that some of the larger municipalities had, and was more of the 'EOC in a box' concept that many localities had opted for. Located in the tiny city's school bus depot and maintenance yard on the outskirts of town, the EOC in a box wasn't much more than a spare closet packed with computer terminals, white boards, and stationary supplies in a back corner of the building. Without a set of keys to get in, the councilman waited outside of the main door in the darkness for other team members to arrive.

Only three weeks into his term, Kelly was still working on getting up to speed on the various procedures and processes of city government when the city clerk plopped a two-inch thick binder on his desk and announced, "This is our emergency action plan. You're supposed to know it."

He had skimmed it, but was far from 'knowing it.' He only hoped that others were more versed in it than he was.

Soon, he began seeing the headlights of vehicles as they arrived and navigated into the pitch-black parking lot. He removed the headlamp from his head and waved it to let them know where he was standing.

Next to arrive was another council member, Janice Frank, followed by the director of public works, Jack Spar, who at least had keys to the building and could let them in. He did not however, he informed them, have the keys to compound that held the backup generator.

"That's the utilities department," Spar stated matter-of-factly. "It's their baby, and they're real fussy about anyone else touching it."

"Are they on their way in?" Councilperson Frank asked.

"Dunno," he replied. "Supposed to be."

Just then, the interim city manager, Joel Tomlinson, arrived and walked up to them. He had been the head of the zoning commission and planning department and was recently catapulted into the position when the previous city manager had resigned under a cloud of scandal.

A married man, the former manager not only had a sordid affair with the head of the parks and rec department, he also embezzled hundreds of thousands of dollars from the city's coffers, leaving them in the worst financial position since the sub-prime mortgage crisis. A lawsuit was pending to try to recover the money, but hopes were not high.

Avarice and lust aside, it was an unfortunate state of affairs as the former city manager had been the lead on the EOC project and had not only secured the federal funding for it, but was also the official in charge. Most importantly to all of them assembling, he had been instrumental in developing the emergency management plan they were now supposed to implement.

"Well," Wayne Kelly stated to all of them, but specifically to the interim city manager. "I guess since the other manager resigned—"

"He was fired!" Councilperson Frank corrected him.

Kelly, paused, took a deep breath and then continued. "Since he was fired, I would guess that you are in charge Mr. Tomlinson, correct?"

"I guess," the interim manager responded.

"Have you read the manual?" councilperson Frank asked.

"I've perused it," Tomlinson admitted.

"Has anyone read it completely?" Kelly asked.

All around him, the beams from their headlamps wagged from side to side.

Exasperated, Kelly followed up. "Well, does anyone here know what we're supposed to do?"

Again, their beams just moved from side to side.

"(sic) Organizations need a more granular version of their response so employees and key members of the crisis management team would know how to activate it should the director be unable to do so."
Source: https: //www.asisonline.org/security-management-magazine/ articles/2018/09/a-failure-to-plan/

CHAPTER THIRTY-SIX

San Roque, California
Thursday, 4:03 a.m.
+ 1 hour, 28 minutes

Demetrius Johnson lost count of the number of times he had been up last night and this morning. That was just what you did when you were seventy-one and blessed with an enlarged prostate; you gave up counting trips to the can.

So, after feeling 'the urge' for the umpteenth time, he once again rolled over, threw off the covers, and reached for the knob on the lamp on his bedside table.

This trip to the loo was going to be different though as, after rotating the knob several times, he came to the realization that the bulb must had burned out.

Undeterred, he stood, felt his way through the doorframe, and turned down the hallway toward the bathroom. Halfway down, he reached for the switch to turn on the overhead light and found that it was out as well.

"Great," he cursed under his breath. "A damn blackout."

He continued on in the darkness and eventually found his way into the bathroom, completely his routine business.

After divorcing his third wife twelve years ago, DJ, as he liked to be called, had decided to remain a committed bachelor and live alone for the rest of his life. He enjoyed the solitude a single life afforded, and he had a modest home in a nice quiet neighborhood to live out his remaining days.

Realizing that he was now wide awake, he decided to stay up and continue on the crossword puzzle he had started last night. He put on his robe and felt his way into the kitchen where he kept a flashlight.

Reaching the kitchen, he rummaged through the junk drawer, found his light, and switched it on; dead.

"Crap!"

His pack of cigarettes and lighter were still on the counter where he left them, and he felt for them and flicked on the lighter, giving him at least a modicum of illumination.

He couldn't hold the tiny tab on his lighter down forever though and quickly went through another drawer to retrieve a candle. After it was lit, he lit a cigarette off of the flame and carried the candle over to the kitchen table to start back on his crosswords.

He was closing in on the clue for an eight-letter word for 'tough' when he felt yet another urge to 'go.'

"Son of a…" he muttered, grabbing the book, his pencil, and the candle off of the table to take with him, reasoning that the solution might just come to him in there.

In his haste and in the dimness of the bathroom, DJ didn't notice the upturned corner of the bath rug when he stepped in. His foot caught on it, and before he could recover, was falling toward the bathtub. In the process, he instinctively let go of the candle.

His chest hit the edge of the tub and cracked several of his ribs, taking his breath away in the process. What he didn't notice was that the fallen candle had stayed lit and ignited first the rug, and then the fabric of his robe. Soon, the flames began racing up his side and he instinctively grabbed at the shower curtain to try pull himself up.

The shower rod, unable to support his weight snapped in half and the curtain came down on top of him, its plastic material quickly igniting and adding fuel to the growing fire that was soon enveloping him.

"Help! Fire!" Demetrius Johnson screamed, hoping that one of his neighbors would hear him.

CHAPTER THIRTY-SEVEN

Lakewood, California
Thursday, 4:11 a.m.
+ 1 hour, 36 minutes

Alan Binder continued his rants at the limo driver, telling him he needed to go faster as Marianne continued to frantically search for open stores on her phone.

Finally, she said, "I think I've got one," and soft tapped the number on the screen to call it.

A few seconds later, Alan heard her say, "Hello...Yes...Are you still open?"

A few seconds later, she asked, "...And do you have candles?"

"Great."

She terminated the call, disconnected her seat belt and leaned forward in the limo to tell the driver where to head to. He punched the address into his GPS and they began to hear the monotonous drone of the instructions as they were recited.

"How long before we get there, driver?" Alan demanded to know.

"Uh, twenty-three minutes."

"Bullshit!" Alan snapped at him. "You get us there in ten, or I'll make sure you never drive a fucking limo again!"

By now, the driver had heard enough of Alan's complaining and against his better judgement, pushed the accelerator down. Alan and Marianne felt the speed of the car suddenly increase.

Marianne returned to her seat and was fumbling to find her seat belt in the darkness when all of a sudden, the limo came to a violent and instantaneous stop. In the inky blackness, the driver couldn't see a train crossing ahead. With no backup source of power, the signal lights and arms were out and they slammed right into the side of a moving freight train.

Marianne screamed and was thrown into the rear facing seats and the divider.

"Fuck!" Alan yelled.

The front left corner of the limo wedged itself between two freight cars and was dragged down the track by the car's bumper. The driver's air bag had deployed and besides being stunned, he was unable to see what was going on.

The limo continued to be dragged down the track for about one hundred feet before it slammed violently into a large concrete base.

The force of the impact dislodged the limo from the train and it rolled over and over down a steep berm alongside the track. All of the side windows shattered into a million pieces and Marianne was thrown from the car. Her body flew into a nearby cinder block wall, hitting it straight on with her head. She was instantly unconscious.

The limo finally rolled to a stop at the bottom of the berm. It was upside down and as soon as Alan could regain his faculties, he undid his seat belt and crawled out through the window opening on the driver's side of the car. Thankfully, the rear compartment dome lights had come on.

As he crawled out on his hands and knees, his hand went into a pile of something that was soft and squishy a few feet from the car. He thought for a second it was animal waste, but when he examined it further in the dim light put out by the limo's interior lights, he saw that it was brain matter.

"Argh!" he cried and shook his hand vigorously to get it off of him, hoping he didn't fling any onto his pants or jacket.

Still crawling on the ground, he made it up to the front compartment and realized then what had happened. The driver's head had been crushed by the door pillar when they hit the concrete base and the entire front of the car had been pushed into him. His head was distorted and his brains were slowly oozing out from a gaping fissure in his skull.

"Marianne!" Alan called out.

Not hearing a response, he stumbled around in the darkness calling her name.

"Marianne...Marianne...Marianne!"

In the darkness, he saw a form lying next to a wall.

He ran toward it and slipped and fell as his foot rolled out from a glass bottle on the ground.

"Shit!" He yelled out.

He climbed back to his feet and then continued towards the form.

"Marianne!" he cried when he reached her. "Are you okay?"

She didn't answer, and Alan began to panic. He leaned down, grabbed her wrist and felt for a pulse. She had one, but it was very weak. Probably just knocked out temporarily he told himself.

Thinking that he still should probably call for help, he reached into his pocket to call 911, but his phone wasn't there.

"Crap!" he said, and then started looking around wildly in the darkness.

Not finding it, he returned to Marianne and looked down to her hand; it was still clutching the phone she was using to call for the candles.

He grabbed it out of her hand and swiped the screen; it was locked.

"Marianne...Marianne! Give me the code to unlock your phone!"

But she couldn't respond.

CHAPTER THIRTY-EIGHT

Santa Clara, California
Thursday, 4:15 a.m.
+ 1 hour, 40 minutes

Emperium Data Center supervisor, Angela Spinelli's cell phone buzzed just moments after the power went out. She had an app installed that would immediately let her know if there was any problem at the site, including, if it was an interruption to the facility's 13.5 MW of incoming power.

She was dressed and heading to the site within a matter of minutes, but her travel was hampered from driving in pitch blackness and having to cautiously navigate the intersections with no working signal lights. Flipping through the stations on her car radio, she heard static from all but a few, and what they were saying wasn't good. That it wasn't just a localized or regional event, but statewide or greater, and possibly – the announcers were already speculating; a terrorist attack.

Spinelli had developed an ulcer over the past year or so since she had taken the position managing one of the two hundred or so data centers in the high-tech state, and now it was beginning to act up.

Pulling up to the 100,000 square foot building, she could hear the hum of the big Caterpillar diesel generators in the distance. They were massive units, eight in total and together could gulp fuel at the rate of twelve-hundred gallons per hour. A 20,000-gallon fuel tank was on site, but at the current rate without being replenished, it would only buy them sixteen hours before the servers would experience 'hard shutdowns' that would corrupt the data stored in them. She gripped her stomach, realizing they had to get fuel in fast or they were doomed.

Her on-site night manager, Dan Lavelle, met her at the front door as the security guard unlocked it and let her in. They walked briskly toward the large monitoring room for the facility. The room was the hub where status alarms for the 250,000 servers and various other equipment such as switches and modems came in.

"Status," she said simply, wishing not to waste any time on pleasantries.

"Went down at two-thirty-five a.m." he began. "UPS transfer was seamless, and the gen-sets kicked on as designed."

"Any data corruptions?" she asked.

"Not that we can detect, yet," Lavelle stated.

They stepped into the room and saw the half dozen or so night shift operators at their monitor station.

"Alarms?" Spinelli asked.

All but one of the operators shook their heads no. The lone holdout, whose duties included power, environmental, and fire or flood alarms turned to her.

"Only the incoming power ma'am."

Good, Spinelli thought to herself. They didn't need an AC failure on top of everything else. Thinking of the air conditioning units, she knew that they would be more taxed when the sun came up in a couple of hours and the gen-sets would suck even more fuel.

"Fuel supplier?" she asked, turning to Lavelle.

"Already called as per the protocol. But they said we'll have to be in the queue; all the SV's and SJC data sites want fuel as well. Everyone's in the same boat."

"Did he give an estimate at least?" Spinelli prompted, knowing that they were now all fighting for the same precious commodity.

"He said that *if* all his drivers show up, hopefully by tonight. Tomorrow at the latest."

"Shit!" she cursed, and gripped her stomach again. She had already done the math in her head and knew that they wouldn't make it to the evening.

Seeing her discomfort Lavelle asked thoughtfully, "You okay?"

"Yes," she replied, although knowing what she would have to do, caused her insides to burn.

"She looked up to the site supervisor. "Call everyone in; all shifts. And get out the data backup and shutdown procedures. It's going to be a long day."

"Even a moment's disruption can have devastating effects on power sensitive customers such as internet service providers and data centers, resulting in data corruption, burned circuit boards, component damage, file corruption and lost customers."

Source: U.S. Dept. of Energy Office of Power Technologies, *Electrical Power Interruption Cost Estimates for Individual Industries, Sectors, and U.S. Economy, February 2002*

CHAPTER THIRTY-NINE

Lakewood, California
Thursday, 4:17 a.m.
+ 1 hour, 42 minutes

Without being able to unlock Marianne's phone, Alan Binder had no choice but to try to find his own. By now, his eyes were adjusting and with the light from the stars overhead, his chances were at least better than they were a few minutes ago.

Still, he had to crawl around on hands and knees to get close enough to items to identify them, tearing the knee in his slacks on the loose gravel in the process.

Dammit! He thought. These fucking things cost me $1200.00 at Dior Homme on Rodeo Drive.

Finally, after several long minutes of picking through discarded bottles, cans and fast-food bags, he finally spotted something with the right size and shape. He picked the object up and sure enough, it was his phone, thrown about twenty feet from the limo.

He pushed the button to activate the screen but the display remained dark. He felt over the surface of the screen with his hands and then realized that it was cracked and that the phone didn't work.

"Shit!" he hissed, thinking to himself, the latest iPhone and now it's broke. He can't call 911… or even Barbara to tell her that he was going to miss the party. He made a mental note to sue both the railroad and the limo company for a new phone and a pair of slacks - maybe even for the loss of a movie role.

Defeated, he stumbled back to Marianne, hoping that maybe she had regained consciousness.

"Marianne…Marianne! Can you hear me?" He tried shaking her. "What's the code to unlock your phone? I need to call 911."

She could do nothing but moan, and turn her head slowly from side to side.

Realizing he had no other option at this point, he picked her up and started to carry her over to the road to hopefully flag down a passing motorist.

Although she was built slightly and probably weighed under a hundred pounds, she was still dead weight, and Alan had an extremely tough time trying to carry her, especially across the loose gravel that bordered the train tracks.

He remembered the last time he had been in decent shape was for his movie, *The Comeback Kid*, where he played a boxer trying to come out of retirement. But that was a couple of years ago, and he worked out with a professional trainer five hours a day. Since then, none of his roles had demanded any sort of physical conditioning. He was paying for his torpidity now.

A few agonizing moments later, he finally made it to the street and set Marianne down as gently as he could on the sidewalk. He began to scan up and down the street.

A car's lights headlights appeared off in the distance and were coming toward him. Feeling hopeful, Alan stepped out further onto the road and started waving his arms to flag down the driver.

The car drove right past him without even slowing down.

"Damn it!" He cursed after them. "Don't you know who I am?"

CHAPTER FORTY

Some headed for the hills as soon as the magnitude of the attack sunk in. Some headed to the grocery stores and gas stations. Still others, hunkered down at home. But some showed up at Second-A Gun Store, fearing the worst of society and wanting to stock up on all the guns and ammo they could find.

Brian Thomas, the owner of Second-A knew this intimately, and from the moment he woke up to go to bathroom and realized that the power was out, he knew he had to get to the store as soon as possible to protect it. No power meant no alarm system, and a store that stocked over seventy-five long arms, fifty odd handguns, and probably 100,000 rounds of ammo, would be a sitting duck and a juicy target for looters when they came.

Feeling his way back to his bedroom in the dark, he grabbed his Glock 19 off of the nightstand and switched on the under-barrel Streamlight, immediately flooding the bedroom in illumination. After making sure the room was empty of intruders, he next grabbed the Glock G-26 subcompact from under his pillow, and the bug-out-bag he kept under his bed. Two assault rifles with extra clips from one of his gun safes rounded out his necessary supplies, and he headed out.

To his surprise, and thankfully, the store had not yet been targeted but he knew that it wouldn't last for long.

He entered through the back door and after sweeping the interior for intruders took up a vigil sitting in the dark and waiting for the looters to arrive, his loaded AR-15 cradled in his lap, and his Glock 19 in a holster on his hip.

Now, an hour later and still with several hours to go before his regular opening time, they were starting to mass at the door. He could see silhouettes back-lit by the starlight overhead, but also by the scattered punctuation of random light from high intensity flashlights.

In spite of the sub-par lighting however, Brian Thomas could tell by their voices and actions that these weren't looters; they were some of his best customers, and they began yelling for him to open.

"C'mon, open up Brian," one of them called out.

"Yeah!" others chimed in.

He set his AR down carefully across his chair and walked to the front door. Most of the group gathered outside were white males, but there were a small number of Latinos, Blacks, and Asians mixed in as well. They ranged in age from the mid-twenties to seventy, but most were baby-boomers. Many sported NRA and Trump 2024 shirts, and some had MAGA hats. Some, he knew, were already carrying guns.

"I can't," he yelled through the glass. "The point of sale is down and I can't get onto the DOJ website."

"Fuck the DOJ!" one of the men yelled angrily, to the cheers of the others crowding at the door. "All they ever did was try to take our guns away!"

"I'll pay cash," another man said, pulling out a thick wad of bills from his pocket. "Whatever you want, for as many three-o-eight as you can sell me."

"Same here," another man said. "Two-two-three."

"And I'll give you this," one man said, removing a bar of gold from his pocket and shining the beam of his flashlight onto it.

Brian knew what it was, and what it was worth. Many preppers stocked up on gold, figuring with a societal collapse, greenbacks would be worthless. And maybe they were right. He stared at the bar of gold for a long time.

"What are you going to do?" one man challenged him. "Not let us defend ourselves. God dammed commies are gonna come for us. North Koreans or Ruskies are probably behind this shit. And we need to be prepared."

"Or fucking Antifa!"

"Yeah," the crowd yelled in unison.

"'Sides that," another man said. "You can either sit here forever and hope you can hold off the bad guys, or you can let us good guys get the guns and ammo we need, and let us *help you hold them off*."

"Yeah!"

Brian Thomas believed in the second amendment—his store was named for it, and he knew that his livelihood came from these folks who believed the same. He couldn't let them down.

"Okay," he said finally. "One at a time—and no hoarding! Who was here first?" The man with the gold bar raised his hand.

"I was," he said.

Brian unlocked the door. Let the man in, and then closed and locked it behind him. Then he turned back to the crowd.

"I need to keep some things for myself though," he told them all."

"Sure, sure. We understand," several of them said.

Then one man in the crowd pulled out a Smith and Wesson semi-automatic pistol. "And don't worry," he said. "We got your back."

"Yeah!" several others said, and six more guns appeared.

CHAPTER FORTY-ONE

Lakewood, California
Thursday, 4:36 a.m.
+ 2 hours, 1 minute

In spite of his antics and yelling, several more cars and a semi-truck, all with their high-beams on, roared by Alan without stopping. Marianne still hadn't regained consciousness, and he had to keep telling himself that it was just temporary. She was young, he reasoned, and healthy. She would bounce back.

Just then, he heard the sound of crunching metal and shattering glass as two cars collided in a nearby intersection, its signal lights dark. One car's horn started blaring into the night like a wailing child.

At this point, Alan figured he had nothing to lose and decided to leave Marianne and run over toward the wreck. Maybe, he thought, they would have a phone and could call 9-1-1 for him.

He ran as fast as he could to the darkened intersection, and by the time he reached the scene of the crash, he was drenched in sweat and dying for another scotch.

In his favor, he approached the two cars just as a Sheriff's car rolled up to the scene. Luckily, the deputy might have been close by on patrol and heard or saw the accident. One driver involved in the wreck was already out of his car and surveying the scene. The other was still in the driver's seat but moving about. Through the light from one of the car's askew headlamps, it didn't look to be much more than a good fender bender.

Even though he had a permit for his Glock, Alan thought the sight of a firearm could complicate matters if he came running up to a peace officer out of nowhere with his weapon visible. Therefore, he wisely buttoned his coat before approaching him. The deputy had scarcely exited his patrol car when Alan got his attention.

"I need help," he said desperately, yelling over the sound of the blaring horn. "My assistant and I were in a horrible accident with a train at the crossing. She might be hurt real bad. I need to get her to the hospital, and I don't have a working phone."

The deputy listened and then took his flashlight and aimed it at Alan's face.

Unlike most people, the veteran actor was used to being under spotlights and didn't cover his eyes or turn away, though he blinked a couple of times.

"You're Alan Binder, aren't you?" The deputy asked, just as the blare of the horn, mercifully ceased.

"Yes, I am," Alan said, relieved someone finally recognized him.

"But please call an ambulance or something. My assistant's hurt really bad."

"Ambulances are swamped," the deputy said matter of factly. "We'll probably have to transport ourselves. I need to check these two out and then we'll attend to your friend. It's been a crazy night as you can imagine."

The deputy quickly checked out the two drivers in the accident and determined them to be non-critical; just a couple of scratches and some bruises. The cars still were somewhat mobile and the deputy instructed them to pull off to the side and to try to straighten things out with insurance and so forth.

"Get in the patrol car," he instructed Alan, and they drove off toward the train tracks where Alan had left Marianne.

The deputy switched on his spotlight and located her lying on the sidewalk within seconds. She hadn't seemed to move at all and Alan hoped this wasn't a bad omen.

He and the deputy got out of the patrol car and after pulling on some latex gloves, the deputy did an assessment, checking her pulse, breathing, etc.

"Ma'am...Ma'am..." the deputy called out to her, while simultaneously lightly tapping her cheek with two fingers to get her to come to, but this time she didn't even moan or turn her head

"She's alive," he finally said, "but non-responsive. We'll have to transport her ourselves," he told Alan.

"So, she's just unconscious right? She'll be okay?"

"No way of telling," the deputy said noncommittally, not giving Alan much comfort.

"Was anyone else hurt in the crash?" he then asked.

"The limo driver, but he's dead."

"I still have to check him out before we leave," the deputy said almost too routinely for Alan's taste. Like most people in the presence of first responders, he became impatient at the deliberate, seemingly glacial pace at which they did their jobs. It was only due to their training and experience that they didn't run around in a panic, rush into things blindly, and make a bad situation worse.

"I told you; he's dead!" Alan repeated, his voice rising.

The deputy wasn't having any of it and said, even louder. "I have to check him out! Now where is he?"

Alan huffed and pointed down the track. The cops took his flashlight and walked through the darkness the hundred feet or so to the limo.

Alan, insulted that he wasn't taken at his word, stayed behind and tried to comfort Marianne. With the police cruisers spotlight on her, he could see her more clearly. She had a large gash on the top of her head, and blood had matted her dark hair to her scalp. Her left arm was also askew, and he wondered if she had dislocated or broken her shoulder. The only hopeful sign he saw was her chest rising and falling as she breathed, albeit shallowly. She'll be fine, he told himself.

"He's deceased all right," he heard the deputy say as he reappeared from out of the darkness a few moments later.

Alan bit his tongue and resisted the temptation to say, *I fucking told you so.*

CHAPTER FORTY-TWO

Lakewood, California
Thursday, 5:14 a.m.
+ 2 hours, 39 minutes

Like millions of others in California that first fateful morning, Barbara overslept. Old fashioned as she was, she still relied on a bedside alarm clock as she still didn't trust her cell phone. Plus, not having the phone within easy reach, helped her avoid the temptation of checking it every so often. On this particular morning however, it would have been a prudent choice.

Having an urge to use the bathroom was what got her up instead. It was then, in the nearly pitch darkness of her bedroom and apartment that she realized the power was out. She felt for the drawer handle of her bedside nightstand, pulled it open and rooted through the contents until she found her emergency flashlight.

She flicked on the switch and discovered that the batteries were nearly dead and that it could only cast a feeble dull orange glow. *What was that old joke?* she thought. Question: What's the definition of a flashlight? Answer: A cylindrical storage container for dead batteries.

After using the bathroom, she realized that it might be a smart thing to see what time it truly was and headed to the kitchen where she kept her cellphone charging on the counter. She swiped the display.

"Crap!"

She took the phone and the failing flashlight into her mom's bedroom to wake her up.

"Mom," she said, gently shaking her. "Mom."

Her mom slowly roused.

"I'm late mom," Barbara said hurriedly. "The power went out and I overslept. I'm going to have to rush out of here and I didn't want you to oversleep and not be able to get the kids to school on time"

"All...alright," her mom said groggily.

Barbara headed out of her mom's bedroom, guided by the weak beam of the dying flashlight, but then she remembered that her phone had a flashlight app. It took her awhile, moving around the screen icons, but then she found it and switched it on. Compared to the dull orange of the flashlight, the blinding beam the cell phone produced was like comparing a hydrogen bomb to a kitchen match.

Getting dressed by the narrow single beam of the cellphone wasn't too difficult, but trying to do her makeup with it was next to impossible. The light scattered in the tiny confines of the bathroom and reflected off of the mirror creating wicked shadows. She had trouble trying to set it up to get just the right angle and most of the time it had her face bottom-lit like kids telling scary stories in the dark with a flashlight.

No matter how bad she looked though, getting to work on time was her highest priority, and so she threw some cosmetics into her purse to hopefully redo her face once she got to the store.

She was rushing out the door and moving at a trot by 5:27 a.m.

CHAPTER FORTY-THREE

Cerritos, California
Thursday, 5:28 a.m.
+ 2 hours, 53 minutes

The drive to the hospital was a crazy one. Alan sat in the back holding onto Marianne as the deputy's radio squawked continuously with new calls for service. Plus, it took longer than usual. Even with the car's siren and lights on, with the signal lights out, they still had to cross intersections more carefully than normal. Just like the limo driver had wanted to do, Alan mused, before pushing the thought from his head.

He also didn't try to make conversation. Not that he thought the deputy would have wanted to talk to him anyway; his last picture had been about an ACLU attorney on a crusade to expose dirty cops. Not exactly a feel-good film for the boys with the badges.

The deputy's personal cell phone went off just then. Unlike other civilians, deputies had the right to use their phones when they drove. He also knew that cops routinely used their personal cells and things like Whatsapp to communicate in private, lest any damning conversation would be captured on the transcripts of radio transmissions.

The deputy looked at the number on the screen and must have recognized it because he readily answered

"Hey, what's up?" the deputy asked

There was a pause as the person on the other end said something. Alan could only hear one side of the conversation, but suspected it was another deputy.

Alan saw the deputy look at him warily in the rear-view mirror and then say, "Yeah, I've been thinking the same thing." The deputy responded cautiously. "Might have to. We'll talk later."

A few silent minutes later, the patrol car wheeled up to the emergency entrance of St. Elizabeth Medical Center—which was so dim as to look closed down. The deputy gave the siren a couple of 'whoops.'

A moment later, a medical tech in light blue scrubs looked out and held up a hand. Soon, he and another man were hustling out with a gurney. In a few moments they had carefully slid Marianne off of Alan's lap, and had her placed on the gurney. They rushed off with her towards the ED entrance.

"I'm going to have to drop you off here" the deputy told him. "I don't know if you heard, but we had a state wide power outage and it's going to get crazy."

"Yeah, I did," Alan said, climbing out of the back of the patrol car. "Thanks."

The deputy nodded dismissively and turned his attention back to the display screen in his patrol car. Alan got the impression that he wanted to put a lot of distance between himself and the actor from the 'liberal bastion' of Hollywood as quickly as possible. He was sure that it also didn't help that he had once participated in a *Black Lives Matter* protest at the suggestion of his manager.

As soon as he shut the door on the patrol car, it tore off with a squeal of its tires and Alan ran to catch up with the hospital techs.

The techs brought Marianne through a large side door that led directly into the ED with Alan trailing them. The room was large and had a central hub area containing a long counter with about ten computers for the staff to do their work. All of the computer screens were dark and the only personnel Alan saw at the stations were two staff members in scrubs, hurriedly flipping through paper charts and making notes. It seemed as if half of the overhead lights in the room were out and it was very dim.

Surrounding the central hub were numerous partitions with curtains for privacy which contained the beds for the patients. It seemed that most if not all of the beds were taken up with people in various stages of distress. Some had bandaged heads while others had arms in slings. One elderly man had his leg in traction. All of the patients seemed to be moaning and groaning at various pitches. A few were weeping.

Mixed in with all of the sounds of human misery were the beeps and chimes of the monitor alarms going off. It was chaotic and the nurses, techs, and doctors were scrambling about here and there, clearly overwhelmed.

Eventually, a young male nurse made his way to Alan and Marianne.

"What happened?" the nurse asked, while simultaneously starting to assess her.

"We were in a horrific car crash," Alan said. "And she got thrown from the car. I think she might just be unconscious and wake up in a bit," he added hopefully. "But I didn't want to take any chances."

The nurse looked back up at him skeptically for a long moment, then Alan could see his nostrils flare slightly, not in a fit of anger, but more like he detected an odor.

Before he could ask, Alan spoke up.

"I wasn't driving," he told him.

The nurse nodded slowly, albeit skeptically.

Just then, the double doors on the side of the ED popped opened. Two EMTs burst through the opening, pushing a man on a gurney who was screaming at the top of his lungs.

"Burn! Burn!" one of the EMTs shouted, as they came through the doors.

Instinctively, the nurse and Alan looked over at him. The actor instantly regretted he had done so.

The man looked like something out of a horror film. His hair had been burned completely off, and his scalp and at least half of his face was blackened like a piece of seared meat. In several places the skin was splitting open and revealing the pink tissue underneath. His T-shirt looked as though it had melted directly onto the skin of his torso and both of his arms were burned like kindling sticks. He was thrashing about wildly on the gurney.

Immediately, several nurses and an ED doctor jumped onto him. The techs started to try to hold him still as the doctor began to bark commands.

"Morphine! Stat!" He yelled.

The nurse attending to Alan and Marianne calmly turned his attention back to them. He grabbed a clipboard with a form on it from the counter of the central hub workspace and pulled a pen out of his pocket.

"What's her name?" he asked Alan routinely.

"Marianne."

"Marianne what?"

Alan was stumped by the question and tried to think.

"Marianne what?" The nurse asked, even louder.

"I...I don't know her last name," Alan Binder had to admit.

CHAPTER FORTY-FOUR

After experiencing numerous power outages throughout the years, both natural and man-made, Barbara remembered that most of them were, generally speaking, localized to only a couple blocks, and even then, some houses were spared while others weren't. But as she walked along the familiar residential streets, she began to realize that it was much more widespread than she had witnessed before. There were no lights on in *any* of the houses she passed, and she saw several residents standing outside with puzzled looks on their faces.

The street lights were out as well and ditto for the traffic lights at the few intersections she had to cross. In the distance, she could hear the occasional honk of a car horn or a siren.

Several people were lined up at the front door of the store when she arrived. The front door was locked and would remain so for another twelve minutes, or would it? Through the large front windows of the store, she could see the interior was still dark.

She entered through the side door of the store to avoid the crowd out front and stepped into the pitch blackness of the windowless storage room. She reached into her purse and retrieved her cellphone to switch on the flashlight app again when it promptly slipped out of her hand and went skittering across the concrete floor.

"Crap!" she muttered, and then had to get down on her hands and knees to feel for it. It only took her a few moments, but still it seemed like her day was being cursed from every which angle.

What else could go wrong? she thought darkly.

She made her way out of the storage room with its pallets of foodstuffs and paper goods and was able to switch off her phone once she was in the main store. The large expanse of front windows allowed some light in, and the ceiling had several skylights. She had never really thought much about them before, but now they were a lifesaver as she was able to walk toward the front with relative ease.

There were three cashiers and a box-person waiting at the registers when Barbara arrived. They looked a little rattled, but thankfully no one looked at their phones to see just *how late* the boss was. Outside was a different story as the crowd was substantial and growing by the minute. They had worried looks too.

"Sorry," Barbara said by way of greeting them. "I have an old-fashioned alarm clock, obviously dead."

One of the cashiers, a twenty something year old named Becky, held up her cellphone then and smirked knowingly at her. The dig wasn't lost on Barbara.

"I know...I know," she admitted. "My daughter is on me constantly to put more trust in it." Then added, "By the way; does anyone know what's going on?"

There were several shrugs, and mumbled, "Just that the power is out."

Becky added, "I tried using my phone to call my friend and find out, and it just keeps dialing."

One of the box-boys said, "I heard on the way over on the radio, that it was a huge power failure, possibly the whole state. But even the radio station wasn't for sure."

There was a loud pounding on front door just then, which rattled the glass. A man was angrily pointing to his watch. "It's past six o'clock," he said loudly. "C'mon, open up!"

Barbara turned to the others. "Have you told them without electricity, the registers don't work, and that we can't open?"

"Yeah, but they didn't like it," another cashier said. "A couple of them said they would pay cash."

Barbara nodded and moved over to door to try to explain the situation again.

The crowd was not moved, and if anything, became more agitated. One woman yelled through the glass, "My baby needs formula!"

It was then that the still fresh memories of the mess of the Covid-19 pandemic came rushing back to Barbara: the empty shelves, limiting customers, rationing, a couple of fights. She wondered if it would be as bad as that.

"I'm sorry," she said as convincingly as she could. "There's nothing we can do about it."

She moved back to her employees. "Anybody get anything on their phones to tell us more?"

They all pulled out their phones and swiped at the displays. Barbara was answered with a bunch of shaking heads.

"Okay, well keep trying, maybe they'll get it back on soon."

She started to think then of the million and one things she had to do in a power outage. First was to keep doors closed until power is restored. In meantime, get out money for cash drawers so they are ready when it comes back on, and at some point, contact head-quarters to get dry ice delivered for the refrigerated and freezer cases.

She turned to a head cashier, Julie, who also filled in as assistant manager. "Julie, come with me to the office and try calling the main office on the landline to see if they can get us some dry ice deliv-ered to save the freezer section. Also see if they can get a generator delivered if the power is going to be out for a while. I'm going to get the cash out for the registers for when the power comes back on."

Then she turned to Becky. "Go to the hardware aisle and grab a flashlight for everyone off the shelf and put some batteries in them."

Becky nodded and started to step away as Julie went with Barbara. Suddenly, everyone's cell phone started to go off with a loud alert tone.

Everyone froze and stared down at their phone displays. Barbara pulled hers out and started to unlock it. She didn't need to.

The alert was an emergency text from California's governor which read:

A suspected terrorist attack has damaged the entire electrical grid in the state of California as well as some neighboring states. Only small pockets of power remain on. I urge you as citizens to remain calm and to know that your local government, the state of California, and the United States government are doing everything in their collective power to restore power and to keep its citizens safe. Again, please remain calm and be patient. We will have further updates as the situation becomes clear. Sincerely, Governor Hunter Doyle.

"Holy shit!" Matt said.

They all looked at one another and then turned toward the panicked sounds that were coming from outside the front of the store. The growing mob had received the same dire message on their phones.

And then, all hell broke loose.

CHAPTER FORTY-FIVE

Pittsburg, California
Thursday, 6:05 a.m.
+ 3 hours, 30 minutes

As he always did, from the moment Walter Gronsky awakened, he laid there for a long while with his eyes closed, pretending to be asleep. Then, very stealthily, he reached under his pillow and felt for his Glock. He switched on the high intensity light mounted on it, and then place his finger into the trigger guard and depressed the safety tab. He was ready for action.

He opened his eyes, sat up, and pulled out the gun in one swift movement, sweeping the room of threats.

Finding none, he silently rolled out of bed and got to his feet—albeit in a crouching position, and before he switched on the lights, cleared the rest of his apartment: bathroom, kitchen and living room, of any intruders.

Then satisfied, he stood up and exhaled, happy to survive another night.

He reached over and switched on the kitchen light; it didn't work.

He looked at the clock display on his microwave and noted that it was out as well. Ditto for his stove.

Just then, the alarm tone from his cell phone went off in the bedroom, startling him. He swung quickly around and went onto one knee, leveling the Glock toward the open bedroom doorframe.

Realizing it was his phone, he stood once again and with the aid of the Glock's under barrel light, returned to the bedroom. He picked up his phone, and read the governor's emergency text.

"Bullshit!" Walter Gronsky cried. "You ain't fooling me! You sons a bitches! And I ain't going down without a fight. Terrorist attack my ass!"

He quickly began gathering all of his stuff. It was time to bug out and start fighting the revolution.

CHAPTER FORTY-SIX

Lakewood, California
Thursday, 6:07 a.m.
+ 3 hours, 32 minutes

By design, or by accident, the force of so many human bodies pressing against the front door glass, shattered it. The tempered safety glass, designed to prevent injury from knife-like shards, exploded in a million tiny pieces that went scattering all across the inside of the opening. Barbara heard several of the cashiers scream. She might have also.

A few of the men that had been closest to the glass fell forward and into the store and had to catch themselves from hitting the floor. As soon as they recovered, they began to make their way past the registers and into the aisles.

Instinctively, Barbara attempted to stop them, but one of the men moved her out of his way, albeit gently.

"Call nine-one-one," she said to any of her clerks and to all of them. Several started punching in the number.

Just then, another man looked at Barbara desperately.

"You've got to let us stock up," he said. "They just said it was a terrorist attack. The whole state is out of electricity, hell, maybe the whole country. We're going to need supplies."

Without waiting around to see if he made his case, he moved passed her and grabbed a cart.

"Nine-one-one says that it's overloaded," one of the clerks called out to her.

"Keep trying," Barbara yelled at her as she and several other clerks attempted to stop the crush of people moving through the shattered door frame. As it was, it was like trying to hold back a tidal wave with a fishing net.

Many of the customers were ones that Barbara recognized as regulars. Many of them looked genuinely embarrassed that they had come in with the mob in this manner. But all of them had worried looks on their face,

"I'm sorry," one woman said to her, placing her hand on Barbara's forearm. "But I need to be prepared."

Prepared, Barbara thought sadly. Ever since the big earthquakes of the seventies, residents of California had been implored to maintain a stock of supplies that could last them a minimum of three days in a disaster. The truth was, most people had only enough to see them through one day, if that.

Then she thought about herself, she maintained a couple cases of water, some canned goods, spare batteries, etc. But how prepared was she? Maybe not much better she thought.

Barbara smiled at the woman compassionately and gave her a look that said, I understand. Then she stepped out of the way.

"Nine-one-one is still overloaded," the same clerk called out to her.

"Forget it," Barbara said. Then she turned to the other clerks hopelessly attempting to stop the influx of the crowd.

"Let them go," she said, resigned. The last thing she needed now was for one of her employees to get hurt trying to fight customers.

And speaking of fighting customers, she was glad 'Mean-Dean' wasn't here this morning. He probably would have been in his glory: a regular Spartan taking on an entire army single-handed. Thankfully, he wasn't scheduled to work today, and even then, only after school, but was school even in session?

She thought about her own kids and pulled out her own phone. She tried calling her mom, but as expected, the cell towers were jammed. It's useless she realized, everyone was in the same boat; trying to figure it out what was going on and not knowing what the future would bring.

She typed in a quick message to her mom and pressed, 'Send,' not knowing if the message would go through or not.

The initial crowd had by now come through the doors and were in the aisles throwing stuff into their carts. She figured that more would come as soon as they saw the opened entrance, but for now, she had to deal with the mess she had.

She turned to the box-boy and said, "Get a broom and a dustpan and clean up this glass, okay?"

He nodded and headed off to the back of the store.

Some of the people started coming back toward the front of store in an attempt to check out. They may have been desperate, but at least they were honest—so far.

Carts were filled with cases of bottle water, toilet paper, candles—even some religious and scented ones, diapers, baby formula, protein and snack bars, peanut butter, canned vegetables, tuna fish, and Spam. Some, expecting not to be able to cook conventionally, had even thrown bags of charcoal and cans of lighter fluid into the mix.

One of the checkers, stepped behind her register. A woman pushed her cart up and started to unload her items onto the conveyor belt, but the belt didn't move. Stymied, the woman instead started to manually shove the items in front of her.

"Umm, ma'am, do you have cash?" The checker asked, somewhat sheepishly.

"No, only my debit card."

She leaned over the card reader and examined it; it was completely dark.

"I'm sorry," she said to the woman. "The point of sale is down also. You don't have any cash?"

The woman shook her head sadly just as a man two customers back held up his wallet and said, "I have cash."

Hearing this, another checker stepped behind a different register and said, "I'll take you over here."

The man jumped out of line and started unloading his goods onto the belt, pushing them toward her.

Out of habit, the checker picked up the first item and passed it over the bar code scanner, which didn't work either.

"Excuse me," she said. "Do you know how much this was?"

"Nah," the man said, shrugging. "I just grabbed it."

The checker looked at Barbara for guidance.

Barbara looked at all the carts filled with a myriad of items. It would take forever to check all the prices. Plus, she hadn't even opened the safe to get out the beginning cash.

A yelling match between a couple of customers toward the back of the store erupted just then.

Barbara looked toward the direction of the shouting, but wisely resisted the initial reaction to get involved. She turned back to the man in line.

"Can I just guess?" she asked him. "It'll take forever to try to get all the right prices."

"Hell yes! I just want to get out of here."

Me too Barbara thought ironically. She looked at the cart and did some quick math.

The argument at the back in the store began to sound like it had devolved into a physical fight. There were sounds of punches being thrown, and cans crashing on to the floor.

The box-boy set his broom and dustpan to the side, and started to move toward the melee. Barbara stopped him.

"No!" she said sternly. Then she turned back to the man with cash and said, "Forty bucks?"

"Done," the man said and pulled out two twenty-dollar bills. He shoved them into the checker's hand, tossed his items back into his cart, and disappeared out the door.

"If you have cash, come to this register," Barbara said pointing to the register. "And we'll try to check you out."

A couple of other people wheeled their carts over, but most apparently had only plastic.

"What about me?" the woman with the debit card asked.

"I don't know!" Barbara said at her, a bit too roughly. She immediately felt bad about it and said, "I'm sorry."

The woman started to cry just as another fight broke out in the store.

A 2019 study conducted by the Federal Reserve found that consumers used cash in only 26% of transactions, down from 30% in 2017.

Source: https://www.frbsf.org/cash/publications/fed-notes/2019/ june/2019-findings-from-the-diary-of-consumer-payment-choice/

A U.S. Bank Cash Behavior Survey found that 50 percent of respondents reported carrying cash less than half of the time. And when they do carry cash, nearly half of consumers surveyed keep less than $20 on hand, and 76 percent keep less than $50.

Source: https://www.usbank.com/newsroom/news/digital-payment-platforms-primed-to-topple-cash.html

CHAPTER FORTY-SEVEN

Lakewood, California
Thursday, 6:21 a.m.
+ 3 hours, 46 minutes

Jake Sullivan attempted to wring the last little bit of sleep out of the early morning, but the sun and growing din from the street denied him that pleasure.

Since the blackout happened, he had listened to the top of the hour newscasts on his boom box. That it still worked told him that it wasn't an EMP burst. If that would have been the case, the electronics in everything, including his radio, would have been fried.

Then, at a little after six, he heard the emergency message from the Governor. That pretty much sealed it; the world had gone to shit.

Even without the newscasts or the Governor's message confirming what he had suspected, he could sense a different vibe in the world around him. The sounds he heard were different this morning. Without power, all of the traffic signals would be out. And without the signals to efficiently control the flow of traffic, gridlock, and the chaos and anger it spawned, would quickly manifest itself in the application of the commuter's non-lethal weapon of choice; the car horn.

He had been in many third world countries during his years of service, countries that lacked any sort of traffic control and he had heard the same irritating cacophony. Now he thought darkly, a new third world had sprung up around him.

He rolled up his mummy bag, carefully peered over the top of the transformer enclosure and, not seeing any prying eyes, tossed everything over and climbed out.

He packed his sleeping bag and radio back into his stroller in the bushes and, knowing that the discarded consumables that he relied on for survival could be quickly drying up, made another foray into the restaurant's dumpster. If they were out of power they couldn't open, and that meant no leftover food. He would have to be less discriminating and harvest some of the customer's half eaten food while he still could.

Although the homeless were often labeled as lazy bums, he knew from several years of living on the street that in order to have a good chance of survival, you had to work very hard to sustain yourself and must always be thinking ahead.

And speaking of thinking ahead; he considered his boom-box. He had just replenished his stock of batteries yesterday, but knew that batteries would soon become a precious commodity. He still had $28.46 left from his recyclables scrounging, and he did the quick math; barely enough for three four-packs of C cells.

He retrieved his baby stroller with the remainder of his possessions from the bushes and headed back to Johnson's Supermarket.

CHAPTER FORTY-EIGHT

Hunter Doyle III swept into the conference room with the same take charge attitude and boldness that got him into the California Governor's Mansion. He came from a prominent Irish political family in Chicago and had been the heir apparent to secure the gubernatorial mantle back there. But he grew tired of the endless battles with labor unions, corrupt lobbyists, but mostly the cold and the snow, and so moved west to sunny California where he soon threw his hat into the ring.

His brash, 'tell it like it is' nature appealed to voters who had grown weary of the Hatfield/McCoy relationship of the two major parties and so in a historic landslide, Doyle became only the fourth independent to serve the Golden State.

Liberals simultaneously loved him and loathed him, as did conservatives. But at the end of the day, everyone had to admit that if anyone could get the job done, it was a ballbuster like Hunter Doyle.

Like any politician however, he still had his detractors. Before long, he had earned the derisive nick-name of 'Hunter-Killer,' after the notorious WWII German U-Boats. But it was moniker Doyle took perverse pleasure in owning; if he had to break a few eggs to make an omelet, so be it.

Fresh from the CAL-OES communications center where he had recently repeated his emergency alert message on TV, Radio, and short wave, he sat down at the head of the long conference table flanked on one side by Shanice Dixon and on the other by his personal aide, who sat ready to take notes.

The remaining seats at the table were now filled as well as all the chairs against the wall as more people had arrived. Some people were standing. Doyle wasted no time and took control of meeting immediately.

"I know a lot of you here, so we're not going to waste endless time by going around the room and introducing ourselves," he started out. "If you have something useful to say, just say which agency you're with and spill your guts. We'll deal with formalities later. Understood?"

There were nods from all around the room.

"Good, so what the hell happened last night?" the governor said.

Everyone in the room turned to Gary Dicey who was seated at the far end of the table. Dicey cleared his throat, introduced himself, and then launched into a narrative about what he had observed; the time, what went down, and the criticality of the HPT's. He ended the recitation with his own suspicions about it being a terrorist attack based upon the coordinated timing and what he was told by the plant operators about the truck pieces and the ball bearings. In all, it took only two minutes to tell.

Doyle nodded. "If it looks like a duck right, Mr. Dicey?"

"Yes sir."

"That's why I sent out the alert. No sense hiding from this thing. With twenty-three HPT locations and the LADWP sites and SMUD all taken down within seconds of each other, I don't need to wait for a big investigation to tell me this was a terrorist attack. So, do we have anything left running Mr. Dicey?"

"Just a couple of micro grids at a university, an airport, and on Alcatraz, sir," Dicey answered. "Other than that, California essentially has no power."

"Really, a defunct prison is one of the few things still working?" Doyle stated incredulously. "Okay, next question; how long to fix these HPT things and get the grid back up and running?"

The DOE rep raised his hand.

"Department of Energy, Governor. Unfortunately, these transformers cannot be repaired, only replaced," he said.

"Fine. How long will it take to get them in?"

"A year sir, maybe less if we can push the manufacturers."

"A year!" Doyle screamed. "A fucking year! Are you kidding me?"

"I wish I was sir," the rep said darkly. "They're custom made, and only a handful of companies can make them. And those companies are all overseas. We don't even manufacture them here anymore."

Doyle shook his head miserably. "Well, that's just dandy; one more industry we let slip right through our fingers."

The DOE rep continued on without belaboring the issue of the state's burdensome regulations on industry. "We would have been luckier if this was a solar flare or a cyber-attack, we might only be down for one to four days. Whoever did this, knew exactly what they were doing."

"And we don't have any spare…HPTs laying around somewhere, another state maybe?"

"We're checking sir, there's a program called STEP, the Spare Transformer Equipment Program, which maintains inventories of critical, long lead time electrical equipment. They are already working with the utilities to see if we have any that match. But even if we do, it will only be a couple most likely, and it will take several weeks to test them and have them transported to site."

Doyle turned to Gary Dicey.

"How many of these HPTs did you say were destroyed in the attack?"

"Our best estimate so far sir is at least eighty-five, but we're still waiting on PG&E, Edison, and so forth, to get their crews out there to verify."

"Shit! Eighty-five in one attack? Well, can we run the grid without them?"

The DOE rep and Dicey shook their heads in unison and said, "No." Then the rep explained.

"From the standpoint of *could* you have a grid without them? Yes. But that's not the grid we have. If we wanted to go that route, it would take years, maybe decades to redesign and then build it. We might be able to do some rerouting of circuits and black start some of the power plants that went down after the attack, but it would be only isolated pockets of power here and there, and even then, it wouldn't be very balanced and therefore unreliable."

The DOE rep then returned to the topic of the replacement lead time. "Sir, we have already given a heads up to the HPT manufacturers and told them they have to fast track them, but even then…"

He let the statement die off.

Doyle turned to his assistant. "Get on the phone to the president and have him push those manufacturers and threaten the worst trade sanctions they ever saw if they don't get their asses in gear to get us these HPTs."

"Yes sir."

The assistant got on her phone and hurriedly stepped away from table.

Doyle turned back to the DOE rep and pointed his finger at him.

"I don't give a damn what you have to do, but you have twenty-four hours to find and test those spare HPTs and get them on their merry fucking way! Do you understand?"

"Yes sir."

Doyle took a deep breath and looked at Behnken, the rep from STAC.

"I guess we should talk about it while we're all here. Do we have any more threats popping up? Poisoning the water system, a dirty bomb?"

"No threats sir. It's pretty quiet out there."

"I guess that's some good news," Doyle quipped.

The rep from the State's Terrorist Assessment Center made a face and Doyle picked up on it.

"You don't think so Mr. Behnken?"

"No sir, I don't," he said darkly. "We don't think they're planning any follow up attacks; because they don't need to."

"The failure of U.S. power infrastructure, specifically, HPTs could present vulnerability to the electric grid. Currently, the United States heavily depends on oversea manufacturers for its demand for HPTs; supply and procurement of HPTs can be challenging, as it can take more than 12 months to replace an HPT due to its long and complex procurement process."

Source: *Energy Sector-Specific Plan Department of Homeland security 2015*

STEP: *Spare Transformer Equipment Program.*

Source: *https://www.eei.org/issuesandpolicy/transmission/Pages/ sparetransformers.aspx*

Black Start: *The process of restoring an electric power station or a part of an electric grid to operation without relying on the external electric power transmission network to recover from a total or partial shutdown.*

Source: *https://en.wikipedia.org/wiki/Black_start*

CHAPTER FORTY-NINE

Hercules, California
Thursday, 7:12 a.m.
+ 4 hours, 37 minutes

Like many immigrants who had arrived in the country illegally, twenty-five-year-old Jose Verdusco had few employment options other than performing day labor for the sundry construction workers, gardeners, painters, etc. who were looking for cheap help to perform a job.

While not inspiring or lucrative, the work was usually steady, and he was able to send several hundred dollars back to his family in Mexico every month. But his world was different today. After noticing that the lights were out in the tiny, cramped apartment he shared with several other men, Jose thought, like many, that it was an isolated event. Or that the slumlord who owned the building had neglected to pay the electric bill once again.

It was only after he arrived and took up a spot with some of the other regulars at the far end of the parking lot of the local Home Depot that he realized the magnitude of the outage.

Even though this particular store had a backup generator and was able to function, albeit in a diminished capacity, he noticed that the traffic was lighter than normal. And even when someone did enter the store, they didn't come out with lumber, bags of concrete, or drywall for a job.

Instead, they exited with their huge carts loaded with cases of bottled water, tanks of propane, or generators. Few, if any, of the contractor's pickup trucks that passed by them at the exit, stopped to pick up any workers.

"Ven aka!" another day laborer called out to the others. The man was standing next to his dilapidated pickup truck with the radio switched on inside.

Jose and several others trotted over to the man, who reached in and turned up the volume. The radio was tuned to a Spanish language radio station in the area and the announcer was speaking in rapid fire Spanish, his voice laden with urgency.

"...*ataque terrorista. Todo el estado de California está sin electricidad. Las autoridades no tienen idea de cuándo se restablecerá la energía...*"

("...terrorist attack. The entire state of California is without power. The authorities have no idea when power will be restored...")

Without electricity to run the saws, cement mixers, or myriad of other power tools they used, Jose and the other men realized that whatever hope they had for a better life in the United States, had possibly evaporated in front of their eyes.

Before long, several began to talk about heading back to Mexico. Jose wondered if he had enough fuel to make it to the border.

CHAPTER FIFTY

Jake Sullivan arrived at Johnson's Supermarket and was simultaneously surprised, and yet not surprised to see the store's condition and the bedlam that was raging around him.

He stepped through the opening of the shattered front door and saw the expressions of frustration and fear on the faces of the clerks and the store manager who were trying to hold it all together. Some customers were in fact attempting to pay with cash, while others simply walked out with their carts filled. None of the employees made an effort to stop them.

Further inside the store, it was dark and difficult to see, with only the skylights in the high ceiling offering a modicum of illumination. Still, Jake could peer in and observe a scene of total confusion and pandemonium as people scrambled to grab anything they could think of to survive. Already the shelves containing can goods and paper products were bare, and the aisles are littered with spilled cans, knocked over boxes and broken jars leaking their contents.

He recognized some of the people in the aisles as regulars, but in emotional states he had never before observed. Almost all had worried looks on their faces, some with tears streaming down their cheeks and quietly sobbing. Still others had almost zombie-like, 1000-yard stares, expressions hauntingly familiar to the ones he saw on some of his fellow soldiers in Afghanistan as they were overwhelmed in battle.

And finally, some individuals seemed to have to already cast off the basic norms of civility. They are jostling and grabbing for items off of the shelves, knocking over merchandise, and sometimes other people in the process. The free for all reminded him of some of the Afghanis he saw clamoring for food when a Red Cross convoy would come in. Two women got into a shoving match over a couple of rolls of toilet paper as he watched.

He made his way to the battery display near the front of the store, and was shocked that some were still there, albeit with only one four-pack of C cells left. He picked them up and started making his way to the register.

The woman who he knew to be the manager was attempting to collect cash at the register. Jake made eye contact with her, held up the pack of batteries, and then extended his hand, proffering the money.

Surprisingly, she didn't accept the money and instead just looked at him with what he felt was a sense of admiration and respect; he had always been honest and never tried to steal like so many others on the street.

"That's okay," she shook her head. "Nobody else is really paying. Why should you?"

Jake pushed the money into her hands anyway and started to walk out.

"Wait," she called after him.

Jake stopped and looked back to her.

"Were those the last ones?"

He nodded.

She then lowered her voice. "Do you need more?"

Jake nodded again.

"Wait here," the woman said, and then grabbed a flashlight and headed to the back of the store.

CHAPTER FIFTY-ONE

Hanford, California
Thursday, 7:20 a.m.
+ 4 hours, 44 minutes

The last of the generators that Ready Power Inc. had in their inventory rolled away and disappeared through the opening between the high chain link fence.

Dana Curry, the owner of Ready Power had been up since a little after three when her cell phone began to buzz like crazy. Since then, she, and the only other worker she could roust at that time of the night had tested, hitched up and rented out the thirty or so generators of various sizes and capacities that they had.

They did in fact save one for themselves though, and had it hooked up and running at the electrical panel in order to keep the lights on in the office and to allow the gas pumps to fuel the units before they rolled out.

"I need to rent a generator," a man said, surprising her as he stepped into the small office.

"Everyone does," Curry quipped. "Unfortunately, I just rented out the last one."

"Well, I really need one," the man insisted. His voice wasn't raised, but he said it firmly, as if he wasn't going to take 'no' for an answer.

Curry sighed. It had already been a long night.

"I'm sorry, but like I said; the last one got rented. We're trying to get some from out of state right now."

"Well, I really need one," the man repeated. "My mom is on an oxygen concentrator."

"I'm really sorry," she said, hoping that she was coming off as sincere "I'll put you first on my list."

The man simply stood there, not moving from his spot. Then he cocked his head slightly; he could hear the sound of the store generator running.

"But you do have one left," he said. "I can hear it running."

"Yes. But we need that to run the store."

The man then reached into the inside of his jacket, pulled out an automatic pistol and aimed it at her.

"Not as bad as my mom needs it," he said.

CHAPTER FIFTY-TWO

Gardena, California
Thursday, 7:22 a.m.
+ 4 hours, 47 minutes

Stuart Gorsky could never remember getting such a good night's sleep—or such an early one. An incurable insomniac, he normally stayed up till the wee hours of the night, reading tech magazines, surfing the web, or talking via shortwave band to some of his contacts throughout the world.

But the lack of sleep finally caught up to him last night, and he begrudgingly crawled into bed at the ungodly hour of nine-thirty. Then, some thing, or some *feeling*, woke him up.

He got up and headed to the bathroom, noticing that the light was not working. Checking other switches throughout the house produced the same results, and verified to him that the power was off.

Thankfully, he had a bank of solar cells on the roof connected to a battery bank and an inverter that would provide 120 volts power to his computer, but most importantly to the Flex 6400 transceiver connected to it. The high-tech device would allow the radio enthusiast to transmit and receive on a multitude of channels, all through the convenience of a PC or laptop.

Besides being a licensed HAM operator, Gorsky was also a CERT (Community Emergency Response) member, as well as part of a radio network that would help to communicate with the authorities and first responders in a disaster or other emergency.

He booted up his computer and the transceiver and as soon as they were active, switched to the network frequency and called in.

"This is George Two-One-Zero to net control. Is anyone monitoring? Over."

The response came back nearly immediately. As the person spoke, their voice signature was displayed on the computer monitor in a colorful series of peaks and valleys that undulated like waves on the ocean.

"This is Frank-Seventeen acting as net control. We've been waiting to hear from you George Two-One-Zero. We have a situation. You may have noticed that all of the power is out. Over."

Stuart Gorsky felt embarrassed. He rarely, if ever, was out of contact.

"Sorry about that Net control. Had everything switched off last night. Yes, I did notice the power being off. What's the situation? Is this a PSPS? Over."

"Negative George Two-One-Zero. This is the real deal. We have had a terrorist attack on the grid and the entire state is down. I repeat; a terrorist attack that took down the whole state. We are being activated by the EOC. Please secure your home, and report to your assigned area of operation. Over."

Gorsky stared in horror at the computer display in front of him, the man's voice signature now flat. He couldn't believe what he was hearing; a terrorist attack, his entire state out of power. How had this happened?

But then he realized that the answers would have to come later. And that emotions had to be put on the back burner. He had, after all signed up for this, and he had a job to do.

He took a deep breath, made a sign of the cross, and then said, "Roger that. Gearing up and heading out. ETA to AOO; approximately fifteen minutes. Over."

"Roger that," Net control replied, then added. "Be careful out there George Two-One-Zero. Over."

Ten minutes later, Stuart Gorsky was out the door with his CERT backpack, his Kenwood NX-1300, and plenty of spare batteries. It looked to be a long day.

CHAPTER FIFTY-THREE

CAL-OES
Mather, California
Thursday, 7:23 a.m.
+ 4 hours, 48 minutes

The main conference room at CAL-OES had increased in population exponentially as more and more key players and stakeholders either showed up, or conferenced in. Shanice Dixon began laying the groundwork for the response that they would be managing.

"EOC's are being activated in the affected areas," she explained, then added, "Which is basically everywhere. They are going to have to do assessments of their own situations and send them up the chain through the different regional op centers. Until they tell us what they need, there's no sense sending supplies, fuel, or whatever to them and wasting precious time and resources and having to haul them back."

"It sounds like we're wasting precious time now," Doyle fired back. "By being reactive instead of proactive."

Shanice bit her lip and kept her expression even. She knew Doyle's reputation for being brusque, and she was ready.

"Sir," she began earnestly. "With all due respect, we *are* being proactive. We've already started working with FEMA in anticipation of the coming onslaught. They are already mobilizing the Army Corp of Engineers' 249th Engineer Battalion and are starting to transport generators from around the country. We are lining up our suppliers to try to keep existing generators supplied with fuel. The Red Cross has already been notified and are mobilizing to set up food banks and triage clinics to hopefully help take some of the burden off of hospitals. Our Ham radio network of volunteers who will be relaying info as it comes in is already activated. As you may have already experienced yourself, even though our phones have WPS emergency priority, the cell service is overloaded and the service is spotty."

"How long will the cell towers last?" Doyle asked.

Standing along the side of the room, a rep from the FCC spoke up.

"A day, maybe three tops," he said. "Mind you, I'm only speaking here about the towers that simply rely on backup batteries in an outage—which is the vast majority of them. The other towers that have been hardened with back-up generators will obviously stay running as long as we keep them fueled. The problem is that everyone wants fuel."

"What about regular phones, landlines?" Shanice asked.

"Still up and running in most cases," the FCC rep replied. "A lot of the phone companies have switched their emergency power to fuel cells that use natural gas, which so far has not been affected. But unfortunately, less than half the households have landlines these days and just rely on their cells. Besides that, if you use a cordless handset, it won't work anyway because the power is out to the base station."

"So pretty soon we'll have forty million people who we can't communicate with, correct?" Doyle said to Shanice.

"Yes sir, not directly," she admitted. "But our primary entry points; the key radio stations that are hardened and high powered, are still on the air and it good shape. And they will be the designated communication link between you and the citizens. People can always tune in on their car radios to get info."

"Okay," Doyle said. "One bright spot. What about food and water?"

A woman's voice chimed in from the conference speaker. "Pamela Rosensteel Governor, Health and Human Services. We know that from our studies, that *if* people are prepared and manage it correctly, they should be good for a week or so. The problem is that plenty of people in California don't have enough of the spare food or water on hand that we recommend. The city of Los Angeles in fact, ranks near the bottom of emergency preparedness for major metro cities. This is due in some cases from simple economics, but also from apathy, and a false sense that it won't happen to them."

"Or that the government will always bail them out," someone in the room added.

The liaison from FEMA spoke up. "Our Atlanta warehouse has several thousand pallets of bottled water and two-point-four million MRE's and they are being loaded onto trucks for transport as we speak."

"Two-point-four million meals doesn't sound like much to feed forty million mouths," Doyle observed darkly. "Unless you are planning on pulling off a miracle like the 'Loaves and the fish.'"

Shanice took a deep breath and admitted, "Yes sir. It would only be able to feed Sacramento for two days. The local EOC's should be activating their food banks as well, but that will only go so far."

Everyone was silent and still, not wanting to speak or breathe. Disaster preparedness, whether on the local, state, or federal level, was typically engineered for confined areas, a hurricane here, an earthquake there. Not since the cold war and the civil defense networks prepped for all out global nuclear war had anything on this scale been expected or planned for. They all knew they were staring down the barrel of an incident of epic proportions.

Finally, Shanice broke the silence. "We're looking at other options right now Governor Doyle," she said grimly.

WPS —Wireless Priority System
Source: https://www.fcc.gov/general/wireless-priority-service-wps
Majority of households in US have cut their landlines
Source: https://www.latimes.com/business/technology/la-fi-tn-landline-cellphone-20180606-story.html
Less than 40% of Californians have the recommended amount of water on hand for emergencies and disasters.
Source: https://www.caloes.ca.gov/ICESite/Documents/CAPrepEQStudyFacts.pdf
Los Angeles residents rank 17 out of 24 in metro area emergency preparedness.
Source: https://www.prnewswire.com/news-releases/how-prepared-are-americans-for-emergencies-301043819.html

CHAPTER FIFTY-FOUR

Lakewood, California
Thursday, 7:39 a.m.
+ 5 hours, 4 minutes

Heading back to one of his favorite places to hang out during the day, Jake Sullivan checked out the recycling center where he would regularly redeem his plastic and glass bottles for money. It was shut down as well, eliminating his only source of income, not that money would seem to matter much right now.

All around him were the sounds and sights of chaos and panic. The streets were totally gridlocked with the signal lights out. It would take five minutes or longer just to move up and wait your turn to get through an intersection, only to fall right into another long line for the next one. Some drivers, impatient to get through, had even taken to driving up on the sidewalk or center median, with others still, throwing caution to the wind, were heading straight into oncoming traffic. A few cars had crashed into one another with the drivers outside and arguing, while some cars were stalled out and abandoned. Moving or not, everyone was driving with sense of urgency and confusion.

Through the windows of the vehicles, he could see people with their cell phones to their ears, trying desperately, he imagined, to communicate with family, friends, or their employer, or to simply find out what was going on. He doubted that they could get through.

And although there was a palatable tension in the air and everything around him seemed in disarray, Jake had never felt so safe and unconcerned to wander the streets. He even thought it was serene. The police who sometimes rousted him would be too overwhelmed, and ordinary people could not be bothered with him today. After all, who had time to worry about a bum when their whole world was crumpling around them?

CHAPTER FIFTY-FIVE

First Federal Bank
Salinas, California
Thursday, 8:18 a.m.
+ 5 hours, 43 minutes

Like everyone else in the state, Elizabeth Davis had awoken to no power, got dressed and ready in the dark, and then headed into her job to see what she could do. As the branch manager of the First Federal Bank in Salinas, California, she arrived as she always did about 1 ½ hours before the bank was scheduled to open at 9:30. She soon discovered that there was pretty much nothing she could do.

Watching from a safe distance in her car in the parking lot, she could see that the windows of the bank were all dark, as well as the screens on the two ATMs located near the entrance. Dark screens notwithstanding, this still didn't stop people from trying to withdraw money from the machines. And when they realized that they didn't work, they moved over to join the growing queue by the bank's front doors, expecting them to open. They would be sorely disappointed.

Besides the ATMs being down, Davis knew that the alarms would not work, that the vault would not open, and that none of the computer terminals would be functional. The bank was, for all intents and purposes, shuttered.

Just then, she heard a knock on her passenger side window.

She turned to see her assistant manager, Rebecca standing outside her car. She popped the locks and Rebecca opened the door and climbed inside. Just then, a man punched the ATM screen and swore in anger before stepping away and joining the growing line at the entrance.

Rebecca witnessed the man's ire as well and said simply, "This could get pretty ugly Liz."

"Yep," Davis agreed, then turned to her second in command.

"So, what have you heard?"

"The entire state is out, and they don't know what it was, but suspect terrorism."

"Same here. And nothing about when we'll get the power back?"

Rebecca shook her head, "No. Maybe they don't know yet."

"Or maybe they do, but they're afraid to tell us." The manager added ruefully.

Rebecca shrugged noncommittally, then gestured to the phone in her boss's hand.

"Have you called the district office to see what they say?"

Davis held up the phone indifferently, as if it were useless. "Been trying," she said. "But nothing goes through. I'm sure the towers are all jammed, just like after an earthquake."

Her assistant nodded and they both turned back to watch the scene unfold at the entrance to the bank. A few of the people were pushing their faces up to the glass and trying to look in. One man pounded his fist on the window, thinking someone might be inside and that he could get their attention.

Davis looked around at the parking lot and saw some familiar cars with people sitting inside. She knew her employees were wisely camped out in their cars as she was. People get antsy very quickly if they feel they can't access their money, and so consequently, it made no sense to stand at the door and try to explain to them that without power, the bank couldn't open. They didn't want to hear it, and it would just bring trouble.

Davis checked her watch; it was past 8:30. She turned to Rebecca.

"Do me a favor," she said. "Very quietly, go around and tell everyone that if we don't see the lights come on inside the bank by nine, to just head home. There's no reason to sit here forever."

"Agreed," Rebecca said and pulled on the handle to open the car door.

"And then you do the same," Davis admonished her as she stepped out.

"I'm not leaving until you do," Rebecca retorted, and then closed the car door and began to make the rounds in the parking lot.

Davis turned back to keep an eye on her customers. If someone recognized Rebecca from across the lot and made a move to approach her, she would intercede and run interference for her. It was her job.

As she watched she thought about the world they had built based on technology that always worked, and power that always stayed on. It was efficient and convenient of course—even seductive, but as soon as that fragile dependence faltered, it threw the world into a tailspin.

Debit cards and payment apps like Venmo and Apple-pay only exacerbated the false sense of security as people became so enamored with their ease of use and reliability, they migrated away from carrying cash.

As she thought about it, she reached into her own purse, pulled out her wallet and did a quick inventory of her own funds.

Not including the coin, she counted $57.00.

Elizabeth Davis stared back out the window at her bank, wondering nervously just how far *her* money would go.

CHAPTER FIFTY-SIX

Folsom, California
Thursday, 8:49 a.m.
+ 6 hours, 14 minutes

When it became apparent that he was no longer was needed, Gary Dicey was released from the meeting at CAL-OES. Shanice thanked him for attending, and shook his hand warmly. Gary took the opportunity to ask her if she would need him to return.

"Probably not," She replied, then handed him a fully charged sat phone.

"If I need you to come in, or do a conference call, I'll get in touch with you via the sat. Thank you, again."

He switched on the phone, nodded, then left.

***

He drove the short distance from Mather back up to Folsom on US-50-E in a fog. Unlike the surface streets bogged down by a lack of working signal lights, the traffic here flowed smoothly. Still though, there was a sense of dread in the air.

It was light now and people were just waking up to the realization that they had no power. The commuters around him drove with a mix of confusion and urgency as they tried to figure things out. Many would arrive at their places of employment or at their children's schools only to be turned away, returning to their homes even more bewildered. The world they all knew had changed.

Even though he had given his turnover and been relieved at Cal-ISO, rather than head straight home, Gary Dicey returned to his long-time employer.

He badged in and headed into the main control center before doing anything else. It was his domain and he felt as protective of it as any mother with her baby. The building was still on emergency power, and would continue running as long as they needed it to.

Just when that would be was anyone's guess.

All of the alarm indicators were still as bright red as ever on the big board, but the audible alarms had ceased, and it was deathly quiet. It gave the room an eeriness, like a tomb.

Only two operators were sitting in front of terminals, but they weren't really looking at them; there was nothing to look at.

Gary knew both of them and they acknowledged him cordially, but he could see by their grave expressions that they understood the gravity of what had happen overnight.

"I sent almost everyone home, Gary," He heard a familiar voice say from behind him.

Dicey turned, and saw that it was David Forney, the Vice President of Operations for the facility. He was a very capable and decent man, whom Gary had learned to have a great admiration for.

Dicey nodded gravely. "It only makes sense," he said somberly.

Forney nodded and put his hand on Gary's shoulder. "I'm sorry for what you went through Gary. I know it had to be hell."

"Thanks."

Forney removed his hand and jerked his thumb toward the main conference room.

"I know you already gave your turnover about what happened, but we'd still like to meet with you for a short debrief, if you're up to it."

"Sure" he said. "I'll be in there in a few. I just want to look around if you don't mind."

"Absolutely," Forney said. "Take your time. After the meeting you go home and get some rest. I'm sure you need it."

Gary nodded and the Operations VP walked away.

Dicey did indeed take his time strolling around the cavernous control room, staring at the big board and all of the alarms. Other than when they did a routine display test, he had never seen so many alarms at one time.

He stared at the Google Earth Sat display. By now the sun was up and the state looked no worse for the wear. It looked fine in fact, peaceful, as if it were just another day. If you didn't know it or weren't on the ground, you would never know that you were looking at a state now in total disarray and on the precipice of falling into total ruin.

He finally turned and waved to the two lone operators before heading toward the conference room. Reaching for the knob but before turning it, he took one more long look back, wondering if it was his last.

This was the nerve center of California's energy, the hub, the place where he had spent many long days and nights. It was like a second home to him really. His coworkers were like family to him, kindred spirits in the mission to keep the lights on for forty million Californians. Now, they were all effectively out of a job. The patient they had all so assiduously labored over to keep alive, had suddenly and inexplicably died. The grid, and the state that it served, was now as lifeless as a corpse.

CHAPTER FIFTY-SEVEN

By 9:00 o'clock in the morning, the SOC (State Operations Center) had undergone an amazing transformation. All of the workstations were manned by CAL-OES employees wearing the colored-coded vests of their designated roles: green for logistics, red for operations, and yellow for executive. Besides the state employees, scores of FEMA employees had been brought in and embedded alongside to aid in the response and recovery effort. The big TVs screens on the main wall were still tuned to CNN and several local stations, in the hopes that they might provide actionable intelligence from the scene.

What the news media seemed to do instead though was what they were famous for; to seize on the moment and deliver the same emotion laden, breathless reporting that had become de rigueur for the instant 24-hour news cycle. To anybody who was able to watch them, the broadcasts typically had the effect of heightening the growing panic and adding fuel to the fire of an already dire situation. Without saying it, many of those in the room trying to manage the event were grateful that few California residents were able to tune in on their own TVs and be swept up in the hysteria.

Although they didn't get a lot of the fame, and weren't as visual, the network of shortwave operators had been the true Godsend for real time info. Spread around the state and with most of the operators having generators or at least some sort of backup power, they were the boots on the ground that CAL-OES desperately needed at this point to communicate both in and out.

The official intel though came from the network of operation centers that CAL-OES maintained throughout the state. Phones were ringing constantly as the regional ops reported in. But the news they delivered wasn't welcomed; all of the local and county-wide operations centers that communicated up to the regionals were overwhelmed with calls for both status updates and for assistance, the latter being mostly for generators and diesel fuel.

Hunter Doyle had already moved some of his personal effects into the private suite designated for him located above and just off to the left of the control center, but other than making a few calls he had scarcely been in it. He was a hands-on guy and wanted to hear for himself just what was going on, and what he was hearing wasn't good; the state that he had been in charge of for only fifteen months was now in total disarray.

But it wasn't just what he was hearing or the reports he was getting, it was the body language and the facial expressions of the people around him in the SOC that told a greater story; this was an epic disaster and totally beyond anything they had ever trained or prepared for.

"Excuse me Governor," an OES worker in a yellow vest said from beside him. "We're meeting in the main conference room in a few minutes."

Doyle grunted his acknowledgment and followed them up the stairs and into the conference room on the second floor.

Once again, the room was filled with personnel sitting around the long table and seated at chairs against the wall. Like a game of musical chairs, some people had been left standing. A seat had been left vacant for him next to Shanice. Doyle took his seat and wasted no time.

"So where do we stand? HPT's first," he said.

The rep from DOE cleared his throat and briefly looked at his notes.

"We've reassessed the damage and it looks like by some miracle, three of the HPTs survived unscathed.

"How long to start them back up?" Doyle asked.

"Three or four days...hopefully. Other equipment was destroyed in the process and the utilities are going to have to do some fancy rerouting to be able to deliver the power—and, without the other HPTs, it's going to be of limited range."

"Can we get a map of where the power will be restored?" Shanice asked. "It may help us with the recovery."

"Already being developed," DOE said.

155

"Good," Doyle said and then moved on. "Now what about the spare HPTs, the program you spoke of...STAR...STEP, whatever?"

"STEP, sir," he corrected. "Two more HPTs were available that had the right capacity and impedance. They will be tested and be loaded onto the heavy haulers within a day. On site, we'll have to modify the footprints and do some other things, but they should work just fine."

Doyle allowed himself to exhale; at least some things were going okay.

"So out of the eighty-five that got hit in the attack, we've got five that we could get back on line?" he said.

"Yes sir."

"Good work," Doyle said. He turned away from the DOE rep to address the greater group. "I'll fill you in on the last part of this HPT mess. The president and the State Department have been working the phones all day talking to the leaders of Germany, France, and Japan and they have all promised to delay production on all their existing orders of HPTs and fast track what we need. What exactly the term 'fast-track' means in some of those countries though is a matter of opinion. Bottom line, we're still in it up to our necks. So, the next question is generators to get us through this. How many will we have to work with in total?"

The head of CAL-OES logistics, Stephanie Holmes, was sitting next to Shanice. She looked down at her notepad briefly then spoke up.

"At last count sir, there were approximately sixteen thousand existing generators in the state that businesses had already installed throughout the years, many in what we would deem critical infrastructure; hospitals, police, communications, etcetera—so that helps us. But many don't have them, and will need them soon. Also, FEMA did a study a while back that predicts that up to fifteen percent of them will fail within twenty-four hours of operation, so that drops our usable number by close to a fifth."

"Great," Doyle said miserably, and Holmes continued.

"We can get close to an additional five thousand gen-sets. FEMA has seven hundred units of various sizes, and we can probably get another three thousand from our captive suppliers and another five hundred to a thousand from Canada and Mexico. The 249th Engineer Battalion will do the installs where we need them. Additionally, other countries such as China, India, and Europe have promised to send us what they can. Australia is planning to airlift us a bunch of the NSW 5B quick deployment solar arrays, and Elon Musk has pledged to get us as many Tesla Powerwalls that he can muster."

She looked up from her notes then. "But it will all take time to get here and be installed sir."

Doyle knew about the inherent lag in disaster aid, especially international, so he didn't belabor it. Instead, he threw out the next question no one wanted to think about.

"Will that all be enough?" He asked to no one in particular, and noticed a few people subtly avert their eyes or grimace.

After reading the expressions, Doyle didn't need an answer, but Shanice took the ball.

"We don't know yet sir; we're still waiting on hard numbers and specifications to come in from the Regional Ops. But we are expecting that the demand will soon far outstrip our supply."

"So, sixteen thousand existing, that's all?" he asked, frustrated, his voice rising. "For a state this large? How come more businesses haven't installed them by now?"

"CARB sir," a representative from the Commerce Department said bitterly. "The California Air Resources Board. The environmental regulations for permitting and operating gen-sets in California are so strict, that most business decided to just roll the dice and hope for the best."

Several of the eyes in the room turned toward a rep from EPA, who was standing against the wall.

Feeling the collective ire in the room, he muttered under his breath, "Well, we have to try to keep the air clean, don't we?"

"At what cost?" The Commerce Department rep fired back.

"All right, all right, enough already," Doyle barked. "Screw the air at this point. So can we round up any more generators than what you've told me about?"

"It's getting tougher sir," the logistics head chimed in. "Some business jumped on the bandwagon early and have already ordered some ahead of us."

Doyle considered the situation briefly, then turned to his aide.

"Contact the president right now and tell him that we need him to use the Defense Production Act to stop any generator rentals or purchases from going to other parties, either here or out of state.

Everything needs to go through either us or FEMA." He turned to the FEMA rep in the room. "Agreed?"

"Yes sir."

Knowing Doyle's intolerance for wasting time, the aide quickly got up from the table and moved out of the room to call the White House.

That seemed to satisfy the governor, but then another, bigger bombshell was dropped by the rep from DOE.

"Governor, we have a bigger problem than just the number of gen-sets we have available. It's the fuel for them. If you may, I've asked a rep from API, the American Petroleum Institute, to conference in and explain."

"All right," Doyle said.

"Tom are you there?" the DOE rep said to the conference unit.

"Yes, I'm here," a voice came back. "Governor Doyle, Tom Jordan from API. I'll get right to the point."

Doyle, Shanice and nearly everyone present seemed to tilt in closer to the speaker on the table.

"Of the dozen or so refineries that operated in the state," he began. "Only two thirds have cogeneration plants that allowed them to continue running after the takedown on the grid. The rest of them had to shut down and will not be up until the grid is restored, a timeline that we understand is already stretching at least a year into the future. Based on the configuration of the refineries and their crude and product slates, this effectively reduces the production of much needed diesel fuel by one quarter to one third. And obviously, none of the generators will run without fuel."

"What about getting fuel from out of state?" Shanice asked.

"Only by rail or by truck," the API rep explained. "And that's not very efficient or fast."

"No pipelines to pump it in?" Doyle asked.

"The California product pipelines only run one way—and that's out of state to Nevada, Arizona, Oregon, and Washington; and it's only to tank farms and terminals. In fact, the southern and northern California product pipelines aren't not even connected."

Doyle fumed, biting his lip. He wanted to ask why all of the refineries didn't have cogens and why the damn pipelines didn't even connect the north and south. But he knew the probable answers— regulations: right of way, environmental, anti-trust. He had come into office promising to slash California's burdensome regulations, but it was like trying to rob a bank by stealing a penny at a time. He let it go.

"All right," he sighed wearily. "Let's move on; what other options do we have?"

A few ideas were floated by the rep such as reconfiguring product slates to shift to higher diesel production and he said that he was following up on them currently. Also, a tanker ship carrying finished product to Asia had been turned around and was heading back. ETA: one week.

But the reduction of available fuel wasn't even the most vexing problem regarding keeping the generators running; trying to distribute it all was going to be a nightmare.

"We've got two challenges as far as distribution goes," Holmes reported. "The first is the pipelines that connect the producers—the refineries, to the terminals that can load the tanker trucks to get it to the end users. Those pipelines have pumping stations that use electricity to keep the product flowing. And in most cases, there are no BUG's or 'Back Up Generators' on site."

"Can we get them generators? "Shanice asked.

"Yes, they are in route as we speak. We made a command decision early on to put them at the top of the pyramid—so to speak—as no other fuel will get delivered without them."

"Good call," Doyle said.

"The pipelines also have electrically operated valves that are control remotely," Holmes continued. "Now, they'll have to be manually cranked open or closed. It's called, 'doing a lineup,' in their vernacular. And, it will take time to get workers on site and make sure the valves are all in the right position. The pipeline companies have promised us they are on it right now."

"Good, it sounds like you are all over it as far as our two distribution issues go," Shanice said proudly. "Thank you, Stephanie."

"Unfortunately, that's not the second issue." the head of logistics said darkly.

"Then what is?" Doyle said.

Stephanie Holmes took a deep breath and then continued.

"There are only so many fuel trucks available to deliver the fuel," she said. "And even if they were running day and night, I don't think they could keep up with the demand with the existing generators, let alone another five thousand coming in. Just the burn rate from critical infrastructure alone accounts for almost three thousand tankers every day. We've contacted other companies from around the country to have them get their trucks and drivers in state, but again, it's going to take time."

"National Guard?" someone in the room suggested.

"Already working on it," Holmes told them. "But they've got their own units to keep supplied."

"Plus, we'll also need them at some point to help stage and guard fueling points when we get to that point," Shanice added. "*And* to possibly run armed escorts for the tanker trucks."

"So, we've got limited generator capacity, limited fuel, but an even more limited ability to deliver it," Doyle recapped, then added bluntly. "We're going to have prioritize this."

There was a long silence that hung over the room.

Finally, Shanice broke it.

"Yes sir, we're going to need to meet after this meeting to discuss," she said. "I've got the Unified Command Group assembling either in person or Zooming in, and you'll need to be there."

The others present at the room understood the gravity of the director's statement; with limited resources to respond to a crisis of this magnitude, the Unified Command Group had to make the hard decisions about who would get what and when. They would essentially be playing God, deciding who would live, and who would die.

Defense Production Act: https://www.fema.gov/disasters/defense-production-act

California refinery cogeneration capabilities.
Source: https://www.eia.gov/outlooks/steo/special/pdf/california.pdf
Critical infrastructure fuel tanker demands.
Source: https://www.fema.gov/sites/default/files/2020-07/fema_incident-annex_power-outage.pdf
"The failure rate of backup generators will increase to approximately 15% after 24 hours of continuous use."
Source: https://www.fema.gov/sites/default/files/2020-07/fema_incident-annex_power-outage.pdf

CHAPTER FIFTY-EIGHT

Saint Elizabeth Medical Center
Cerritos, California
Thursday, 9:31 a.m.
+ 6 hours, 56 minutes

"Surgery?" Alan repeated incredulously back to the nurse.

If anything, the ED had gotten even busier and more helter-skelter than before. Besides the beds parked in the curtained partitions, gurneys and beds were now cramming the aisles in between the partitions and the central hub. The congestion made the situation even worse as the techs, nurses and doctors had to navigate around them. Marianne was off to the side in one of the partitions and at least had a curtain that offered her a modicum of privacy. A portable tree of IVs drained their various liquids into her, and monitors pulsed and beeped endlessly. According to the nurse, she was currently sedated and resting.

"*Possibly,*" the nurse emphasized. "She's bleeding internally and for now, we think we can cover it with regular transfusions and monitoring. But if it doesn't stop, and her blood pressure drops too low, she'll have to have surgery."

Alan felt his knees go weak. For several hours he had tried to not think too much about Marianne's condition, or of the limo driver who died. And when he did think of them, he made excuses. The driver was driving, so it really wasn't Alan's fault; it was the fault of the company, who should probably be sued.

When his thoughts turned to Marianne, he had been trying to convince himself that she had just been knocked unconscious, and would soon snap out of it. Now though...

"Just do it then," Alan sighed, resigned. "You have my permission. I'll sign whatever you want."

"Unfortunately," the nurse continued. "The hospital is in no condition to perform *any* surgeries - either elective or emergency, right now. In fact, we are trying to discharge all non-critical patients out of their beds to conserve energy. So, we'll just have to wait to transport your friend out to another facility to have her operated on."

"Why don't you just transport her now, instead of waiting?" Alan asked, irritated.

"Because there are no other hospitals available in the state. The whole state is out of power, and everyone is in the same boat."

"Well, I don't care about other fucking hospitals," Alan said angrily, pointing at Marianne. "I care about her! And so, you either perform the surgery, or get her transported right now, God dammit!"

The nurse took in a deep breath, and then let it out slowly. "We're trying," he said flatly, and started to walk away.

"Bullshit mister!" Alan screamed, grabbing him by the arm to prevent him from moving away. "You'll do more than just try!"

The nurse reached over and easily peeled Alan's hand off of his arm. He was a lot stronger than Alan expected.

"Sir," he said tersely. "We're doing the best we can!"

"Do you know who I am?" Alan screamed at him.

By now, the nurse had had enough of this pompous ass. It was one of the first things you learned in medicine; that no matter who you were in the outside world, in here; everyone bled, defecated, urinated, and had their skin bruise and their bones break the same way.

"Yes, I know who you are!" He fired right back, his voice rising to match Alan's. "But right now, you are just another human being in a sea of human beings we are trying to care for! Your fame doesn't mean shit right now!"

"Well, let me tell you—" Alan started to say.

And then, the lights went out.

CHAPTER FIFTY-NINE

Berkeley, California
Thursday, 10:03 a.m.
+ 7 hours, 28 minutes

As a card-carrying member of Gen Z, Arron Wilson fully embraced technology and the new economy. He didn't own a car—Uber. He didn't carry cash—Apple Pay. He never cooked and rarely kept food in the house—GrubHub. He didn't own a TV or even a radio, preferring instead to get all of his information from Facebook, Instagram, and Twitter. He had never read a newspaper in his life.

His parents paid for his rent-controlled apartment, "Doing it," they had insisted, "Just until he could get on his feet," a posture that two years after finishing college with a dubious degree in fine arts had so far eluded him.

When he awoke that day in the small loft, he thought that other than the planet hurtling headlong into a climate crisis, nothing was awry in his world. He did hear more than the usual amount of car horns from outside his window though. Didn't these people know he wanted to sleep?

Checking his iPhone as he always did before climbing out of bed, he saw that he had no Wi-Fi signal, and, that most of the posts on his Facebook and Instagram accounts had not updated. He hit refresh and waited. Instead of them updating he saw a warning that said, *"An error occurred and the requested action could not be completed at this time."*

Miffed, he climbed out of bed and went to reset his modem.

When he found it though, it was dead. He tried unplugging and re-plugging it to no avail, and then switched it to another receptacle. Next, he tried the lights; dead.

He didn't know where the breaker panel was, what a breaker panel was, or even what to do if he somehow stumbled onto it. He owned no tools—not even a screwdriver, and the thought of being prepared for an emergency or disaster was antipathetic to him; that was the government's responsibility.

His time and money were better spent going to music festivals and protesting for social justice and animal rights. Besides that, the vegan or gluten free emergency foods that he needed to survive were practically non-existent.

Instinctively, he went to his Nespresso coffeemaker on the counter and hoping against hope, tried that as well. Nothing.

"Darn," he thought.

He threw on his Birkenstocks, grabbed his keys, and headed out the door dressed in his pajama bottoms and his Che Guevara T-shirt. He was in the middle of a 'cleanse,' and needed his coffee, specifically, a pour-over made with Daktari Kenya Gathugu beans.

Stepping out onto the street however, he was greeted to a chaotic scene straight out of some of his favorite zombie apocalypse films.

The traffic signals were out and he saw panicked looks on the faces of people as they tried to navigate their cars through the clogged intersections. Everybody, even those walking seemed to be moving with a sense of urgency. Horns honked incessantly.

What the heck was going on, he thought and navigated to the Uber app on his phone to see if he was going to be able to get into work today. It was hosed up as well and just kept cycling.

His pulse quickened and he started walking a little faster, thinking that once he got his coffee, he would be able to calm down a bit. Certainly, Starbucks would have backup generators or solar power or something at their stores, because people had to have their coffee...right?

He was across the street from his favorite location when he saw the hastily written sign taped up in the window.

"SORRY. BIG POWER FAILURE. CLOSED."

Beginning to panic further, he went through the frequent contacts on his phone, dialed and got nothing but a recorded message saying that all circuits were currently busy and to please try again later.

He quickly switched from phone to text and typed in:

"Mom. Please call me. I don't know what to do."

CHAPTER SIXTY

Saint Elizabeth Medical Center
Cerritos, California
Thursday, 10:17 a.m.
+ 7 hours, 42 minutes

When the lights went out, Alan and everyone who wasn't a patient or staff had been hustled out of the ED and herded to the pickup area outside the hospital.

But it wasn't just the people from the ED; Alan saw dozens of others waiting outside. Many were wearing hospital gowns or looked hastily dressed in their street clothes. Most of them were standing and milling around. The lucky ones sat on the few benches or planters available. Many looked forlorn and confused, and it seemed like everyone had a phone pressed to their ear, trying in vain to contact someone—*anyone,* or to at least find out what the hell was going on. Most of those dressed in only their hospital gowns had their arms wrapped tightly around their chests in an effort to stay warm. Some of the people were quietly sobbing.

Just then, a car roared up and a man jumped out of the driver's seat, leaving the car running and the door wide open. He ran over to one of the benches, yelling, "Mom! Mom!"

An elderly woman looked up at the sound and immediately, tears filled her eyes.

The young man approached her, knelt down and wrapped her in a comforting hug.

"I...I didn't know what was going on," the man said, clearly emotional himself. "So, I just decided to show up."

"Well, I'm so glad you did" the woman said, her chocked voice filled with relief. "They just, kind of...kicked us out, you know," the woman explained. "The power failure and...and...everything..."

The dam broke and the woman began to sob. The young man held her tighter, comforting her. Then, he pulled her slowly up off the bench and guided her to his car.

Alan spotted an opportunity to make an escape and approached the man and his mom.

"Excuse me," he said, as sincerely as he could. "I really need to get home, and was wondering if you could give me a lift?"

"Well, uh...uh, where do you live?" the young man asked hesitantly.

"Beverly Hills. It's really not that far," Alan said, unconvincingly.

"Well, I'm going the opposite way, and the traffic is terrible right now with all the lights out. I'm sorry."

The man continued to help guide his mom into the car. At one point, a sweater she had draped over her shoulders slid off and fell to the ground. Alan defiantly walked away without offering to pick it up.

"Well thanks for nothing," he said. "Fuck!"

The man got his mom secured in the car as some of the others cheered them for their good fortune; if only everyone could get picked up, they thought.

Alan watched the car drive away, and with it; his chance to get home.

Sure, he thought bitterly. *Cheer for them, the fucking nobodies of the world.*

Once again, he was feeling trapped and helpless. He began to stomp around the periphery of the growing crowd. More people were openly crying now and it pissed him off even further. *What the hell do they know about misery,* he mused?

How did I end up in this shit? I needed to get to that party, damn it. I needed that role. That fucking manager of mine had me take those two shitty films and I needed that God damned role!!

He began muttering to himself under his breath. He didn't care if others were looking at him. He didn't even care if they knew who he was. Fuck them! What would they ever do for Alan Binder other than say he was a washed-up actor and that his movies sucked?

He was dying for a drink, and for the cigarettes that he had sworn off for the umpteenth time. Suddenly, he felt his breathing start to quicken. It didn't seem like he could get enough air in his lungs.

"My fucking ex-wife!" he continued ranting, to himself and to the world. "If that bitch hadn't have cleaned me out, I wouldn't have had to take those crappy films to pay the fucking bills!"

Sweat began to form on his face and under his armpits.

"And if I wouldn't have had to take those shitty scripts, then I wouldn't have needed to get to the party. And I wouldn't have pushed the driver to get there…and the driver…and Marianne…"

His chest tightened up like a strap was being pulled around it, and his stomach became upset. Fuck he needed a drink. He needed a drink, and a good film, and he needed…he needed -

He let out a guttural wail and crumpled to the ground. The whole world was spinning, sounds were blurred like he was under water. He couldn't breathe. He couldn't breathe and his chest was killing him. He saw a few people gathering around him, but they seemed like they were miles away.

Damn it! I needed a good picture to save me! Alan Binder, thought to himself. *Just one, good, fucking picture!*

His eyes rolled up into his head.

And then, just like the final curtain coming down in a performance, everything went dark.

CHAPTER SIXTY-ONE

Near Carmen City, California
Thursday, 10:52 a.m.
+ 8 hours, 17 minutes

Walter Gronsky had escaped the confines of the city and the subservient society that bound him. He didn't mind leaving behind his job as a tool and die maker (which was caput anyway), his crappy apartment with his few belongings, or even the minimal amount of money he kept in the bank. As it was, the Jews controlled all the money in the world and would probably soon deem US currency worthless, printing their own notes with some kike bastard like Simon Wiesenthal on the face.

He loaded everything he needed into his jeep, wiped down his fingerprints and then booby-trapped his apartment with several homemade IEDs. He purposely left the keys in the door, gleefully imagining the carnage as the first looter or government Jack-Boot seized the opportunity and entered his home without permission. His final tasks completed, he set out east toward the Stanislaus National Forest, and to the secret bunker he had maintained for several years.

The traffic was a mess on the streets with the street lights out and all of the useless lemmings thrashing around trying to get to their jobs—jobs that now ceased to exist. Finally, though, he made it through the gridlock and got on to State Route 4 east.

Traffic thinned out considerably on the highway and he made good time to his first location, an undeveloped patch of land near the defunct town of Carmen City. But before he parked, he rolled all of the windows down on his jeep to reduce reflections and drove past the plot of land and around the area several times to check for any prying eyes.

Determining the area to be secure, he pulled off road and parked his jeep under a tall Oak. He switched off the engine, but kept the keys in the ignition just in case he had to make a run. Then he sat and waited silently for fifteen minutes, his right hand gripped around his cocked and ready Glock pistol.

Not spying anyone taking notice of him or coming to ask questions, he quietly exited the vehicle, removed his small rucksack, and tucked his Glock into his holster. Apropos of creating a lower profile with his Jeep, he had previously removed all the chrome and had it painted a flat olive color so as to better blend into his surroundings.

Never one to take chances though, he took the extra step and pulled a camouflage net over the top of the vehicle, and then tucked it in under the wheels. Taking one last look around, he hoisted his rucksack onto his back, pulled out his Glock and headed out up the hill and to the first of his cache sites.

He took his time getting to the site, choosing an oblique route that went up and around the hill rather than taking a straight line and giving the location away. Every so often, he stopped, listened, and looked back to where the jeep was parked. Walter congratulated himself that his vehicle was being more indiscernible the further he went.

Reaching the top of the ridge, he ducked down into the low Chaparral so as to not 'outline' himself against the skyline and studied the surrounding area again. It may have seemed excessive, but he had planned for this day for years and didn't want to fail now out of carelessness.

Seeing no threats, he crouch-walked down the hill through the stand of Chamise and Black Sage toward the first cache, dropping to his knees when he felt he was close. He re-holstered the Glock and pulled off his rucksack. From inside, he removed a metal detector along with some headphones. He switched it on and began simultaneously crawling and sweeping the ground to pick up the signal of metal.

Besides his own cache, he had also buried several decoys: old saws, car parts, cans of nails, and even some salt blocks, around the area so as to throw off any nosy treasure hunters.

It took a little while and after several false alarms from his own decoys, he came to the correct spot under a Scrub Oak. What set this bush and site apart from the others around it was a small brown tie wrap attached around the base of the trunk. A person would have to have been crawling around on their hands and knees to see it and even then, they might not understand the significance.

Waving the detector around the area just to the east of the trunk, he heard the screeching sound as the detector picked up the signature of his buried treasure: a four-inch diameter PVC pipe containing several dozen Krugerrands, three hundred rounds of .223 ammo, and most importantly, an acetate map overlay with secret markings showing him the location of his other eight caches.

Walter Gronsky switched off the detector, pulled out his foldable shovel and started to dig, smiling happily that his plan was coming together.

CHAPTER SIXTY-TWO

Lakewood, California
Thursday, 11:11 a.m.
+ 8 hours, 36 minutes

By eleven o'clock that morning, Johnson's Supermarket was a shambles, with a third to half of the shelves emptied. Some 'customers' even trekked into the storage area at the back of store looking for more stuff. All of the frozen food was starting to thaw, and the refrigerated section was beginning to stink as food began to rot. An industrious column of ants had already appeared, found their way into the ice cream section, and were feasting on their windfall.

Several more skirmishes had broken out between customers, but at least no one had threatened Barbara or her employees. It was quickly apparent that as long as they let people take what they needed, they would leave them alone. And if they were honest enough to try to pay for it, well, that was all she could hope for at this point.

Her mom was finally able to get through and respond to Barbara's text. Her response read: *Schools closed kids home + safe*

That was welcome news, the first she had heard all day, but it came at a cost.

With all of the schools closed and class not in session, 'Mean-Dean' and a couple of his buddies from the team had shown up to help out and to 'keep order,' as they referred to it.

Seeing what he considered tantamount to a personal affront, the big linebacker was incensed that customers were walking out unmolested with product from *his* store! Barbara told him not to worry and that it was all insured anyway, but he was undeterred, and tried to force his way past her in order to intercede. Already beyond the limits of her patience, she shoved him roughly - as hard as she could, and stuck her finger right into his big meaty face.

"Get the hell out of here right now and don't come back until I tell you! Do you understand?"

Dean Timmons was shocked by his supervisor's tone and the profanity laced command she delivered, but not as much as she was. Barbara realized then just how much stress she had been under and she immediately felt bad about blowing up on what was otherwise a good employee. Still, the shock of her forceful tirade did the trick.

"Alright," Dean said finally, and huffed away, defeated and angry he wouldn't get to 'kick some major ass.'

"C'mon guys," he said to the others and they marched out through what was left of the front door.

Her calls to the main office to get assistance; plywood for the front door, dry ice for the freezers, and so forth were met with a perpetual busy signal and so finally she gave up. On the plus side, a couple of the semi-trucks were finally able to make it through the traffic snarls about mid-day and backed into the loading dock to offload with much needed replacement products.

But even they were not immune to the desperation of the masses as several people climbed up onto the dock and began tearing the plastic wrap off of the pallets to get at the merchandise as soon as it hit the dock. This triggered another fight between the driver and one of the men who tried to take stuff off of a pallet and Barbara found herself playing nurse as she took care of the driver's battered face.

At one point during the day, when she realized that it was hopeless and that no help would arrive—either from the main office or the police, Barbara had taken the unusual step of telling all of her employees that had shown up that day to take turns and grab what they needed for themselves from the back room and to stash it in the trunks of their cars. After all, she thought, the situation was growing increasingly dire and her employees had served her valiantly today. They needed to survive as well.

Even more completely out of character for her, she had even partaken and grabbed a bunch of items and locked them in her office where she could come back later and get them. Included in her stash were two boxes of Tampax for her daughter, Olivia.

She knew that there was always a minor bit of pilferage (shrinkage was the term) from store employees sneaking a bit here and there, but in twenty-plus years of working in grocery stores, Barbara Williams could proudly say that she had never so much eaten a banana without paying for it. Now, that impeccable record of honesty and virtue had been forever erased.

Afterward, she sent several of her employees' home to be with their families, keeping just two cashiers to work with her until their shifts ended. The truth be told however, few customers had cash and so they weren't ringing up much and were really just watching the store being looted. But as long as she and her employees could stay safe, Barbara intended to maintain her post and not abandon the store until her replacement arrived.

Before long though, she would realize that her dedication to duty was nothing more than a fool's errand; the night manager texted her to say she would not be coming in. So much for loyalty.

CHAPTER SIXTY-THREE

Bakersfield, California
Thursday, 11:17 a.m.
+ 8 hours, 42 minutes

Sam Renner had five fuel deliveries to do today, but because of the traffic snarls was only at his second

The Bakersfield Costco store, being one of only the few places in town with a working store and pumps, had residents flocking to it in droves, and in the process, clogging up the road leading in.

Sam sat high up in his semi-truck cab, waiting for the line of cars to move in front of him. He could see the pumps and the fuel tank fill covers, but he just couldn't get to them to make his drop.

Just then, one of the employees walked up to his truck. He recognized her as the daytime manager, Heather.

She made a motion to roll down the window.

"What's up?" Renner asked.

"Were out," she says, regular tank went first, now we're out of super too.

"Well, I've got loads of both if I can just get through," he told her.

"I know," she said, "But the people who were at the pumps or in line when we ran out refuse to move, and say they are not giving up their spot."

"Crap!"

CHAPTER SIXTY-FOUR

"You're leaving them to twist in the breeze!" The commissioner of the CHP yelled back.

Another meeting was being held in the conference room, possibly the most pivotal of the many meetings they had had so far. The discussion was about how the generators and diesel fuel deliveries would be prioritized and, despite the fact that Shanice had arranged to have some food at the meeting from the CAL-OES emergency supply to hopefully calm everyone's nerves, tempers were already flaring.

Besides Doyle, his Chief of Staff, and OES management, the Unified Coordination Group consisting of reps from: Cal-Fire, the CHP, The California National Guard, and the FEMA Region Nine Administrator, were all present to put their stamp of approval on what decisions would be made.

But Doyle broke with protocol by also allowing reps from the designated sixteen CI, or critical infrastructures: Communications, Emergency Services, Food and Agriculture, and Healthcare, etcetera to be present. He knew it could get testy, but he wanted them all to be able to make their case for the limited resources they had - and make it they did. Quite naturally, everyone had their own babies they wanted to save.

Agriculture argued for the farmers in California, saying that they should be given priority to keep the food supply going. Bankers made the case that without money to buy critical items, the populace could not survive. The information sector wanted their data centers and server farms to keep humming along, or as they said, the high-tech sector was doomed in our state. In fact, Facebook and Google had already threatened to leave California and never return unless they got the fuel that they needed to stay functional.

Everyone present was given about five minutes to make their case and Shanice, Doyle and the members of the UCG listened patiently, but in the end, there was only so much fuel and delivery systems they had at their disposal, so the hard choices had to be made and some sectors would be sacrificed to serve the greater good.

There were three tiers in the FEMA guidelines as far as allocation of resources went, but they were only guidelines and every situation was different. Doyle had seized control and surprised some and angered others by skipping over the tier 1 benefactors, namely the supporting of fire and police.

"I'm not leaving them to twist in the breeze," the governor fired back. "I said that they will have to conserve what they have."

As a sworn peace officer, the CHP Commissioner felt a unique brotherhood with other law enforcement personnel and endeavored to be their advocate. He was echoed in his comments by the head of Cal-Fire, who also lobbied hard for first responders.

"Conserve!" the Commissioner shot back. "Do you know what our guys are going through out there? There's already widespread looting in some areas. If we can't get fuel for our cars or stations, it's going to be full scale rioting!"

"I know it's tough," Doyle admitted. "I've heard about the looting. Let those thugs steal all the phones and watches that they want. It's all insured. And pretty soon, they'll realize that nobody has any use for them."

The Commissioner sat glaring at Doyle. The governor then surprised him by asking, "How many sworn officers do we have in this state?"

The question briefly threw off the Commissioner. "Ugh, seventy to eighty thousand."

"So, eighty-thousand, to control forty million people? You guys had a hell of a time just handling the BLM riots, and that was just a couple hundred. Imagine forty million people that are starving or dying of thirst! People will be killing their own neighbor for a bottle of water. Forget about a riot; it will be full scale war!"

Doyle, breathing hard, turned to Stephanie Holmes. "How long before things get really bad with these generators and fuel running out?"

"A day or two," she said sadly. "Three tops. The phones are ringing off the hook with EOCs demanding fuel for everyone from their fire and police departments, to hospitals, and everybody else under the sun. Besides that, we're also hearing growing reports of AWOLs."

"Do you know who specifically?" Shanice asked.

"Truckers, the guys who deliver the fuels, but also police and fire, doctors, nurses, prison guards – even the refinery workers who we need to keep making the fuel. At some point everyone will just look at their own situation and decide to stay home to take care of their families, or to escape the state completely. It's happened before during some of our major earthquakes, and even Hurricane Katrina."

Doyle rubbed his hand over his jaw, he hadn't shaved in close to a day and he was already growing a beard. His eyes, like others in the room, were bloodshot.

"All right," he said. "People are bailing out, but we can't; we have a job to do and are the last line of defense for millions of people. Understood?"

There were nods all around.

"Good."

He stood up then and began pacing around the room, his head down and thinking out loud.

"We need to think basics here, not just what we were comfortable with in our old lives. Forget our TVs, our cell phones, social media...forget about even going to work – that's all over for now."

He stopped then and looked up at the group. "What are the bare bones for human survival?"

"Food and water," several said in unison.

"And health care, and medicine," the rep from Health and Human Services insisted. "Just with diabetes alone, we have over two million in this state and the pharmacies are basically shuttered. Without proper refrigeration, the insulin will start to go bad."

"And we've got to think of the guys repairing the HPT stations," the DOE rep said. "They are going to need shelter, food, water - some communications of some sort, if they are going to be able to do the repairs."

"Good point," Doyle said, and then Shanice stepped in.

"Sir," she said. "Taking care of the repair crews is something well within our wheelhouse. We can handle it just like the camps we set up for our wildfire crews."

She looked toward the head of Cal-Fire. "Tony, can you work to help us organize them?"

Still fuming about his first responders taking a backseat in the priority list, he replied with a simple, "Sure," bitterness lacing his voice.

"So, then that's what we're going to focus on," Doyle said decisively. "The repair crews as well as medicine and water. As far as food; I may not be a math genius, but two-point-four MREs from FEMA are a drop in the bucket. We can't rely on that."

"And they need water more than food," a rep from the State Water Resources Control Board added.

"Exactly," Doyle said. "We have water pumps to keep running, and sanitation systems to continue to work. That's the priority. Then, if we can somehow...*somehow*, get some of our existing food supply chains moving again, we can keep more people alive than anything else we do from this point on. Agreed?"

Again, there were nods, although the Cal-Fire and CHP reps remained stoic.

"Good," he said. "Now that we've got our priorities set, I want a detailed plan in two hours."

And then he marched out of the room.

Police Chief: Two-hundred-forty-nine New Orleans Officers Left Posts Without Permission During Katrina
Source: https://www.wave3.com/story/3904630/police-chief-249-new-orleans-officers-left-posts-without-permission-during-katrina/

CHAPTER SIXTY-FIVE

Cell Tower KNKA-327
Fresno, Calif.
Thursday, 12:17 p.m.
+ 9 hours, 42 minutes

The SunHo SHR-6000 BTS (Base Transceiver System) had automatically switched to its string of backup batteries at 2:35 AM. Since then, the 800-Watt unit had been taxed to its limit as an inordinate amount of call requests clogged its queue.

The gel cell lead acid batteries, though well within their lifespan, ran down quickly from their nominal voltage of 48 volts DC. Eventually they were drained to the point that they reached the threshold voltage of 38 volts.

The unit shut down, and with it, one segment of the city's mosaic of cell service was now lost. As customers phones began to roam, other BTS sites would have to pick up the slack, and unless they had auxiliary power units such as diesel generators or fuel cells, those towers would soon be overwhelmed, and would suffer the same fate.

Numerous customers lost critical cell service during PG&E planned PSPS (Public Safety Power Shutoff)
Source: https://www.kqed.org/news/11785039/heres-why-you-lost-cell-service-during-the-pge-power-shutoffs
FCC does not mandate minimum power backup or compliance from providers
Source: https://www.fcc.gov/document/mobile-wireless-resiliency-order

CHAPTER SIXTY-SIX

Executive Director of the Port of Los Angeles, Gene Reynolds stared up to the cargo container hanging motionless high above the deck of the Express Munich. The sight reminded him wryly of the pendulum of a faulty mechanical clock that had stopped working, and it was just about as useful.

Along with the container hanging in the air, the rest of the ship's 150,000 tons of cargo would go unloaded until either power was restored, or the massive generators that they needed to run the huge overhead cranes could be brought in and connected. There were, in fact, a couple of generators on site, but they were small and were only used to power lights to allow for a safe evacuation of the facility in the case of an outage.

A study had been done several years ago to look into building a micro-grid to generate electricity for the port in just such an emergency; a "Resiliency Plan," it was called. But now, half a decade later and after numerous meetings, steering committees assembled, and analysis performed, the only thing that had been generated was a bunch of reports, PowerPoint presentations, and some career advancements.

Reynolds turned and looked down the long dock at some of the other ships tied off there. Like the Express Munich, their cargo would remain idled as well, resulting in yet another huge supply chain disruption like the Covid pandemic.

Except, he thought, this one would be more devastating. Back then they were merely behind and at least were functioning. Now, they were, literally and figuratively, "dead in the water." And as the busiest port in the US, moving over 20% of all imports coming into the country, they were the entry point of America's supply chains.

"Doesn't look good, does it?" a familiar voice said from behind him.

Gene Reynolds turned to see, Ed Koons, the Chief of the Port Police who was also the Executive Director of Public Safety and Emergency Management at the giant facility, walking toward him.

"It sure doesn't," Reynolds acknowledged. "Any word on the generators coming from DHS?"

"They say that they are getting them loaded and will be hitting the road shortly. ETA; about three days, four tops."

"And then we still have to get them hooked up, and keep them fueled—which from what I am hearing already is going to be a huge challenge with everyone under the sun fighting over what diesel there is."

"Well, we may just have another option," Koons said softly.

The executive director stared at him intently. Koons was one of the best Reynolds had ever worked with; dedicated, driven, but also smart. He could often come up with ideas from outside of the box.

"I'm all ears," Reynolds said.

"We use navy ships," Koons explained. "They've done it before, in World War Two. The newest ships—the DDX class of destroyers, have enough capacity to power this whole port and then some."

Reynolds stared at the Chief with an abundance of admiration. He remembered that Koons was a military history buff, so he knew what he was talking about.

"Really," he said, astounded.

"Yep," Koons nodded. "It'll save us from having to be reliant on regular fuel deliveries—and *that* could keep us humming along without interruption."

"I like it," Reynolds said emphatically. "Of course, the permission to move a warship to power up our port is going to have to come from the top, with the president and the military's top brass signing off on it. Then of course, we'll have to go up the chain of command and get the governor to put in the request formally. We just can't jump over him."

"Nope," Koons agreed, nodding. "You know what a control-freak our boy, 'Hunter-Killer' is."

The two men shared a laugh at the governor's expense. But it was an uncomfortable laugh for Reynolds. Not because he had trouble making fun of the foibles of politicians, but because he knew, at this very moment, with the state and country's supply chains headed into the abyss, what America really needed, was someone in control.

"...there are no backup power sources currently configured to power the Port's critical terminal operations in the event of a loss of LADWP power."
Source: https://kentico.portoflosangeles.org/getmedia/60e68acf-1483-470f-b1ba-6d171ae67d08/draft-pola-e-map_july-2014
DDX Class Destroyers or submarines, could be used to power facilities, including ports
Source: https://ocw.mit.edu/courses/electrical-engineering-and-computer-science/6-691-seminar-in-electric-power-systems-spring-2006/projects/ship_to_shore.pdf

CHAPTER SIXTY-SEVEN

Lakewood, California
Thursday, 1:21 p.m.
+ 10 hours, 46 minutes

Jake Sullivan was at his favorite bench in the public park. It was his favorite not for the view, or the shade a large oak tree provided, but because the bench backed up to a high chain linked fence that the other homeless could not sneak up on him from behind.

Since living on the streets, he had been attacked four times; twice at night while he was sleeping, and twice during the day. Once, the weapon of choice was a piece of iron pipe, three times it was knives.

In every instance, his military training had allowed him to repel his attackers and they had not bothered him again. Word of his defensive skills, he hoped, would be spread amongst the homeless population and serve as a warning to others not to attempt it.

His radio was switched on and he listened to the latest news through his ear buds, in order to conserve batteries. A press conference at the White House was in progress with reporters hammering the president: How did we not see this coming? How long would it take given that the equipment was not readily available? How could the government continue to support the state of California and forty million people for that long?

"I promise you that we are working on it right now and that we have put the full resources of the country into this," the president responded.

"But what if those resources aren't enough to sustain the population?" a reporter fired back. *"Are people going to start dying of starvation or thirst?"*

"It has only been twelve hours since the attack and we are aggressively working on our response," the president repeated, then added testily, *"And I would appreciate it if the media would not expect miracles."*

"But we are not expecting miracles."

"Mr. Presi—"

Suddenly, and uncharacteristically, the president then cut off the reporter.

"I'm sorry but this press conference is over. I must get back to work to deal with this crisis. Thank you."

As the president left the room, Jake heard the sounds of confusion and shuffling chairs as the reporters were left in the lurch. The White House Press Secretary apparently went to the podium to attempt to pick up the slack, but he knew no more than anyone else in the room at this point. Jake switched off his radio and stared out to the green grass and trees in the park.

The world was crumbling around him. Or maybe, he pondered, it was just a reset of society as people knew it. The bar of what defined human existence would now be lowered. In fact, it was being brought down to his level; basic, primitive survival.

A raven appeared from out of the sky just then and landed not far from him. It hopped around, picking in the grass for scraps of food that some picnickers had left behind.

Jake watched the bird, realizing that with supermarkets being emptied and restaurants closed, his major source of food from dumpster diving would soon dry up. He was okay with that and could adapt. There were plenty of ravens to kill and eat, along with squirrels, rabbits, opossum—maybe even a coyote.

He was society's bottom feeder, and would do just fine.

CHAPTER SIXTY-EIGHT

CAL-OES
Mather, California
Thursday, 3:16 p.m.
+ 12 hours, 41 minutes

Even with the agreement to maintain the repair crews, and food, water, and medical systems functioning, there was still some residual debate amongst the members of the UCG meeting. The rep from the FCC argued lamely that cell towers should be kept fueled at all costs to allow people to keep in touch.

Doyle rejected the argument outright and reminded everyone that the world survived long before there were cell phones, or for that matter, even phones, period.

He also surprised everyone—and earned their respect, when he said to not continue to refuel the generators at the governor's mansion, and in fact, remove the unit outright.

"My wife and kids are going to have to deal with this like everyone else" he said. "They can light candles and eat canned food. We need that generator and fuel for higher priorities."

"And speaking of that," Doyle continued. "I just passed on a request from the head of the Port of LA to the president, who signed off on it. The navy is going to have one of its ships brought in and docked to supply power to keep the port running and keep supplies coming in. I told the head of the port that I would approve it as long as it wasn't being used to unload a bunch of useless crap Americans can live without. So that buys us some more diesel."

"And the generators they were going to use," someone added.

"Exactly," Doyle agreed. "And the other ports are going to try to do the same. So, what else do we have?"

There was continued discussion and updates, and the one thing everyone agreed on was that CAL-OES needed to be sustained, as well as the tent cities for the repair crews fixing the equipment.

Then they moved on to the life sustaining services they had determined to be a priority.

Potable water and sewage were relatively easy to figure out. They would have the individual regions delegate to the county and city EOCs to find out exactly where the water was out, what size of a generator was needed, and then work on getting it delivered and hooked up.

Hospitals were also somewhat easy as they simply had to contact them and inform them of their priority status for fuel deliveries.

It was a thornier task trying to figure out how to keep the food supply chain moving. There were twenty-five large distribution centers in the state, and most of them had generators and fuel on site, so they just had to keep them supplied.

Ditto for the one-hundred-thirty-one Costcos and twenty-nine Sam's Clubs in the state that had existing gen-sets and were continuing to function—some even with operating gas stations

But there were over six thousand smaller or independent grocery stores in the state – many without back-up power. The decision makers at CAL-OES would have to comb through the list and try to prioritize, based upon population density and so forth, who stayed open and who didn't.

On top of that, the product all had to move to these stores, so they had to consider keeping the semi-trucks supplied with fuel and to get through traffic. The Adjutant General of the California National Guard offered up their services to supply both armed escorts for the trucks as well as working with the CHP to clear the routes of congestion.

All in all, it sounded good, and so after the meeting adjourned, Shanice allowed herself the luxury of making a phone call to her husband. She moved into her office, pulled out her cell phone and dialed *272 to initiate the WPS (Wireless Priority Service), and then her husband's cell number. The phone rang so many times she thought it was either dead or going to go to voicemail when her husband, breathlessly answered it.

"Sorry baby," he said, breathing hard. "My phone's been pretty much useless, so I didn't have it nearby. How's it going there?"

"Crazy, as you can imagine," she answered. "But we do have a plan going forward that we think is going to work."

"You mean to get the power back on?" he asked incredulously.

"No," she admitted. "That's going to take quite a while."

"So, I've heard," he said. "I've been listening to that little emergency crank radio you got us – nice gadget by the way, and I heard the president's press conference. Did you listen to it?"

"No time," she said. "But I heard he got hammered pretty hard."

"Yeah, a reporter from the Associated Press must have gotten wind of how long the lead time is on these HPR things – "

"HPTs," she corrected, chuckling to herself. "I've had a crash course on the grid, by the way. But go on."

"So anyway, this reporter really called him out. He said that he wasn't being truthful and that California was going to be without power for over a year. Is that true baby?"

Shanice bit her lip, a habit she had when she didn't know what to say. She was silent for so long her husband thought the call had dropped.

"Shanice...Shanice? Are you there?"

"Yes, I'm here," she said. "Sorry."

"So, is it true; a year with no electricity?"

She took a deep breath and then said, "Yes."

"So, what are we going to do baby?" he asked. "What's going to become of us?"

The question struck her hard, especially since her husband, a man who she had never known to have any fear, suddenly had a tremor in his voice.

"I don't know," Shanice Dixon said. "I really don't know."

CHAPTER SIXTY-NINE

Lakewood, California
Thursday, 4:06 PM
+ 13 hours, 31 minutes

After locking up whatever meager cash they took in for the day in the safe in her office, and sending her two remaining employees' home, Barbara grabbed one of the boxes of Tampax and snuck out through the side entrance, wondering if she would ever return.

She had struggled with her decision to leave her post, but in the end, she realized that it was a hopeless situation. She had done her level best to hold onto the ship, but she wasn't about to wait there forever until someone relieved her—if they ever would. Worse yet, she wasn't about to put her life and that of her employees in danger. If management ever came up with a plan to deal with the crisis and wanted her back, she would return, but not until then.

The street outside was not as busy as the morning, but it was still chaotic. Any cars that were trying to travel the streets were inevitably stopped at the gridlocked intersections to wait their turn—some chose not to and this led to further the rancor. Horns seem to honk incessantly. Several cars were stalled in the street, and a couple of vehicles were still in the intersection where they collided. She barely looked at them as she walked, lost in her own thoughts.

More of her customers had reported to her that they had heard on their car radios that it was indeed a terrorist attack and that the entire state was without power. For how long, no one could—or would, say. Barbara thought of all of the emergencies that threatened California: Earthquakes were at the top of the list with their destruction—and in some cases, the death that they wrought.

But an earthquake was a different type of disaster in that you could feel and visually witness the damage from it. A large trembler would knock houses off their foundations, cause bridges and overpasses to collapse, and rupture gas and water lines as well as disrupting electrical power. It was visual and real. This was different, a sublime event, even ghostly. As she walked, she realized that the world around her was still as physically intact as it had been just yesterday, it was just lifeless now, like an empty movie set.

As she went, she glanced up at the overhead power lines, realizing that, unlike an earthquake or a windstorm that dropped trees onto them, they were still intact. The difference was that nothing flowed through them. The lines even appeared to be more taught than usual between the poles. She remembered hearing once that during heavy demand, they actually sag. Now, with zero demand, they were straighter than she had ever seen them before.

"The world is ending! The fucking world is ending!"

The sound came from across the street. There was a middle-aged man gesturing wildly and screaming about the world ending.

When he spotted her looking at him, he turned his attention to her.

"Repent now!" he screamed. "You don't have much time!"

Even though he was a good hundred feet away, Barbara hoped he wouldn't dart across the street and confront her, or worse. She looked away and sped up her pace as he continued his dire soliloquy.

"Repent now, you sinful bitch!"

CHAPTER SEVENTY

Santa Ana, Caliornia
Thursday, 4:25 p.m.
+ 13 hours, 15 minutes

Mike Harrigan was proud of his purchase. Other than test run it on Christmas morning, he had waited a long time for this moment of vindication.

At the time, his wife had thought it a useless and frivolous request for a present, but then, he thought her fascination with miniature Hummel figurines was a waste of money as well. Like most couples, they bit their respective tongues and compromised.

The Sun Fast Power dual-fuel 7000 portable generator, manufactured in China, had been running steadily for over ten hours. Mike was proud that not only did he have lights and a working TV, not a single bit of food had gone bad in their refrigerator. Plus, his beer was staying just as cold as ever.

He knew that he had to keep his power source a secret from his neighbors though, and so rather than run it outside, he kept it running in their attached garage along with enough propane to keep them going for about a week, or until the utilities got their act together and got the power turned back on.

To celebrate his foresight and independence, he had been downing beers as it he sat in front of the TV watching the drama unfold. He was nine cans into the case and starting to get drowsy. His wife was next to him in the other recliner and had already fallen asleep reading one of her trashy romance novels.

Before long, his eyelids got heavy, and closed as well. But it wasn't because of his drunkenness or a lack of sleep. In the nearly half-day that his generator had been on, it had been running 'rich,' and the incomplete combustion spewed dangerous amounts of carbon monoxide into the attached garage. The deadly, odorless gas silently made its way into the main house and before long, into the couple's lungs and bloodstream.

The Harrigans never woke up, and were both dead before the bottle of propane had run out.

Carbon Monoxide (CO) is responsible for almost 25% of all propane related fatalities.
https://www.propane101.com/carbonmonoxideandpropane.htm
Portable generators can emit as much carbon monoxide as 450 cars, according to federal figures.
Source: ProPublica via: https://news.yahoo.com/generators-poison-thousands-people-u-110012528.html

CHAPTER SEVENTY-ONE

Near Carmen City, California
Thursday, 4:31 p.m.
+ 13 hours, 56 minutes

By 4:30 that afternoon, Walter had located and retrieved about seventy percent of his caches. They were buried in various locations near his hideout, but not so close as to help someone find it.

He 'owned' three acres in a heavily wooded area off of an unmaintained dirt road. The land was undesirable to the average developer as it was located far from any utilities, and was sloped up against one of the rolling hills that ran in the area. For Walter, it was a perfect spot to avoid others and to defend his freedom.

Never one to leave behind paper trails, the land was actually owned under an LLC that he created out of state under a false identity. Therefore, not only did no one know he owned it, but as a bonus, he never paid any of the property taxes on it. As remote and impractical as the land was, he never lost sleep thinking tax assessors might try to go after him. Fuck the money-grubbing government! He thought.

After pulling off the road and up to his property, he once again repeated his security ritual of waiting and watching. Once again, he determined the threat to be low, if not non-existent. The few houses that were built in the area didn't have a clear-line view to his property and if someone wanted to come on to his land and nose around, he had made sure that they would have to make an extra effort to get close.

Utilizing unconventional—and most importantly, *nondescript* barriers to keep anyone from getting too far onto his property, he had strategically planted several native bushes to serve as bramble. The plants were prickly, thick, and difficult to get past. Additionally, he set out random coils of old barbed wire just below the grass line to serve as 'tangle-foot' and to slow down any intruders. One thing he didn't do was to post "No Trespassing" signs on the property, feeling that they only served to advertise to others that someone owned it, and that there might be something valuable to make it worth their effort to enter.

To the casual observer or untrained eye, the property looked to be nothing more than a patch of raw land on the slope of a hill. But it was what was under the hill that really mattered.

After purchasing the land several years ago, Walter had rented a backhoe, scraped a new road to it and carved out a large flat spot in the hill. As soon as the excavation was complete, he drove an old used school bus he had purchased onto the site.

He removed the gas tank and the tires, placed the bus flat on the ground and bolted an ingress/egress tunnel that he had fabricated onto the roof where the buses escape hatch was located. ¼" steel plate was welded over all the windows to keep them from shattering and then he filled the area all back in with dirt, covering the bus entirely and leaving the tunnel his only way in and out.

More native plants and bramble were planted and before long, the land looked as natural and virgin as it had been for centuries.

Satisfied it was safe to make a move, he climbed out of his jeep, grabbed some of the caches and began trekking up the hill to his bunker.

For good or for bad, this would be his new home for the time being. Until either the revolution was won, or Walter Gronsky, patriot, died trying.

CHAPTER SEVENTY-TWO

City of Industry, California
Thursday, 4:32 p.m.
+ 13 hours, 57 minutes

What should have taken John Donegan only four hours to do on a normal day, was stretching into nine and counting. As a senior field operator for the Southern California Region of the Kindle-Morgan Pipeline Company, he had to make the runs to correctly check the line ups of the various switching valves along the pipeline to make sure that the product reached the terminals in nearby Ontario, as well as to the cities of Colton, Nyland, and even March Air Force Base.

Under normal circumstances, some of the MOV's (motor operated valves) would have been remotely switched, but now even these had to be hand cranked into position as well as the myriad of other block valves. Add to that, the mess with traffic just trying to drive from the control center in Carson, and it was turning into one hell of a day.

Listening to the news reports on the radio as he made his way through traffic, Donegan knew that his job was more critical than ever. With the grid completely shut down, fuels for generators would be the vital link to helping people stay alive and get through this.

He pulled his company truck up to the manifold of pipes and valves and began checking his line-up card to make sure he opened and closed the correct valves and in the proper sequence.

The first two went well as they were gear reduced manual valves, but he hit a snag when he moved over to one of the MOV's. As it was normally operated remotely and used an electric motor to open and close the gate of the ten-inch valve, the manual override clutch assembly had not been used in some time. The lever to engage the clutch was sticky and the big handwheel was difficult to turn, probably as a result of a lack of use and preventive maintenance.

Barely budging as he attempted to turn it, Donegan hooked a valve wheel wrench, colloquially known by oil workers as a 'peno-li', onto the outside ring of the valve handwheel. Gaining leverage with the device, he pulled with all his might and then suddenly, the wheel broke free, although not in the manner he had hoped for; the small shear pin that held the collar of the handwheel to the shaft of the valve had snapped.

"Shit," he cursed as the handwheel now spun easily around, completely useless.

Even with all the other valves opened, no matter how much product was ready to flow, nothing would get through until the valve got repaired. He depressed the button on his two-way radio.

"E-17 to control; we've got a problem here."

CHAPTER SEVENTY-THREE

Lakewood, California
Thursday, 4:33 p.m.
+ 13 hours, 58 minutes

Barbara Williams arrived home without further incident, but was still rattled by the encounter with the deranged man. She noted, as she closed the door and locked the deadbolt behind her, that their apartment was dimmer than normal for this time of day.

Her mom had all the blinds pulled up to let in the maximum amount of light, but even with that, it had a muted grayness to it, just like her mood. She also realized in a few hours it would be getting dark, and that they needed to take care of whatever business they could as soon as possible.

Her six-year-old son, Freddie, was playing with some toy cars on the carpet in the living room. Her daughter, Olivia, was slumped in a chair, holding her phone in her hand and staring at it vacantly. Barbara sensed a fear in her daughter's face she hadn't seen before.

She kissed Freddie on the top of the head and he barely acknowledged her, which was his de rigueur response and which actually gave Barbara a sense of relief; normalcy, she thought. Then she made her way over to Olivia, handing her the box of Tampax.

"Here you go honey," she said, kissing her on the forehead. "I've got another box at the store that I stashed."

Olivia took the box and nodded mutely.

Barbara made her way into the kitchen where her mom was sitting at the table.

"Crazy?" her mom asked.

Barbara pulled out a chair and sat in it wearily.

"Oh yeah, it was crazy all right," she nodded, and then buried her face into her hands. She took a deep breath and tried to relax. She didn't really want to think about seeing the store broken into and looted, but she couldn't get it out of her mind; the sound of the glass shattering, the customers charging into the aisles, the fights over simple things. The rush on stores during the opening days of the pandemic was one thing, but this was far worse. It was an ugly display of human behavior and she was glad her children weren't witness to it.

"Mom," Olivia called out from the living room. "My phone doesn't work. I don't have any bars."

Barbara looked at her daughter, noting trepidation in her voice, as opposed to the usual petty whining. Right now, Barbara would welcome the whining.

"I know honey," she said. "A lot of them don't work. The towers are probably overloaded and maybe going dead. I'm not sure if they have generators or not."

"Are we going to be…okay?" Olivia asked in a very tiny voice. "They said that it was a terrorist attack."

Barbara nodded sadly, 'That's what I heard; the whole state."

"Well, how are we going to…to survive?" Olivia asked, her voice cracking.

Less than twenty-four hours ago, she was an ordinary adolescent, bursting with hormones and on the precipice of womanhood. Gone from her voice was the defiant and challenging teen angst. Now she sounded like a little girl, scared and vulnerable.

"We'll be okay honey," Barbara said trying to reassure her daughter as much as herself. "We've got enough food to last us for almost a week, and I have some more at the store that I can always get."

She added, trying to sound confident, but not knowing how convincing she was, "I'm sure the utilities or the government will think of something and get it fixed right away."

"Olivia just stared at her, before glancing down once again to her inoperable phone.

"And speaking of food," Barbara, thought just then. "You guys haven't been opening the refrigerator today, have you?"

"Just once," her mom admitted. "Olivia and Freddie each wanted a soda, so I thought I would treat them."

"Was it cold?" Barbara asked.

"Sort of," Olivia said.

"Good," Barbara nodded. "We're going to have to be very smart about managing our food so it doesn't spoil. We have to cook and eat the stuff that's going to go bad first, whether we want to or not. Understood?"

Olivia nodded mutely. Freddie was engrossed in crashing his cars into one another on the carpet and said nothing.

Watching her son play, Barbara thought ironically of the similarities she had seen today in the intersection outside the store. At least a dozen cars were involved in collisions throughout the day. She never saw any police or fire respond, or even a tow truck. Several of the cars must have been disabled on the spot and were left there, further adding to the congestion. She briefly considered asking Freddie not to crash his cars into one another and trigger her sad thoughts, but he didn't know what she had witnessed, and she wouldn't deprive him, especially right now.

"Already one step ahead of you," Barbara's mother said, bringing her thoughts back to the food situation. "When I got out the soda, I saw that we still had almost a full tray of that lasagna leftover. Plus, we have stuff to make a salad. The freezer food should be good for another two or three days."

"Good," Barbara said. She leaned back in her chair and closed her eyes. She had had a splitting headache for the past four hours. Even after swallowing some aspirin at the store, it still had no signs of abating.

"But how are we going to cook it?" Olivia asked. "The microwave doesn't work."

"No, it doesn't," Barbara's mom said, then added somewhat righteously. "But believe it or not young lady, we cooked and kept ourselves fed long before microwaves came along. The regular oven doesn't work either, but the burners on the top will if we light them with a match."

Barbara's mom stood up then, "C'mon Olivia, I'm going to show you how to bake on a stove top."

Olivia got up from her chair in the living room and joined her grandmother in the kitchen, where they start assembling pots and racks to bake with. Barbara took the opportunity to get out of their way and moved into the living room, taking the seat her daughter had just vacated.

She settled into its warmth and closed her eyes. Soon, she started hearing the comforting sounds of clanging pots and utensils from the kitchen. Before long, she also felt her mom opening her hand.

"Here," her mom said, placing a glass of wine into her hand.
"Thanks mom."
Barbara took a sip. It was heavenly, and 'sort of' cold too.

CHAPTER SEVENTY-FOUR

CAL-OES
Mather, California
Thursday, 6:17 p.m.
+ 15 hours, 42 minutes

How did this happen?
How much of the state is down?
How long to repair it?
What is the state doing to help people survive?

The questions came in like a torrent, from in the room as well as from outside via conference call.

Hunter Doyle III was giving his first press conference since the attack and was being hammered from all sides. The press conference was being carried live on television (although admittedly, few in the state could probably watch it) on AM and FM radio, short-wave, YouTube, and Zoom.

Besides the governor and his aide, also in the room were the Unified Command group, the CAL-OES director of communications, the rep from STTAC, and Shanice Dixon, who at some point would be called upon to outline the state's response.

Prior to appearing in front of the cameras, the Governor had retreated to his private suite, showered, shaved and changed into a fresh shirt. Mindful of the importance of appearance, he knew that nothing screamed chaos in a crisis louder than a disheveled and harried looking leader. He didn't wear a suit coat, but his tie was smartly knotted, and the sleeves of his dress shirt were rolled up on his forearms. The hard charging leader in control of the situation.

He answered the questions in order as best he could, although the reporters who conferenced in continually talked over one another and those present in the room.

"It was a terrorist attack," Doyle said flatly. "We know that for certain. I will not get into any of the particulars right now, but will let Mr. Behnken from the State Terrorism Threat Analysis Center respond further to that."

"As far as how much of the state is affected, the estimate is that we lost roughly ninety-eight percent of the grid."

An audible gasp was heard in the room from the reporters present, and this stimulated even more questions.

"How did we not see this coming?" a CNN reporter asked pointedly.

"I'm not going to speculate on that and will defer all those questions to STTAC, the FBI and DHS...Next?"

"Is it true it will take over a year to restore the grid?" a reporter practically yelled through the conference speaker.

Doyle took a deep breath, then admitted, "That is what we're hearing, although we are working every angle to try to shorten that repair timeline."

"So, what are you going to do about the forty million people that live here governor?" a female reporter from the Sacramento Bee blurted out, her blunt query coming more of a challenge than a question. "How are you going to take care of them? We are already hearing reports of food shortages as well as a lack of fuel, and even water systems that have failed. How are your constituents going to survive for over a year?"

The woman was a veteran reporter who had fought hard to rise through the ranks of journalism and was well known to the governor and to anyone in California politics in general. Her name was Cory Donaldson, but her nickname was "Cory the Cobra" for the way her questions struck lightning fast and straight to the jugular. Like the others that had come before him, Doyle had tangled with her on more than one occasion.

But politics was not for the faint of heart, and Doyle didn't cower from blistering interrogation. Nor did he punt the ball to Shanice, which would have been an easy way out. Instead, he focused on the facts and the path forward without being pulled into the spiral of panic the media liked to cultivate.

"It has only been fourteen hours since the attack," he began simply. "And in that brief period of time, we have marshalled tremendous amounts of our resources—and rather superbly I might add."

As he said this, he turned and gestured toward Shanice and to the other CAL-OES team members in the room. Shanice smiled demurely; she never cared about praise, only about doing the best job she could.

"As we speak," the governor continued. "Generators are already in transit, as well as fuel trucks, aid organizations, security personnel and others. The DOE is also working tirelessly to finish assessments of the damage and to implement repairs and replacements of the damaged equipment with the utmost speed and efficiency.

With regards to the citizens of our great state, our immediate focus has been on rescue and assessment. We are still combing through reports that are filtering up through our regional EOC's to determine needs. Beyond the immediate needs and looking toward the short term, it has been determined that our best path forward is to focus our resources on the basics of survival."

Holding up his hand, he ticked off on his fingers what those basics were.

"Water, number one," he said, extending a finger. "As basic as air for human survival. Any municipal water or sanitation system that needs power and fuel to keep running will be given top priority."

"Two, food and medicine. We will focus resources on getting our existing supply chains back up and running. This means food distribution centers, transportation, and finally, retail. Some smaller grocery stores will have to consolidate with the larger chains and Costcos, but there is no sense in reinventing the wheel and creating entirely new supply chains, we just have to get our existing ones up and running again."

Doyle continued on for several more minutes, outlining the basics and the bigger strategic plans before turning the podium over to Shanice to dive further into the details of implementation.

She took over and knew that she wanted to maintain a balance of confidence and control without coming across as overly cocky. Like Doyle, she too had attempted to freshen up before the conference. Although truth be told, after being up for fourteen hours with only a couple of hours of sleep the previous night, she wondered how much effect it had.

Luckily though, by now many of the reporters appeared to have gotten their 'sound-bites,' and weren't as interested in the nitty-gritty details she presented. Several left the room and the questions that did come from the remaining reporters were more softball in nature, with a greater focus on specifics. She also didn't hear as many voices barking from the conference speaker, and suspected many of them had already formed their opinions and were busy filing their reports.

Still, as easy as she had it compared to Doyle, she found she had to place one of her hands on top of the other to prevent them from shaking. She also thought she heard her own voice cracking a couple of times. Was it nerves, a lack of sleep, or a reckoning of just how massive this disaster was?

She finished with her piece of the conference after about twenty minutes and handed it off to the STTAC rep to handle specific questions regarding the actual attack. She noticed that as she left the podium, her hands were still shaking and she felt faint.

She hastily exited the room and barely made it to the bathroom before she threw up.

CHAPTER SEVENTY-FIVE

Lakewood, California
Thursday, 8:17 p.m.
+ 17 hours, 42 minutes

Barbara thought their apartment seemed smaller tonight, the boundaries of the rooms existing only as far as the light of the candles they used. To pass the time, they played a board game that was within Freddie's ability and attention span. A lit candle was on the table along with a couple of flashlights for moving about.

She also noted that the evening had less traffic noise as more people stayed off the streets after realizing there weren't any gas stations open. It reminded her of the eerie quiet during the Rodney King riots after the city had declared a nighttime curfew, and few were brave—or stupid enough, to be out during those harrowing five days in April/May of 1992.

More ominously, she did hear what sounded like random gunshots in the distance as well as the occasional siren. As stressful as it was for her, she tried to maintain a brave face for everyone's benefit, but mostly for Olivia's as she seemed the most vulnerable. Although she was a proud and stubborn teenager who would not readily admit to being scared, Barbara knew deep down her daughter sought what all children want more than anything; the comfort and security of a safe existence.

After they collectively allowed Freddie to 'win' several games, she told her children that they had to go to bed at 8:30. Olivia didn't push back as she expected her too, and instead asked if she could sleep in her bedroom with her.

"I'll sleep on the floor if you want," she added.

"Me too!" Freddie chimed in.

"Okay, that's fine. But you can both sleep in the bed with me. We can all fit."

"I wanna sleep on the ground," Freddie insisted. "Like camping."

"Alright," Barbara surrendered. "But first you have to go to the bathroom and pee."

She grabbed a flashlight from the table and started to lead him by the hand into the bathroom.

"I'll do it mom," he said proudly and grabbed the flashlight out of her hand.

While Freddie was in the bathroom, Barbara grabbed another flashlight and made her way down to the parking garage and climbed into her car. She switched on the ignition and had to scan past several stations that were all static until she finally hit on an am radio station that was broadcasting.

The news was still pretty much the same that she had been hearing all day: statewide power outage, suspected terrorist attack, government working on the problem, stay calm, blah, blah, blah...

She closed and locked her car and using the beam of the flashlight, climbed the steps up to the second-floor landing to their apartment. But before she went inside, she stood there for a moment taking in the scene.

It was so dark and quiet; she couldn't believe it. Other than the muted glow of candles or an occasional movement of a flashlight inside, there were no lights on in the other apartments, not even the familiar flicker of TVs. No planes from nearby Long Beach Airport were taking off or landing, and other than an occasional siren or gunshot in the distance, it was eerily silent.

After a while, she turned her gaze upward and looked at the Milky Way Galaxy. A satellite was slowly crossing the sky from horizon to horizon. Traveling up there in the cold, emptiness of space, it seemed so alone. At that moment, Barbara Williams felt the same way.

CHAPTER SEVENTY-SIX

Near Carmen City, California
Thursday, 9:40 p.m.
+ 19 hours, 5 minutes

Properly clearing his bunker of security threats, Walter Gronsky set off to work. After several trips back and forth to his jeep to bring in his caches, he finally removed the distributer cap from the jeep, covered it with a camo netting and descended the ladder into the bunker.

Inside, he stowed the remaining items, and then, satisfied, took a moment to reflect and look proudly at his creation; his brainchild and labor of love that had taken him over two years to complete. Now it was done and in the nick of time.

Even with the seats removed, as large as the forty-eight-passenger bus was, after stocking it with his equipment and other supplies: a bunk for sleeping, two large barrels of water with pump, a small propane powered cook stove, a portable toilet, two-month supply of MREs, a dozen weapons from side arms, to assault rifles, to a match grade .50 caliber sniper rifle as well as 20,000 rounds of ammunition in various calibers, it became very small and confined in short order. But he was a freedom fighter now and was ready, willing, and eager to make the sacrifice. After all, he reasoned, it was small price to pay for freedom from tyranny. He moved over to the corner of the bus and depressed the start switch on his propane powered generator.

He had debated long and hard the pros and cons of using solar panels versus a generator before finally decide to go the mainstream route. Granted, solar cells were simple and required no fuel, but they only worked during peak periods of sunshine and were therefore an unreliable source of power should he have a couple of gray days. Also, they were large, reflective and therefore could easily give away that fact that someone was living on the property. The generator was a dual/fuel unit tied to a bank of 6-gallon propane cylinders and discharged through a muffled pipe that ran underground about a hundred feet from the bus and exhausted to the atmosphere.

Two carbon monoxide detectors kept him safe from poisoning and he typically would run the generator while he was out of the bunker and doing work outside. The unit produced 12000 watts of AC that powered an industrial automotive battery charger that in turn fed a bank of sealed 12-volt DC car batteries. All of the lights, fans, and other equipment in the bunker ran off of this voltage.

Once the generator had started up and was running smoothly, Walter once again left his bunker.

Donning a pair of night vision goggles and with his Steyr AUG 'Bullpup' assault rifle in his hand, he trekked up the hill above the bunker to a large oak tree. Using a slingshot, he launched a half inch steel ball over the top of the tree. The ball had a hole drill through it where a thin wire was attached. The wire was barely discernable during the day, and essentially invisible at night. After the ball with the wire landed on the other side of the tree, Walter grabbed the free end and walked about fifteen feet towards a Chaparral bush. At the base of the bush, he dug a small hole with his hands and connected the wire to another just below the surface.

The wire ran underground back to his bunker, where it terminated on the antenna jack of his shortwave radio, his chosen method to gather intel.

Before the January 6th fight to save the steal, Walter Gronsky typically turned to social media for his updates. But then the companies, led by that kike bastard Mark Zuckerberg, caved in to the government and kicked the only truthful groups off of their sites, in essence nullifying and silencing their first amendment rights. But that fight for the truth continued, albeit in another format.

Satisfied that the connection was secure, Walter buried the hole with dirt. He hefted his assault rifle and his other gear and headed back down to the bunker. He was anxious to listen to the other preppers who broadcast on SW and were now part of the fight for freedom.

Forget the lying government or the social media lackeys, Walter Gronsky was now going to hear what was *really* going on!

CHAPTER SEVENTY-SEVEN

CAL-OES
Mather, California
Thursday, 10:27 p.m.
+ 19 hours, 52 minutes

"You need sleep." Sandra Clayton, the CAL-OES Chief Deputy Director for Operations, told her.

Shanice had been awake now for close to twenty hours, but then, so had a lot of others. This included Clayton, who stood before her glaring like a scolding parent.

"So do you," Shanice said back to her.

"Mike Binkley relieved me, and I caught a cat nap a couple of hours ago—just like you ordered everyone to do," the Deputy Director replied. "Now *you* need to follow your own directive."

It was true that since they had been staffed up from early morning, the order had been given to the heads of the respective divisions to develop a shift schedule so that everyone could get some much-needed rest.

Some, who lived close by had taken the opportunity to head home and check on their families, but others—as they had done many times before during large scale emergencies 'camped out' at the OES campus, finding every unused office, broom closet, or nook and cranny to catch some shut-eye in.

Shanice looked around the SOC and saw her employees manning their stations, working the phones, and basically doing their jobs. There was no good reason to watch over them, and she could feel herself fading fast. Pretty soon, she would start getting punchy and would begin making mistakes; something she could not afford to do.

"You're right," she admitted. "I'm going to go into my office and lay down for a bit then added, gesturing to the SOC "Have you got this?"

"Absolutely."

"Thanks," Shanice said, briefly resting a hand on Clayton's shoulder before turning away and heading up the stairs and into her office.

Inside, she grabbed her sleeping bag from the closet, unrolled and unzipped it and then climbed onto a leather sofa on the far wall, pulling it over her body.

She closed her eyes and attempted to 'will' herself to sleep.

In a few moments, it was apparent that it wasn't working; her mind was a jumble of things she needed to think about, make decisions about, or just simply try not to forget. She needed a respite and turned to her favorite solution.

Throwing off the bag, she got up, retrieved her Nana's bible from her desk and climbed back onto the couch. She opened it to one of her favorite books and began to read.

A few minutes later she was sound asleep, the bible clutched on her chest. The last thing she remembered was James 1:2-4:

"My brethren, count it all joy when you fall into various trials, knowing that the testing of your faith produces patience. But let patience have its perfect work, that you may be perfect and complete, lacking nothing."

CHAPTER SEVENTY-EIGHT

Near Carmen City, California
Thursday, 11:02 p.m.
+ 20 hours, 27 minutes

"Good evening my fellow patriots of The Organization" the voice began.

Patriot Man paused for a moment then announce somberly, *"As you all know by now, the day has dawned.*

I have been telling you for some time now of this plot by our government to supplicate our freedoms, and it has finally happened. The evil forces of the Zionist leaders and our whore government, have struck and struck hard. We are now, my fellow patriots, officially at war."

Walter listened intently, one hand gripped onto the receiver of his Bull-Pup assault rifle, the other making notes on a tablet.

"And for those of you wondering if this 'so called attack' on our electrical grid was the work of outside sources, I can state unequivocally that it was not. Just as in the Sandy Hook charade, the nine-eleven farce, and the Waco slaughter, actors and special effects have been used to 'show' the damage inflicted on our electrical infrastructure. In reality though, it was just our government—our corrupt, spineless puppets of the Jew boys, that did it by simply flipping the switch. After all, if they are able to steal a presidential election from right under our noses, then there's no limit to their tyranny and underhandedness."

Walter was not surprised by the proclamation by Patriot Man; he had realized it from the first moments he opened his eyes this morning, but then his trusted freedom fighter in this struggle dropped a bigger bombshell.

"And, unfortunately my fellow patriots, I'm afraid I have even worse news, worse than what you already know. We are getting reports in of a new machine that has been developed, a machine designed to help our compromised and evil government carry out their hideous plans by first locating and then confiscating all of our guns. That's right, they tried it with laws, with restrictions, with media campaigns and phony reports of mass shootings, but they were largely unsuccessful in their efforts to take away our second

amendment rights. Now they have turned to technology, a new technology that can sniff out the presence of any trace of gunpowder residue. We aren't sure how it works yet, or of any way to defeat it, but it does work. Members of the organization have been able to witness a testing of the device. It is large they say, and is carried under the belly of a helicopter as it flies around sniffing for residue. When it detects a hit, storm troopers move in, neutralize the patriot, steal their weapons, and then hand them over to the murderous raping thugs they have released onto our streets."

Walter gripped the receiver of his gun even more tightly. He looked around his bunker at the other guns he had stashed inside. They were basically his only defense and it shook him to his core to think of them taken from him. Just to imprint the threat deep into his mind, he drew a very simplistic picture of a helicopter with square device under it.

"And I know what you're thinking my fellow patriots; I clean my weapons thoroughly each time I use them, it can't sniff them out. Well, this device is so sophisticated, so sensitive, it can even detect the presence of gunpowder in the parts per billion range, so you'll never be able to hide them, never! My fellow patriots, this is it. This is the beginning of the white genocide! Will you fight with me, or will you roll over? This is our last stand! This, my fellow patriots, is kill, or be killed!"

The broadcast ended and Walter set his pencil back down on the tiny table in his bunker, and turned off the radio. He knew what he had to do. But before he could, he would need a good night's sleep. Tomorrow would be a big day, an important one in the fight for freedom. Walter Gronsky, true American and patriot, would begin ringing the perimeter of his property with IED anti-personnel mines.

PART III:
THE THIN VENEER
OF CIVILITY

CHAPTER SEVENTY-NINE

CAL-OES
Mather, California
Friday, 6:00 a.m.
+ 1 day, 3 hours, 25 minutes

Shanice bolted awake with a start, the alarm on her cell phone stunning her with its melodic chiming, her hands still clutching nana's bible on her chest.

Instinctively, she sat up, noticing that she was extremely stiff. This was understandable as based upon her position on the couch, she probably had not moved all night long.

She leaned over, picked the phone up from the floor next to the couch in her office and swiped 'dismiss' on the screen to silence the alarm. Then, rather than navigating to other screens, she simply held the device in her hand for a long time, staring at it.

What a world of comfort and convenience we had created, she thought. While we once had to have an alarm clock to wake up by, maps to navigate by, and a camera to capture the "Kodak Moments" of our lives, now everything was wrapped up in one tiny package barely the size of a bar of soap.

And it's all great, she thought ruefully, until it no longer works.

Then, embarrassed, she thought of the fact that because of her position, her phone *did* in fact still function. Not the same for millions of others in the state at this moment.

Feeling the call to action, she struggled through her aches and stiffness and climbed up off the couch and headed to the private bath in her office.

While she was in showering, she began to think of the day and plan ahead as she always did. Under normal circumstances, her routine work day was the typical mixture of meetings, emails, decisions, and PR work that she had to do. Now, it was uncharted territory; the largest disaster of any kind in the US, and they were responsible for managing the response. Rather, *she* was responsible.

The thought suddenly made her physically weak, and she had to rest her hand on the tiled wall to keep from fainting. She closed her eyes, and took a few deep breaths until she recovered.

Feeling better, she finished up, dressed and was out the door of her office and headed toward the conference room. The first meeting with the governor, the unified command group, FEMA, and the heads of the various departments was scheduled for seven AM sharp.

She looked at her wristwatch and saw that she had about ten minutes or so to grab a quick bite to eat and have a cup of coffee. But before she indulged herself of sustenance, she headed over to the SOC to see how things were going. Reports from the heads of departments were one thing, but she liked to be down in the trenches to interact with those on the front lines, the people trying to make it all happen.

Inside the big room, it was pretty much as she had left it about seven hours ago. Overhead on the big wall, the monitors were still on with feeds from CNN, the networks and some of the local affiliates showing the same dire scenes, of stores being looted, cars stalled and several structure fires that were burning unabated.

The workstations were now being manned by a new shift that had come on at six a.m. Besides the color-coded work vests designating areas of responsibility, someone had printed out large font paper signs at certain workstations further delineating them as: "GEN-SETS," "FUEL DIST", 'MUNI WATER."

Shanice was pleased that someone had thought ahead, and approached Seth Tailor, a veteran operations person whom she had worked with for close to a decade. Unlike many who worked at CAL-OES, Tailor felt no drive to work up the ranks into management, and chose instead to be close to the ground and doing what he loved to do; juggling as many balls in the air that he could.

"How's it going Seth?" Shanice inquired.

"Fair," he said, shrugging. He grabbed his coffee cup and took a long sip, before turning to her. His eyes were puffy and red, either from a lack of quality sleep from 'camping out' at the campus, or from staring at a computer screen for hours on end. He also had the makings of a couple of day's growth of beard.

"Gen-Set installs going okay?"

He shrugged again. It was a habit he was not normally given to, and Shanice was concerned by his body language.

"They're going," he said noncommittally. "But we get one installed, and then three more requests come in."

"The resources from out of state?" she asked.

"'In route' is all we hear," he sighed wearily.

His computer chimed just then, and he said, "Sorry," before turning back to the screen.

Shanice didn't want to interfere and step away from the workstation. She took a moment to examine some of the facial expressions and body language of others in the room. It was not a comforting picture.

Most, if not all, looked haggard and worn, and it was only day two of managing the response. They were seasoned, battle-hardened professionals who had been through the golden state's gauntlet of forest fires, mudslides, and the occasional earthquake, but nothing it seemed could have prepared them for a crisis of this scale and magnitude. What would it be like a week from now, or a month, even a year? Could they manage? Could *she* manage?

Besides the expressions on the faces she saw, she was also taken aback by the conspicuous sight of a couple of empty chairs. She tried to reassure herself that maybe the people assigned to them were in meetings, or were simply taking a break, but the image stuck with her and nagged.

Then, she glanced at her watch once again, realizing the ten-minute cushion she had until the meeting, had just evaporated into two. She would just have to eat later.

She headed through the SOC and off to the conference room, walking right past the empty chairs, noting ominously that the monitors were not even switched on.

CHAPTER EIGHTY

Lakewood, California
Friday, 7:14 a.m.
+ 1 day, 4 hours, 39 minutes

The next morning, Barbara lay awake in bed for long time, even though, truth be told, as exhausted as she was, she really hadn't slept much. Instead, she mostly lay there silent, staring into the pitch blackness of her room.

Finally, through the window blinds, she could see that the sky brightening outside. Without her alarm clock functioning, she estimated the time to be about seven o'clock. Olivia was curled up sleeping soundly next to her. Freddie—as she knew he would, eventually got tired of 'roughing it' on the floor and had climbed into bed with them sometime during the night. He was lost to this world as well.

But what world would it be? Barbara thought darkly as she lied there with her children. What was left of the state, her city—even her store? Would she have a job left? Would all the food run out or spoil, would the water stay on? Certainly, the government had plans to handle such emergencies, right? They had stockpiles of food, and generators, and fuel and so forth. She had seen the Red Cross and FEMA on the news numerous times swinging into action after major disasters. They would do it here. They would save them. They had to.

She carefully moved Freddie out of her way, and was able to slip out of bed without waking either of her children. She took care of business in the bathroom and then headed into the kitchen.

Her mom was already up and was boiling water on the stove in a medium sized pot. Barbara hugged and kissed her good morning.

"Ready for coffee?" her mom asked.

Barbara looked into the pot of water, which was growing browner by the moment. Then she glanced over at the fancy stainless steel Kurig she had on the counter. It had cost several hundred dollars and was now a useless piece of metal and plastic, like many of the rest of their appliances.

"Sure," she said. "I'd love some. I don't think I had any yesterday and it probably caused my headache."

Her mom cocked an eyebrow at her. "I doubt if anything could have prevented your headache yesterday," she said. "It was pretty bad, huh?"

Barbara pulled out a chair and sat down.

"Oh yes. The worst I have ever seen. Way worse than the pandemic. The store is basically trashed."

As her mom poured them each a cup of coffee, Barbara replayed the horror scene at the store yesterday, ending with the coup de grace of her replacement not showing up.

"I got no help from the main office," she said, exasperated. "I couldn't even get through on the phone, and no area managers came around to check on me. So, I had no one to turn to. And I wasn't about to stay there for a second shift just to watch it get looted some more. What was the point?"

She looked over at her mom then and received the validation she was looking for.

"You did the right thing honey," her mom said, placing a soothing hand on her arm. "No one can blame you, or expect you to stay put forever."

Relieved, Barbara sighed, then took a long sip of her coffee. She added, "Thank God it's my day off today."

The realization that it was her day off triggered another thought, and she set her cup down quickly.

"Oh my God mom. Today is your dialysis. Do you think they're open?"

"I don't know," her mom said. "I certainly hope so."

CHAPTER EIGHTY-ONE

Norco, California
Friday, 7:16 a.m.
+ 1 day, 4 hours, 41 minutes

Like all farmers who worked closely around animals, Jeffrey Mc-Daniel III knew when something was amiss with his stock. There were the constant and normal sounds of cows mooing: calling out to one another, wanting to be fed, to mate. But this was something different; this was the plaintive cries of an animal in distress.

A veteran of numerous power outages through the years, Mc-Daniel immediately fired up his generator and instructed his twenty or so workers to start getting the cows lined up and herded into the stalls in the milking parlor as soon as possible.

Not knowing how long the outage would last, he next began calling his fuel supplier to get another delivery of diesel. The line was busy and it took over two hours of trying to finally get through. The owner of the fuel supply company said that they were doing their best and that already his drivers were being run ragged. "I'll try to get to you was all he could offer." Then the presidential emergency alert came through on his phone, and McDaniel knew he was screwed.

Now, a day and a half later, only 173 of his herd of 1,200 cows were able to get through the milking parlor and have their udders drained before his generator ran out of fuel. The remaining thousand or so, their udders bloated with milk and beginning to harden from mastitis, were crying out in terrible pain. His calls to the fuel supplier went unanswered and he figured they might have simply given up on what would be an impossible task: to supply all the fire and police departments, hospitals, various businesses, and lastly, dairy farmers, with the fuel they needed.

And without fuel for his generator there was no electricity, and without electricity, the milking parlor with its automated wash-pen, milking machines, and cooling tanks would cease to function, leaving him with his own impossible task; to try to milk over a thousand cows by hand. He knew he simply didn't have enough workers or hours in the day to accomplish it.

By now a couple of his workers had already abandoned him, going home to their families. McDaniel could understand that; he once had a family whom he cared for and who cared for him. To the rest of his workers who stuck by him, doing what they could, he called them all together.

"You've all been very good to me," he began. "But unfortunately, in spite of all of our efforts, it doesn't look like we're going to make it."

As he spoke, several of the workers who were bilingual, translated his words into Spanish for the others.

"And so, I want each of you to take as many cows and as much feed as you can, and head on home to your families. At least you'll have some milk every day, and when the feed runs out, some beef."

There were some appreciative nods, and a host of "Muchas gracias" emanating from the group.

It took a couple of hours, but pretty soon, forty or so cows had been loaded up and hauled off. After the last worker left and they said their goodbyes, McDaniel went into his house and retrieved a .308 rifle from out of the front closet. Like all farmers, he would use it from time to time to keep his herd safe from predators; mostly coyotes, but once, from a mountain lion. Along with the rifle, he grabbed all the ammo he had in the house; 1 ½ boxes, or about thirty rounds. Then he headed out to begin the job of putting his cows out of their misery.

The first cow was very painful to put down. Not that he hadn't done it before with sick animals, but it was the reason he had to do it that really weighed on him. Even watching the animal try to move around; its thick spine curved, rocking on its rear legs as it tried to avoid any further irritation to its teats which were suffering from hyperkitosis, it was still difficult to pull the trigger.

His grandfather had started the farm eighty years ago with only a dozen or so cows. Both his father and his uncles worked the farm when they were growing up.

Bamm!

By the time his grandfather had passed, the herd had grown to over 180 cows. His father bought out his uncles - who had had enough early mornings and endless labors, and worked, along with Jeff and his two brothers, to continue growing the family business.

Bamm!

And when his own father passed in 2001, Jeffrey McDaniel III followed his father's business model by buying out his brothers, and continuing to build up the herd.

Bamm!

Like all forms of farming, dairy was always a risky endeavor due to the capricious market forces of supply and demand. But adding to that, in September of 2018, the price of milk crashed, brought on by rapid drop in quota prices paid to farmers. This was followed just a couple of years later by the Covid-19 pandemic which saw prices plummet even further when schools - always a perennial and reliable market for dairy products, closed up and sent their kids home to distance-learn. By that point, McDaniel was just hanging on by his fingertips and hoping to recover.

Bamm!

The financial hardship caused a huge strain on his marriage and last year his wife announced she was done living milk check to milk check and that it was either he sold out and got a 'normal' job, or she would divorce him. Not wanting to be the one to throw away three generations of toil by his family, he watched her as she packed her final things and drove away, never to return. His two kids had gone to college and wanted nothing to do with farming or rural life and now lived out of the state. He was essentially, all on his own.

Bamm!

He checked the pocket of his jacket and found that he had only three bullets left. He took aim at another cow and fired.

Bamm!

"Damn it!"

The cow had moved at last moment and the bullet had just grazed her on the back of the neck. He fired again, knowing that he now had only one round remaining. The animal crumpled to the ground. He felt the muzzle of the rifle with the tip of his finger; it was hot to the touch.

Slinging the rifle over his shoulder, he slowly walked over to the main pen gate, slid the bolt and opened it up.

Let them go free, he thought, maybe they'll have a fighting chance in the wild.

A couple of the cows that could still move with their bloated udders, began to meander through the opening. He stared across the field to where several of the cows had been dropped. Already, ravens were beginning to feast on the carcasses.

He touched muzzle of the rifle again. It had cooled, and was now barely luke warm. Good enough, he thought.

He chambered the final round, and then dairy farmer Jeffrey McDaniel III put the muzzle into his mouth and pulled the trigger.

Bamm!

CHAPTER EIGHTY-TWO

Gaviota, California
Friday, 7:31a.m.
+ 1 day, 4 hours, 56 minutes

Fuel truck driver Lucas Pedroza had to admit that as much as he loved all the overtime he was getting, he was starting to run out of gas himself. Since the power outage had begun two days ago, he had been going non-stop, delivering much needed product to some of the small supplier's high priority accounts.

Of the four regular drivers that Coast Fuels employed, two had not shown up or even called in after the outage. Maybe they had tried, but like everyone else attempting to make a call with their cell phone, the system was overloaded. Or maybe, they just bailed out.

Either way, Lucas, along with the other remaining driver and the company's owner—who had jumped into a truck himself, were doing their best to make up for the high demand, but it was tough. Their regular fuel terminal did not have a backup generator itself, so fuel could not be pumped directly into their trucks, leaving them to use an onboard pump and a long pipe called a 'stinger' to suck the fuel out of the underground tanks.

The lines of fuel trucks at the other terminals that were still running were blocks long and stretched out onto the street. On top of this, the demand for fuel continued to climb from police and fire stations, hospitals, metropolitan water companies, wastewater treatment plants and other various business whom Coast Fuels had standing contracts with. It seemed as if no end was in sight.

Tough as it was though, Lucas hoped that the owner took notice of his hard work ethic and commitment. He had a wife and family to support, and, as an ex-con, it wasn't easy. He had done a partial on his five-year sentence for his part in an armed robbery that he had stupidly allowed his homeboys to talk him into. And even though good behavior and a 'compassionate release' during the Covid pandemic had given him his freedom, there still weren't many employment opportunities for a high school dropout with a felony conviction.

He was overjoyed therefore when the owner of Coast decided to take a chance and hire him. Realizing his good fortune, Lucas Pedroza had been doing his level best ever since not to blow it. His fuel truck—a Chevy Silverado with three 50-gallon fuel tanks (diesel, regular, and supreme) mounted in the bed was always immaculate. His wife kept his uniforms cleaned and pressed, and he was always early to work and, unlike others, was willing to work any overtime that popped up, no matter the time or weather.

Currently though, he was limited in how much diesel he could carry as the other two tanks were partially full of gasoline and the two fuels didn't mix. This resulted in him having to take more trips than normal back and forth to the terminal. The upside though was that without gasoline stations operational, he could use the gasoline in the tanks to fuel his own truck. As soon as they ran empty, he could use them to carry more diesel.

He had just topped off one of the backup generators at the hospital in Lompoc, and was headed back south on Pacific Coast Highway to the terminal in Goleta to get more fuel. There were still some abandoned cars on the road, but the traffic here was lighter than when you got into the bigger cities. He dreaded heading into the more populated areas as he was being flagged down constantly by drivers in other cars wanting to buy fuel off of him. Some held up wads of cash trying to entice him and he knew he could have made some quick money. But he had his orders, and he had messed up his life before by not playing by the rules.

As he drove, he tried to keep his mind focused on the road and his driving, but it was getting more difficult after twenty-eight hours with no sleep. To keep himself busy then, he tried to do the math in his head as to how much his next paycheck would be with all of his overtime.

After several minutes of trying, he realized that it was incalculable at this point and so his mind began to drift instead to some of the things he could finally buy for his family with his newfound windfall.

His wife, Carmen, had wanted to get a new refrigerator for some time and after putting it off as long as possible, he now knew that it would be in the cards for them. The apple of his eye, his five-year-old daughter, Lupita, had also asked about getting one of those American Girl dolls for her upcoming birthday. They were ridiculously priced of course, but now, with all of –

Without realizing it, Lucas had drifted off to sleep and his truck had veered off the highway toward the Pacific Ocean.

Before he knew what was happening or could react, his truck barreled through the small median strip that separated the southbound highway from the Southern Pacific rail line, hitting the tracks and bouncing over them. The jarring of the tracks made him ricochet around in the cab and he couldn't reach nor find the brake pedal to slam on it.

Just a few feet on the other side of the tracks, the terrain dropped off steeply. Lucas finally found the brake pedal and pushed on it with all his might, but it was too little and too late. He plunged headlong down the hundred-foot cliff, straight toward the rocks below.

The truck struck with so much force, that the front end caved in, jamming the engine and the floorboards into the passenger compartment. The force pushed his body back into the seat and with nowhere to go, cleaved his legs right out of his pelvis, thrusting them into his body cavity and severing the femoral arteries in the process.

As Lucas Pedroza, devoted husband, father, and ex-con trying turn his life around, lay there for what would be his final moments, he began to smell the distinctive aroma of gasoline from the ruptured tanks as it leaked into the passenger compartment. In just a few minutes it would reach the still hot exhaust manifolds from the engine, ignite, and slowly incinerate him.

He only hoped he would be dead before then.

CHAPTER EIGHTY-THREE

CAL-OES
Mather, California
Friday, 8:01 a.m.
+ 1 day, 5 hours, 26 minutes

An hour into the first meeting of day two of the attack, things were not looking well. The replacements of the HPTs were moving at an agonizingly slow pace, even though the utilities, the manufacturers, and the federal government continued to offer assurances that the were being "fast-tracked."

"Slow boat from China," Doyle quipped sarcastically when the proclamation was made.

Some HPTs orders from other countries such as India, China, and the Netherlands had been shifted to the US needs, but they would still take some time to reengineer to the US standards and even then, being built on the metric system, the footprints on site would have to be modified to accept the replacements. The few spare HPTs that were available to them through the STEP program had been tested and were in route on heavy haulers, but they still wouldn't arrive for over a week and would take upwards of several more to have them installed. Then it was the matter of what power plants they could black-start and most importantly, could they keep them operating when they did.

The topic next turned to generators. Since the UCG had put muni-water, waste treatment, hospitals, and getting the grocery supply chains up at the top of the priority list, the word had been passed down to the regional and then the local EOCs to come up with a list showing size, location and fuel burn rates. But the data was slow in coming, partly because of the difficulty in communication as well as the fact that some of the local EOCs and some counties had already thrown in the towel and shut down, preferring just to try to manage it on their own. How they were faring in those communities, no one wanted to speculate.

Sensing a feeling of defeat that others were already giving up on them, Shanice spoke up in an effort to try to maintain morale. She reminded everyone that, "We can only help them if they decide to let us. So, let's stay focused on what we can do in the here and now."

Besides the dearth of useful info, several local EOC were also still trying to lobby to provide more fuel and gen sets to their first responders whom they said were being dangerously close to being overrun.

"We've got to keep the water flowing, damn it!" Doyle yelled. "The answer is still no."

Then they got to the fuel situation, which was even worse.

The 60% of refineries that were still operational were pushed to make more diesel. They had complied, but there were design limits to how much they could produce as well as running out of tanks to store it.

Besides the supply side issues, the smaller fuel distribution terminals where the smaller fuel trucks loaded up were not being able to be restocked fast enough by the large bulk tanker trucks which got theirs from the pipeline terminals run by Kinder-Morgan. This led to a situation where many of the small trucks available to deliver fuel to end customers had to spend needless time driving around looking for a place to reload. It was the classic Domino effect of a supply chain breakdown.

"Can they go straight to the pipeline terminals or the refineries and cut out the middle man?" someone offered.

"Yes," the rep from API spoke up. "The terminals maybe, but not all refineries have loading docks, and the ones that do are limited by how many docks they have and how long it takes to fuel a truck—on average, about fifteen minutes each."

Someone chimed in that they saw on one of the news channels a line of tanker trucks a half mile long trying to fuel up at one of the terminals.

"I believe it," the rep responded.

"So, what's better?" Doyle asked. "Having the smaller trucks go straight to the refineries, or wait until the terminals get restocked."

Both the API rep and the CAL-OES head of logistics, Stephanie Holmes, pondered the question.

"I'd say you try to get the bulk tankers fueled up as fast as possible and keep the smaller terminals supplied," API said.

"I agree," Holmes said. "Keep the supply chain you already have. Besides that, the small trucks typically don't have any experience loading at a bulk dock. There would be a learning curve and slow everything down further."

"Sounds logical," Shanice said. "So, we're in agreement that we don't put the word out for the smaller trucks to fuel at the racks?"

Everyone nodded yes.

"But even if we settle the problem of production and bulk delivery," logistic chimed in. "We still have the problem of not enough trucks - and these drivers are getting tired. Some of them have been working for thirty hours. We need to get replacements to give them a break."

"Are we bringing in more from out of state?" Shanice asked.

"We're trying," one of the FEMA reps said. "But if you remember back to Covid, we lost a lot of experienced drivers when demand for fuel went down. That lack of drivers triggered a gas shortage in June 2021, even when there was plenty of fuel to go around."

"And what about AWOLs?" someone brought up. "We're getting more and more reports of people bailing out. Not just truckers, but the refinery and terminal workers we need to keep the facilities running."

"Police, fire, and prison guards too," the CHP rep said. Then added, "Those guys aren't going to stick it out forever with no support."

It was a dig that was meant for Doyle and the Unified Command Group who had made the decision to put water, hospitals and food ahead of first responders. Doyle and the members of the UCG ignored it, not wanting to start the pissing match all over again.

There was a long silence in the room as people considered the ramifications of so many AWOLs, then...

"And what about us?" Shanice asked after a while, afraid to have her suspicions confirmed. "Are any of our people AWOL? I saw some empty chairs in the SOC this morning."

A few of the department heads bit their lips and averted their eyes.

"We lost two," Stephani Holmes, the head of logistics finally admitted.

"Three for us," operations said. "They were crying when they called in. Said they were scared for their families."

Another moment of uncomfortable silence, broken when someone in the crowd standing around the perimeter of the room muttered under their breath, "Well, you can't really blame them."

Doyle's head swung around wildly. "Who said that?" He demanded.

No one answered.

"Who the hell said that!" he repeated, louder.

"I did sir," a voice called out from the back of the room. He stepped forward through the crowd, angling past a couple of people.

"Who are you?" Doyle pressed him.

"Lance Taylor, State Agricultural Department."

"Well get the hell out of here Mr. Taylor!" Doyle screamed, pointing at the door. "We don't need quitters here!"

The man sheepishly turned and left the room silently.

"Anyone else," Doyle challenged. "Anyone else want to abandon your post?"

Nobody spoke, although a couple of people swallowed so hard it was audible.

"Alright," the governor finally said. "Let's continue on."

Shortage of delivery drivers means some gas station pumps could run dry
Source: https://www.nbcnews.com/business/consumer/shortage-delivery-drivers-means-gas-station-pumps-could-run-dry-n1265673

CHAPTER EIGHTY-FOUR

Lakewood, California
Friday, 8:48 a.m.
+ 1 day, 6 hours, 13 minutes

After the kids got up, Barbara made them a breakfast of scrambled eggs and bacon, minimizing the time the refrigerator had to be opened. Her mom had to avoid eating the bacon, and only had some eggs with a couple of slices of white bread.

Freddie had wanted cereal, but after smelling the milk, Barbara said 'no,' and drained what was left of it into the sink.

It was a very quiet meal as everyone was into their own thoughts and concerns. After breakfast, they cleared the table and Olivia asked if she could take a shower before they left on the trip to take grandma to her dialysis.

It would slow them down a bit, but Barbara also knew that feeling clean and refreshed might bolster her daughter's mood, so she agreed.

As Olivia headed off to the bathroom, Barbara's mom started to get Freddie dressed and to make the beds while Barbara got ready to wash the dishes by hand.

As she reached for the faucet, she heard Olivia's muffled voice cry out from behind the bathroom door.

"Mom, there's no water!"

Barbara turned on the faucet at the kitchen sink and only a trickle came out, before it slowed to a meager drip.

CHAPTER EIGHTY-FIVE

Near Carmen City, California
Friday, 9:17 a.m.
+ 1 day, 6 hours, 42 minutes

The anti-personnel mines were a homemade version of the Claymore, a device used extensively during the Vietnam war by US forces. They were small, easy to deploy and could be detonated either remotely, or by the use of trip wires that would catch on the enemy's foot or other body part. Most importantly, they were very powerful and could kill or severely maim an intruder.

Walter had bought an instruction manual from a fellow prepper at a gun sale and had fashioned two dozen of the deadly devices using Hi-Drive 80% dynamite, 7/32" steel "gingle balls" Devcon plastic steel, some pieces of plexiglass, tinfoil, and for detonation, #8 blasting caps.

Now, after a quick breakfast of MRE, he had emerged from his hole and, after accessing the area for security threats and taking down his shortwave wire, was busy at work setting up his deadly booby-traps.

He debated with himself long and hard about whether or not to have the mines go off remotely from a switch that he would activate, or to have them set up with trip wires.

Since there were deer, coyotes and other animals in the area, he knew that he was risking a possible inadvertent triggering event that would not only use up some of his supply, but most importantly, tip off anyone nearby of his whereabouts.

But the tradeoff was that he would have to either set up another elaborate surveillance system such as cameras or ground vibration sensors—which he did not have, or he would have to man a lookout constantly. The concept of 24-hour-a-day surveillance was nearly impossible though, since every soldier needed to sleep after a certain amount of time. Besides that, sitting all day monitoring the perimeter would chew up valuable time, time he needed to maintain his bunker or, before his food supply ran low, to forage plants and to hunt or trap small game to eat.

He also reasoned that he wouldn't be staying at the bunker for very long. He would have to stay fluid and eventually, when he was able to meet up with Patriot Man and the other freedom fighters to consolidate their efforts in the revolution, he would be moving on. For now, though, the bunker and the land it sat on would be his base of operations.

And so, he began the process of carefully laying out his trip wires and arming his devices, thinking excitedly of the first thug or government lacky who would blow themselves to bits when they stepped on one.

CHAPTER EIGHTY-SIX

Fast & Go Gas Station
Bellflower, California
Friday, 10:23 a.m.
+ 1 day, 7 hours, 48 minutes

Enterprising as he was, where others saw chaos and catastrophe, Lonnie Bednarski saw an opportunity.

Twenty-six years old and struggling under a mountain of student debt from a sociology degree which had failed to produce any worthwhile employment for him, he worked several menial jobs just to keep his head above water.

Then, yesterday, when the lights went out and everything ground to a screeching halt in California, he saw an opportunity while driving past all of the shuttered gas stations with signs taped on the windows which read; *NO POWER = NO GAS. SORRY*

It was true that the underground pumps to supply the gas needed power, and that hardly any gas stations had backup generators, but Lonnie knew that there was more than one way to skin a cat.

Of his many jobs, he currently worked at an auto parts store, and yesterday, after the owner had locked the place up because of the power outage, Lonnie snuck back in and pirated a number of items to help him with his brainchild: an in-tank electric fuel pump, a pressure regulator, twenty feet of fuel hose, some wire and electrical connections, and finally, three 5-gallon gas cans.

After assembling his pumping rig, he returned to one of the closed gas stations, opened the fill cover to the tank and dropped the hose down into the precious liquid. A few seconds later 91 octane supreme gasoline began to stream out of the hose and into one of the cans.

Then, he made a sign: *GAS $25 A GALLON,* taped it to the front of his truck and watched gleefully as his desperate customers began to pull in.

All was great as the word quickly spread but then, a few hours after opening and with six hundred dollars already in his pocket, a group of four very rough looking bikers on Harley Davidsons thundered onto the lot.

They defiantly cut straight to the front of the line to the ire of the others who had been waiting. One of the bikers turned and casually flipped them off. Besides their menacing appearance and the obscene gesture, the fact that they were openly carrying automatic pistols on their belts, pretty much insured that no one would dare to challenge them.

After turning off their motors and putting their kickstands down, one of the bikers, who appeared to be the leader, dismounted and slowly sauntered toward Lonnie. He was about six foot five, muscular, and dressed in black leather pants with a denim jacket with the sleeves cut off. His thick arms were covered in tattoos: daggers, skulls, and swastikas. Most noteworthy was a face of the devil snarling and baring teeth, designating him as a member of *The Predators* motorcycle gang. It was a group that was lesser known by the general public, but equally as notorious and dangerous as the Hells Angels or the Vagos. Their motto was, *"Only the strong survive."*

Wordlessly, the leader inspected Lonnie's jury-rigged setup, before signaling to the others to begin filling up. The two bikers each grabbed a gas can and began filling up the tanks on the bikes.

"Uh, you guys need gas?" Lonnie asked sheepishly.

The leader glared at him and nodded. "Yeah, and we're gonna take it. You got a problem with that, man?"

"Oh no...no," Lonnie answered too quickly, hearing his voice rising an octave. "I can help you guys out if you don't have the money. I mean, I had a motorcycle once, a dirt bike."

The leader looked at him and chuckled. "Well, that's just fucking great, isn't it? Kind of makes us like brothers, don't you think?"

The other bikers behind him laughed out loud.

"Well, um. Yeah. I guess."

Sweat began trickling down the back of Lonnie's neck and he felt his bowels loosen. Suddenly, his enterprise didn't seem like such a good idea.

"And you'd help out a brother, right?"

"Well, uh..."

"That's good man, cause we need gas. *And* we need your little rig here, and your truck to run it."

"But that's my—"

The leader suddenly gut punched him, taking away Lonnie's breath and any remaining protestations he had left. He doubled over and gripped his stomach.

Two of the bikers swiftly moved up and grabbed him, dragging him away and out of sight of the remaining motorists and into the cinder block structure that housed the gas station's dumpsters.

Back by the dumpsters, he regained his breath, and was about to acquiesce to the gang's demands. But it was to be a desperate effort that was too little, and too late.

In just a few horrendous moments, Lonnie Bednarski, budding entrepreneur, would cease to worry about his business, his truck, his student loans, or even his crappy jobs. All he would care about was his life, which was quickly spilling out of him from the knife wound in his neck.

"We all topped off?" the leader of the Predators asked the two men when they returned from their gruesome assignment.

"Yeah, were good." One of them said.

"Good," the leader said, gesturing to Lonnie's hand painted sign. "Change it to fifty bucks a gallon."

He laughed. "Prices just went up."

In 2011, California considered a bill (AB 1339 (http://www. leginfo.ca.gov/pub/11-12/bill/asm/ab_1301-1350/ab_1339_ cfa_20110506_115347_asm_comm.html)) to grant a tax credit of up to $2,500 to gas stations that bought and installed an emergency standby generator. The bill was not passed.

Source: https://www.cga.ct.gov/2012/rpt/2012-R-0539.htm
FEMA generator inventory.
Source: https://www.power-eng.com/2019/11/07/fema-seeking-on-site-gen-sets-to-update-emergency-fleet/#gref

CHAPTER EIGHTY-SEVEN

San Ramon, California
Friday, 10:28 a.m.
+ 1 day, 7 hours, 53 minutes

Unlike the majority of kids in California, Bart Rogers and his wife Julie's son and daughter were comfortably camped out on the living room floor and playing Minecraft on their X-Box. On the 70" monitor in front of them, the blocky characters tried to navigate a world where they had to find resources, craft tools, and to do everything possible to survive and stay healthy. How little they knew that their virtual, make-believe world mirrored what was going on outside the walls right around them.

Their good fortune, and the fact that they were able to enjoy these modern creature comforts was the result of intense lobbying by Bart; his wife wanted a new designer kitchen, he wanted to invest in technology to keep them safe when "the big one" hit.

But instead of the massive earthquake that seismologist had been warning California was overdue for—and that the Rogers had been prepared for, it was a nefarious man-made disaster created when just a few hundred copper cables were sliced through by truck bombs—albeit, some very important copper cables.

Regardless of the event, Bart had swayed his wife to postpone her dream kitchen and the Rogers family were now reaping the benefits of eight giant solar cells panels, along with two Tesla Powerwalls to store all of the juice they sucked in. As long as the sun kept shining, they had all the power they could use. But that didn't mean that everything was roses.

Another knock was heard through the front door just then, along with persistent ringing of the doorbell.

"Please!" a muffled woman's voice called out, pleading from the outside of the door. "We know you have power, and we don't. We just need to charge our cell phones and keep our food from spoiling."

From where they sat on the couch in their living room, Bart and Julie stared silently down to their hands, their expressions tight. They recognized the woman's voice as Karen from across the street. She was nice, and friendly, as most of the neighbors were, but they had vowed long ago that they would not give in and try to support the whole neighborhood if the stuff hit the fan. The logic being, their neighbors were equally as well off financially as they were and could have opted to harden their homes instead of constantly buying new toys or taking lavish vacations.

Additionally, they knew that if they did it for one neighbor, they would have to do it for all, and would soon be inundated. As it was, a couple dozen of their neighbors had shown up and beg for power, many with extension cords in hand. Thankfully, their children—like most, were so engrossed with their video games they were oblivious to all of the commotion. Still, the constant begging for help was getting old.

"Please!" Karen cried. "We'll split half our food with you."

The Rogers remained stoic.

The pounding and ringing eventually stopped, to be replaced by the sounds of sobbing as the neighbor stomped off the porch, empty-handed.

"How long do you think we can survive?" Julie asked, turning to her husband.

"Survive?" Bart repeated. "You mean have food to eat? Two or three weeks, but that's not the only thing we have to consider."

"What do you mean?"

"When we run out of food – and we will, will the stores have any to resupply us with? And before long, if they can't keep the water pumps going, we'll run out of tap water too."

Another neighbor, a man, pounding on door, looking for help.

Again, they ignored him and pretty soon he went away, but not before yelling out, "Fucking stingy asshole!"

"And then there's that," Bart said, gesturing to door. "How long before they don't knock?"

Before his wife could respond, he said, "In fact…"

He got up, went into the garage, and came out a few minutes later with a short barreled, pistol grip shotgun and a box of shells.

Julie saw the gun, and her eyes went wide with fright.

"Please honey," she pleaded. "I don't want the kids to see that. It might scare them."

He sighed, "Alright," and carried the gun and ammo into the kitchen, setting it up on top of the refrigerator where their children couldn't see it.

"But I'll use it if I have to," he said, returning from the kitchen. "And that may come sooner than we think."

They were both silent for a long time. Together, they had watched the news on TV and seen how bad it was getting: traffic snarls, stores being looted, smoke from a few fires. A man's uncovered body lying dead on the street.

"So, what's going to happen?" Julie asked, worry straining her voice. "Can they fix it before it gets so bad?"

"I don't know," Bart admitted. "They said it took down some very important pieces of equipment, and that they have no idea how long it will be to replace them. Even off the grid, we are only as good as the society around us."

His hand gestured to the neighborhood outside their walls.

"And obviously, they aren't prepared and are getting more desperate. In a couple more days - three tops, I think this place it going to descend in total anarchy."

He turned to his wife. "And we can't be here when that happens."

"You mean we have to leave?"

He nodded sadly.

"But our home!" she cried out incredulously. "Our life, the kids, it's all we ever worked for."

"I know," Bart agreed with her. "I don't want to leave it all behind either. But it's either that, or eventually we...we, starve, or we die of thirst, or we get killed by our neighbors when they turn on us."

"But what will do? How will we start over?"

"The same way people do in the south after a hurricane. Or in the Midwest when a tornado destroys their house—or even their whole town. They move on and simply have to start over. But at least they're alive."

They both stared in quiet silence at each other for a long time. Bart broke it.

"I'm going to make sure the cars are both charged up," he said decisively. You quietly start getting stuff ready, clothes, some food and water. I'll get all of our important documents out of the safe. All right?"

She nodded mutely, her eyes welling up with tears. She fell into him, sobbing.

Bart held her tight, comforting her, thinking about the part of his plan he didn't share with her. Before they would leave at sunrise the next day, he would take an axe and smash the control unit that monitored the flow of electricity from his solar cells to the Tesla Powerwall, rendering it useless. He didn't spend all this money just to support his free-loading neighbors.

CHAPTER EIGHTY-EIGHT

Lakewood, California
Friday: 10:30 a.m.
+ 1 day, 7 hours, 55 minutes

Even though Barbara had witnessed firsthand some of the effects of the power outage in their community, her mom and children had not. And without TV, computers, or cell phones working to show them dramatic video feeds, it would be a world none of them had seen before: terra incognita.

It was also a world that Barbara had reservations about venturing into, especially with her family. But her mom needed her dialysis treatment and that was that. Certainly, she thought, medical facilities would be available. They were a priority, right? Go, get her mom's treatment, and then hurry back home and lock herself and her family into their apartment; that was her plan.

A more vexing decision was whether or not she should take Olivia and Freddie with and possibly put them at risk, either physically or emotionally. But Olivia was apparently cognizant of what was going on, and had been acting even clingier lately. Even though she had babysat Freddie before, Barbara didn't think she would do well staying at home under the circumstances, and so she made the decision they would all stick together.

On the way to the clinic, all of the stores and gas stations they passed were still closed, their lights off, and the interior's dim. Ditto for the restaurants. Worse than the dark and empty interiors, some establishments had their windows smashed and the debris of looting was evident on the sidewalks and parking lots.

Barbara didn't want her children to realize that she had experienced the same ugliness yesterday, and so she purposely avoided the route that took them by the store. The sight would only trigger endless questions about what happened yesterday and it would just feed into their unease.

Occasionally, they would pass people walking on the sidewalks or in the streets and pushing shopping carts with items in them. Unlike the all too familiar scene of disheveled homeless men or women dressed in rags doing the same thing, these people were well groomed and dressed decently. They were just normal people that had been thrust into abnormal circumstances.

At one point, when Olivia must have realized that they were not taking the more direct route to the dialysis clinic, Barbara caught her staring at her from the back seat. Her daughter had probably figured out that Johnson Foods—and more importantly her mom, had suffered the same vandalism and looting as the other stores. Thankfully, she didn't bring it up, thus sparing Freddie from the thought. Inwardly, Barbara was proud of her daughter's maturity in the situation and smiled at her.

The traffic was thankfully lighter today and they didn't have to wait long to cross the intersections safely, but along the way they saw a couple of cars abandoned in place and even some wrecks that still stood where they had met their demise. Barbara carefully guided her car around them.

"Cool!" Freddie exclaimed upon seeing them and then took a couple of his own toy cars and ran them into each other on his thigh, complete with crashing sounds.

Barbara also spied "Batteries" the homeless man, as he trudged along the sidewalk, oblivious to the new world around him. If anything, he was like the birds that flew in the sky or the squirrels that scampered about the branches of the trees; he was at best, minimally affected and didn't have a care in the world.

Even though the travel was slowed somewhat by having to wait their turn to cross through intersections, they arrived at her mom's scheduled appointment time only to see a paper sign taped onto the front door that read, "Sorry. No power. No dialysis available."

"That's it!" Barbara cried incredulously after reading the sign. "That's it? No generator, no options of where else to go? After giving how much to them in co-pays we're just left out in the cold?"

"That's okay," Barbara's mom said, trying to soothe her. "There are other clinics. Some of them must have generators, we'll just have to find one."

"I have to go pee mommy," Freddie said just then.

"Okay honey," Barbara said absently, then thought about it.

Where could they go to use a bathroom? Everything was closed. Other than at a park, there would be no more public bathrooms available. And would the parks be closed as well, or safe? She didn't know how long Freddie could hold it even if that were an option.

Screw it! She finally thought.

She clicked the door locks open and got him out of the car. They marched around to the back of the dialysis clinic and she told him to pee here, anywhere he liked in fact.

Go ahead, she thought bitterly. *Piss on them like they pissed on us.*

After he finished and they were headed back to the car, she realized there was no time to dwell on the indignity they had suffered; they had to try to find another clinic for her mom's treatment. But how?

Even though she still had power on her phone and they had Olivia's connected to the charger as soon as they got in the car, they still had no signal to do a search online. She thought of a phone book in a pay phone, but where was there a pay phone? She couldn't remember the last time she saw one. How did we ever get so dependent on technology?

"Mom, Olivia, do either of you remember any other clinics that we can try?" She asked as she climbed back into the car.

They were all silent as they all racked their brans trying to recall.

"How about on Carson Street?" her mom suggested. "I remember seeing one there, near the shopping center."

Barbara thought about it and recalled it as well. It was close to her old house, now her ex's house. She started the car and was going to pull away from the curb to head toward the next clinic, but she had to wait as a convoy of beige National Guard Humvees and trucks rumbled by.

The next clinic was a bust, as was the next after that, and the next. Besides that, after several fruitless hours in their quest, they also had used up a lot of gas. She only had a quarter of a tank when they started out, and now the low fuel light was on.

"Everyone keep an eye out for a gas station that's open," Barbara instructed. "Maybe one of them has a generator or something. Then I'm going to head over to the hospital, maybe they can do dialysis there on an emergency basis."

They drove for only a couple of minutes before Olivia cried out. "Mom!"

It was a gas station just up ahead. No lights were on, but there was a line of cars stretching out onto the street. Maybe their luck had finally changed.

CHAPTER EIGHTY-NINE

Saint Elizabeth Medical Center,
Cerritos, California
Friday, 10:32 a.m.
+ 1 day, 7 hours, 57 minutes

Alan Binder came to in the ED department Saint Elizabeth Medical Center.

He didn't realize it immediately. He didn't realize much because he had suffered a heart attack the previous day due to dilated cardiomyopathy, a disease of the heart muscle that makes it harder for the heart to pump blood to the rest of your body. It is most common in middle aged men, and is exacerbated by excessive alcohol use.

"How are you feeling?"

Alan looked up from his bed in one of the partitions in the ED. The question came from a male nurse, the same one he had been badgering ever since he got here.

"Like I had a truck run over me. What happened?"

"You had a heart attack out in front of the hospital. Thankfully, someone ran in and grabbed me. I gave you CPR and we brought you back in. We've got some blood thinners into you, and based on what we saw on the tomography CT scan, we think it was a minor one, probably brought on by stress and exhaustion. You've been out for over a day."

"You're kidding!"

"Nope," the nurse replied easily and then began checking Alan's eyes.

Alan stared back, even though the nurse was a nice-looking young man, he was now sporting a five o'clock shadow and his eyes were red and puffy. Poor guy hadn't probably slept in two days, he thought. His name tag read: Colton McKenna. Up until now, Alan hadn't paid any attention to his name; he was just another person in this world who was there to serve him. But then, no one had ever saved his life, especially after enduring his wrath.

"You should be the one under stress Mr. McKenna," he said apologetically. "Especially after having to deal with major assholes like me. I'm really sorry about all that, I just—"

Colton held up a hand and cut him off.

"Don't worry about it," he said magnanimously. "Everyone is wigged out right now. And it's Colton, by the way."

"I can't imagine, Colton,' Alan said, realizing just then how good it felt to address someone in the familiar. Then he looked around the ED. The lights were back on, albeit dim as before.

"They got the lights back on," he observed. "Is the power outage over?"

Colton shook his head sadly. "The governor sent out a message. This is bad, really, *really* bad. They have no idea when they can have power restored. I don't know if the state can recover. We're still on emergency power and thankfully, we just got a fuel delivery so we can keep going for maybe another twelve hours or so."

"But after that?"

The nurse simply shrugged. He had no answer.

"How's Marianne?"

"Your friend that you brought in?"

"Yes," Alan Binder said, "Yes, my friend." He realized it was the first time he ever referred to her that way.

Colton looked toward the bed Marianne was in, it was just a couple of partitions over from Alan.

"Hanging in there, for now," he said turning back to Alan. "She made it through the night – which is critical. But we really need to try to get her to another hospital out of state, and unfortunately there are no more ambulances to transport her, and all commercial flights are grounded. From what I understand, they are some LifeFlights going in and out, but they are overwhelmed too and in extremely short supply."

"So, if the fuel runs out and the power goes off, she might die?"

"I'm sorry Mr. Binder," Colton McKenna said sadly. "Everyone is doing the best they can. We're just trying to remain hopeful we can keep everything going and save as many people as we can."

The nurse looked away. "I've got some other patients to see; I've got to go."

"Sure," Alan Binder said. "I understand Colton and hey, thanks again."

Colton nodded and started to walk out. He had only taken a few steps when he suddenly stopped, spun around and stepped back to Alan. He closed the curtain behind him and reached for Alan's jacket that was laying on a chair. He pulled it open to reveal his holster and the Glock.

"I found this when I was doing CPR on you. I'm not supposed to let you have it in here, but under the circumstances, I'll let you keep it. I'm sure you've been trained on it."

"Absolutely."

Colton folded back the jacket to keep the gun hidden and then pulled the curtain back to its open position.

"I'll check on you in a couple of hours Mr. Binder," he called over his shoulder. "Try to get some rest."

"Thanks again, and it's Alan, by the way."

"Alan," Colton repeated and disappeared back into the chaos of the ED.

Alan lay there for a long time reflecting. A person who he had been berating and treated so poorly, was the first person to unselfishly come to his aid, saving his life in the process.

He thought painfully about the other people he treated like doormats in his life; waiters, chauffeurs, his housekeepers, fellow actors, the crew, his manager, and of course, Marianne.

He swallowed hard, feeling his eyes well up with tears.

Deep down, he knew that every one of them were decent, hardworking human beings who, in spite of his callousness and cruelty, would do what they had to keep him satisfied in his privileged little bubble of a world.

And what, he thought shamefully, would I ever do for them? Would I offer them a jacket when they were cold? Would I tell them to slow down and take their time getting to a party? Or would I just bully my way through life, stepping on them and squashing them like bugs every step of the way?

He thought of the limo driver who had died, trying to satisfy his unreasonable demands.

And he thought of Marianne, a sweet woman just trying to make it in this world, in this shitty business in this shitty little town. There she was, because of his selfishness and impatience, clinging to life just a few feet away from him.

What would he, Alan Binder, a has-been actor in a town that may not even exist any longer, do for her? What *could* he do for her?

He rolled his head over and stared at his jacket on the chair in his room. Then he began to formulate his plan.

CHAPTER NINETY

Compton, California
Friday, 10:35 a.m.
+ 1 day, 8 hours, 0 minutes

Thelma Washington hadn't had use of a vehicle since the last car she owned had been stolen, used in a string of residential burglaries, and then abandoned. By the time she was notified of its whereabouts, it had racked up three days of impound fees that her meager fixed income was unable to pay, and so she just relinquished the title to it. Now, she wished she hadn't.

Relying on public transportation in her low-income neighborhood had typically served her well. But now, two days into the big power outage, the buses weren't running and she had no choice but to walk the mile or so to the closest drug store to pick up her insulin.

Her legs, devastated by the lack of circulation as a byproduct of her type 2 diabetes, were throbbing from the exertion and she wished with all her might that she hadn't let her supply run so low.

Finally, she saw the familiar signage of her drug store up ahead. But what she then saw hadn't been familiar to her since the riots of 1992; the front window of the store had been shattered, and the iron gate had been pulled away and was hanging crazily on its hinges. A few boxes of items that had apparently not been considered valuable enough to cart off were spilled out onto the sidewalk in front of the store.

She stepped closer to the store, her feet crunching over the broken glass as she peered inside. None of the drug store employees were visible inside, but thankfully, it didn't appear as if any of the looters were in there as well.

Using her cane to help her climb through the opening, she stepped inside, and began to make her way through the darkness toward the back where the pharmacy was located.

Inside, it was an even bigger mess than the front of the store. She had to pick her way over broken and scattered merchandise on the floor and in one case, around a shelf unit that had been completely tipped over, blocking one of the aisles.

She finally made it to the pharmacy counter and to her surprise, saw another young man, was also in the store. He was behind the pharmacy counter and was going through bottles of medications that had been left behind. He'd pick one up, read the label and either stuff it into the front pocket of his hoody, or toss it on the ground.

He noticed her and quickly looked in her direction.

"What'chu want old lady?" he asked her, irritation in his voice.

"Insulin," she replied weakly. "For my diabetes."

"Ain't seen none," he replied sharply, then went back to his scrounging.

"It's not on the shelves," she said. "It's in the refrigerator—behind you."

He turned around and in the darkness of the store, spotted the silhouette of the aforementioned refrigerator. He pulled a cell phone out of his pocket and flashed the light in its direction. He and Thelma could both see that the door had been left open and that the shelves inside were bare. Others had apparently gotten to it before her and depleted the supply.

"It empty, old lady," he said, switching off the phone and returning to his looting. "Looks like you fucked."

She certainly was.

10.5%, or 3.2 million California adults, have diabetes.
Source: https://diatribechange.org/news/cgms-be-covered-under-california-medicaids-medi-cal

CHAPTER NINETY-ONE

Bellflower, California
Friday, 10:40 a.m.
+ 1 day, 8 hours, 5 minutes

"I see it," Barbara said, thinking, at least something was going right today. Maybe they could get some gas and continue their search for a clinic anew. They pulled into the last spot in the line of cars and waited, and waited, and waited. The line moved agonizingly slow.

To save fuel, she turned the car off and only started it when the line moved forward. It was torturous.

She glanced over to her mom and saw that she wasn't doing well. Besides having renal issues, she also had heart and circulatory issues. Barbara knew that combined with her various maladies, without regular dialysis, her situation could quickly become life threatening. She started up the car and pulled out of line.

"Mom, what are you doing?" Olivia said.

Without answering, Barbara pulled their car around the others and drove to the front of the line.

"Mom, what are you doing?" Olivia protested as a chorus of car horns erupted behind them. "You're taking cuts!"

"Your grandma's sick," Barbara said. "She needs help, and we can't wait here all day."

Now at the front of the line, she saw the makeshift operation: some sort of a hose snaked down into a tank underground, a couple of big metal gas cans being filled up, and some very rough looking bikers. Then, she saw the sign with the price and her heart sank.

"Fifty dollars a gallon!" She cried.

The horns behind her were still honking and several angry customers got out of their cars and stomped toward her to give her a piece of their minds.

She popped the locks and jumped out of the driver's seat. To the irked people behind her she yelled out, "My mom is very sick! We have to get her to the hospital"

She went up to one of the bikers, a menacing looking man who towered over her. He looked very frightening, but she hoped he had some modicum of compassion in him.

"I'm sorry for asking this," she said." My mom is very sick and we need to get to the hospital. I only have forty dollars or so. Can I please get some gas? I'm begging you."

The man looked her over wordlessly and then slowly stepped over to the car. He glanced briefly into the passenger's seat at Barbara's mom, but then his gaze drifted toward Olivia sitting in the back seat.

He turned back to Barbara. "Price is fifty bucks a gallon," he said. "But you only got forty?"

"Yes," Barbara pleaded. "I'm so sorry."

"Well then," the biker grinned evilly, leering at Olivia. "It looks like we'll just have to take out the rest in trade."

He suddenly flung the rear door of the car opened, grabbed Olivia by the arm and dragged her out.

Olivia began flailing and screaming. Barbara ran toward him and tried to free his grip from her daughter's arm. He smacked her in the face and she fell to the ground. Another biker pulled her up and bearhugged her, pinning her arms to her side.

Still holding Barbara, he pushed the back door closed with his backside and then leaned against the front passenger door, holding it shut and preventing Barbara's mom from getting out to help.

Another man joined the first biker and they headed off toward the back of the gas station lot and toward enclosure that held the dumpsters, laughing as they dragged Olivia along with them.

"No!" Barbara screamed. "No! No! No!"

A couple of men who had previously been upset with Barbara, saw what was going on, got out of their cars and stepped forward to come to her rescue.

"Hey!" one of the men said to the bikers. "Let them go!"

The biker not restraining Barbara reached under his denim jacket, pulled out an automatic handgun, and fired a shot into the air.

"Mind your own fucking business!" he yelled. "And get back into your fucking cars if you want gas."

Sheepishly, the men quickly backed down and returned to their cars.

Barbara's cries turned into hysterical pleas. She turned to the man holding her

and said, "Please, please. I beg you. She's only fourteen years old!"

"Old enough to bleed, old enough to breed," he quipped.

Then the two bikers laughed.

CHAPTER NINETY-TWO

Bellflower, California
Friday, 10:40 a.m.
1 day, 8 hours, 9 minutes

Jake Sullivan was on one of his regular routes heading through the alley behind the gas station, when he heard the sounds of screaming coming from the dumpster enclosure.

He peered around the corner of the enclosure and spotted one man attempting to sexually assault a young girl; grabbing at her clothes and attempting to pull them off as another man looked on. The man looking on had his back to Jake and was oblivious to his presence.

Jake's mind flashed back to some of the brutalities he had seen committed by the Taliban against women in Afghanistan, especially young ones. His mind instantly and uncontrollably went into a rage and all sound disappeared. He could no longer hear the commotion, or the girl's panicked screams, only a constant hum. His vision became like he was looking through a tunnel.

He reached into his waistband, extracted his Navy combat knife from its sheath, and quietly crept up behind the onlooker. In position after only a couple of silent steps, and without any delay or hesitation, he swiftly reached around with his free hand and grabbed the man's forehead, pulling him backwards.

Before the man could react, he plunged the knife deep into the base of the man's skull, twisting it and severing the brain stem in an instant, exactly as the Army had trained him to do. The man crumpled to the ground, dead before he even hit it.

The second man saw the other man drop dead in front of his eyes. Then he saw Jake standing there with the bloody knife in his hand. Instinctively, he let go of the girl and started reaching into his waistband to pull out his gun.

The girl ran off screaming, but Jake neither heard her or paid any attention to her; he had another threat to deal with. His training kicked in once again and he lunged at the man before he could get his gun fully raised and leveled at him.

Jake swept the man's arm upward, forcing the gun high and out of harm's way. In the same swift motion, he jammed his knife deep into the man's exposed armpit, severing his brachial artery.

Disabled in the one arm and bleeding profusely, Jake knew that the man would pass out and die in a minute or so, but for now he was still fighting with his other good arm. He had had it drummed into his head by the military that the only good enemy was a dead enemy and so he finished the job by plunging his knife between the man's rib bones and into his heart.

Blood erupted violently out of the man's chest and he slumped over onto Jake, dead as a doornail. The gun clattered to the ground, but luckily didn't discharge when it hit.

The second threat neutralized; Jake's hearing slowly began to return. He heard another commotion coming from the gas station's lot; more screaming and yelling. More threats?

He shoved the dead man off of him, and picked up his gun. He checked that it had a round chambered, cocked the hammer and flicked off the safety.

He was about to exit the enclosure and head toward the screaming sounds, when he noticed another body lying on the ground. It appeared to be a young man who had sustained some sort of a traumatic injury; a pool of drying blood surrounded his body. No matter what his story or condition, Jake assessed, there was no time for him right now; there were more threats to deal with.

As he exited the enclosure, he spied two other men standing next to a car parked close by. The two men appeared to be of the same ilk as the two combatants Jake had just killed and he quickly evaluated them as threats by association.

Besides the men and the car, some motorcycles, a bunch of gas cans, and an older pickup truck were sitting off to the side. One man was trying to hold onto the hysterical girl who was squirming wildly in his arms. Another man was restraining a middle-aged woman from behind.

Jake recognized the woman instantly. She was the woman from the store, the one who was always so decent to him when others weren't. She was the one who gave him the extra batteries just yesterday.

While the two men were distracted, Jake dashed over to the backside of the truck. Using the body of the truck as a barrier, he rested his forearms on the hood of the truck and drew a bead on the man holding the middle-aged woman. As soon as the target was acquired, he fired and the bullet hit the man in the side of the head, just above the temple. Blood and brain matter exploded out the other side. The man fell dead, releasing his captive.

The other man, the one with the girl, heard the shot, let go of the girl and started to reach for his own weapon.

Jake shifted his aim to the other man's upper torso and was about to fire when the girl, running to the woman, blocked his shot.

By the time, she was clear, the man had his gun out and pointed at him. The man fired and a bullet grazed Jake's left shoulder, swinging him around. It hurt like hell, but it was a do or die situation and he had no time for self-pity.

He dropped to his knees and aimed around the front of the truck. He fired a low shot, hitting the man in the crotch.

The man screamed in agony, dropped his gun and crouched over, gripping what remained of his testicles.

The man was wounded but not fully neutralized, and so Jake raised back up and fired again, this time hitting the man on the top of his head.

With nowhere to exit, it was a clean wound as the bullet traveled through the man's skull and down through his neck and chest cavity, destroying multiple organs in the process. The man slumped down to the ground.

His gun still raised and sweeping the area, Jake quickly scanned for more active threats. Seeing none, he slowly came back from around the truck and checked each man. Both were terminated.

He picked up the second man's gun and stuck it into the waistband of his pants.

Then he allowed himself to breathe again.

CHAPTER NINETY-THREE

Saint Elizabeth Medical Center
Cerritos, California
Friday, 10:51 a.m.
+ 1 day, 8 hours, 16 minutes

When it looked like a good time to make a break for it, Alan got up out of his bed, grabbed his jacket and his gun and headed out of the ED. Everyone was so busy, no one noticed, including Colton.

Outside he observed more of the same with people standing around, waiting to get picked up by friends or relatives. Every once in a while, when someone was lucky enough to get picked up, the cars were often small and Alan knew that they wouldn't suit his needs. He knew that he might wait forever to find a vehicle big enough and even if he did, would they be willing to help him out?

He began to roam around, seeing if any other options existed; a large van or a truck even.

He had just rounded a corner of the hospital a few minutes later when he saw it.

There, backed up to a loading dock, was a large semi-truck, a Peterbilt with a sleeper cab. The back doors of the trailer were open and a man was dragging out pallets of boxes with a small pallet jack.

"Excuse me, sir?" Alan said approaching him.

The man stopped pulling against the pallet jack and turned to him. He was a lanky man in his 50s or 60s, with a tan, weathered face mapped with wrinkles. He was breathing hard from the exertion of unloading the pallets by hand.

"Yes sir," the man said genially, extracting a handkerchief from his breast pocket and wiping the sweat from his face. He had an accent, Texas or Midwestern, definitely not from here in California.

"I have a huge favor to ask," Alan Binder said.

CHAPTER NINETY-FOUR

Bellflower, California
Friday, 10:58 a.m.
+ 1 day, 8 hours, 23 minutes

After the gunfire ceased, Barbara grabbed Olivia and held her tight. Both of them had bruises on their arms and faces where they had been hit or manhandled. Olivia was screaming hysterically.

Jake stepped over to Barbara and there was instant recognition. She realized that it was 'batteries' the polite homeless man who came into her store occasionally.

Not knowing if other members of the bike gang might soon show up, Jake told her in no uncertain terms, "Get in your car and get out of here now!"

It was the first time Barbara had ever heard his voice.

Freezing with fear, Barbara hesitated. She continued to hug Olivia, who was still carrying on.

"Do it!" Jake said again, firmer.

Barbara looked at Olivia and her mom and son in the car.

"Only if you go with us," she said.

"I can't …"

Barbara unwrapped one of her arms from around Olivia and gripped Jake's arm.

"Please," she pleaded with him. "We need you. I'm so scared. Please!"

Jake stared at Barbara for a long time, considering. He could see the panic in her eyes, the desperation written all over her face. Of all the people he had to deal with in this world: people who yelled at him to get a job, people who would avoid looking at him, the cops that would roust him and make him move on, and worst of all – the other homeless who would try to rob or kill him if they could, she treated him better than anyone else. While others looked down at him with pity, or outright disdain, she always treated him like he was a regular, decent human being who deserved respect.

"Alright," he said finally. "But let me get my things."

He quickly disappeared around the truck and headed back to the dumpster enclosure. Outside of it, he grabbed his rucksack and his boom-box from his baby stroller and then, took one last look at the two dead bikers in the enclosure. It was a scene of carnage, not that he hadn't seen similar—or worse scenes over in "The Sandbox."

Their bodies were twisted in crazy angles and a huge pool of blood had formed that was still growing. Out of curiosity, Jake checked on the other body who had been lying behind the dumpster. He was a young man about the same age as he, and his throat had been split almost from ear to ear. His head was lying motionless in a pool of dried blood, his dead eyes staring up to the sky.

Jake leaned down and did a quick assessment. His skin was cold to the touch, and he didn't have a pulse. By the looks of it, he had been dead for a while and was probably another victim of the biker gang. Too bad for him, Jake thought, but the world had suddenly gotten much more violent—and it was only going to get worse. He headed back to the woman from the store and her family.

By the time he returned, the car's engine was running and everyone was inside and ready to go. The back door was open and he could hear the hysterical sobs of the young girl booming from inside.

The other people waiting in line had cautiously started to return to the scene. They don't know what happened and really didn't care at this point; they only wanted fuel.

Jake jumped into the rear seat, dragging his rucksack and radio with him. As soon as he was seated and had the door closed, he yelled to Barbara, "Go!"

Desperate to leave the scene, Barbara squealed rubber as she hauled out of the gas station. She entered the street and started heading down it at a high rate of speed to get away.

They had only gone a block or so when another car suddenly pulled out in front of them. She slammed on the brakes but was not quick enough to avoid the collision.

Her car hit the other car in the back end, clipping it in the rear bumper and spinning it around.

Barbara's car careened off the other car and slammed straight into a light pole.

CHAPTER NINETY-FIVE

Beijing, China
Friday 2:05 a.m. (11:05 a.m. PST)
+ 1 day, 8 hours, 5 minutes

President Gao Zemin and his trusted advisors sat in the secure room of the Zhongnanhai complex and watched the bank of monitors gleefully as the chaos unfolded 9,000 kilometers away.

Based upon the sat images and reports coming in from news agencies, California was in full disarray with municipal water pumps shutting down, communications all but non-existent, and supply chains crippled. There was rioting in the streets, and neighbor turned on neighbor to take by force whatever they needed to survive. Some were already surrendering to the inevitable and attempting to leave the state, clogging the outbound highways. It was everything the leaders of the People's Republic could have hoped for.

For their efforts and as part of the deal, 300 of the negotiated 600 Krytrons had already been delivered to the Iranians, with the remaining ones in transit. The Iranians would be pleased with their new toys, and rightfully feel that they had finally turned a corner in their efforts to become a nuclear power.

But it would be a short-lived victory. No one, including the Chinese, wanted to see the fanatical Islamic Republic come into possession of the most powerful weapons in the world, and so plans had been drafted to keep the Iranian regime in check.

Already, back channels were being used to quietly "tip off" the Israelis about the shipments of the nuclear triggering devices. Before long, F-35 jets would come screaming into the backyard of the Israeli's longtime nemesis to carry out surgical strikes on their weapons facilities, landing the Iranians right back on square one in their program.

When the dust cleared, the Islamic Republic may suspect the Chinese for betraying them, but there was not much they could do about it lest they tip their hat to the Americans that they were behind the grid attack, thereby triggering an apocalyptic response by the US military.

It was, Zemin pondered wistfully, like the Chinese finger puzzle invented by Lao Tzu in the 6th century BC; the more you struggled, the more you were trapped.

CHAPTER NINETY-SIX

CAL-OES
Mather, California
Friday, 11:16 a.m.
+ 1 day, 8 hours, 41 minutes

Shanice, the governor and other key members of the response team were fresh from their daily press conference, where they once again had taken a drubbing.

In reality, it was a lot like the movie, *Groundhog Day*, where the same questions, challenges, and accusations were levied against them, and the same answers were given.

Shanice knew from experience that this was the time—transit time, or *'lag'* they called it, when CAL-OES was most vulnerable to criticism. It was due to the inherent nature of the trying to get assets ordered, procured, transported, and finally, in place. Almost everything: generators, fuel trucks, medical supplies, MREs, water, even the spare HPTs were in transit now and there was, unfortunately, no way to blink their eyes or tap their toes and have it all suddenly appear. The reality of the situation did not appease the media however, who seemed to demand faster and faster results.

As the buck stopped ultimately with him, Doyle took the usual brunt of the barrage. Battle hardened as he was, he handled it with his usual no nonsense manner, but Shanice—and even some others might have noted, he was beginning to show signs of strain himself. His eyes seemed especially red and puffy, and his tie wasn't knotted as tightly and was slightly askew. One could only imagine the sound bites his disheveled appearance, however slight, might generate.

As de rigueur as the attack was on the governor, Shanice thought that the media had eventually gotten around to putting her into their sights as well. The questions—and sometimes outright challenges, directed at her were now greater and in higher ferocity.

She stayed on script however, answered the questions honestly and evenly, and most importantly, tried not to let the strain show on her as well. By ten this morning she already had given birth to a splitting headache and the brutality of this interrogation was doing nothing to help it.

When the press conference mercifully ended forty minutes later, the team left the small comm room and headed back out into the SOC. Out of habit, they all looked up to the monitors in the front of the room to check out the latest status from on the ground.

Thankfully, the networks and locals were not replaying the conference in its entirety, so no one had to endure reliving what they had all been through.

Just as they were taking in the various news feeds, the ABC network splashed a SPECIAL REPORT notice on the screen. It was followed by the words: DARK STATE: DAY 2 OF THE GREAT CALIFORNIA BLACKOUT.

"Just dandy," Doyle quipped miserably, verbalizing what all of them were thinking. "The bastards already have a name for it."

Together, they stood there transfixed as the news anchor delivered his dire report. The sound was muted, as it was on all of the TV monitors, so they followed along reading the closed caption at the bottom of the screen.

"...day two of what is already turning out to be the worst disaster and act of domestic terrorism on US soil. Forty million Californians are now without power and are quickly running out of gasoline, food and water with no end in sight."

Cutting away from the somber looking news anchor, the screen then changed to a side-by-side comparison of a Google Earth satellite image of the western United States at nighttime, before and after the attack. The images had lines overlayed that showed the borders of California. The effect was striking.

The before image showed a Golden State that was more white than dark, with the Bay Area, Los Angeles, and San Diego completely saturated by huge blotches of illumination.

The after image was equally striking, as the area between the state's borders was nearly completely black, punctuated by only the tiniest pinpoints of light here and there.

The contrast in the two images was palatable and put into stark perspective, just how large this disaster was.

Shanice stood there frozen by the images, no longer reading the crawl at the bottom. For her it was the horror of all horrors displayed in graphic detail. It was all so real, and undeniable; her state was in real trouble.

Her head suddenly seemed very light, and she lost the focus of her eyes. Her legs suddenly felt like rubber, failing her body from the waist down. At the last moment, she tried to reach out to grab onto somebody to hold herself up, but it was too late.

She collapsed on the floor of the SOC.

CHAPTER NINETY-SEVEN

Santa Ana, California
Friday, 11:17 a.m.
+ 1 day, 8 hours, 42 minutes

Todd White never learned to read a map.

Part of this was due to the dyslexia which had dogged him his entire life, but also, like most Americans today, he relied on technology to guide him to his destinations. Google maps was one of his best friends.

But despite his limitations with spatial reasoning, he had survived well as a full-time employee of the Red Cross in Phoenix, Az. driving a box truck and keeping the One Hundred Forty-year-old organization's various blood donation centers, offices, and warehouses supplied with everything from syringes, to paper clips, to the ubiquitous, "I DONATED," stickers. After all, it was familiar and routine to him.

Now though, lost in a strange city and trying to locate the local foodbank with a map and a set of directions that looked no more decipherable to him than a wall of hieroglyphics, the twenty-seven-year-old began to question his decision to volunteer to help out with the California disaster.

He pressed the redial key on the sat phone he had been given and put it on speaker. It rang a few times before being answered by a young woman he worked with named Sheila.

"Hello Todd," she said, somewhat impatiently. "Are you there yet?"

"No," he answered exasperated. "The map you gave me is wrong."

He looked down briefly then at the trucks instrument cluster; he was under an eighth of a tank and the low fuel light had been on for the past half hour as he endlessly drove around in circles.

"And I'm getting low on gas," he added.

He heard her huff on the other end of the phone. She had personally printed up all the maps and directions for the drivers and no one else was having trouble except for Todd. It was the third time he had called her in the past hour.

"Alright, she said. "Get to an intersection and tell me where you are at. Then I'll tell you where the fuel truck is at so you don't run out."

He continued driving down the unfamiliar street until he came to an intersection and pulled over under the sign to read it. Reading was a relative term though and although the sign clearly indicated he was at the intersection of McFadden and Dower, to Todd it looked like, *DcafdMed* and *Wdore*.

"I...I can't really pronounce it," he said, hedging. "It's not very clear."

"Well then spell it to me, I'll look it up here."

He recited the letters to her as he saw them, and she fired back. "There is no such street. That's not even a word Todd!"

She huffed again and then said to him, "Just go to another one!"

He accelerated again to try to get to another intersection with hopefully simpler names, but after only going about a hundred yards, the truck sputtered and then quit.

"Oh man," he said, loud enough she could hear him on the sat phone.

"What? Don't tell me you ran out of gas."

"Yeah, I think I did," he said, ashamed of his disability and how he was letting people down. He started trying to crank the engine over, but it never caught.

"Well, you'll just have to find out where you are and I'll try to get the fuel truck to you." Sheila said. "I can't wait all day."

She abruptly hung up and he continued trying the start the engine. The sound of the starter motor whining attracted the attention of a group of rough looking people on the sidewalk near him, and they began to slowly saunter over.

He didn't like the look of things and continued trying desperately to start the truck to no avail. Finally, they reached him, and before he could lock the door, they had opened it and dragged him out. He knew the supplies would never get to the food bank.

CHAPTER NINETY-EIGHT

Bellflower, California
Friday, 11:17 a.m.
+ 1 day, 8 hours, 42 minutes

The violent collision with the light pole caused the air bags to deploy, sparing Barbara and her mom from serious injury. But Jake, Freddie, and Olivia, seated in the rear and not wearing seat belts, flew forward into the back of the front seats.

When she was able to compose herself, Barbara asked, "Is everyone okay?"

Everyone was too stunned to answer.

"Mom?" Barbara said louder, shaking her by the shoulder. "Are you okay?"

Her mom turned to her and took her glasses off. The airbag had driven them into her face. She now had two black eyes and a small laceration on the bridge of her nose.

"Yes," she mumbled. "I'm alright, I guess."

Barbara could hear the weakness in her mom's voice and thought it could have been from the trauma of what they had just endured. But then, she had seen this in her mom before when she missed her dialysis: general weakness, confusion, lethargy. Barbara pressed on and went down the list.

"Olivia?"

Nothing.

"Olivia!"

Barbara turned in her seat and looked at her daughter; she was in a state of shock. First the sexual assault, now a vehicle crash. It could't get much worse.

"Olivia, are you okay!" Barbara practically yelled.

Olivia nodded her head slightly, not looking at her mom but staring into her hands in her lap. Barbara pressed on.

"Freddie...Freddie!"

Jake examined him and announced. "No bruises or blood. He's fine, he's just shaken up, I think. He's crying and that means his lungs work."

Barbara looked at Jake then. "Are you okay?" she started to ask, then noticed the blood on his arm and recalled the gunfight. "Oh my God! You've been shot. We have to get you to a hospital!"

"No, we don't. It just grazed me. I'll be fine."

Freddie was still wailing and Jake turned to him. He couldn't help but think of the innocent boy he killed in Afghanistan. There was no bringing that child back, but maybe Jake thought, he could save this one, maybe he could protect Freddie and his family. The thought filled him with cautious optimism.

"Hey there Freddie. My name is Jake."

He extended his hand to shake. Freddie took it limply and shook it.

"How old are you Freddie?"

"Six and a half," he said, sniffling.

"Six and a half?" Jake cried incredulously. "I thought you were at least eight!"

Freddie brightened up at the compliment, and looked over at Jake. He wiped his tears from his cheeks with the back of his hands. "Really," he said?

"Yeah," Jake said. "Really. But I have to get out now and look at the car. Can you wait for me Freddie?"

"Sure."

Even from his view in the back seat, Jake could see the hood crumpled up and steam rising up from what was left of the radiator. The other car had since taken off.

Jake started to get out and had to force the rear door, which had been buckled in the crash. It screeched in protest with every inch it was pushed open.

Outside, he saw the true extent of the damage to the front of the car; the right wheel was twisted and shoved up under what was left of the fender. And the front end was completely caved in, with various liquids draining onto the street.

The car was totally disabled and couldn't be driven. The light pole was sheared off at the base and had fallen over onto the sidewalk. At least it hadn't fallen on the car and crushed them.

Barbara got out herself and walked around to see the damage. It made her heart sink; the only thing she had to help her family survive and to her mom get to dialysis was this car - their only lifeline. Now, they didn't even have that.

The world was crumbling around her, not in the literal sense of buildings collapsing like in an earthquake, but a collapse of society. Her store was in shambles, People were taking everything that wasn't nailed down. Her daughter had almost been raped. They had almost been killed. And her mom needed dialysis.

Barbara Williams, the glue of her family, didn't know if she could take it much longer. She was quickly becoming overwhelmed.

Her heartbeat started pounding in her head and she began hyperventilating. The world began to spin out of control. She couldn't take it anymore. She couldn't take it!

She let out a guttural wail and started to sob uncontrollably. Her body collapsed and she fell into Jake. He caught her and then pulled her close to him, stroking her head.

"It's okay," he said softly. "It's okay. We'll get through this."

CHAPTER NINETY-NINE

Saint Elizabeth Medical Center, Cerritos, California
Friday, 11:22 a.m.
+ 1 day, 8 hours, 47 minutes

Back inside in the ED, Alan hunted down Colton and quickly found him standing and talking to another nurse, a young female with brownish-blond hair pulled up into a tight bun. Colton did a double take when he saw Alan up and dressed.

"You're supposed to be in bed Mr. Binder. What are you doing up?"

"I'm feeling much better, actually."

Colton had seen plenty of patients "self-discharge" through the years and didn't have the energy at this point to argue with Alan about it.

"I know your tired Colton and want to get home," Alan continued. "But can I talk to you first, in private?"

Colton sighed and pointed towards the partition/room Alan had recently occupied. Even though beds were at a premium, housekeeping still had not changed the sheets or wiped down the room.

After they got into the room, Alan closed the curtain behind them and wasted no time getting to the point.

"Now you told me that it's iffy if you guys can keep the power on and save Marianne, correct?"

Colton nodded and said nothing, although something changed in his expression. As exhausted as he was, his eyes narrowed slightly and his pupils dilated enough that Alan could see them.

"And that all the LifeFlights are already booked and unavailable," Alan continued.

The nurse became visibly suspicious.

"What are you getting at Mr. Binder?" he asked.

"If I told you that I could get Marianne transported to safety, will you help me?"

Colton suddenly raised his hands in alarm.

"Whoa! I'm not her doctor Mr. Binder. I can't make the call to dischar—"

Alan pulled the lapel of his jacket slightly to the side, revealing the gun in its holster.

"I'm saying that you can...and that you will," Alan Binder said firmly.

CHAPTER ONE HUNDRED

Bellflower, California
Friday, 11:23 a.m.
+ 1 day, 8 hours, 48 minutes

It took a while, but eventually Barbara calmed down. By now, Olivia and Freddie were out of the car and hugging her as well. Other cars were driving by, but no one stopped to ask to help or see if they were okay; everyone was worried about their own lives at this point.

Finally, she took one big breath of air and pulled away from Jake, steeling herself. With the back of her hand, she wiped the tears off of her face and looked at him appreciatively.

"Thank you," she said. "Thank you so much for being here."

"No problem," he said humbly, then asked, "Where do you live? Near the store, right?"

"Yes," She said, nodding "You see me walk home sometimes, don't you?"

Jake nodded, and then added, "And that's quite aways away. Do you think your family could make it that far?"

Barbara shook her head. "I don't know. I don't think so. My mom is not well, she needs her dialysis. And Olivia and Freddie, I don't know if they're in any condition to walk that far."

"Is there anybody you could call to come get you?" Jake offered.

"The cell phones don't work. I think the towers are dead."

Jake nodded mutely; he hadn't owned a cell phone in years.

Barbara took a deep breath and looked around. The area was her old stomping ground when she was still with her ex, Tom. She remembered the stores, the streets, the neighborhoods. She turned back to Jake.

"I know what we can do," she said.

CHAPTER ONE HUNDRED-ONE

Saint Elizabeth Medical Center
Cerritos, California
Friday, 11:23 a.m.
+ 1 day, 8 hours, 48 minutes

Colton McKenna stared at the pistol under Alan's jacket. In his many years in the ED, he had seen some crazies, but none of them were armed. He wished now he had never given the actor his gun back.

Still, thinking about the other patients and staff in there, he didn't want to cause any alarm and so muttered under his breath, "You're fucking nuts, you know that? You'll never get away with this."

"Yes, I will," Alan said. "Yes, *we* will, because you are going to help me save her life. I've got a truck standing by right now at the loading dock ready to help us transport her out of state. I just need you to help me wheel her out."

"Mr. Binder," Colton sighed, his voice taking on a conciliatory tone. "Even if we could wheel her out and get her into this truck of yours, she needs regular transfusions about every four hours."

"When was her last transfusion?"

Colton thought about it, it was tough for him running on zero sleep. "Uh, thirty to forty-five minutes ago."

"So ,she doesn't need one for another three hours, correct?"

"Yes. But you couldn't drive out of state in that amount of time. Even Vegas is five hours under the best of circumstances."

"We don't need to drive out of state, just to Long Beach."

"Oh," the nurse said' cocking a skeptical eyebrow. "And what do you have in Long Beach; a hospital that I don't know about?"

"No," Alan Binder said, smiling. "Not another hospital; a private jet."

CHAPTER ONE HUNDRED-TWO

Barnes, California
Friday, 11:52 a.m.
+ 1 day, 9 hours, 17 minutes

The backup generator for the wastewater pump lift station "Charlie" outside Barnes, California switched on automatically when the power went out at 2:35 AM. Since that time, it had mainly idled as the level of raw sewage had not built up sufficiently in the wet well that collected it to trigger a pump-out into the discharge, or "force-main" pipe.

But now that the 78,000 residents of the town had risen and performed their bodily functions, the high-level switch activated and the submersible pump switched on, putting a greater strain on the generator and burning more fuel.

Workers for the sanitation department had dutifully tested the generator on a quarterly basis as required, but this typically meant isolating the generator, starting it up, and playing on their phones as it sat idling. Unlike a true test, the procedure did not "load" the generator as it was now experiencing.

And although the generator had been tested and run, it had not had the diesel fuel filtered or "polished" in over two years. This resulted in condensation forming in the tank, leading to a growth of microbial colonies. Now that the fuel demand was high, the fuel filters for the engine began clogging as more and more microbes were captured. Finally, the filters could no longer pass enough fuel to satisfy the engine and it shut down.

Upstream of the low point lift station, toilets continued to be flushed and showers taken, and the wet well continued to build a higher and higher level. When it could no longer be pumped out to the treatment facility, the raw sewage had no place to go and began backing up into the pipes and into the resident's homes.

Importance of fuel polishing in diesel generators
Source: https://www.wpowerproducts.com/news/how-fuel-polishing-keeps-diesel-tank-clean/

CHAPTER ONE HUNDRED-THREE

Saint Elizabeth Medical Center
Cerritos, California
Friday, 12:14 p.m.
+ 1 day, 9 hours, 39 minutes

They made it fast, as fast as possible. Colton pushed the bed while Alan moved along side of him, pushing the monitor unit along with a tree of IV bags with tubes leading into Marianne's body.

"Where'd you say the truck was?" Colton asked as they moved through the dimly lit halls. Around them, more patients were being moved, either pushed in their beds or by way of Med-Sleds, cloth emergency transport devices, used in rapid evacuation procedures.

"On the loading dock."

Colton nodded. "Follow me," he said, just as a nurse wearing a carrier holding two infants came around the corner.

When they reached the end of a long hallway, Colton instructed Alan to move ahead of him and hold open the doors

They stepped through and into the shipping and receiving department, which looked as though it had been abandoned. Pallets with boxes sat all around and clipboards lay on top of desks with the computer monitors dead. The cavernous space was dark except for the sunlight streaming in from the two open doors on the loading dock.

Alan was thankful to see that the trucker had not had second thoughts and taken off. He was standing outside, leaning against the fuel tank of his truck and smoking a cigarette. He tossed it to the ground and crushed it out when he saw Alan and Colton.

"Didn't know if ya was gonna make it or not," he said affably, then turned his attention to the bed with Marianne on it.

"This the young lady you's telling me about?"

"Yes, sir," Alan said. "And we have to get moving as soon as possible."

It took all three of them to work in concert to get Marianne's bed loaded into the sleeper cab of the truck, even at that, it barely fit through the narrow side doors. Initially, they considered loading her into the now empty trailer, but with the traffic snarls on the roads that the driver described, they thought they would have a better chance making it through traffic with just the tractor part of the rig.

Once they had her loaded, Alan turned to the nurse and said, "Alright, thanks Colton. I'll take it from here."

"No, you won't," Colton said. "I'm going with you."

"You don't have to, I just—"

"She needs to be monitored Alan, and I can do that while we drive. Now let's get going, we don't have any time to waste."

"All right, you made your case. And by the way, I'm sorry about pulling the gun on you. I didn't mean to scare you."

"You didn't scare me, Alan. You're not that great of an actor. I knew you'd never use it."

They both laughed as they climbed into the truck.

CHAPTER ONE HUNDRED-FOUR

Cerritos, California
Friday, 12:17 p.m.
+ 1 day, 9 hours, 42 minutes

The walk from the scene of the car crash to her ex's house was only about a half of a mile. They grabbed everything of value from the car and left it where it was, like everyone else was doing with their disabled vehicles.

Jake took her mom's arm and helped her while Barbara kept her arm wrapped tightly around Olivia. Freddie was busy chattering to Jake about his toy cars. Jake, for his part was very accommodating and this kept Freddie's attention.

Initially, Barbara's main concern was getting her mom's kidney issues taken care of. But now, with the trauma of the sexual assault, Olivia was in a state of shock and acting in a catatonic manner. Barbara had no idea how long her torpor would last or what to do to help her, other than to comfort her.

When they finally arrived at the house, Barbara realized that she needed her daughter to pull it together. When he repurchased the house from her, Tom had changed all the locks and replaced them with pushbutton keypads. The locks were mechanical in nature and didn't rely on electricity or batteries, so that was good. The only problem was Barbara didn't know the combination.

They stepped onto the porch and Barbara turned to Olivia.

"Honey," she said very gently but distinctly. "I need you to punch in the code for the door, okay?"

No response. Just a distant look.

"Olivia, the code?" Barbara repeated, somewhat stronger. *"We need to get in."*

Nothing.

"I know it mommy," Freddie said and stepped forward.

He turned to Jake and bragged, "Daddy has me do the buttons sometimes."

Freddie quickly punched in the code and sure enough, the door lock clicked.

He turned the handle, and they stepped in.

CHAPTER ONE HUNDRED-FIVE

Near Carmen City, California
Friday, 12:20 p.m.
+ 1 day, 9 hours, 45 minutes

The task of properly setting out the Claymores and arming them with trip wire was going much slower than he thought, and Walter Gronsky was dripping from sweat after just a couple of hours or so of working. So far, he had only set out four of the two dozen devices he had manufactured.

Besides the sloped and brushy terrain he had to work on, he also had to contend with his own tangle-foot underneath and had so far caught on it twice and tripped. Besides the physical impediments, he was operating in broad daylight and had to keep one eye open for the enemy. On the bright side though, he thought that if it was this difficult for him to navigate in what was essentially his own backyard, how tough would it be for an intruder.

As was standard operating procedure for antipersonnel mines on the battlefield, he had started setting the devices at the outer perimeter of his property and working inward toward his bunker, thus ensuring that he didn't have the added problems of having to step over any of his own trip wires in the process.

As each unit was set up, he put an "M" designating where a mine was located on a crude map he had drawn of his property, along with the numerical designation 1-24. A dashed line showed the direction and location of the trip wire. And unless something changed, and he had to move them, the map would become his bible to safely navigate on his land.

Still another consideration he had to make was to have a viable path that he could follow through his minefield and back to the safety of the bunker. The most obvious and easy routes were the most tempting, but he had to avoid using these as they would be the ones most likely used by the enemy. Therefore, he had to lay out a—

There was a sound in the distance, the snap of a twig. Walter immediately dropped down and rolled into a nearby bush, his weapon raised and at the ready.

When he was sure he was adequately camouflaged, he slowly raised up and scanned the area for the source of the sound, his pulse and breathing quickening.

He quickly worked to calm himself down and to focus on the special training he had received at the survivalist camps he had attended: no movement of the body or head, use your eyes only to survey your AOO (Area of Operation), assess the situation, and most of all, be patient and let the enemy make the first move, and therefore, the first mistake.

It was going to be a long day.

CHAPTER ONE HUNDRED-SIX

Cerritos, California
Friday, 12:25 p.m.
+ 1 day, 9 hours, 50 minutes

Barbara Williams hadn't been inside the house she had once co-owned since she had to sell it back to her ex, several years ago. He had said she could come in if she wanted to, but her pride kept her from ever crossing that threshold ever again. Therefore, she had no idea what to expect.

It was a four bedroom, two story, track home with a large living room at the front of the house and the kitchen and family room leading out to a covered patio in the back. Three bedrooms were upstairs with the fourth on the main level. In many ways, it was like every other house in the subdivision, ('cookie-cutters' people would derisively refer to them as) but now it was a sanctuary from the world imploding outside. Barbara had never felt so comforted to step into it. She double locked the door as soon as they were all inside.

Thankfully, the house was tidy and neat—which Olivia had shared with her, but most of the furniture was different, and what had not been replaced had been moved around. A woman always likes to feather a new nest as she sees fit, Barbara thought wryly. She took a moment to look around, but didn't allow herself the luxury of wasting time gawking.

"Mom, sit down," she said first, pointing to an arm chair that had been added.

Jake, slowly released Barbara's mom, and helped her into the chair.

"My feet hurt mommy," Freddie said. "I want to sit too."

"Alright," Barbara said. "I'm going to see if the water works."

She started to release Olivia, who whimpered in protest.

"Nooooo," she cried in a very small voice.

"I'll go check the water," Jake graciously offered, and started to head out of the room.

Freddie, whose feet suddenly didn't seem to bother him any longer, then announced, "I'm going too," before bounding out of the chair

"Thanks," Barbara said, and then moved Olivia over to a couch and gently sat down next to her.

Settled with Olivia, Barbara took the time to look around a little longer. Even though the furnishings had been rearraigned or replaced, it was still the home she remembered: the smell, the way the light streamed through the windows. A flood of memories came rushing back, good ones and not so good ones.

Jake and Freddie suddenly appeared with filled water glasses.

"Water works," Freddie reported with a flourish, as if he had personally seen to it that it did.

"If you need to know anything about the house, just ask this guy," Jake laughed, setting a glass in front of Barbara's mom and gesturing to Freddie. "He knows where everything's at."

He set the two remaining glasses in his hand in front of Barbara and Olivia. Barbara took hers and drained about half of it heartily. Olivia simply stared at the top of the coffee table.

Barbara set her glass down and allowed herself a faint smile directed towards Freddie. "My little man," she said proudly. This caused Freddie to beam.

He took a quick drink of water and said, "I'm going to get my toys," and disappeared out of the room, bounding up the stairs to the second floor.

Barbara's mom stared at the glass of water in front of her, but didn't touch it. Without her dialysis treatment, she had to watch her liquid intake. But Barbara also knew that she couldn't let her get dehydrated either.

"You really have to have some mom," she said gently. "I know you have to watch it, but we can't have you getting dehydrated either."

"Right," she said finally and Barbara noticed her words were somewhat slurred. She picked up the glass shakily and drank about a quarter of it in one sip, then another quick sip before she set it down. Her eyes were staring straight ahead and she was suddenly listless.

"Mom," Barbara said. "Why don't you lay down in the down-stairs bedroom?"

"No, I need to –," she said slowly.

"No mom, there's nothing to do right now. You need to lay down and save your strength."

Barbara turned to Jake.

"She has kidney issues, and need's her dialysis. We were trying to find a clinic that had power when…when…"

Barbara couldn't finish, and started to choke on her words; the horror of Olivia being dragged off to be…to be…

Jake sensed that she was going to lose it and intercepted.

"It's okay," he said strongly. "It's over, all right? You're all safe now. We're gonna be fine."

"Thanks," Barbara said, sniffling and sucking back her tears.

Olivia looked up then and stared at Jake. Then she bolted up off of the couch and hugged him.

"Thank you!" she cried.

It was her first words uttered in over an hour.

CHAPTER ONE HUNDRED-SEVEN

Lakewood, California. En route to Long Beach Airport
Friday, 2:11 p.m.
+ 1 day, 11 hours, 36 minutes

Alan and Colton were thankful that the truck driver had wisely ditched his trailer rig as the going was still tough on the streets, which helped to fuel everyone's anxiety.

Adding to the sense of dread was the driver's CB radio, which was full of chatter from other drivers sharing info about the incident.

"whole state of California out, anybody know where there's diesel?"

"I just fueled in Ontario. They gotta generator to keep the pumps running, but ya better hurry. They don't know if the fuel delivery's gonna come in."

"I can't make it that far," the first driver said. *"I'm in Anaheim now."*

"Try a Costco" someone else offered. *"They got generators."*

"I'm at one now," another chimed in. *"Tween people raidin the store and trying to get gas, lines backed up for a half mile. Been sittin for close to an hour now."*

Alan gestured to the radio and asked, "What's the range on that thing?"

The driver eased out the clutch as the line of cars ahead of him inched forward.

"Bout twenty miles or so, but if I get a good skip, could be hundreds."

"So, you can hear from out of state?"

"Only at night when the conditions are right and the signal skips off the atmosphere somehow. I don't really understand it all. But you gotta remember, drivers pass on the info from rig to rig, so I might be hear'n someth'n that happened in Colorado and got passed on from one driver to the next."

"Kind of like, an information pipeline," Colton observed.

"Yup," the driver agreed.

Just then, the line moved again, but before the driver could let out the clutch to move forward, another car cut right in front of him.

"Asshole!" Alan barked.

The driver, as unflappable and laconic as anyone Alan had ever met, just shrugged. You had to have patience to drive a big rig, people cutting you off, not letting you into their lane, it was just part of the job.

"What are they saying about what it's like outside of California?" Alan asked. "We can't get much news."

"Other states like Nevada, Arizona took a hit from what they call 'oscillations' or somth'n when this all happened here in California, but they's comin back up slowly."

"What do they say about our state?" Colton asked.

The Driver turned and looked at of them pitifully. "They said get out when ya can."

The driver gestured back to Marianne, who at least seemed peaceful as she lay prone on her emergency bed.

"You alls doin the right thing getting your friend outta here. 'For long, people are gonna wise up and you won't be able to get out of the state."

Alan and Colton looked at each other darkly.

"How's she doing?" Alan asked, partly to change the subject.

"Stable," Colton said, "And honestly, that's all we can hope for."

At last, they reached the intersection, and the driver flipped on his right blinker. All they had to do was make it the short distance onto the freeway, which according to the driver, was far better than the surface streets.

Before long they had reached the on-ramp and were on their way. Alan put his hand on the driver's shoulder.

"Thanks again," he said sincerely, a phrase that up until this point in his life had been foreign to him.

"F'get it" the driver said, and then started humming a tune.

CHAPTER ONE HUNDRED-EIGHT

CAL-OES
Mather, California
Friday, 2:33 p.m.
+ 1 day, 11 hours, 58 minutes

Shanice Dixon came to several hours later, not recognizing her surroundings for a few moments. Then, she realized it was Doyle's governor's suite in the CAL-OES building. She was laying down on the queen-sized bed and had been stripped down to her panties. Her skirt, blouse and brassiere were folded neatly on the nightstand next to her. The blanket had been pulled up to just above her breasts.

Also sitting next to her was Martin Hagen, a Lieutenant and one of the paramedics from Cal-Fire who was housed in the building and currently embedded with them for the duration of the response and recover effort, however long that might be.

"How are you feeling?" He asked as soon as he saw her become alert .

He was like a lot of firemen, fit, good looking, with piercing blue eyes and a disarming smile. No lonely Saturday nights for this guy, Shanice thought.

"Sleepy, a little woozy...and honestly, pretty hungry," Shanice said.

"Hungry is good Ms. Dixon, and we're going to get something into you besides this," Hagen said, referring to the IV tree next to the bed. A bag of saline solution was doing a slow drip into the tube that ran down into her. It was the first Shanice had noticed it and looked down to her right arm, rotating it to see a catheter stuck into the top of her hand and held in place with gauze tape. She also noted then, the adhesive electrodes from an EKG test stuck onto her chest and shoulders.

"You haven't been eating well from what I hear," the Lieutenant continued. "And you were running on empty. You were also very dehydrated. That's probably why you passed out. All your other vitals are good, although we did take some blood and are having the hospital run a panel on it just to be sure."

Shanice started to sit up then.

"Well, while we're waiting for that I have to get back to wo – "

Hagen's strong forearm, reached out across her chest, stopping her progress.

"No, you're not," he said forcefully. "Not until we get some good food into you and get the blood tests back. You're staying right where you're at."

"But I need to … "

"Uh, uh." The paramedic insisted.

"And that's an order," Shanice heard someone else call out from the other end of the room. She couldn't see beyond Hagen, but recognized it as the governor's authoritative voice. Then he stepped around, and faced her.

"I'm sorry governor," Shanice heard herself apologizing. "I don't know what happened."

Doyle held up a hand. "I know what happened Atlas," he quipped. "You're trying to carry the weight of the world on your shoulders."

"Not the world," Shanice corrected him wryly. "Just one big-assed state."

The three of them laughed, and it broke the tension somewhat.

"Whatever," Doyle laughed. "But you're going to stay here, get some rest and some food into you. And we're going to make sure your blood tests are good before we deem you fit to come back to work."

"But what if I—" Shanice started to speak, and Doyle cut her off.

"We need you Shanice," he said. "But we don't need you in the condition you were in; running yourself ragged. So, you either get some rest and some food in you, or I'm going to have to replace you. Is that what you want?"

"No," she said sheepishly, her eyes casting down and away from the two men. She wanted to cry, but wasn't about to break down in front of them. Finally, when she had recomposed herself, she looked back up to them.

"Alright, I'll follow orders. But can one of you do a favor for me?"

"Sure," they answered in unison.

"Actually, two favors, I guess. One, don't call my husband and tell him what happened."

Doyle nodded. "Alright. We haven't yet and we won't, if you want."

"Thanks," Shanice said.

"What's the other favor?" Doyle asked.

A few minutes later, Shanice had her nana's Bible open and propped up on her chest.

CHAPTER ONE HUNDRED-NINE

Thornwood, California
Friday, 2:41 p.m.
+ 1 day, 12 hours, 6 minutes

The current political climate had taken Officer Mack (Big Mack) Bradley of the Thornwood Police Department off of the street, but the current situation had thrust him right back onto it.

A relic from the by-gone days of 'kick ass and take names' policing, Bradley was more comfortable crossing the line of department policies and procedures, than he was he staying on the right side of it. He was currently on the third administrative leave of his twenty-plus year career for the questionable shooting of a suspected black gang member and had been going stir crazy when the patrol car unexpectantly pulled up to his house. To his surprise, the chief of the department climbed out of the passenger side of the car, carrying Bradley's confiscated gun and badge with him.

With so many officers going AWOL, and the situation growing more chaotic by the minute, the chief had no choice but to break with protocol and ask Big Mack Bradley to return to the force and pinch hit for him in the clutch.

"Don't fuck this up" he said begrudgingly to him as he handed him his gun and badge back.

He was informed that he was to help provide security at one of the local big box stores that was now designated as a hub to distribute essentials such as water, batteries, toilet paper, baby formula, and other sundry items to the residents of the low-income community.

Just as with Covid, only so many 'shoppers' were to be let in the store at one time. Not out of public health concerns, but as a way to control the crowds that lined up for blocks outside. Besides that, coveted items were being strictly rationed with hastily made signs taped up in the store that read: "1 case of baby formula per person," or "Toilet paper—4 rolls per person."

Along with five of his fellow officers, a handful of store employees, and a few national guard troops, there were three distinct jobs to be manned.

One was at the entrance, making sure only so many people were in the store at a time. The other was at the registers making sure no one tried to take more than their limit of certain items. And the third, and the one that "Big Mack" lobbied for, was to play rover in the store, monitoring some of the various locations where the most valuable goods were displayed to make sure order was being kept.

Mack loved it, and would rather be where the action was than performing what he considered to be, "usher" duties at the front of the store. This position, along with the badge on his chest and the gun on his side, made him feel invincible once again.

Already he had broken up a couple of fracases in the paper goods aisle and was now riding herd over the shelves of baby formula. It was an item that brought with it the highest emotions, as women would do just about anything to safeguard their child.

To Officer Mack Bradley, it was the best of all worlds as he was essentially getting paid to be entertained by the low-life welfare moms as they fought it out for a can of food for their illegitimate brats. On top of that, when California recovered and he finally got his day in court for gunning down the gang-banging scumbag, the board may just look favorably upon him for stepping up when the chips were down.

"That's mine bitch!" A woman yelled out suddenly in front of him.

Another woman evidently had reached into the cart of the woman and pulled out a pack of toilet paper from her cart. She was now clutching it to her ample bosom and was refusing to give it back.

"They ain't no mo!" the offending woman, protested back. "I needs it."

"Not as much as me, now, give me my shit back bitch!"

"I give you shit!" the other women said, dropping the package into her cart.

The two women began squaring off and Bradley instinctively reached for his nightstick.

He thought though that he would let them get into it for a bit; pulling hair and ripping clothes, before he stepped in.

They really were like savages he thought condescendingly. *Gorillas in the Mist*, he used to quip when he answered calls for domestic disputes in the mostly minority housing projects that blanketed the area.

The women were just reaching for each other when they suddenly stopped and looked his way. Mack thought it was odd, because they didn't seem like the type to be intimidated by his authority. And when they both smiled at him and moved off like old friends, he knew something was amiss. Then, he felt the cold steel of a gun barrel on the base of his neck.

"Raise yo fuckin hands, and turn around real slow mother-fucker!" a man's voice instructed.

Officer Mack Bradley did as he was told, turning around very slowly and hoping to reason with the perpetrator and talk him down. Maybe they just wanted some extra shit-paper or something.

The hope for a diplomatic solution quickly evaporated however when he saw who the perp was, as well as another half dozen guns pointed in his direction.

It was 'Daddy Five', the leader of the Assassin Crips Gang, and a home-boy of the man that Bradley had killed. The notorious gang leader slowly backed away, but kept his gun leveled at Mack's face, as did the other gang members.

"You kilt our fuckin homie man," Daddy Five said.

"He pulled a gun on me, and was gonna fucken kill me," Bradley stated matter of factly. "What was I supposed to do?"

"Walk the fuck away, and stay out of other people's shit—that's what!" Daddy Five a-said. "But you didn't. And now we gonna finish that homie's job."

Then, they all pulled their triggers.

CHAPTER ONE HUNDRED-TEN

Long Beach Airport
Long Beach, California
Friday, 2:47 p.m.
+ 1 day, 12 hours, 12 minutes

Even though he had heard from Marianne that the pilots were grounded when they landed eleven hours ago, in reality, Alan didn't know if the situation had changed. Mindful the revelation of his concerns might have affected Colton and the driver's decision to participate in his plot, he wisely kept it to himself.

He was therefore very relieved to see the Lear Jet still parked in its spot off of the tarmac when they pulled up. It had a GPU, or ground power unit, hooked up to it and the main cabin door was open with the stairs deployed. Whether or not the pilots were still there and available to fly was another thing.

He had played a pilot once in a movie about an aircraft being hijacked to finish off what the 9/11 plotters had started, but that was done in a simulator with a green screen. If the pilots weren't there, he couldn't fake his way out of this one.

"Right there," Alan pointed.

The driver drove the tractor up within fifty feet of the plane.

He got out of the tractor followed by Colton and the driver.

As the two of them moved over to the side door of the sleeper cab to start to get Marianne out, he held up his hand.

"Before you get her out, let me get this all set up."

They nodded and stood by as Alan approached the plane.

"Hello, hello," he called out through the aircraft's open doorway.

In a few seconds he heard some movement from inside and then one of the pilots stuck his head out of the opened door. His expression changed to one of disdain as he saw Alan standing on the tarmac.

Alan, held up his hand. "I know," he admitted. "I was an asshole to you guys. But we have a medical emergency. My assistant has been very seriously hurt in an accident, and we need to get her out of state and to a hospital. Everything here is shutting down. So please," he pleaded. "Don't do this as a favor to me, do it for her."

"I'm sorry Mr. Binder, we can't." the pilot said. "We're under FAA orders; TFR, Temporary Flight Restrictions. No flights in or out until they figure this out. Sorry."

"So, you won't do it for her?" Alan said, as much as he asked.

The pilot shook his head.

"Sorry."

"Then you'll do it for this," Alan Binder said as he pulled his jacket open to reveal the Glock.

CHAPTER ONE HUNDRED-ELEVEN

Johnson Foods Distribution Center
City of Industry, California
Friday, 2:58 p.m.
+ 1 day, 12 hours, 23 minutes

Carlene Fox felt as if she was drowning, or at least treading water with nowhere to go. She had been the manager on duty at the Johnson Markets 450,000 square foot distribution warehouse when the lights went out, and had been there ever since.

Following the protocols for dealing with an outage, she had her employees start up the on-site diesel generator and initiate a power transfer in order to keep some of the lights, the computer terminals, but most importantly, the giant refrigeration units, running.

That done, she immediately called their fuel supplier to get them into the queue for more diesel, and then began the task of trying to understand what had happened and just how long they would be without power for. Unfortunately, when it became apparent to her, her employees, their suppliers, and the contract workers, just how bad the situation was, the dominos really began to fall.

Half of her staff had now gone AWOL, and the truckers that did show up to deliver the goods to keep the shelves in the stores filled, fell to a trickle of what a normal day would be. To add to it, her replacement got word to her that she wouldn't be able to come in as her husband had cancer and they had to try to find a functioning hospital to administer his regular chemo treatments. That left her to try to keep things going until she either abandoned ship herself, or dropped from exhaustion.

The handful or so of truckers who had shown up and were able to get deliveries through the clogged roads, described dire scenes of chaos, as well as many of the Johnson's forty-one stores being ransacked and abandoned.

They also described feeling vulnerable out on the road. In one case—*thankfully so far*, a truck had been ambushed with a homemade spike strip, broken into, and looted. The driver, fortunately, followed the company's policy, surrendered his vehicle, and walked away unscathed. The government had promised national guard troops to offer protection as well as run escorts for the semis, but so far, that had yet to materialize.

Then, two hours ago, the order had come down to do something Carlene Fox had never imagined she would hear; switch off the giant refrigeration units and let over one-hundred-tons of refrigerated and frozen goods thaw out and go to waste.

At first, she couldn't believe her ears, but then after hearing the logic behind the decision, it all made sense. Even if some of their larger stores did have generators to keep the items cold or frozen, with diesel becoming increasingly hard to get, they couldn't count on being able to keep the product from spoiling.

On top of that, the end consumers, their customers, typically didn't have any way to keep the food frozen or even cold, so why keep protecting it and waste precious fuel? Of all the items that were being panic bought, or in many cases—outrightly taken, frozen or perishables were not one of them. "Cans were king," someone had quipped.

Now, walking through the wide aisles on 'the cold side' of the cavernous warehouse, she began to see - but mostly smell, the ramifications of pulling the plug on over four-hundred-fifty-tons of refrigeration capacity.

The putrid smells as some of the frozen dinners and vegetables spoiled were bad enough, but the pallets of stacked ice cream were even worse as they would collapse under their own weight without the contents being kept in a solid state. The fallen containers would split open, and then spill their now liquid contents all over the floor, creating not just a sticky mess, but an irresistible banquet for insects and vermin.

She had sent several employees to the warm side to bring back all of the ant spray and roach motels that they could find to try to set up a perimeter defense, but already the ants had penetrated their fortifications and were gleefully feasting away.

"You're living better than anyone these days," Carlene Fox said to the line of eusocial invaders.

CHAPTER ONE HUNDRED-TWELVE

Long Beach Airport
Long Beach, California
Friday, 3:01 p.m.
+ 1 day, 12 hours, 26 minutes

The pilot looked at the gun incredulously, and then to Alan's face, then back to the gun, and then finally to Alan's face again.

"You realize this is air piracy don't you Mr. Binder, and that you won't get away with it."

Alan said nothing, but reached his hand into his jacket and placed his hand on the grip of the gun. Very slowly he started to extract it from its holster.

Just then, the copilot poked his head around the corner, his eyes going wide at the scene unfolding in front of him.

"This is air pirac—"

"You already said that," Alan cut him off. He pulled the gun out of its holster and held it by his side. The three men were all staring at one another for a long moment.

Alan broke the silence.

"Now, get this damn plane ready to fly! She needs to get to the nearest hospital out of state, and we don't have much time."

CHAPTER ONE HUNDRED-THIRTEEN

Near Carmen City, California
Friday, 3:29 p.m.
+ 1 day, 12 hours, 54 minutes

After what had seemed like an eternity, Walter eventually determined there was no threat and resumed the deployment of his DIY Claymores. At one point during his vigil, he had found that he was zoning out from staring so intently at the terrain in front of him and could was longer be an effective observer.

To combat the visual fatigue, he resorted to an old Navy SEAL trick. At a certain point, using your central (focal) vision to watch for movement becomes ineffective. By turning your head slightly from your field of view, you utilize your peripheral vision, which is far superior at spotting movement.

It was now past three o'clock and he would have only another hour or so of daylight to work under. By now, only a third of the mines had been laid out, wired up and armed with trip wires. He was getting tired, frustrated, but worst of all, tempted, knowing that there were other, easier tasks that he could do in the bunker: finish cleaning his weapons of the cosmoline grease he had coated them in, checking the condition of his generator, and various other housekeeping chores.

But none of the other tasks were as important as setting up his perimeter defenses, and so he soldiered on.

Just as he was crouching down under a bush to attach the trip wire for one of the mines, a rabbit suddenly darted out and took off down the hill.

It caused him to jump and reach for his gun, but then he realized what it was and watched it scamper away, hoping all the while its hind feet didn't catch on a trip wire and set off one of his mines in the process.

When it didn't and he could no longer see it, he relaxed a bit. Taking satisfaction in the fact that at least there were small game that he could trap and survive on. Then he returned to his work, hoping to get at least a couple more bombs set up before dark.

CHAPTER ONE HUNDRED-FOURTEEN

Long Beach Airport,
Long Beach, California
Friday, 3:37 p.m.
+ 1 day, 13 hours, 2 minutes

Alan had relied on Colton's expertise who had suggested that Las Vegas was probably their best shot for a hospital, both timewise and capability.

After they were informed of the destination, it took some time for the pilots to calculate the fuel requirements and to get the plane fueled up. What complicated matters in what would have normally been a routine equation, was that fact that because of the TFR, the airspace might be monitored by fighter jets who could suspect them to be hostile and possibly shoot them down. Therefore, they would have to fly low to the ground, using the terrain following feature of the plane to avoid detection, but in the process, burning up more fuel.

With Alan monitoring the pilots to make sure they didn't try anything funny as they went through their pre-flight checks, Colton and the truck driver loaded Marianne into the main cabin of the plane on her bed.

"Never been in anything this nice," the truck driver said as he examined the sleek leather and wood interior of the plane. "Heck, never even flown on first class," he added with a laugh.

The pilots said nothing, but gave the driver a thin smile. Alan reached out to extend his hand to him.

"Again sir, thank you so much," he said. "You just may have helped save this woman's life."

"f'get it," the driver waved a hand dismissively. "Happy to help. You just get that little missus on her way now."

"You sure you don't want to come with us to get out of the state?" Alan offered. "We have room."

"Nah," the driver said. "Gotta stay with my rig. She ain't much, but she's my bread n butter."

At that, Colton extended a hand and he and the driver shook.

The truck driver disappeared out the door and down the stairs.

"Y'all have good flight," he called out as he walked away.

Completed with their checks, the pilot turned to Alan.

"You sure you don't want to reconsider?" He asked. "You will be arrested and in a hell of a lot of trouble that even your fame won't be able to get you out of."

"What fame?" Alan said darkly.

The pilot returned to his seat, the outside door was closed, and the engines began to spin up.

A few minutes later, they were down the runway and wheels up.

CHAPTER ONE HUNDRED-FIFTEEN

Cerritos, California
Friday, 3:40 p.m.
+ 1 day, 13 hours, 5 minutes

Barbara tended to Jake's bullet wound as well as to the bruises on her face and arms as well as her moms, which had taken the most abuse. Together, they looked like quite a rag-tag group, but appearances didn't matter at this point, only survival.

Freddie did indeed know where everything was in the house, and gave Barbara and Jake a tour. Together they collected all of the flashlights they could find, along with spare batteries, candles and matches.

They also checked out the garage which had two cars parked inside; Tom's new Corvette—which magically appeared as soon as the ink was dry on the divorce papers, and a two-year-old Range Rover that evidently belonged to his girlfriend.

With the water working, Barbara had insisted that Olivia take a shower. She had read somewhere that the victims of sexual assault often feel dirty, and that they had an intense desire to 'wash' their attacker off of them.

Olivia acquiesced, but only if her mom sat there in the bathroom with her. Barbara accommodated her and afterwards got her some new Kotex from a box under the bathroom sink. She hoped it would begin to heal the emotional wounds.

Next, she got Freddie into the tub with some of the toys he kept at the house. He would play for days in the water if she let him, but it was getting dark and she didn't need for him to fall down the stairs - flashlight or not, so, much to his chagrin, she cut it off after a half hour.

Her mom had gotten up from her nap after three hours and looked somewhat better, but her strength and ability to concentrate was slipping fast. Barbara knew that she only had a couple of days without dialysis before the situation became dire. She had to figure something out. Besides her renal issues, she also had heart issues, and the medication was back at their apartment. This day was looking nowhere like she had imagined it.

CHAPTER ONE HUNDRED-SIXTEEN

Over the Mojave National Preserve, California –
103 miles from Las Vegas
Friday, 5:22 p.m.
+ 1 day, 14 hours, 47 minutes

The flight over the expansive California desert was lower and slower than any of them had ever experienced.

The plane was using its terrain following feature and would rise and fall to maintain an altitude of just 1,000 feet off of the surface. It used a lot of fuel and the ride was bumpy due to the thermals that came off of the desert floor, but it was the only way to avoid radar. They also had to avoid taking the most straight-line route and had to, as the pilot quipped, 'thread the needle' between the twin threats of Fort Irwin Army Base and 29 Palms Marine Base, which would be under high alert due to the terrorist attack. This added almost 100 miles to the normally 230-mile trip, but it was the only way.

Back in the main cabin, Alan asked Colton, "How's she doing?"

"About the same, stable," the nurse replied. "But in these cases, stable is always good, especially since we are transporting her."

They hit another patch of turbulence just then. Alan and Colton, both felt themselves get a little lighter in their seats. Instinctively, they both reached over to Marianne's bed to stabilize it.

"Sorry," the pilot called from inside the cockpit. "We should be through the worst of this in a bit."

"Got it," Alan called back. "No worries, were doing okay back here." Although in reality his stomach was queasy, whether it was from the turbulence, the drugs from his recent heart attack, or a hangover, he couldn't say.

A few minutes later, the ride smoothed out and Alan took the opportunity to go forward. He knelt down in the small opening in the bulkhead separating the cockpit from the main cabin.

The pilot sensed his presence and turned to him. "You need to be in your seat Mr. Binder, and buckled in. We can't predict the next bump."

"I will," he promised. "I just wanted to say thanks again. And when we get on the ground, I want you to contact the authorities and tell them that I hijacked you and that you had no choice, okay? I don't want you guys to get in trouble."

The pilot and copilot shared a look, but said nothing. Alan couldn't tell if they had softened due to the fact that he was trying to help Marianne or what.

"Just wanted to tell you that," Alan repeated. "I'll move back to my—"

"Shit!" The copilot said just then. He pointed out the left side of the jet's windscreen.

Alan looked over at the same time as the pilot, and then they all saw it: an E-3F AWACS (Airborne Early Warning and Control) plane flying about five miles off in the distance.

"What is that, and what does that mean?" Alan asked, gesturing to the AWACS, but feeling he already knew the answer.

"It's an AWACS," the pilot sighed. "And it means were smoked."

"You mean, they can detect us?"

"They can find a needle in a haystack," the copilot chimed in.

"So, what do we do now?" Alan asked.

The pilot looked down at his instruments and, after noting their current location and remaining fuel, said, "We maintain our course and hope for the best."

"And what's 'the best?'" Alan asked.

The pilot turned to him and said, "That we don't get an air-to-air missile fired right up our ass."

CHAPTER ONE HUNDRED-SEVENTEEN

CAL-OES
Mather, California
Friday, 5:27 p.m.
+ 1 day, 14 hours, 52 minutes

The applause started with just a few handclaps, then grew quickly in measure and in volume. Pretty soon, the members of the SOC had risen up from the chairs at their work stations and were giving Shanice Dixon, their leader, a standing ovation. Doyle was there as well, clapping as loud as anyone.

Shanice was embarrassed by the unexpected show of affection. She waved her hands to quiet them down.

The applause subsided slowly, then finally ended.

"I'm humbled," Shanice said modestly. "Thank you so, so very much."

She paused and took a deep breath before continuing.

"And I've also learned a valuable lesson. And that lesson is that none of us in here are supermen, or superwomen. We need to do our jobs, yes, but not incapacitate ourselves in the process. We will do our constituents, our customers, our residents of this great state, no good if we are down from the count."

A few heads nodded and there was murmured agreement.

"From now on, I want you all to promise me that you will take care of yourselves, physically, but also mentally, emotionally, and if you are so given, spiritually as well. We owe that to the people of California, but we also owe it to ourselves and our families."

There was a small bit of applause following.

At that point, Shanice turned to a man who was standing behind and off to the side of her, motioning him to come forward.

"This is Dr. Simon Ayres, he's a clinical psychiatrist who specializes in trauma. I think we have all realized by this point that we are facing a challenge far larger than anything we ever dealt with. Larger than the largest wildfire, the earthquakes, even the pandemic.

And I ask you all, to please use his services as you see fit. There is no shame in this as we are all under tremendous pressure. Dr. Ayres has been given an office near the comm room, and will be embedded with us for as long as we need. Understood?"

Again, there were nods and the soft rumble of agreement.

"We also have several members of the clergy," Shanice continued. "Christian, Judaism, Islam and the Buddhist faith, that have agreed to be called upon as needed for spiritual counseling. We will also be working at setting up regular religious services for those of us who wish to attend. As many of you may know, I am a Christian, and I know that I will be missing my regular services as some of you may. We will be making any and all efforts to accommodate everyone's needs."

Many of those in the room stood in stunned silence. The thought of a mental health professional and clergy available to them was more than any of them had ever seen or experienced in their years of service. But then again, so was this event.

"Are there any questions?"

There were no questions, but several of them were smiling and nodding their heads. A few even clapped again.

"Thank you," Shanice said sincerely. "Thank you for being the best team any person could ever ask for, and for keeping the ship righted in my absence. And now…?"

She looked over to Doyle who nodded and tapped on his wristwatch.

"And now I have a meeting to attend. Thank you all again."

Shanice joined Doyle by his side and together they walked to the conference room.

"Touché," was all he said to her.

CHAPTER ONE HUNDRED-EIGHTEEN

Over the Mojave National Preserve, California –
82 miles from Las Vegas
Friday, 5:29 p.m.
+ 1 day, 14 hours, 54 minutes

They continued on in a tense silence for the next several minutes. Alan stayed forward as one; he didn't want to unnecessarily rattle Colton, who had to continue to monitor Marianne. And two; he wanted to see for himself what unfolded.

Just then he saw the pilot hold his hand up to the side of his headset.

Alan glanced down and saw a spare headset that was laying behind the copilot's seat. He picked it up and listened in.

...the United States Air Force. Civilian aircraft one, one, delta, tango on heading zero four three, you are in violation of a TFR. Identify yourself and state your purpose. Over."

At the same time that they heard the transmission, the copilot looked out the window and pointed. In the place of the AWACS plane they had spotted earlier, was an Air Force F-22 Raptor fighter jet about 200 feet off to the left side of the aircraft. An array of missiles was mounted underneath the plane's stubby wings.

"United States aircraft, this is one, one, delta, tango," the pilot responded. "Premier Air Services Corporation. We are on an emergency flight. We have a severely injured person who needs urgent medical attention and are the process of transferring her to a hospital in Las Vegas. Over."

"Understood," the fighter pilot responded. "Maintain current speed and heading, and standby for instructions. Over."

The pilot, copilot and Alan all exchanged worried looks. Alan turned away briefly to see how Colton and Marianne were doing in the main cabin. The nurse was thankfully turned away and was focused on the readouts of the monitors hooked to Marianne.

The pilot, pushed a button on his headset and said to the copilot, "He's probably going to instruct us to land at the next available airport. Start checking our options."

"Roger," the copilot said and turned to the map data to see where they could land.

The F-22 pilot's voice came back on in their headsets.

"One, one, delta, tango, we do not have confirmation of a mercy flight with your tail numbers, did you file a flight plan? Over."

"Negative sir. There wasn't time. Over."

"Stand by one. Over."

"Why does he keep having us standby?" Alan asked.

"Because he has to go up the chain. He can't make the decisions himself."

"Well, that's kind of—" Alan started to say, but was cut off by the fighter jet pilot's voice in his headset.

"One, one, delta, tango, you are instructed to alter course and land immediately at Lima-India-Delta-Oscar-Lima-seven. Over."

"Roger, copy Oscar-Lima-seven. Over," the pilot said

Alan, confused by all the pilot jargon, asked, "What's that? All that stuff you said?"

"That's the identifier for the airport he wants us to land at," the copilot said. "Which is in Jean, Nevada."

"Jean!" Alan yelled, gesturing to the main cabin. "We need to get her to Vegas! Tell him we have to get there or she dies."

"I'm not in charge here!" the pilot yelled back at him. "He is" He jerked an angry thumb at the heavily armed jet fighter just off their wing. "And if we don't do what he tells us to, we're going to get shot down—and *everyone* is going to die!"

Alan was fuming. He jerked off his headset and turned back to the main cabin.

"Colton," he yelled out. "Is there a hospital in Jean, Nevada?"

Colton thought about it for a moment and then shook his head.

Alan turned back toward the cockpit. Damn it, he thought. This isn't about getting to a fucking party, or about buying candles, or about getting another bullshit role—this is about saving her life and I own this! And if I can't save her...

He put his headset back on and caught the tail end of the instructions from the fighter pilot

"...stay on your port wing and follow you in—"

"Alan reached into his jacket pocket and pulled out his gun. He leaned forward into the cabin, put it up to the pilot's forehead and angled it so the pilot in the fighter jet could see it.

"What the fu—" The pilot started to say, but then Alan pressed the transmit button on his headset cord.

"US Airforce plane, this is the hijacker of this mercy flight. Look at me!"

Through the Lear Jet's windscreen, Alan saw the pilot of the F-22 turn his helmeted head toward them. He wanted him to see that he meant business.

"And I have forced this aircraft at gunpoint to help me save this patient's life," he continued. "And if you do not allow us to continue on the Las Vegas then not only will this patient die, but I will shoot the pilot and the copilot and allow this plane to auger into the ground. And you will have the blood of five people's lives on your hands! Now is that what you want to be remembered for? Over!"

There was a long pause and then finally the jet fighter responded with a halting, *"Stand by one. Over."*

CHAPTER ONE HUNDRED-NINETEEN

Cerritos, California
Friday, 5:50 p.m.
+ 1 day, 15 hours, 15 minutes

After cooking a couple of steaks on the BBQ they found thawing in the freezer, Barbara got her mom settled in the downstairs master bedroom along with Olivia.

The bedroom had once been hers and Tom's and she knew she wouldn't feel right sleeping in a room where her ex and his new girlfriend had sex.

She decided she would sleep upstairs with Freddie, who was rapidly running out of steam. But first she wanted to have an uninterrupted conversation with Jake, and so she got Freddie hustled off to his upstairs bedroom, where, after the excitement of the day, was soon fast asleep.

On a "recon mission" with Freddie, Jake and he had discovered a bunch of solar powered lights in the backyard and brought them inside. They put one in each of the bedrooms as night-lights and then set the remainder along the staircase in the event that one of them had to come downstairs during the night. As soon as the sun set and the house became dark, the lights started coming on one by one. It wasn't much light, but it would have to do. Barbara stepped past them gingerly as she came down the steps.

Jake was standing in the living room, peering out the curtain and watching the street. One of the handguns was in his hand and draped at his side, the other was still tucked in his waistband. His left arm where the bullet grazed him had been cleaned up, disinfected and had a small bandage on it. Jake insisted that he was fine and had no need to go to a hospital.

Barbara peeked from around him and stared out onto the street. Other than the glow from candles or flashlights inside the houses, there were few signs of life. The street lights were out and you didn't see the cozy flicker of TV sets pulsing through the curtains.

Occasionally though, the sound of gun fire could be heard. Some, too close for comfort.

"It's like an empty movie set, huh?" Barbara observed. "Buildings, but no life."

Jake nodded. "None that wants to venture out at least."

A lit candle burned on the coffee table along with one of the few working flashlights they had found. Barbara made her way over to the couch next to the table and took a seat.

"Why don't you sit?" She said to Jake.

He said nothing and continued staring out.

"Please," Barbara said. "I'd like to talk."

He sighed and then slowly returned the curtain to its resting spot. He moved away from the window and sat down on the far end of the couch from her. He set the pistol down on the coffee table next to his prized boom-box, The barrel of the gun was thoughtfully pointed away from Barbara.

"I want to thank you again," she said. "For doing what you did. You saved my daughter, and all of us really. I owe you so much. It could have been so much worse."

Jake shrugged.

"So, your name is Jake," Barbara continued, hoping to get some sort of dialogue going. "That's a nice name."

"Thanks."

"Where are you from?" she asked, genuinely interested.

"Oklahoma originally," he said. "But we moved around a lot. My dad was in the military."

"And you were too, right?" Barbara added.

"Yeah. Up until a couple of years ago."

He turned and stared at her then; a pain filled stare. "And I don't talk about it," he said firmly.

"That's fine," she assured him.

Either to stay informed, or to avoid further conversation, Jake switched on his radio and set the volume down low. Together they listened. It was pretty much the same dribble.

"...*state and federal government working to normalize things and to bring about swift repairs to the grid. Supply chains will soon be back on line with big box stores such as Costco and Sam's Club serving as distribution centers. Strict rationing will be imposed to insure that—*"

Then, there was a knock at the front door.

CHAPTER ONE HUNDRED-TWENTY

McCarran Airport
Las Vegas, Nevada
Friday, 6:03 p.m.
+ 1 day, 15 hours, 28 minutes

The tarmac at McCarran Airport in Las Vegas was ready for them when they arrived. In addition to the ambulance, they had requested to transport Colton and Marianne to the hospital, several fire trucks were on the scene, along with a contingent of police cars including a BearCat G3 assault vehicle containing a SWAT unit.

On the flight inbound, Alan was adamant that the pilots and Colton say that they were forced against their will to comply and that this was not their idea.

"Just tell them the truth," he insisted. "Don't worry about what happens to me."

The pilots begrudgingly agreed, but reminded Alan that he would be facing air piracy charges, which could put him away for a long time.

"That doesn't matter to me any longer," Alan Binder said.

Colton tried to push back and wanted to say that he was part of the conspiracy so that Alan would not have kidnapping added to his charges. But the actor was insistent that Colton didn't need to lose his nursing license and face criminal charges himself.

"You're too important right now Colton," Alan told him. "People need you. I'm just an actor. I'm expendable."

"And a good one," Colton smiled.

"I thought I didn't convince you back there in the hospital that I would really shoot you if you didn't go along with me?" Alan said, surprised.

"Maybe so, but you convinced the fighter pilot that you were serious. And in the end, that's the only person that really mattered."

As they were on approach the F-22 pilot considerately reminded the Lear jet pilots to lower their landing gear. He had heard plenty of stories of other planes being escorted down by military jets and in the stress of it all, forgetting to lower their gear.

When he saw the gear go down, the F-22 peeled off.

"One, one, delta, tango, your wing is clear. Good luck gentlemen. Over and out."

When they finally rolled up to a stop 100 feet or so from the emergency vehicles, they were instructed to come out one at a time, with their hands up and fingers laced behind their heads.

Colton, went first, followed by Alan and then finally the pilots.

After they were deplaned, they were told to separate, turn around, and drop to their knees.

They all complied, and one by one were searched for weapons or bombs.

"Officer, I'm the hijacker, and my weapon is inside the plane on the seat closest to the door," Alan told the policeman who was searching him. "The clip is removed, and there are no bullets in the chamber."

The officer said nothing and only grunted, which Alan could take either way.

After being searched and cuffed, a group of SWAT officers charged up and surrounded the plane. Before any of them went up and into the plane's fuselage, a bomb-sniffing police dog climbed up into the cabin and did a search. Only when he came back without indicating that anything was awry, did the officers themselves enter the plane. One of them poked his head back out a few moments later and called out.

"Just like they said, female patient, on a gurney with monitors tied to her."

At that, two paramedics were given the go-ahead to enter the plane to begin extricating her.

"Officer," Alan said, getting the policeman's attention and jerking his head towards Colton, "That man there is the nurse that I also kidnapped. Please let him go to the hospital with the paramedics so he can update them on her injuries and condition."

The officer listened and then without saying anything, walked off to speak to someone behind Alan's back. A few minutes later, the same officer came up to the man guarding Colton and said a few words to him. The officer leaned down, helped him to his feet, but didn't remove the cuffs.

Colton was led away by the officer and the two of them intercepted the paramedics just as they got Marianne's gurney onto the apron. Colton started filling them in on her situation as they wheeled it away to the waiting ambulance.

From behind him, Alan heard Colton's voice call out. "I'll take care of her Mr. Binder. She'll be fine."

A sergeant approached Alan and helped him up to his feet. His expression changed as he now had a better look at him.

"You're Mr. Alan Binder," he said, as much as asked. "The actor, Alan Binder."

"Yes sir," Alan responded.

The sergeant nodded and, smiling said. "I thought so." Then, he continued with the bad news.

"Well, Mr. Binder" he sighed, "These are obviously very unique times, but you understand I'm still going to have to place you under arrest for the crime of air piracy."

"I do," Alan said. "And I understand."

The sergeant nodded and began reading the charges against Alan, along with his Miranda rights.

The actor turned hijacker barely heard the sergeant's recitation as the charges were read to him.

All Alan Binder cared about was that someone recognized him.

CHAPTER ONE HUNDRED-TWENTY-ONE

Cerritos, California
Friday, 6:05 p.m.
+ 1 day, 15 hours, 30 minutes

Instantly, Jake was alert. He switched off the radio, picked up the pistol, and stood up.

"Did you tell anyone you were here?" He asked in a low voice.

"No," Barbara said emphatically, keeping her voice low as well. "And my ex wouldn't know. I haven't even tried to contact him. I've had too many other things to deal with. Besides, he's stuck in Hawaii until they allow commercial flights again."

"Right," he said.

Another knock. Then a muffled voice from the other side of the door. "Tom? Samantha? Are you guys' home?"

Jake looked at Barbara, who explained. "It's one of the neighbors, Bob." She whispered. "He lives across the street."

"Tom? Can you help me? We're running out of food."

Barbara started to move to the door to answer it, but Jake reached out and stopped her.

"We're on our own here," he says.

"But if he needs food—"

"Then it's food out of your mouth, as well as your mom, Freddie, and Olivia. Do you want that?"

Another knock, more forceful, more of a pounding.

"I know someone is in there," Bob said. "And we need help. I smelled the bar-b-que earlier."

"He's not going away," Barbara said. "I have to answer it."

Jake looked at the door then back to her.

"Okay, but get rid of him. Tell him we have no food to spare."

He grabbed the flashlight out of her hand and set it back down on the coffee table.

"Here, take this."

He pulled out the pistol that had been tucked into his waistband and tried to hand it to her.

Barbara recoiled. "I–I can't take that!" she said incredulously.

"Yes, you can," Jake insisted. "And you will. Everything has changed now."

"I–I don't even know how to use a gun."

More pounding.

"Damn it, Tom! My family needs help!" Bob screamed. "And I'll break this door down if I have to!"

Jake pushed the gun into her hand and wrapped her fingers around the grip. She looked at him, terrified.

"You won't have to use it. Just keep it by your side. He'll see it and know that you mean business. I'll be right behind the door."

Barbara nodded and swallowed hard.

She walked toward the front door and slowly undid the bolt. She opened the door only enough to see out.

It was dark on the porch, but the moon provided just enough illumination to make out Bob's outline and features.

"Tom?" Bob said, then caught himself when he saw her.

"Barbara? Barbara, is that you?"

"Yes."

Baffled, Bob stammered a bit. "Ugh, you and Tom aren't - "

"No," Barbara said firmly. "He and his girlfriend are in Hawaii and won't be back. We needed a place to stay."

"Well, um, it's great to see you again."

Barbara knew he was just placating her to try to soften her up, which was his nature. Bob and his family always had the best of everything, and didn't mind subtly reminding everyone. Barbara and Tom had always felt that the family lived beyond their means, and maybe this was proof of it. They had a fancy designer kitchen, but ate out all the time or had food delivered. They probably had nothing in their refrigerator or pantry.

"Yes, it is," Barbara said evenly. "And I'm sorry; but we don't have any food to share," she added.

"No wait a minute Barb, I know that – "

Barbara, opened the door wider so that the pistol was visible in her hand.

"I said, no," she repeated, more stridently.

Bob took a step forward towards the threshold, he was going to push through if he had to.

316

Behind the door, Jake sensed what was going on and was ready to spring into action. He didn't have to.

"I said NO!" Barbara yelled and raised the pistol up, pointing it at Bob's face.

Instantly, he halted in his tracks and raised his hands. He began backing away.

"All right," he said. "All right…We're just…hungry, the kids, and Sarah."

"So are we," Barbara countered.

Then, her own voice sounding foreign to her, she commanded, "Now go!"

Bob slowly backed down the front steps one at a time. Only when he was on the walkway did he feel safe enough to lower his hands – and to take a cheap shot.

"You selfish fucking bitch!" He hissed. "Tom was smart to dump you. You got everything you deserved!"

Barbara stepped back and slammed the door so hard the front of the house shook.

Then she locked the door, dropped the gun, and threw up.

CHAPTER ONE HUNDRED-TWENTY-TWO

Long Beach, California
Friday, 6:21 p.m.
+ 1 day, 15 hours, 46 minutes

Paul Handle hated the prick across the street from him.

For the two decades he had lived in the neighborhood, Ross O'Leary, or "Bucky" as he liked to be called, loved to lord over his neighbors about how his family had been the first to settle here when the subdivision was built in the 1940's. To hear "Bucky" tell it, you'd think he had some sort of a God-Given right to dictate to others on the block how their lawns should be mowed, when they should put out their trashcans, and where they should park their cars.

Paul Handle wouldn't have any of it, and now he was going to get back at that pompous ass. His car was nearly out of gas, and he figured old Bucky was the just the guy who should supply it to him.

Sitting in his favorite chair in his living room, Handle stared out into the pitch blackness of the neighborhood watching the O'Leary house for any signs of candles or flashlights beams bouncing about inside. After he hadn't seen any activity for about an hour, he extinguished his cigarette, moved through his garage and grabbed his two five-gallon jerry gas cans and a length of gas hose.

Silently, he stepped out the side door of his garage, through the gate and out onto the street, pausing a bit to let his eyes adjust to the limited light from the stars above. A veteran of combat in the jungles of Vietnam, the seventy-one-year-old had operated under far worse conditions on night patrols through the triple canopy searching for VC and NVA. Here, he was only stealing a little bit of gas. Piece of cake.

He stepped across the street and to Bucky's pickup truck. Mrs. O'Leary's car was kept in the garage, leaving the other parking space open for her husband to fawn over with his model train set-up, a pastime Handle had always considered silly and childish.

He pulled open the fuel door on the truck, unscrewed the cap and snaked the hose down through the opening until it bottomed out in the tank. With the caps unscrewed from his jerry cans, he put the free end of the hose into his mouth and began sucking, feeling the resistance of the fuel as it traveled upward against gravity.

When he felt the weight of the hose shift in his hand, he quickly transferred it into the opening of one of his cans and let it flow.

He heard a splash of fuel hit the bottom of the metal can, but then the sound ceased just a few moments later; he hadn't gotten enough flow going.

"Crap!" he muttered under his breath.

He reinserted the end of the hose into his mouth and tried again, this time pulling even harder. He was still sucking when the fuel suddenly rushed out the end of the hose and into his mouth, and he inadvertently inhaled the liquid deep into his lungs.

An irritant, the gasoline instantly began blocking oxygen from being absorbed into the small blood vessels of his lungs. He began to choke and cough. His lungs, already damaged from a lifetime of smoking, were unable to absorb any of the precious O^2.

He dropped the end of the hose onto the ground and tried to stand up, thinking somehow that he would be able to breathe better this way.

He wasn't and he was quickly getting dizzy, his eyes watering. He gasped for breath, staggering about in the growing pool of gasoline at his feet. What shallow breaths he could take in were filled with the fumes from the gasoline.

He struggled to keep his balance, his strength leaving him with every second that passed. The gasoline in the meantime, was dissolving the asphalt coating on the street and making it slick.

Paul Handle's world began to spin, and darkness closed in on his vision. His feet slipped on the slick gasoline/asphalt pool and he fell forward, his head slamming onto the top rail of Bucky's pickup bed. He crumpled to the ground and lost consciousness, never to regain it.

CHAPTER ONE HUNDRED-TWENTY-THREE

Cerritos, California
Friday, 6:23 p.m.
+ 1 day, 15 hours, 48 minutes

After cleaning up Barbara's vomit, they extinguished the candles and moved to the back patio, using the flashlight they shared as minimally as possible. The moon and the abundance of stars provided just enough light to move about. They sat on patio furniture set around a gas fire pit. Even though Jake had already checked it for propane, they didn't light it.

"You did good back there," Jake said.

Barbara chuckled quietly, "Yeah, right up until the point when I threw up."

"Most guys in battle the first time do the same thing," he reassured her. "Or they piss or shit on themselves; you were lucky."

"I guess so," Barbara said and laughed, too loud for Jake's comfort. He put his finger up to his mouth and indicated to her to keep her voice low.

"We need to be quiet," he said. "The less people know we're here, the better."

Barbara nodded and they were both quiet for a bit. Finally, Jake broke it, his voice barley above a whisper.

"You know," he said. "The next time, they may not knock, or they may be bring their own guns."

Barbara looked at him, she knew he was right.

"It sounds like you've seen this before."

In the muted darkness she saw his head nod. He stared at the cold fire-pit.

"In Iraq. I was there in the first invasion force. We—or rather the Air Force—would take out the electrical grid before we even got there. They used carbon fiber threads or something, I think. Anyway, it totally knocked everything out so we could go in. But it also decimated the civilian population."

Barbara nodded and let him continue; if he was going to spill it about his military service, she wasn't going to distract him.

"Everyone thinks that people only die in a war from bombs or bullets," he went on. "But a lot of them, especially the civilians, die from disease, starvation, dehydration, or exposure."

Barbara took in a big breath of air and exhaled heavily. It sounded like he might be describing their fate.

Then Jake dropped the bombshell.

"We have to leave," he said flatly. "We have to get out of the state."

"No," she said. "We can't leave. They'll fix it, the government will—"

He cut her off. "The government is completely overwhelmed right now. You can read between the lines of what they are saying. Help is on the way, be patient, be patient. That's all they can say. They can't tell us the truth. Otherwise, it would make matters even worse."

"But – "

"But nothing," Jake insisted. "I've seen countries fall apart. I was there. Besides getting your mom into a dialysis clinic, you saw what happened to your store yesterday. That's going to happen everywhere, if it hasn't already. And the trucks won't be able to get through to replenish the shelves because they can't get fuel. And people won't have any money because all the ATMs are down. Then all the fuel will run out on the generators that are keeping the water running, and the sewage pumped. It's going to be mass panic. I've seen it before."

Jake jerked his thumb toward the front of the house. "Neighbor on neighbor. If you - or more importantly, your family, are hungry or sick, or dying of thirst, you'll do want ever it takes to get what you need. It's human nature. I've seen people over in the Sand Box killed over a bottle of water."

Barbara wrapped her arms tightly around her chest. She suddenly felt very cold.

She nodded mutely and looked down to the fire pit. She hated to admit it, but deep down she knew he was right. She imagined the government trying to handle the situation, but it was just too overwhelming. An entire state? Forty-million people? What could they do?

"The civilians in Iraq and Afghanistan are way tougher than people here," Jake continued. "They're used to strife and suffering. For lots of them; it's all they've ever known in their lives. Here, it's a different story. We're so—"

"Soft?" Barbara offered, turning to face him.

"Exactly. We're so much more reliant on technology, efficient supply chains, safe food, clean water and sanitation. And the instant people don't have it, they push the panic button."

"Like they already have," Barbara added.

"Exactly, but that was just from a loss of being able to use their phones, gas their car or use their debit card at the grocery store. Those are just the luxuries in life we enjoy, wait till it's the *necessities*."

Jake took a break and paused, taking a deep breath.

"And when that happens," he continued. "I won't be able to protect you and your family against everything and everyone. I already checked the clips in the guns, between the two we only have fifteen shots left. That's not much against an angry armed mob."

She nodded, lost in her thoughts and thinking of how her life had been turned upside down in just the past forty-eight hours. Two days ago, she was content to provide a good life to her mom and kids, now she was struggling *just to keep them alive*.

Jake was silent and let her digest it all. He knew that it was a tough thing for anyone to take; leaving behind the only life they knew. But he also knew it was the only chance for survival.

Barbara looked up after a long while and turned to him.

"When?" Was all she said.

CHAPTER ONE HUNDRED-TWENTY-FOUR

Near Carmen City, California
Friday 7:05 p.m.
+ 1 day, 16 hours, 30 minutes

Refreshed after cleaning up and having an MRE for dinner, Walter settled in and switched on his shortwave radio, anxious to get more news about the fight for freedom. Instead, all he could hear was static. Even on some of the higher-powered channels he listened to, it was the same hiss of dead air. Then he remembered that in his haste to finish with the Claymores he had forgotten to re-string his wire antenna over the tree.

As tired as he was, he knew he needed the fresh intel from his sources about troop movements, convoys, soft targets to hit, etc. and so he donned his NVG's once again, grabbed his equipment and his weapon and headed back out.

The air had cooled considerably by now and he felt chilled from his sweat as he trudged up the hill, the terrain a ghostly pale green on the twin displays of his goggles.

Finally, he reached the designated tree, placed the ball and antenna wire in the pouch of his slingshot, pulled and released. Instead of flying over the tree though, his shot went low and ended up going into the tree.

"Shit," he muttered quietly to himself and set to work to free the ball and wire from within the tree.

Unfortunately, the ball was stuck in the branches of the tree and had not fallen through to the ground where he could detach the wire, pull it back through and then reattach it and try again.

His efforts took a considerable amount of time and energy and he had to yank the wire this way and that to get it loose. He had an extra wire and ball in the bunker that he could have used, but he didn't want to waste time going back down the hill to get them.

Finally, the apparatus broke free and he was able to line it up once again and fire. This time, with success.

He quickly connected the wire to the underground cable leading back to the bunker and was just about to head down when he stopped suddenly and looked up toward the sky.

There it was, a satellite, directly overhead and slowly making its way across the sky. By its path, Walter could see that it would fly right over him where he stood on the hill.

"You're watching me aren't you, you sons of bitches."

CHAPTER ONE HUNDRED-TWENTY-FIVE

CAL-OES
Mather, California
Friday, 7:25 p.m.
+ 1 day, 16 hours, 50 minutes

"Are you ready for some good news?"

The question came from Steve Phillips, one of the leads on the transformer replacement team. He was standing there alongside the rep from DOE.

Shanice exhaled a big breath and then quipped, "Well, that's a silly question. Of course. What have you got?"

Phillips spoke up. "Well, it seems as if two of the HPTs at the Metcalf sub-station in Coyote only have a few windings that were cut—*and* they can be repaired on site."

"Great!" Shanice practically yelled. She wanted to hug the two men, but knew she needed to maintain her professionalism.

"We need to bring in a coppersmith," the DOE rep said. "To re-fuse the windings, but engineering has assured us that they will work."

"A coppersmith?" Shanice repeated, surprised. "I didn't even know there was such a thing."

"Yep. Believe it or not, and a few are still around. Usually, to make jewelry of other such things," DOE explained. "But they're also found at those historical theme parks doing demonstrations of how things worked 'in the old days.' This particular one is out of Williamsburg, Virginia...supposedly, he's the best in the country and..."

The DOE rep looked at his watch, "...is in the air on a military jet enroute as we speak."

"Excellent work guys," Shanice said, shaking their hands profusely.

"And it still needs to be tested," Phillips said. "We have a testing unit in Reno, Nevada now and can have it airlifted first thing tomorrow. It's a large, ungainly thing and needs a Sky-Crane to move it, but the Army National guard one-fifty-second has one available and it will be in the air tomorrow at first light."

"Great!" Shanice heard herself repeating, then asked. "Is the governor informed?"

The two men turned to each other and smiled, before turning back to her.

"No, Ms. Dixon," Steve Phillips said. "We thought you should have the honors."

This time she did hug them.

CHAPTER ONE HUNDRED-TWENTY-SIX

Cerritos, California
Friday, 8:29 p.m.
+ 1 day, 17 hours, 54 minutes

For the next half hour or so, Barbara and Jake went through their plan. What they needed to bring, when they would leave, what route, etcetera. The big question mark was how they would get there. Barbara's car was totaled and when they checked the garage earlier and spotted Tom's Corvette and the Range Rover, they didn't see any keys in the ignition.

They moved back into the house and tried to check all of the spots they could imagine where the keys might be hidden, including places Barbara and Tom would use when they were still married.

The going was tough though, especially trying to use the flashlight to help them search. Already the batteries were running low and they only had four cells left.

Finally, Jake held up his hand to halt their quest.

"This is no good," he said. "We're stumbling around here and using up the little battery life we have left. We should wait until the sun comes up."

"But what if we can't find the keys?" Barbara asked.

"Then we'll find another car, steal one if we have to. Maybe we can make a deal with your neighbor; all of our food for one of his cars?"

Barbara nodded, not able to fathom what they were discussing; stealing a car or even having to make a deal with that jerk, Bob. But if anything, Jake was a survivor and knew what they had to do.

Jake stopped just then and pondered something.

"Do you think if your ex hid the keys in the house, Freddie would know where they might be?"

Barbara considered it. "He might, he certainly has his fingers on everything else. Should I get him up?"

"No. Let him sleep. It's been a long day. In fact, you should get some rest too."

"What about you?" Barbara asked. "You need to sleep too."

"I'm alright," Jake said. "I need to stay on watch."

"But you can't just keep going," Barbara protested. "You're human too."

"Maybe so," Jake said. "But in battle, we would go sometimes for days without sleep. You just had to do it, and I'm trained for it."

"And that's what this is, isn't it?" Barbara said. "This is a battle."

"Yeah," Jake said ominously. "The first battle in an even longer war."

CHAPTER ONE HUNDRED-TWENTY-SEVEN

Near Carmen City, California
Friday, 10:14 p.m.
+ 1 day, 19 hours, 39 minutes

The soft hiss of radio silence filled the bus, which had seemed to grow smaller with each passing moment, every frequency he tried, every retune he attempted. He could hear none of his fellow patriots. What did that mean?

He didn't want to think about it, but before he assumed the worst, he had to be methodical and check out his equipment.

He rebooted the device three times; no change.

Even though the rechargeable batteries in the unit tested good, they still could not be ruled out as the culprit and so he tried changing them out to a fresh set. Still nothing.

The antenna connections were checked and rechecked. He even trekked twice back up onto the hill to clean and reattach the connections there.

Silence.

Finally, he took a chance and unplugged the unit, opened it up and peered inside. He knew nothing about electronics, but maybe something obvious would jump out at him. It didn't.

Finally, he put the unit back together, hooked up the charge cable to it to keep the batteries fresh and left it on. Maybe his bunker would soon be filled with the familiar sound of Patriot Man instructing them on what to do next.

He laid down on his bunk, trying to sleep, but even as exhausted as he was it was difficult.

Maybe, Walter Gronsky thought with dread, he would never hear his leader's voice again.

Premature failures of the Tecsun PL-660 PLL World Band Receiver
Source: https://www.eham.net/reviews/view-
product?id=9935&page=2&per-page=10

PART IV:
HOUSE OF CARDS

CHAPTER ONE HUNDRED-TWENTY-EIGHT

Near Carmen City, California
Saturday, 3:40 a.m.
+ 2 days, 1 hour, 5 minutes

There was a detonation, an explosion that even through the walls of the bus and the dirt blanketing it, Walter could hear.

Instantly he was awake and alert. Following his training, he rolled out of bed and hit the floor, his weapon already in his hands.

In the pitch blackness and feeling with his hands under his cot, he located and then donned NVG's and switched them on. To maintain a low profile, he rolled onto his belly and crawled on the floor to the front of the bus.

Where the front windows of the bus had once been, he had welded steel plates. But within the plate on the passenger's side, he had cut out a narrow slit to use as a gun port, similar to those on tanks and APCs. The slit was covered by another steel plate with hinges at the bottom, and latches on the top to keep it closed when not in use.

Listening first for muffled footsteps or other sounds, Walter leaned off to the side and very slowly and quietly, unlatched and lowered the gun port cover.

He waited a few minutes and when no bullets or RPG rounds came screaming in, he slowly moved toward the opening and peered out.

Through the imagining of the low light device, he scanned the area, spotting no telltale silhouettes or movement. But the military had worked hard to develop special digital camo that hampered the effectiveness of NVG's and so he crawled back down the floor of the bus, grabbed his Handheld Thermal Monocular, as well as one of his assault rifles outfitted with a silencer and a night vision scope.

He carefully crawled back up to the front of the bus, and retook his position, scanning the terrain with the thermal imaging device hoping to pick up the heat signature of a body in the bush. In the background, he could still hear the soft hiss of radio silence, filling the bunker like gentle waves.

The sound did little to sooth his frayed nerves, and instead made him come to grips with some grim possibilities.

One: Patriot Man had been detected, captured, and possibly killed.

Or worse yet; he had been tortured, and had given up the locations of some of his followers. Followers just like Walter Gronsky.

CHAPTER ONE HUNDRED-TWENTY-NINE

Gapton, California,
Saturday, 4:18 a.m.
+ 2 days, 1 hour, 43 minutes

After the backup generator powering the municipal water pump had failed in the first hours after the attack, the Gapton Public Works Department tried calling the company that sold them the unit to request an emergency repair. Their repeated calls went to voicemail, and were never returned.

With the town's overhead storage tank running dangerously low, they next turned to the local emergency operations center to request a new gen set be delivered and installed. This was pushed up the chain to the regional ops center, to CAL-OES, and then finally, to the Army's 249 Engineering Battalion. Gapton was one of the first locations in the queue to be promised a replacement gen-set.

Now, in the inky blackness of the pre-dawn hours, the quaint hamlet looked more like a ghost town or an abandoned movie set than a cozy little community that boasted, *"The Friendliest Town in California."*

Staff Sgt. Lewis Jordon drove the M-97 Cargo Truck through the empty streets with only the vehicle's high beam headlights to illuminate the way. Next to him in the passenger seat was Specialist Matt Salas. They were part of the 249th's PRT (Planning and Response Team).

"Pretty friggen dark," Jordon said.

"Empty too," Salas added. "Everybody's just hunkered down, I guess."

"Or gone."

The two men turned to each other in the dark confines of the truck's cab and shared a look. They had seen firsthand the endless lines of cars heading out of California as they drove in overnight from their post in New Mexico.

"Where are we supposed to meet this guy?" Jordon asked.

Salas consulted his "dagger," a colloquial term for the handheld GPS unit used by the military.

"Twelve-eleven Bower Street. That's it up ahead. Turn right."

Jordon swung the vehicle wide to the left to navigate the sharp turn and a few moments later they had rolled up to the offices and maintenance yard for the Gapton Public Works Department. An 8-ft high chain link fence with barbed wire surrounded the facility on all sides along with a large sliding gate located on the street side. The gate was closed and secured with a thick chain and beefy padlock.

They pulled up to the gate, and Jordon set the brake and put the truck into neutral as the two men climbed out of the cab. Salas pulled out the sat phone assigned to them and punched a number on the speed dial.

"What's this guy's name we're supposed to meet?" Jordon asked as the call started to go through.

"Bob...something. Bob Evans—I think. He's the head of public works, and knows where the well pumps are located."

The phone rang, which meant a nearby cell tower still had enough juice to put the call through. According to plan, Evans would have had his work cell number tied into the priority system and as long as he kept it charged and there was a working cell tower nearby, they should be able to communicate with him.

But, after twenty or so rings there was no answer or even a voicemail recording.

"What now?" Salas asked, after terminating the call.

"Try again in about five." Jordon shrugged.

"Okay, I've got to take a leak anyway," Salas said, as he handed the sat off to Jordon, before disappearing into the darkness to relieve himself.

By the time he returned, the Staff Sgt. was trying to make contact again, and with the same results. Next, he tried the city's emergency operations center; no answer.

"I'm calling command," he said finally.

Thirty minutes later, they were on the road again, after being ordered to move on to the next location in the queue. Gapton would never receive its generator.

CHAPTER ONE HUNDRED-THIRTY

Cerritos, California
Saturday, 6:22 a.m.
+ 2 days, 3 hours, 47 minutes

If Barbara Williams slept at all, it was in spurts and very floaty. She had just so much to think about: Olivia being sexually assaulted, leaving the life she knew, her mom's condition, did Tom and his girlfriend take the car keys with them, or if they were in the house, would Freddie really know where they were hidden?

She felt herself dozing off once again when suddenly, she felt a presence next to her, like someone was looking at her.

Her eyes flicked open and it was Freddie, looking every bit as rested as any six-year-old boy without a care in the world.

"Hey mom," he said brightly.

"Hey there, my little man," she said, stroking his soft cheek with her hand. "How are you today?"

"I'm good," Freddie assured her. "I want to go down and see Jake again."

He started to climb out of bed, but then Barbara stopped him.

"Freddie, Jake and I wanted to know if you could help us?"

"Sure," he chirped, happy to be considered an asset.

"Do you know where daddy might have kept the keys to the cars in the garage? Does he hide them?"

"Yeah," he said easily. He bounded off of the bed, and said, "And I know exactly where they're at."

He nearly sprinted out of the room and Barbara tried to jump up to catch him, but she was stiff and sore, and wasn't moving as spryly as him.

She heard the sounds of footsteps bounding down the stairs and by the time she was out of the room, he was already on the ground floor and disappearing around a corner toward the kitchen.

Barbara finally caught up to him just as Jake was rounding the corner of the doorway.

In spite of what he had said, Jake looked worn out. His face drooped and his eyes were bloodshot. Even though they had talked about leaving at first light, she wondered if she could talk him into postponing their departure so he could get some sleep.

"Up there," Freddie pointed to a kitchen cabinet over the sink. "I hear them go chink-chink when they put them in there. It's their secret place."

Jake reached up and opened the cabinet doors.

"The blue one," Freddie instructed, pointing to a small decorative teapot.

Jake reached up and pulled down the ceramic pot, hearing the welcome sound of metal scraping around the inside of the bowl.

He brought down the bowl and they removed the cover. Sure enough, two sets of keys and fobs were in there; one for the Corvette and, more importantly, one for the Range Rover.

"Bingo," Jake said.

"I told you," Freddie said proudly, just as his mom leaned down and smothered his cheek with kisses.

Like any normal boy, he recoiled at her affections and pulled away.

"Yuck!" he said.

CHAPTER ONE HUNDRED-THIRTY-ONE

Los Baños, California
Saturday, 6:51 a.m.
+ 2 days, 3 hours, 50 minutes

Steve Hays parked his Ford F-250 pickup on the dirt road that bordered the northern-most boundary of his farm, switched off the diesel engine, and climbed out. He stood for a long time accessing the scene, a hot wind from the south fluttering the brim of his Stetson. Finally, he took a deep breath and ventured out into his rows of crops, the toe of his boot kicking up dry dust where moist soil should have been.

A tomato farmer for over thirty-two years he had seen his share of crop disasters: disease, recalls, infestations of Hornworms, but he had never dealt with anything like this.

With an average rainfall of only ten inches per year, Hays was like most of his fellow farmers in California's Central Valley who relied almost entirely on irrigation pumps to keep their crops healthy with copious amounts of H_2O.

As he walked between the rows of tomato plants, he began to see what several days of a lack of water had done. The leaves on the plants were starting to wilt, and already the tips of them were starting to yellow, tell-tale signs that his crops were dying.

He had recently ordered a new backup generator for his irrigation pumps but it hadn't arrived yet, and now, because of the blackout, it probably wouldn't. In the meantime, he had rolled the dice and run down the fuel in his existing gen-set to about an eighth of a tank. His calls to his fuel supplier had gone unanswered, and with what little fuel he had remaining, the generator could only keep his pumps on for about ten to fifteen minutes, barely enough to get the ground wet.

Like most farmers, both he and his wife drove diesel vehicles and Hays had briefly considered siphoning the fuel in their tanks to feed his generator. But then he realized that it would be too little-too late and that he might need the fuel to run for supplies, or just to make a run for it.

Somberly, he turned and walked back through the rows of the plants toward his truck. When he reached the dirt road he turned back and took a long, wistful look at his field; 460 acres of prime central valley farmland, enough fertile soil to produce over 22,000 tons of tomatoes annually. And now, after decades of toil and sweat, of working day and night toward an unsure future, that potential was evaporating in front of his eyes as quickly as the meager bits of moisture in his plants.

Finally, he turned his face upward toward the cloudless sky and did what tillers of the soil had done for millennium; Steve Hays prayed for rain.

California Tomato farmers produce an average of 49 tons of product harvested per acre. An amount equaling 11.5 million tons per year.

Source: https://www.nass.usda.gov/Statistics_by_State/ California/Publications/Specialty_and_Other_Releases/ Tomatoes/2019/201908ptom.pdf

CHAPTER ONE HUNDRED-THIRTY-TWO

152nd Air National Guard
Reno, Nevada
Saturday, 07:13 a.m.
+ 2 days, 4 hours, 38 minutes

Major Terrence (Skip) Duffy gazed at the peculiar looking load slung under the belly of his Sikorsky CH-54 Tarhe for the umpteenth time. The Tarhe was the military version of the twin-engine, six-bladed civilian heavy lift helicopters known as the Skycrane. Duffy had already performed his pre-flight external inspection of the ungainly looking aircraft and as usual, found no issues. His Crew Chief, First Sgt. Bob Kimmel, was one of the best he had ever worked with.

Still, a pilot's life, and that of his crew were riding on the integrity of your aircraft every time you lifted off - and you didn't take chances. The old pilot's adage - beaten into his head by his flight instructors, echoed with every new mission: *"Takeoffs are mandatory, landings are optional."*

"What do you think Skip?" Bob Kimmel asked, stepping up to him and gesturing to the strange apparatus strapped under the belly. "Odd looking duck, isn't it?"

Odd, indeed. The Beckwith Hi-Pot tester, used for testing high-voltage transformers, was the size of a small SUV and had any number of bizarre looking appendages protruding from it: corkscrew shaped cooling fins, angle-cut tubes that looked like they were pirated off of a church organ, and insulating discs stacked like plates.

"It sure is," Duffy agreed. "But I guess this monstrosity is pretty damn important right now with what's going on in California."

Kimmel slapped him playfully on the shoulder, and laughed.

"Yup. And that's why they picked you, boss; they needed the best."

The banter was no joke however. Although he was one of the younger pilots, Major Duffy graduated top in his class and had thousands of hours in the CH-54 flying in all kinds of weather and conditions. He had been alerted to the mission late last night, and was informed that it was of the utmost priority.

"Got our flight path filed," Lt. Keith Brands, Duffy's CSO (Combat Systems Officer) announced as he stepped up to the two men. "She's topped off and were ready to spin up."

"Let's go then," Duffy said as the two men climbed into the cockpit and began with instrument checks. Diligent as always, 1st Sgt. Timmons took several steps back and looked on to make sure there was no hiccups.

There were none, and a few minutes later, the big Pratt & Whitney turboshaft engines were at speed. Major Terrence Duffy gave a crisp salute and a thumbs up to Timmons, and then lifted up on the collective lever while simultaneously depressing the left pedal slightly to counteract the torque of the rotation.

The Tarhe was 'wheels up' and headed to Coyote, California by 07:22 PST.

CHAPTER ONE HUNDRED-THIRTY-THREE

Cerritos, California
Saturday, 7:20 a.m.
+ 2 days, 4 hours, 45 minutes

With the discovery of the keys, things moved very rapidly from that point on. Jake took both sets and after checking the fuel levels of each vehicle—the Vette was nearly full and the Range Rover had about a half a tank, he began siphoning from the vette into a gas can and then pouring it into the Range Rover. He had to work in shifts and although he had agreed to let Freddie, "help" him, he had to keep the youngster in control and out of harm's way.

In the meantime, Barbara got her mom and Olivia up.

Her mom, looked slightly worse and had hardly any energy. Olivia appeared better, but still with a look of emotional distress on her face. Besides her mom's dialysis, when they got to civilization, Barbara figured she would have to get her daughter into some sort of therapy.

Barbara wanted her mom to continue to rest while they got things ready to leave, but she was having nothing of it and insisted on helping out, albeit with diminished effectiveness. Together they loaded up all the bottled water, non-perishable food, some toiletries, and blankets into a couple of storage containers to be put into the Range Rover.

It was only when she told Olivia that they were going to be leaving the state that things got hairy.

"Mom, I can't leave my school and all my friends!" She protested.

"Honey, we have to," she said. "It's—"

"But mom!"

Barbara was about to respond, when her mom uncharacteristically spoke up, mustering what strength she had left.

"Olivia," she said firmly. "Mind your mom. There is no more school, or society, or pretty soon, food or water left in the state. We have to leave if we are going to survive."

Olivia stared at her grandmother for a few moments, then to her mom. Finally, with tears in her eyes, she nodded mutely and continued loading the boxes.

"We're all done," Jake announced as he stepped into the kitchen.

"Yep, all done," Freddie repeated.

"This is what we have," Barbara said, gesturing to the boxes. "Can you think of anything else?"

Jake looked inside and pushed a few items around.

"No," he said. "That looks good. We've got a full tank in the Range Rover and another two and half gallons in a can in the back. That should be plenty to get us to Nevada."

"And civilization," Barbara said.

Jake looked at her and nodded slowly, "Hopefully, he said.

They used the bathroom one last time and then loaded the boxes into the back of the Range Rover. The electric garage door opener wouldn't operate so Jake was going to have everyone loaded up and have the motor running before he had Barbara pull on the red emergency override handle so he could lift the door open manually.

"Wait a minute," Barbara suddenly said as they were getting into position. "I have to do one last thing."

Jake didn't say anything, but she could tell by his expression that he was anxious and impatient to get going.

She rushed back into the kitchen, found a pad of paper and a pen, and then wrote a letter to her ex-husband, apologizing for taking one of his vehicles and his food. She hoped he would understand.

CHAPTER ONE HUNDRED-THIRTY-FOUR

Near Carmen City, California
Saturday, 7:40 a.m.
+ 2 days, 5 hours, 5 minutes

Walter Gronsky waited until dawn before determining that no threat existed. It could have been a small animal that inadvertently set off the Claymore, or the wind blowing a low hanging branch into the wire, or an electrical short circuit that triggered the blasting cap. Or...was that what the enemy wanted him to think, luring him into an ambush as he went to investigate?

Either way, at some point he would have to investigate, determine the cause, and replace the detonated unit with a fresh one.

He slowly closed the gun port, hefted his rifle and other equipment and moved to the rear of the bunker to stow them.

As he walked, his body stiff from sitting so long, he looked longingly to his bunk; the blankets were askew and the pillow was still on the floor where it had fallen when the explosion woke him up, but it looked tempting all the same. What he wouldn't give for several uninterrupted hours of sleep.

But he had a mission to complete, and so after a quick breakfast of an MRE and some instant coffee, he was ready to get back to work.

Outside, the cool air felt refreshing on his skin and reinvigorated him somewhat, but for how long he didn't know.

After rechecking the area once more and not detecting any security threats, he consulted his map of the minefield and then began systematically inspecting each device.

He had only inspected three when he suddenly heard a sound in the bushes behind him. He spun around quickly, dropped down, and flicked off the safety on his assault rifle in one fluid motion. This time though, he didn't wait and watch and instead squeezed the trigger and let loose a barrage of bullets into the bushes.

On full auto-fire, the gun's 30 round magazine was empty in a matter of seconds and he pressed the eject button, dropping the clip to the ground. He inserted a fresh clip, rechambered the action and waited and listened.

There were no further sounds; no snapping of twigs, rustling of branches, or even the cries of a small animal, or a man.

But then, there was another sound, an unnatural sound, rhythmic and low, thumping.

He turned his head trying to locate its source. Then he realized it was behind and above him.

He turned back around and gazed toward the horizon. To his horror, he saw it; a helicopter about a mile off and coming right toward him. It was large and lumbering, a military helicopter of some sort. And worst of all, it was carrying a large piece of machinery underneath it.

He suddenly remembered Patriot Man's warnings. It was them; the government with their God-damned device! They were coming to take his guns!

"Shit!"

Instinctively, he raised his rifle to line up on the target, but then realized that the small caliber would probably be ineffective against it.

He dropped the rifle where he was, and sprinted back to his bunker. It was time to bring out the big guns.

CHAPTER ONE HUNDRED-THIRTY-FIVE

CAL-OES
Mather, California
Saturday, 7:43 a.m.
+ 2 days, 5 hours, 8 minutes

The morning meeting in the CAL-OES conference room began with an in-depth report of the HPT situation given by the DOE rep. By now, the utilities had been able to do a proper assessment of the damage from the truck bombs and were reporting in. Besides the HPTs, plenty of other equipment: switchgear, power lines, insulators, and so forth had been damaged as well. Luckily for the ancillary equipment, there were either spares on hand or if not, the components were easily available. Not so with the HPT's.

Even with the transformers from the STEP program, and the fact that two of the Metcalf units could be salvaged, the fact remained that less than five percent of the grid could be restored within several weeks, and even then, it would only be in isolated pockets.

"So, you're saying that essentially, ninety-five percent of California will be without power for a year?" Doyle asked directly.

"Yes, sir," the DOE rep replied. "That's the situation. I'm sorry, but I wish it wasn't."

Doyle sat silently staring out across the table, not seeing anything. Finally, he shook his head sadly and buried his face into his hands.

It was eerily quiet in the room. Some people glanced at one another, but most just kept to themselves. Secretly, everyone would have preferred Doyle's rants or heard him barking commands. To see him uncharacteristically shrinking in front of them, was tough to stomach. From the back of the room, a woman began to softly sob.

Shanice sat still, feeling helpless herself. Part of her wanted to cry as well, or to put her hand on Doyle's shoulder, but she had to remain strong and stoic, no matter what it took.

She imagined more bad news to come in the meeting. She had seen a few more empty chairs in the SOC, and had heard people lamenting how impossible their task was. Each day that passed meant people were getting hungrier, thirstier and more desperate. Equipment and supplies were in transit, but that all took time. Even then, communications were breaking down minute by minute and key stakeholders were often nowhere to be found when they needed them. The word "failure" was now being openly spoken.

Finally, Doyle steeled himself, took a deep breath, and pulled his hands away from his face.

"Alright," he said flatly. "Next item."

CHAPTER ONE HUNDRED-THIRTY-SIX

Lakewood, California
Saturday, 7:45 a.m.
+ 2 days, 5 hours, 10 minutes

Jake drove the Range Rover and, to avoid people as much as possible, took them through the side streets and alleys. He knew from years of living in the shadows, they would not be as well travelled.

He also, Barbara noted, avoided going past the gas station where all of the horrors occurred the previous day. Jake might not have thought that she noticed, but Barbara gave him an appreciative look just the same.

Still, they saw plenty of other signs of just how bad things had become; the occasional abandoned car, and in one case, a man's body lying in the gutter off in the distance A small group of crows were busy picking at it. Jake quickly turned onto another street that took them away from the scene. Neither Olivia or Freddie needed to witness that.

The detour took them to one of the major thorough fares and that's where they first smelled it, a foul odor like raw sewage.

"Ugh," Olivia exclaimed, covering her nose with her t-shirt. "What's that?!"

Freddie said. "It smells like a fart."

Barbara was about to admonish him, when Jake's hand went up, pointing; The street ahead of them was covered in a brown liquid that was spewing up from the manhole covers.

"The sewer system's overflowing," he said matter of factly. "The pumps that push it to the treatment plans must have stopped."

Barbara looked at him and nodded, acknowledging that the horrors he had painted for her the previous night, were coming to fruition.

Jake slowed the car enough so that the sewage wouldn't spray up onto them, but not so slow someone could catch the car and try to take it from them.

When they had gotten through the flood, he accelerated as fast as possible to get them to their next destination; Barbara's apartment.

Along the way, Jake had instructed Barbara that while he guarded the car and her mom and Freddie, she was to take the other pistol and her and Olivia were to go into the apartment and quickly load up with only a few important items: any legal documents such as birth certificates, passports, and bank statements, any and all prescriptions, any family photos, and finally, two changes of clothes and undergarments for each of them. Everything else was purely prosaic and could easily be replaced.

Jake backed the car into a spot for quicker escape and got out, the pistol at his side. Barbara and Olivia followed.

He handed the other pistol to Barbara and said, "Go, make it fast. Throw everything into pillow cases. If you're not down here in ten minutes, I'm guessing something is wrong and I'm going in."

"Got it."

CHAPTER ONE HUNDRED-THIRTY-SEVEN

Near Carmen City, California
Saturday, 7:46 a.m.
+ 2 days, 5 hours, 11 minutes

In his haste to get into the bunker to get a more powerful weapon, Walter missed the bottom rung of the ladder and twisted his ankle when his foot landed hard on the floor of the bus.

"Arrgh!" He screamed and instinctively gripped his ankle. But this was no time for self-pity or licking his wounds. If he didn't bring down that helicopter, then he was doomed, as was probably the revolution!

He grabbed his Barrett M107A1 sniper rifle off of the rack, chambered a .50 caliber armor piercing round in the breech and climbed back up the ladder as fast as he could. With each painful step, he could hear the thump-thump of the rotor blades getting closer and closer. Soon it would be right on top of him and he would be neutralized.

He exited the hatch and rolled onto the ground, extended the front bi-pod and bringing the rifle butt tight into his shoulder.

By now, the chopper and the gun detector device were only a couple hundred yards away and heading straight for him.

He lined up the reticle crosshairs of the sniper scope on the front windscreen and straight at the pilot's head. He had such a clear shot; he could even make out a satisfied grin on the little bastard's face. Then, Walter Gronsky squeezed the trigger.

CHAPTER ONE HUNDRED-THIRTY-EIGHT

Lakewood, California
Saturday, 7: 47 a.m.
+ 2 days, 5 hours, 12 minutes

Barbara and Olivia quickly headed into the apartment courtyard and towards the apartment. There was a swimming pool at ground level and they saw a man, who they did not recognize as a tenant of the building, scooping out pails of water. He was middle aged and dressed decently in a pair of jeans and a windbreaker, although he had the makings of several day's growth of beard by now.

The man stared at the two of them as they moved past the pool and up the stairs into the apartment.

Inside, the apartment, they went right to business.

"You take the bedrooms and get all the clothes," Barbara said. "And I'll get the documents, the pictures, and the pills."

"Okay mom," Olivia said and Barbara thought she detected a stronger tone in her daughter's voice; maybe she would bounce back faster than she thought?

They were done in about seven minutes and Barbara took the time to take one last quick look at the place they had called home for the past two years. It wasn't much, she admitted, but it was theirs and had some good memories in it.

Finally, they hoisted the pillow cases onto their shoulders and started out.

Barbara opened the door and stopped abruptly: the man from the pool was standing in the doorframe. He had a gun in his hand, and it was pointed right at them.

CHAPTER ONE HUNDRED-THIRTY-NINE

Near Carmen City, California
Saturday, 7:47 a.m.
+ 2 days, 5 hours, 12 minutes

He had the perfect shot, the perfect gun, and the perfect round. What Walter Gronsky didn't have was the safety switch of the rifle, set to the "fire" position.

He squeezed the trigger but instead of feeling the comforting mule-kick recoil of the big sniper rifle, all he felt was resistance.

"Shit!!"

He reached up and flicked the safety off and attempted to reacquire the target, but by now, it was passing straight overhead and heading away from him.

He spun around, took up another position on the ground and tried to line up again, albeit at the rear of the airship, thinking maybe he could put a round through the engine and bring it down anyway.

He was lined up and tracking it, looking for the prime target area on the big Sikorsky when it disappeared behind a tree.

"Bastards!" Walter said as he jumped to his feet and attempted to get into a new firing position.

It was a tremendous effort though as the gun weighed nearly thirty pounds and his sprained ankle was slowing him down, in effect his foot dragging behind him.

"I'll get you, you sons of bitches! I'll get you!" he screamed as he made his way through the bramble and toward the top of his hill.

He was almost there, and getting close to acquiring another shot, when his dragging foot suddenly caught on something, the momentum of his body carrying him forward, and tugging on it.

As designed, the force on the trip wire of the homemade Claymore—designated number "M-7," closed a set of contacts connected to the battery. The battery delivered its voltage to the blasting cap which instantly detonated, setting off the one and half pounds of high explosives.

At that point, it was all physics and there was no turning back; the blast wave sending a fusillade of steel balls at over 21,000 feet per second, directly at Walter Gronsky.

CHAPTER ONE HUNDRED-FORTY

Lakewood, California
Saturday, 7:50 a.m.
+ 2 days, 5 hours, 15 minutes

Even though she still had the gun Jake had given to her, Barbara had dropped it into the pillowcase and knew that she couldn't draw her weapon out in time to save them. It would be a shootout and she and Olivia would lose. So, she tried to accommodate the man standing in their doorframe.

"Wha...what do you want?" she asked, hearing tremor in her own voice.

"Food," the man said slowly, almost dreamily. "All I want is food, for me and my family."

She thought about it, they didn't have much left that was probably good, but what they had in the house, he could have; they had taken enough from her ex's house to get them out of state.

"Alright," she said slowly, trying to sound reassuring. "I understand. And you can have anything that's in here."

Then she nodded at the gun still pointed at them. "But you have to lower your gun and move out of the way, okay?"

The man stood there for a long time, not responding. His eyes were glazed and he looked delirious.

"Food," he finally repeated. "I have to get food for my family."

"Right," Barbara said slowly and clearly. "And you can have ours—all of it, but first you have to lower the gun so we can leave. Okay?"

The man sniffled and wiped his nose with the back of his hand.

"My child's sick...she's hungry," he rambled on.

"I understand," Barbara said, wondering if she was getting through to him, or if he was too far gone.

"That's terrible," she said soothingly. "And we want to help you. You can have all of our—"

Boom!

CHAPTER ONE HUNDRED-FORTY-ONE

Bradshaw, California
Saturday, 7:51 a.m.
+ 2 days, 5 hours, 16 minutes

Ben Klein estimated he had been in line now for well over two hours. Next to him was the Kinder-Morgan Bradshaw Terminal, a thirty-five-acre facility consisting of sixteen tanks for storage of fuel, as well as the three loading racks he needed to fill the twin 4,500-gallon tanks on his semi tanker truck. Ahead of him though was at least another quarter mile of trucks who all wanted the same thing. And with only three loading racks, the process was agonizingly slow and he had to pee.

Finally, the line moved and he slowly let out the clutch, allowing his truck to lurch forward and catch up to the one ahead of him.

Realizing his bladder couldn't take much more neglect, he put the truck into neutral and set the emergency brake. He reached over and grabbed the traveling urinal he kept in the glove box.

As he was relieving himself, he noticed a commotion up ahead. Several of the other tanker drivers were out of their trucks and talking with one of the security guards who patrolled the line.

After a few exchanges, the guard threw up his hands in a helpless gesture and the two drivers, stormed back to their rigs disgusted.

Then, Klein saw something he couldn't imagine happening. The rigs belonging to the other drivers, pulled out of line and disappeared down the street. Then, the other rigs behind them did the same.

Klein began to think that maybe the terminal was opening another loading rack or something, but then he saw a cardboard sign taped to the back of one of the tankers.

The sign read: *"Sorry. Last truck. Running out of fuel."*

CHAPTER ONE HUNDRED-FORTY-TWO

Lakewood, California
Saturday, 7:52 a.m.
+ 2days, 5 hours, 17 minutes

The man's head exploded in front of Barbara and Olivia as the sound of a gunshot echoed off the walls of the apartment courtyard.

The force of the shot caused his body to arch into them and fall through the open doorway. They jumped out of the way just as he fell facedown between them, the entrance wound at the back of his head gushing blood. Olivia started to scream just as Jake came running up the stairs with the pistol in his hand. He quickly stepped over the body and moved right past them into the living room.

"Any more?" he yelled.

"What?" Barbara said incredulously. She was starting to feel dizzy and nauseous. Olivia was on the verge of hysteria and was hyperventilating.

"Any more hostiles!" Jake screamed, sweeping the pistol around the room from side to side in large arcs. "Are there any more hostiles in here?"

"No!" Barbara screamed. "And did you have to shoot him for God's sake! He just wanted food. I was calming him down."

"He was a threat," Jake said firmly.

"A threat? A threat!" Barbara yelled. "He was a human being with a family that was hungry. His child was sick. We were going to just let him have what was left."

She lost it then, shaking her head angrily. "Do you have to be so...so...God-damned trigger-happy?!"

Jake turned to her slowly and stared at her, her words ringing in his ears.

It all flooded back to him then; Afghanistan...the boy...his chest exploding...trigger happy...all the killing...kill, kill KILL!

"Aargh!" Jake cried out in pain. He slumped over and began to sob uncontrollably, the gun dangling from his hand.

Barbara suddenly regretted everything she had said. She had no idea of the pain and suffering Jake had endured, the horrors he had seen.

She began to move toward him to try to repair the damage any way she could.

"It's okay Jake," she said soothingly. "It's okay. I didn't mean what I said."

"Yes, you did," he choked out. "And you're right; I'm not okay. I haven't been okay for a long time...and I never will be."

He rose back up and turned to face her and Olivia. Then he placed the barrel of the gun underneath his jaw.

CHAPTER ONE HUNDRED-FORTY-THREE

Stevenson Mortuary
Fortuna, California
Saturday, 7:53 a.m.
+ 2 days, 5 hours, 18 minutes

Keri Stevenson-Helms, tried once again to get the chemical mixture to flow into the corpse on the prep table in front of her. With no backup generator, and without electricity to power the pump, she was resorting to the old-school method of gravity feed to embalm the body.

"Nothing?" her husband, Ron, asked as he held the Maglite for her during the procedure.

"No," Keri sighed, massaging the cadaver in an attempt to get some sort of flow going. "I haven't done this since I tested and got my license, and that was over twenty years ago. And then..."

She let the statement die off, gesturing to the deceased on the table. He was an older man, obese, and had obviously enjoyed plenty of comfort food in his sixty-eight years. Besides causing the undo strain on his heart—which lead to his demise, a plaque producing diet also made it more difficult to get embalming fluid through the arterial network. And without a pump to force it through, this case was nearly impossible.

Keri shook her head in frustration. "Forget it," she said, and pulled off her latex gloves.

Her grandfather had started the business back in 1922 to serve the bourgeoning community of Fortuna, an agricultural and lumber town located on the Eel River in Humboldt County. When he died, her father took over, planning to maintain the family's legacy by passing it on to her brother when he passed away himself. That occurred only eight years ago, quicker than anyone had anticipated.

But her brother, who, like most reluctant scions, had been forced to work in the Stevenson Mortuary since he was twelve, wanted nothing more to do with the body business, and sold all his interest to Keri as soon as their father's estate was settled. Keri had been proudly serving the community ever since.

Now though, with no power to perform the needed tasks, she felt she was failing her customers.

She grabbed a headlamp off of the table, switched it on and said, "Let's look at the other cases again. Maybe we can figure something out."

She and Ron stepped out of the prep room and headed down one of the hallways in the twelve thousand square foot facility. On the way, they passed the retort room, where bodies were cremated. The big oven was silent now, its display panel dark. Even if they wanted to, they couldn't operate it without electricity also.

It was an eerie feeling walking through the empty, darkened halls with only headlamps or flashlights for illumination. Not because of the close proximity to the dead—she had grown up around that. Rather it seemed as if she and her husband Ron were somehow intruders, like thieves breaking and entering under the cover of darkness.

They stepped into the next room and to the large refrigerator designed to keep the bodies at a precise forty-one degrees—except it no longer was. Even with keeping the door closed, with three days of no power, the internal temp was already up to sixty-three degrees.

Keri checked the custody record hanging on the clipboard outside the reefer and consulted it again.

There were three more cases inside, each stacked on the heavy-duty shelves lining the interior walls of the reefer. One was already embalmed, so they didn't have to worry about her. But the other two had not been, and would soon begin to decay and putrefy.

Including the man on the table in the prep room, that meant they had three soon-to-be rotting corpses to deal with. Transport to another mortuary or morgue was out of the question as the whole state was out of power and everyone else was in the same boat.

In the dim light, Keri Helms looked up at her husband. He was realizing the same dire choice they had to make.

"In all my years in this business, I've never let anyone not have a decent burial or cremation," she said.

"I know," he nodded solemnly.

"And I'm not going to start now," she added defiantly.

An hour later, shovels in hand, they were out behind the Stevenson Mortuary on a small grassy knoll that bordered the property. They were doing what custodians of the deceased had been doing for centuries; they were digging the graves for the bodies.

California mortuaries are affected by power outages.

Source: https://www.ktvu.com/news/funeral-fallout-pge-power-outages-dont-just-affect-the-living

CHAPTER ONE HUNDRED-FORTY-FOUR

Lakewood, California
Saturday, 7:57 a.m.
+ 2 days, 5 hours, 22 minutes

"No!" Barbara screamed. "No, Jake. Please!"

"I'm not okay," he repeated. "And I never will be. I'm a killer. The government made me one. And I can't be fixed."

"Yes, yes you can be fixed. We can get you some help. We just have to get out of here so we can get you some help. Now put the gun down Jake. Please put the gun down."

"Put it down Jake," Olivia sobbed. "Please."

He stood there looking back and forth to each of them.

He closed his eyes and then covered the trigger with his finger.

"Stop." a soft voice called out from the landing. It was Freddie. They all turned to see him standing just outside their door.

"Go back to the car," Barbara ordered him. "Go back now Freddie!"

"Don't hurt yourself Jake," Freddie said. "You're my friend, and you're helping us."

Jake, still with the gun under his jaw, stared at Freddie, letting his words sink in. A child is so innocent, he thought. They say what they really feel. Could he really abandon him when he and his mom and family were so vulnerable? Jake had his demons for sure, but was silencing them for good the most important thing right now? Or was getting Barbara and her family out of here and to safety more important?

"Please," Freddie pleaded. "I don't want to see my friend get hurt."

Barbara noticed that Jake relaxed a bit. His muscles, which had been so taut, loosened, his shoulders slumped and the focus of his eyes changed. Freddie words seemed to really resonate with him, but she still she didn't want her son here, at this moment, possibly in harm's way.

"Thank you, Freddie," she said calmly. "Jake appreciates being your friend. But right now, I want you to go back to the car, please?"

"But a man's trying to take it," he said.

Suddenly, Jake pulled the gun down from his jaw and sprinted past all of them and down the stairs.

Grab the pillowcases, Barbara told Olivia, and was soon hot on Jake's heals.

By the time she got back to the car, Jake already had his gun on a man of about thirty years old who was trying to get into the car. Barbara's mom was still inside and was recoiling in fear.

"Move back right now," Jake ordered the man.

The man put his hands up and said, "I'm not armed, okay? I just wanted to see if I could get a ride from you."

"No." Barbara said firmly, from behind Jake. "We don't have any room. Now get the hell out of here now and you won't get hurt."

Olivia and Freddie arrived just then and stood next to their mom, watching the tense scene unfold. "All right," the man said, backing away slowly. "Just don't shoot, okay?"

"I...I don't want to, but I will if I have to," Jake said. Barbara thought he might have said it as much for her as for the man trying to take their car.

The man backed up a few more steps then turned and trotted away.

As soon as the man turned the corner, Jake said, "Everyone in, now!"

Even after the man disappeared, Jake kept his pistol raised and aimed toward the area in the off chance that he would try to double back and ambush them.

Barbara's mom popped the locks from the inside switch and Olivia and Freddie piled in, followed by Barbara.

Only when everyone was inside, did Jake lower his weapon and climb into the driver's seat. Then he saw that the keys were missing.

He quickly checked his pockets.

"Crap, the keys! Where are they?"

"Here you go," Freddie said, handing them over the rear seat to him. "I thought I should take them with me."

CHAPTER ONE HUNDRED-FORTY-FIVE

On the road to Nevada – 275 miles to go
Saturday, 9:41 a.m.
+ 2 days, 7 hours, 6 minutes

Thankfully, they made it to the on-ramp to the 91 freeway east—the first of two highways for their escape, without issue, and were on their way.

Still, they passed through a scene of desperation and destruction straight out of a war zone: abandoned and wrecked vehicles, windows broken out in restaurants, liquor stores, and drugstores, and a few more bodies lying still on the street. No place, or no one, it seemed, was immune. Off in the distance, smoke from an occasional fire could be seen rising in the sky.

Another enterprising person had set up a fueling business at one of the gas stations that they passed, but they were glad to be able to avoid it and the horrific memories it would bring back.

Inside the car, it was very quiet. No one was speaking or making any sounds except for Freddie who was occupied with his toy cars that he was driving all over the inside surfaces of the car.

Barbara's mom was looking even worse as time went on. She was very listless and her skin had taken on an ashen pallor. Barbara had gotten her to take a couple of her pills and while they wouldn't address her renal issue, she hoped to at least keep some of her other medical issues at bay.

After seeming to recover a bit, Olivia now seemed to have withdrawn once again. Barbara could hardly blame her as she had experienced and seen more horror and ugliness in the past twenty-four-hours than most people would in a lifetime.

And speaking of horrors, Barbara was worried about Jake as well. Would he have another meltdown and hurt himself, or even them? She wanted to try to talk to him about it to see if she could help, but it was not the time or place.

Instead, she merely placed her hand on top of his as he held the shift lever and drove, not in a romantic or sexual manner, but just to let him know that she was there and that she cared.

He was startled at first and flinched when she reached over, but he didn't try to rebuff her or remove her hand either. Instead, he let her keep it there as he drove wordlessly, eyes straight ahead on the road, and on the mission.

* * *

The traffic, which had been relatively light when they began, was now growing more congested with every mile they travelled. More vehicles appeared to be traveling the same direction; the one leading out of town and out of the state. The other side of the highway was a different story; there were convoys of military vehicles heading inbound as well as first responders and occasionally, a large semi-truck or tanker. All of the trucks had police or military escorts with them.

Barbara looked over to Jake with a worried look; would they be able to get through? He simply shrugged, like someone who had seen it all and didn't get too rattled.

At the town of Corona, they transitioned onto the 15 North, one of the major highways and part of the huge interstate system. It ran all the way from the Mexican–US border near San Diego all the way up to Alberta, Canada. On most weekends it was clogged with travelers hoping to have some luck at the blackjack tables or slot machines in Las Vegas.

Now though, Barbara imagined most of their fellow travelers headed to 'Sin City' were hoping for a different kind of luck; to escape California.

The towns of Rancho Cucamonga and Fontana seemed to meander past them agonizingly slow before the road started its long climb up through a gap between the San Gabriel Mountains to the west and the San Bernardino Mountains to the east. At the high point of the pass was the Cajon Pass, at 3,777 feet.

It was here they crested the pass to begin the long downhill into the towns of Victorville and Barstow and onto Las Vegas. It was also here that they had a commanding view of the Victor Valley below, and to the miles and miles of traffic heading out of state, a river of cars that stretched all the way to the horizon.

Barbara, and everyone's spirits, sank when they saw the traffic.

"Oh no," Barbara's mom said weakly.

CHAPTER ONE HUNDRED-FORTY-SIX

Simi Valley, California
Saturday, 10:38 a.m.
+ 2 days, 8 hours, 3 minutes

Crystal Timmons stood on the porch for long time before knock-ing.

In her entire life, she had never done anything like this before. In fact, she had never even *imagined* anything like this before.

But the water at their three-bedroom home had been out now for two days, and the situation was getting dire.

A single mom with two young daughters, they had already gone through the case of water she kept in the house for emergencies, and had drained and drank what little remained in the toilet tank. She had even attempted to drain the water heater to gain the thirty or so gallons stored in it, but she could not get the valve to turn. The stores had run out of water the first day of the blackout and she had no idea when or where any emergency supplies would be coming from.

Her children were so thirsty they were beginning to cry now and were probably on the verge of dehydration. Her own mouth was so parched she had to make a Herculean effort to swallow, which she did, before she steeled herself enough to knock on her neighbor's front door.

A few moments later, the door swung open and he was in front of her, his frame filling the doorway.

His name was Bill Batty and he was Crystal's neighbor from across the street. He was a big, beefy man with a ruddy face and dark leering eyes. They were eyes that she never liked as she always felt as if they were undressing her when he would see her going off to work or taking her kids to school. The same eyes that stared at her hungrily when she had brought a Bundt cake when his wife had lost her battle with ovarian cancer.

His wife deceased for only two days, he had looked her body

over hungrily and had to mention that, 'It was going to be getting lonely around here.' She always felt dirty being in his presence, but never as much as right now.

"Yeah?" he said brusquely. His accent was eastern, Boston or Philly.

"You have a swimming pool, right?" Crystal said matter of factly, noticing how her voice croaked from being either nerves or from being so parched.

"Yeah," he said. "And people around here know that too. That's why they been over here all day with buckets to fill."

Then he smirked.

"But they always bring something to trade, food or whatever."

He looked down to her empty hands briefly, then added, "But I see you didn't bring nothing."

"I don't have any food to spare," she said evenly, then added, "But, you know..."

A huge grin broke out on his face. "Yeah," he said, licking his lips. "I know. I was wondering what took you so long. Go get yer buckets or whatever. We can make a trade alright. Hee, hee."

She did her best not to show her disgust and kept her expression even as she turned and walked off the steps back to her house, feeling his eyes checking her out as she stepped.

It's for the kids, she kept telling herself as she crossed the street. *A parent has to do whatever they have to for their kids.*

She stepped back up onto the porch of her own house, opened the front door and headed into the kitchen to get some containers to put the water into.

Then she heard it; a loud hissing sound coming from somewhere in the house.

She traced the sound to the bathroom and saw that air was coming out of the faucet. She must have left the valve open at some point and now, air was rushing out as well as an occasional spray of water. The pipes were banging in the house and she could hear the same sound coming from the empty toilet tank behind her.

Then...water! Beautiful, life-giving water!

At first it was just a few slugs, then, it came out in a steady stream. The toilet tank began to refill as well and she called out to her children. They came bounding in and they each took turns cupping their hands and drinking what they could.

Crystal ran into the kitchen and got glasses for all of them. They filled them, and drank ravenously over and over until they couldn't any longer.

The toilet tank had refilled and she flushed it to get rid of the disgusting sight and smell of two days of human waste. Then, re-hydrated and somewhat sated, she looked longingly at the shower/bathtub. She hadn't bathed in two days and felt disgusting, wishing with all her being to climb in and take a nice long shower.

But she didn't know how long the water would be on, so she did what she had heard people do when preparing for an upcoming disaster; she closed the stopper, turned on the faucet and began to fill the tub as a reserve source.

While it was filling, she went back to the front door and locked it so 'lover-boy' Bill across the street wouldn't get curious as to what happened and do a follow-up.

Then, she did something totally out of character for herself. She flipped her middle finger in the direction of his house.

"To hell with you, you disgusting creep!" she said.

CHAPTER ONE HUNDRED-FORTY-SEVEN

Cajon Pass, California – 209 miles to Las Vegas
Saturday, 11:31 a.m.
+ 2 days, 8 hours, 56 minutes

With no other routes available to them, they had little choice but to soldier on through the greatest traffic jam any of them had ever seen. The travel was stop and go in the beginning, but as more cars joined the herd by merging off of the interconnecting highways and roads, it slowed to a crawl, and then finally, to a stop. They were barely north of Victorville, still 140 miles just to get to the state line, and to what they had hoped would be their salvation. They were hopelessly stuck.

"Do you think it will clear up?" Barbara asked Jake, fearing the answer he would give.

"Hard to say," he said, trying to sound hopeful. "It could be an accident, or it could be this way all the way to Vegas. We won't know until we get past Barstow."

"That looks like that might be a very long time," Barbara said.

"Maybe," Jake said in a strange tone, then looked out the window to the desert that surrounded them. "This thing has four-wheel drive, doesn't it?" He asked Barbara.

She shrugged her shoulders and was about to say, 'she didn't know' when Freddie chimed in.

"Yeah, it's those buttons there," he said pointing to a cluster of controls that were on the center console. They were marked with symbols that were completely foreign to Jake. He had driven many vehicles in his life, including military ones such as Humvees and APCs, but he had never seen anything as advanced as this. It was a whole new ball game.

"Do you know how to activate it, Freddie?" Jake asked hopefully.

"No, I don't," Freddie answered sadly, embarrassed that he couldn't help.

"Maybe it's in the owner's manual," Barbara offered.

"Yeah," Freddie said excitedly, pointing to the passenger's side glove box.

"It's in there."

Barbara popped the door open, and there it was. She pulled it out and started to read through it.

CHAPTER ONE HUNDRED-FORTY-EIGHT

CAL-OES
Mather, California
Saturday, 12:17 p.m.
+ 2 days, 9 hours, 42 minutes

The large TV monitors in the SOC were still running continuously, which was both a good and a bad thing.

On the one hand, the feeds that came in from some of the networks still with boots on the ground was rapidly becoming their best source of real time intel. But the flip side was that it served to constantly reinforce to those working in the room just how desperate the situation had become. Some of the team members of CAL-OES had since refrained from even looking at it.

Shanice had not however, and stood at the back of the room, watching in silence. A few others were around her watching as well, but she really didn't notice them. Up on the screen was the horror of the attack playing out in real time. Besides scenes of full-scale looting of grocery and convenience stores, many of the big box stores that they had planned on using as main distribution hubs were being overrun. A few law enforcement and national guardsmen tried to control the panicked crowds, but they were overwhelmed. Reports were coming in of shots being fired at several of the stores, by-whom and at-whom was anyone's guess.

In one long shot taken at a Sam's Club in Concord, California, a man's motionless body lay on the ground just a few feet from the entrance.

Shanice shook her head and looked away, fighting back tears. Already her stomach was aching from the stress, even though she had been sure to maintain her food intake. The woman standing beside her cried out, "Oh my God," and began sobbing uncontrollably.

Shanice reached over and tried to put a comforting arm around the woman's shoulders to comfort her, but the woman just pulled away and rushed off.

When Shanice looked back up to the news feed, it had switched to a shot of the outbound highways as people attempted to leave. The traffic was gridlocked and went on all the way to the horizon. Several cars must have stalled or broken down and were sitting idly on the side of the roads. A few motorcycles and even a couple of bicycles moved along the shoulder, but other than that, it was if the cars were stuck in concrete.

The camera zoomed in on a tight shot of a man and woman, standing on the side of the road trying to flag down a ride. The women held a baby in her arms as the man desperately waved his wallet and a couple bottles of water in the direction of the grid locked cars. No one opened a door to offer them a ride.

A plan had been floated this morning by the CHP to use the "Contra-Flow" method to alleviate some of the outbound traffic. The plan involved cutting down the in-bound side of the highway to only one lane and allowing some of the outbound vehicles to use it to get out of state. It was a model successfully implemented by southern states during large scale evacuations ahead of hurricanes, but was not currently a plan that California had developed. Still, Doyle readily approved the idea and the CHP was attempting to create a plan and implement it as fast as possible. But it would all take time and manpower, luxuries they all knew they were running out of.

Even if the plan did help to alleviate the congestion and get people out of state faster, the bordering states of Nevada, Arizona and Oregon were already reporting that they were overwhelmed with refugees, and could not handle any more. Oregon had even floated the idea of closing the border with California.

'Refugees,' Shanice thought sadly; that's what the people she was tasked with protecting now were considered.

Contra-Flow Lane Reversal History
Source: https://en.wikipedia.org/wiki/Contraflow_lane_reversal
"Contra flow has been implemented as a component of hurricane evacuation planning in certain southern and southeastern states, but is not a common feature of many disaster evacuation plans because of the need for a long lead time prior to the evacuation event during which the contra flow can be established."
Source: https://ops.fhwa.dot.gov/publications/evac_primer_nn/primer.pdf

CHAPTER ONE HUNDRED-FORTY-NINE

Barstow, California – 156 miles to Las Vegas
Saturday, 12:20 p.m.
+ 2 days, 9 hours, 45 minutes

It took her a while, but Barbara eventually found the proper section in the owner's manual. After activating the manual AWD system, they made their way over to the shoulder of the road and took off into the dirt. After a short distance, they found a paved road that they took north to its terminus before turning back onto dirt and gravel.

It was bumpy at times, but they were making fair progress by skirting the freeway and Jake seemed to enjoy himself like it was old times. Freddie definitely enjoyed the sudden off-road adventure, but Barbara wasn't sure of her mom, who was looking worse every minute.

They drove past the local landmark, Bell Mountain, and then picked up Barstow Road, which would take them directly into Barstow. From there, they would cross over the 15 to see what the traffic situation was like on it.

If some of the towns they had passed on the way seemed disheveled, Barstow was even worse and looked like it had been through the ringer. With less amenities than the major population centers, it had suffered mightily with the crisis.

The town looked abandoned. All of the storefront windows were shattered with evidence that widespread looting had occurred. Cars were abandoned, And occasionally. a body could be seen lying on the ground.

At the junction for Barstow Road and the 15 Freeway, they slowed to a stop and peered out over the overpass; the 15 Freeway North was still jammed as far as the eye could see.

"Oh my God," Barbara exclaimed, "It'll take days to get there at this rate."

Jake sighed his agreement with her, then said, "We'll just have to keep off-roading. And I think I know which way to go."

"Yeah!" Freddie squealed.

CHAPTER ONE HUNDRED-FIFTY

CDCR-LAC
Lancaster, California
Saturday, 1:03 p.m.
+ 2 days, 10 hours, 28 minutes

Captain Hugh James of the California Department of Corrections and Rehabilitation was rapidly losing what little respect he had for his fellow correctional officers at the three-thousand inmate state prison. Plenty of them he knew, played the game and burned their sick time, and COs, as they were known, had one of the highest rates of AWOL for essential workers in a disaster, but this was getting ridiculous—and scary.

The first shift immediately following the attack and the outage, had seen a reduction of twenty eight percent of personnel calling in or not showing up to work. By the third shift, on day two, the AWOLs had risen to forty-five percent. Now, three days into the disaster, and on the fifth shift since the attack, they were down close to only thirty percent of their normal manpower—essentially a skeleton crew to guard some of the most dangerous criminals in the California system.

The outage and precipitous reduction in manpower had forced those who were still manning their posts, to go into emergency 'modified program' mode. Instead of being able to leave their cells for meals, bathe in the community shower, or go outside to the yard for exercise, the inmates in each of the housing units were locked into their cells indefinitely—and they were not happy about it.

Inside the large common area, which was surrounded by two levels of about a sixty cells total, the din of yelling and banging by the trapped inmates was deafening. A prison was a loud place in general with all of the surfaces either being made of concrete or steel, but Captain James had never heard it so raucous in all of his twenty-one years in the institution. It was giving him a splitting headache.

On top of the forced detention, the kitchen, which was on limited power from the facilities generators, was slow in getting the meals prepared and delivered. Several of the trustee inmates worked in the kitchen and Captain James knew they were performing as best they could, but with the impact of the power outage plus the fact they had only thirty percent of their normal staffing and the fact that each meal had to be cell served (slid through a locked opening in the steel door) to the confined inmates, meant that they were running way behind schedule.

He heard a garbled sound emanate from the PA system just then. He knew that it came from the CO manning the observation tower inside the common area, but the cacophony of sound made it nearly impossible to make out what was being said.

Captain James turned toward the angled windows that faced outward from the observation tower and saw the CO mouthing the words, "food."

He nodded and headed toward the small tunnel under the tower toward the door to the outside yard to meet the kitchen staff with another meal delivery.

He reached it at the same time the CO above him activated the switch to unlock the door. The mechanism activated with a loud bang. A few seconds later, it was pushed open and two of the kitchen staff wheeled their stainless-steel carts through with the trays of food.

Captain James had known them for about two and seven years respectively and had a good relationship with the short timer. The one with the longer sentence, who was deemed LWOP, or Life Without Parole, he was not too sure of. When men had nothing left to lose, they—

One of the carts slammed into him violently, hitting him in the gut and knocking the wind out of him. It bent him over at the waist onto the cart. In the tunnel below the observation tower, he wasn't visible and he knew with all the noise, the CO above him wouldn't know what was happening, or hear him call out.

The captain's training kicked in, and he reached for the large container of pepper spray mounted on his belt. But before he could retrieve it, a 'shiv,' or prison fashioned knife plunged into his neck, severing his carotid artery.

Still fighting to regain control, he felt the knife plunge repeatedly into his arms, his chest, and his eyes, until he could fight no more and fell face first onto the floor to bleed out and die.

The last thing he felt was one of the inmate's hands removing the ring of keys from his belt.

Five minutes later, the two men had breached the observation room, killed the CO, and activated the switch that opened all the cell doors.

Correctional Officers have one of the highest rates of AWOL during a manmade or natural disaster.
Source: https://journals.lww.com/joem/Abstract/2010/10000/
Factors_Associated_With_the_Ability_and.8.aspx

CHAPTER ONE HUNDRED-FIFTY-ONE

Near Fort Irwin, California – 157 miles to Las Vegas
Saturday, 1:23 p.m.
+ 2 days, 10 hours, 48 minutes

Jake continued heading north past the 15 overpass, through the town of Irwin Estates and with a couple of turns here and there, soon had them on Irwin Road.

"Where are we going?" Barbara asked.

"Toward Fort Irwin, the big military base. I used to be stationed there."

"Can we get in then?" Barbara asked hopefully. "Can we get my mom some help there?"

"Unfortunately, no," Jake said. "This is a major terrorist attack and they won't let anyone in. They are locked down and on high alert."

"But my mom—," Barbara protested.

"No," Jake answered firmly. "They have their mission and their orders. That's the military way. Civilians, well, I'm sorry."

"So then why are we heading there if they won't help us?"

"We're not going all the way. There are some off-road trails outside of the base that some of the guys I was stationed with used to ride on. It might be bumpy and slow going, but as long as we stay on those roads, we can get closer to the Nevada border than if we stayed on the highway."

He turned and looked toward Barbara. "It's really our best shot."

* * *

With no traffic heading toward the base, the travel was fast. Along the way they saw numerous signs posted that announced that they were on a 'Tortoise Desert Wildlife Management Area' and that visitors were forbidden to approach the endangered creatures. Jake took the opportunity to explain how they had to walk on eggshells around the lumbering creatures, avoiding them, cancelling live fire exercises, etc.

"It really pissed off a lot of the soldiers," he said.

After about a half hour, Jake turned off the main road and onto a dirt one that he seemed familiar with.

"This is as close as I want to get to the base," he said. "There will be patrols and they won't want us getting too close."

"Will this road get us all the way to Nevada?" Barbara asked.

"I'm not sure," Jake said. "We may have to take other roads as well."

They had only gone a short distance, when they hit a bump that caused the Range Rover to get slightly airborne.

"Woo-hoo!" Freddie exclaimed.

Barbara turned to check on her mom and Olivia in the backseat to see how they were managing with the rough ride.

Olivia was still quiet and withdrawn, but Barbara knew it wasn't the driving that was getting to her; it was the combination of the trauma she had seen and endured, and their exodus from the only home she had known. Like all of them, her world had been turned upside down and the thin veneer of civil society had been quickly stripped away, revealing the ugly base levels of human existence and survival. Nobody should have to experience this, Barbara thought, especially a young person.

More worrisome was her mom's condition, which had continued to degrade; her body was limply being thrown around with the roughness of the road, and she barely attempted to steady herself. She was lethargic and appeared to not even know what was going on.

Jake noticed the look of distress on Barbara's face. "Sorry," he said. "I can slow down if you want for your mom, I know it's tough going."

Barbara thought about it for a bit. "That's okay," she said. "The sooner we can get there, the better."

After another half-hour or so, Jake did slow down due to the roughness of the roads that continued to worsen with each passing mile. Then, the road stopped altogether.

"There was another side road we passed back there," Jake said. "I'll have to backtrack some."

"Are you sure were going in the right direction," Barbara asked.

Jake held his watch up to sun and checked the orientation of the hour hand to the sun's position, putting the sun directly between the time and noon on the face of his watch.

"Yeah," he said. "That way is south." He pointed toward the rear right side of the car. "We're heading northeast, like we should be."

"You can tell all of that from looking at your watch?" Barbara said in amaZemint.

Jake nodded. "Old military trick, and one of the first things they teach you in nav school."

"Cool!" Freddie said from the back seat. "I want to do it. Can you teach me Jake?"

"Sure. But can you tell time?"

"Kind of," Freddie admitted sheepishly, although in the age of smart phones and digital displays, telling time on an analog watch was rapidly becoming a lost art.

"Okay. When we have a chance, I'll show you," Jake said and then spun the Range Rover around and headed back to the side road.

A short time later though, that road dead-ended as well and they were forced to backtrack once again.

It was the same for two other roads and before long, they had lost a lot of the distance they had initially gained.

Jake stopped the Range Rover, put the shift lever into park and got out.

"I've got to think," he said to no one in particular. "...and to pee."

"Me too," Freddie chimed and burst out of the back door.

"Freddie!" Barbara yelled, fearing he would get into some sort of mischief.

"Let me check for snakes first," Jake said, holding up his hand to stop him. "I'll tell you where its safe, alright?"

Freddie stopped in his tracks, but then added, "Alright. But if you find a snake, I want to see it."

Jake did a quick assessment of the area and then came back to Freddie and pointed to a bush.

"Over there," he said.

By now, Freddie was already starting to jump up and down and hold his privates. He really had to pee and raced over to the bush.

"I have too also," Olivia said and slid out of the back seat.

Barbara had been holding it for some time herself and so she got out. But before she took care of herself, she checked on her mom.

"Mom," she said gently but firmly. "We stopped to go pee, let me get you out."

She looked at her daughter with vacant eyes. It was like she didn't see her.

Freddie had finished and was coming back to the car, pulling up his pants. Jake gestured to Olivia where it was safe to go, and then turned away to give her some privacy.

He called out to Barbara, "Get your mom first, and then you," he said.

"Don't you have to go?"

"I can wait. Just get her fixed up."

Barbara nodded and then said, "Freddie, get back in the car."

"But I want to – "

"In the car Freddie," Jake said more firmly. "Do you want to be a good soldier and learn things like telling direction with a watch?"

"Yeah."

"Well, the first thing a soldier has to do is follow orders."

With the glory of military adventure awaiting him, Freddie acquiesced and climbed back into the Range Rover.

"By now, Olivia had finished and then Barbara pretty much dragged her mom out of the car and led her over to the bush.

It was an effort, but she was finally able to get her mom to urinate a bit. Barbara got her back into the car, and then was finally able to go herself.

Jake went last and when he turned back to head to the car, Barbara was there waiting for him, about halfway between the car and the bush.

"What are you thinking?" she asked in a low voice so that her children and mom couldn't hear.

"I don't know," Jake said. "Without the satellite navigation system working in the Range Rover, I can't tell which roads will keep going and get us there, and which ones will peter out on us."

Barbara didn't say anything, she knew he was trying and she really didn't have anything of value to add.

Jake turned toward the west. "If we were on base though," he said, thinking out loud. "I know the roads there like the back of my hand, and I know I could get us there."

"But you said that they wouldn't let us on, right?"

Jake nodded. "Not as civilians, or in a civilian car."

Still staring toward the base, his eyes narrowed, and he bit on his lower lip. Barbara could tell he was in deep thought and didn't say anything.

"I think I know a way," he said, before turning toward her and smiling.

CHAPTER ONE HUNDRED-FIFTY-TWO

East Bay Fertility Clinic
Berkeley, California
Saturday, 2:30 p.m.
+ 2 days, 11 hours, 55 minutes

The controlled rate freezers were the first to fail.

The units, about the size of a household washing machine, are used to 'freeze down,' or slowly bring down the temperature of specimens to -196 °C without allowing damaging ice crystals to form. Afterwards, the specimens could be transferred to the main cryo-tanks for long term storage.

In essence, the machines were super freezers that operated like any other cooling system; using compressors, evaporators, and condensers. But they all ran on electricity, and there was none to be found.

East Bay Fertility had four controlled rate freezers. One for human eggs, one for sperm, and two for blastocyst, or embryos that have been created in a laboratory. In a matter of hours after the power went off, the units had warmed up and the specimens were lost: twenty-six eggs, thirty-one vials of sperm, and eleven blastocyst that had recently been created.

They were gone, and co-owner and founder of East Bay, Samantha Euclid knew that there was no bringing them back. Now, as she walked through the row upon row of stainless steel cryo-tanks in the darkened storage area at the 5,000 square foot facility, she wondered if they would lose these specimens as well.

Although the cryo-tanks were essentially large insulated thermoses that held liquid nitrogen to keep the various specimens preserved indefinitely, they utilized monitoring systems that kept tabs on tank level and temperature. So sophisticated were the systems, they could automatically re-order liquid nitrogen from their bulk supplier on an as-needed basis. Like everything else though, the monitors relied on electricity, and the displays had gone dark.

Samantha's wife, Mary came up to her then, a headlamp on her head of short cropped red hair. She flipped the beam up so as not to blind her partner.

"How many are low?" Samantha asked, fearing the answer.

Since the monitoring systems were kaput, the two women were forced to rely on the old-fashioned method of visual checks to see if they needed to top off the liquid nitrogen in the tanks. Besides being more labor intensive than automatic level indication, it had the deleterious effect of also allowing the precious liquid nitrogen to 'boil off' when the cover was removed, further exacerbating a bad situation.

"Five at last count," Mary announced sadly. "One of the blastocyst tanks, I'm afraid, is already below the second rack."

"Meaning they're gone already," Samantha said, and Mary nodded.

What she didn't ask her wife was whether or not the blastocyst tank was the one that contained the embryos, two girls and one boy, that they had created and stored for their own future use. When you were responsible for the hopes and dreams of so many people, it would be selfish to think of yourself first.

"And nothing from the supplier about when they can get out here to top off the tanks?" Mary asked.

"Nope. I keep calling and calling, but the phone just rings." Samantha said darkly. "Either the hospitals are the priority, or they've just bailed out."

Feeling her wife's distress, Mary reached out and put her arm around Samantha's waist, pulling her close.

Samantha smiled at the comforting gesture, but said nothing. She slowly gazed out at the rows of gleaming tanks, all running low and with no solution in sight. When they all finally failed—and they would without the addition of more liquid nitrogen, it would mean the collective destruction of over five-hundred sperm, egg, and embryo. And with them, the last resort for so many childless couples.

Samantha Euclid understood that in any large disaster, whether man-made or disaster, there was always the potential for a loss of life. She just never imagined that it would be 'potential' lives that would be lost.

Tank failures in cryo-storage facilities
Source: https://www.wired.com/story/what-keeps-egg-freezing-operations-from-failing/

CHAPTER ONE HUNDRED-FIFTY-THREE

Fort Irwin, California – 143 miles to Las Vegas
Saturday, 3:02 p.m.
+ 2 days, 12 hours, 27 minutes

Jake drew a simple map on a piece of scrap paper they found in the Range Rover.

"If I'm not back in 2 hours, follow this map and get back on the fifteen," he said, handing the map to Barbara. "It'll be your only hope at that point."

She nodded, staring at him and wondering if she would ever see him again. Then gave him a long hug. She knew he was trying, and for all his issues, that he was a good person inside.

He broke off after a few moments, hoisted his rucksack, and then took off, marching toward Fort Irwin.

The going was tough and along the way, he passed numerous Mojave Rattlesnakes and Sidewinders, as well as several endangered desert tortoises.

When he got close enough to the barbed wired fence that was the physical boundary of the base, he picked up one of the tortoises and carried it under his arm.

He cut through the fence easily with a multi-purpose tool he carried in his backpack and slid through it, bringing the tortoise with him.

From this point on, he was on a secure government facility and so he crouched down and kept a low profile as he made his way to one of the roads that hugged the perimeter of the base.

When he got close enough to the road, he checked for traffic in both directions and then, seeing none, bolted out to the middle of the dirt road. He turned the tortoise upside down, setting it on the top of its shell and preventing it from lumbering off.

"Sorry buddy," he said. "I need you to help me out."

Then he disappeared back into the low brush, assumed the prone position and waited.

He was rewarded for his efforts when about twenty minutes later, when he saw a cloud of dust roiling up in the distance. And before long, he spotted the front grill of a Humvee emerge from the cloud. He crossed his fingers.

CHAPTER ONE HUNDRED-FIFTY-FOUR

Fort Irwin, California
Saturday, 4:20 p.m.
+ 2 days, 13 hours, 45 minutes

PFC Scroggins and Lance Corporal Pená had been assigned to patrol the eastern most perimeter of the Fort.

They had done patrol duty plenty of times before, but this was different. The state of California had been attacked by terrorist and by extension, the United States which they were sworn to protect. They, like all of the base personnel, were on heightened alert and the Secretary of Defense had raised the threat level of the nation to DEFCON 2, the second highest level. DEFCON 1 was reserved for nuclear war.

Two M-4 carbines were held down by webbing straps on the storage box behind them as the men scanned the terrain around them. The weapons had full clips with a round chambered, and each soldier carried a full complement of additional ammo.

Pená, who was driving, saw it first.

"Shit," he said.

Instinctively, Scroggins moved to grab his weapon. Pená stopped him.

"Nah", he said. "It's just a fucking tortoise."

"Well run over the fucker," Scroggins said. "I always hated how those bastards fucked us up."

"No, not gonna do it," Pená said. "We'll do the right thing."

"What?" Scroggins cried incredulously. "We're at DEFCON 2! We don't still have to do that shit, do we!"

The military in general, and Fort Irwin specifically, endeavored to maintain goodwill with environmentalists and the public by working to protect endangered species. To that end, the two men would have to stop, secure the area, and report the sighting up the chain of command who would bring in a reptile specialist to safely relocate the animal, lest it become injured.

"They didn't say not to," Pená sighed. "And a good soldier always follows his last order."

"Crap," Scroggins said. "You're just bucking for more rank. You big suck!"

"Fuck you," Pena laughed, then added as he climbed out. "And I've got to take a leak anyway."

"Get the tape," he called out as he stepped away from the Humvee.

CHAPTER ONE HUNDRED-FIFTY-FIVE

Fort Irwin, California
Saturday, 4:33 p.m.
+ 2 days, 13 hours, 58 minutes

Jake watched from his concealment as the Humvee stopped about seventy-five-feet away from the tortoise. Two soldiers emerged, a lance corporal and a private. One pulled down his trousers and peed on the road a few feet from the Hummer. The other emerged with rolls of yellow caution tape to set up a cordon around the tortoise. Luckily for Jake, they didn't dismount the vehicle with their weapons.

He waited until they were far enough away from vehicle and setting up the tape before he pulled out his gun and made his move

"Hands up," he said when he was close to the Hum-Vee.

The two men jumped at the sound, not expecting to hear another voice out here in the middle of nowhere. They were even more shocked to see it was a civilian with a gun pointed at them.

"Corporal," Jake said to Pená, "Get on ground." To Scroggins, he said, "Private, strip off your shirt—and make it fast, or I shoot your friend here, before I shoot you."

PFC Scroggins took off the camouflaged shirt quickly, then Jake ordered him to toss it over to him.

"Your boots, and your cover too," Jake said, using the military jargon for a hat.

Scroggins did as he was told, tossed them over, and then asked, "You military?"

Jake didn't answer and simply said, "Switch places now, and do the same."

The two GIs did as they were told, and when Jake had everything he needed, said, "Now flip that poor tortoise back onto its feet."

Pená leaned down and flipped the tortoise upright and it waddled away. Thankfully, it didn't evacuate its bladder, which was a good thing.

He grabbed the clothes and climbed into the Humvee. Inside, he grabbed their weapons and, with practiced efficiency honed by years of field stripping the same weapon while blindfolded, removed the bolts from each weapon, rendering them useless.

He started the big vehicle and drove past them on the road, tossing out some water bottles that were in the vehicle as he went past.

Then, a hundred feet or so further, their weapons, minus the bolts.

Jake then did the math in his head; unless they are spotted by another vehicle and got a ride, it would take them at least an hour to walk back to headquarters. Most importantly, he knew they wouldn't be in a big ass hurry to get there and tell their superiors that they had just had their Humvee jacked—on a military base of all places. He knew that they'd get their asses reamed, and maybe lose a rank, but they'd survive.

Hopefully by then, he and Barbara and her family would be across the state line.

CHAPTER ONE HUNDRED-FIFTY-SIX

Outside Fort Irwin, California – 143 miles to Las Vegas
Saturday, 5:17 p.m.
+ 2 days, 14 hours, 42 minutes

When Barbara and her children saw the Humvee pull up to the Range Rover, they thought that they had been detected and that the Army wanted to know what they were up to, but then Jake jumped out of the vehicle dressed in one of the soldier's camo shirts and hat.

"Get the stuff and get in," he said, opening the rear hatch and the tailgate.

"Wow!" Freddie exclaimed when he saw the Hum-Vee. "Cool!"

Olivia and Jake started transferring the boxes into the back while Barbara helped her mom.

"I don't dare to ask were you got this," Barbara said wryly, as she moved her mom slowly to the vehicle.

"I turned in all my aluminum cans," he joked, then noted that Barbara's mom seemed barely able to walk at this point. Even with his humor, he realized that their situation was no joke; they had to get across the state line and to a functioning hospital or dialysis clinic soon.

With the boxes loaded and everyone settling in, Jake was in the process of closing the rear of the vehicle when Freddie stopped him.

Hold on he said and stepped up on the bumper and reached in. He fished around in his backpack and produced a toy Humvee which he proudly showed off to Jake.

"Cool, huh?"

"Yeah, cool," Jake agreed. "But we gotta go, so hop in. You sit on the box in the middle, got it?"

"Yea!"

A few moments later they were off and headed back up the road.

Jake turned to Barbara. "Here, he said, handing her the remaining camo shirt and hat.

"Put these on and tuck your hair up under your cover."

"My what?" she asked, as she started pulling on the shirt.

"Sorry, your hat; I'm back to talking military."

She did as she was told and pretty soon, they looked like another couple of soldiers out on patrol, albeit with some civilian passengers on board. Jake knew that would set off alarm bells, especially during a lockdown on the base.

"If I tell you to, you guys have to duck down in the back okay," Jake told them. "If anyone spots civilians in this thing, they'll be very suspicious."

"Yes sir," Freddie said saluting. Olivia simply muttered a weak, *"okay."* Barbara's mom said nothing.

They reached the perimeter fence and Jake barreled through the hole he had punched in it just a few minutes earlier. They were now officially on a secured and locked-down US military base, in a stolen vehicle, driven by a dishonorably-discharged soldier. It didn't get much worse than that.

CHAPTER ONE HUNDRED-FIFTY-SEVEN

Fort Irwin, California – 97 miles to Las Vegas
Saturday, 6:03 p.m.
+ 2 days, 15 hours, 28 minutes

They moved quickly as Jake was well acquainted with the roads from his time here and before long, had traveled from one maneuver road to the next and were pushing the Humvee to the limits of its governor at fifty miles an hour.

"Will this road take us all the way to Nevada," Barbara asked.

"No. At some point, we'll leave the eastern perimeter of the base and be back on public land. But I know the roads there. We used to go off-roading on the weekends sometime."

"Once," he laughed, recalling a fond memory. "We had a contest between a couple of the guys on a Friday night. One group drove to Vegas the conventional route on Interstate 15. The other group—the one that I was in, drove on these roads to see who could get there first."

"And who won?" Barbara asked.

Jake turned to her and smiled. "We did," he said proudly, and then turned back around.

"Oh crap!" he said.

In the distance, they could see another Hum-Vee approaching them on the road.

"Get down, and stay down!" he motioned to those in the back.

Freddie ducked down and Olivia pulled Barbara's mom down, before ducking herself.

"What should I do?" Barbara asked.

"Don't do anything but look bored and pissed off, like a million other grunts. In fact, lean back like you're sleeping."

Barbara followed his directions and tried to slouch down in the seat as Jake had instructed. The seat was incredibly uncomfortable, and she couldn't imagine anyone being able to sleep in it. But she also knew that one of the first things a soldier learned to do was to sleep anywhere, anytime.

She kept her eyes open behind her sunglasses and watched as the vehicle approached. Thankfully, it didn't seem to slow down or indicate that it was going to block them. As it went by them, Jake flipped them off and they returned the gesture. Barbara was stunned at the display, but figured it was, "a guy thing."

When it was far enough behind them and didn't stop or turn around, Jake gave the all clear and everyone sat back up in the back.

"That was close," he said, glad they hadn't been alerted by the other soldiers.

Barbara let out a big breath of air, not even aware she had been holding it in. "How much further until we reach the edge of the base?" she asked.

Jake looked around and made an assessment based on the landmarks he saw. It was already starting to get dark.

"We should be there in about twenty minutes," he said, "Hopefully, we won't see any more patrols."

"Yes, hopefully," Barbara agreed. They had struggled and come so far; she didn't want to think about failure at this point.

CHAPTER ONE HUNDRED-FIFTY-EIGHT

CAL-OES
Mather, California
Saturday, 6:11 p.m.
+ 2 days, 15 hours, 36 minutes

"Damn it!"

The curse came from the logistic table in the SOC. Ben Thomas, a seasoned and talented ten-year veteran and one of the members assigned to generator fuel supply, threw down his headset in anger.

"We have no comms!" he bellowed, standing up from his workstation. "This is impossible!"

Shanice was in the SOC having a sidebar with one of the DOE reps and heard the outburst as well.

Ben Thomas's immediate supervisor, Stephanie Holmes, also in the room, heard the ruckus and moved quickly to try to calm her employee down.

They had a short discussion and she must have instructed Ben to take a break and cool down, because he stepped away and out of the room.

Shanice turned to the DOE rep and said, "Excuse me," before stepping away herself and walking over to the logistics supervisor. When she was close enough, she motioned with her head for Stephanie to follow her into one of the many breakout rooms that ringed the SOC. She didn't want a discussion about an employee's behavior to be in public.

When they were inside and had closed the door, Shanice took a deep breath and asked, "What happened back there?"

Stephanie shook her head sadly. Shanice noticed the dark circles under her eyes. Many of the women working the crisis had since given up applying makeup to enhance their appearance.

"It's...it's getting very tough," she stammered with a choked voice that sounded as if it were on the verge of breaking down completely. "Working cell towers are all but non-existent, we don't have enough sat phones distributed, and even some of our HAM operators have gone silent."

"She looked up pitifully to Shanice. "And without communication…"

The logistics supervisor let the statement die off. Shanice knew what she was saying. Without good communication, no organization - law enforcement, first responders, medical staff, or even the military, couldn't function effectively. You were essentially, 'flying blind.'

"I know," Shanice said. "And believe me, I understand. I know how tough it is for everyone."

Then, the CAL-OES director sighed and added wearily, "Can you try to put together a list of the communications gaps Stephanie? So, we can see exactly what we're dealing with."

The logistics head nodded mutely, and looked up at her boss with a pitiful look, not verbalizing the obvious question; *What good was knowing the gaps, if you had no way to fill them?*

CHAPTER ONE HUNDRED-FIFTY-NINE

Fort Irwin, California – 66 miles to Las Vegas
Saturday, 6:48 p.m.
+ 2 days, 16 hours, 13 minutes

As Jake had promised, they reached the eastern perimeter a short time later, and after having everyone brace themselves, he sped up and punched another hole in the chain linked fence to get out of the base, much to the delight of Freddie.

A short distance later, they crossed Death Valley Road, north of Baker, California. It was totally dark now and they could start to see the glow of the lights from the towns of Primm and Las Vegas in the distance. They were only forty-five miles to the state line.

A deep sense of emotion swept through the vehicle; they had not seen light in so many days. It was finally civilization.

The closer they got, the more they were drawn to the light.

"Is there a dialysis clinic in Primm?" Jake asked Barbara.

"I don't know," she said. "We never had a need to check on it."

"Does anyone's phone work?" Jake called out. "We might have service here."

It had been so long that any of them had used a phone that they hadn't even switched them on. Wisely though, they had kept them charged up on the drive in the Range Rover.

Barbara and Olivia each switched on their phones. As Barbara was waiting for hers to boot up, she told Olivia to turn on her mom's phone as well. Even though they all had the same carrier, they were different models of phones and maybe one would get through before the other.

"A long minute later Olivia announced, "I've got bars! Oh my God!"

"What about internet?" Jake asked.

"Trying," Olivia said. Then, "Got it."

"Google dialysis clinics in Primm, Nevada honey," Barbara said.

With the speed of a young person's texting skills, Olivia soon had the search entered.

"Only Vegas it looks like," she said sadly.

"What about hospitals?" Barbara asked.

Olivia typed in the new search and it returned the same results. "No, they're all in Vegas."

Barbara slumped in her seat, knowing that it might mean another hour or more of travel.

Jake thought more about it, reaching back into his memory for any other option.

"Wait a minute," he said. "There's another town, outside of Primm, north of it. Sandy... something - Sandy Valley. It's real small, a retirement community. Only a couple thousand people and not too far."

"And they have a dialysis clinic?" Barbara asked incredulously.

"No," Jake said. "But they have an airport. And more importantly, airplanes."

CHAPTER ONE HUNDRED-SIXTY

CAL-OES
Mather, California
Saturday, 7:00 p.m.
+ 2 days, 16 hours, 25 minutes

Shanice tried to call her husband every evening at the same time, 7:00 pm, to check in, but also to be soothed by the sound of his voice. It was the one 'perk' or luxury she indulged herself in.

On this call however, she took her husband by complete surprise as soon as the call thankfully went through.

"What is it like?" she asked simply,

There was a long pause, confusion.

"What? What do you mean 'what is it like?'" her husband asked when he could regain his composure. "What is *what* like?"

"Being there, out in the world," Shanice explained. "We're here in a cocoon, a bubble really, and are only getting sporadic reports. I want to know what it's like from your perspective, being out there 'in the battlefield' so to speak. What does life *feel* like to you now?"

"Feel like? Well, basic survival, I guess. I'm using those supplies you insisted we stock up on, so I have plenty of water and food for now. And I haven't answered the door when neighbors came knocking asking for me to share. But really, it's incredibly boring. And I feel...you know, useless not being able to work and function like normal. I guess it's like being a prisoner."

"A prisoner," Shanice repeated slowly.

Then, to herself, she thought, *Yes; Prisoners. Forty-million prisoners.*

CHAPTER ONE HUNDRED-SIXTY-ONE

Sandy Valley, Nevada – 40 airmiles to Las Vegas
Saturday, 7:21 p.m.
+ 2 days, 16 hours, 46 minutes

Jake and company pulled into the airport and saw a Cessna 172 bathed in the headlights of a pickup truck parked nearby. A middle-aged man and woman were standing next to the truck.

As they had driven to the town, they had contacted the Sky Ranch Estates Airport and explained their desperate situation.

One of the local pilots had offered to fly them straight to McCarran Airport in Las Vegas and from there an ambulance could take them to one of the dialysis clinics located in the city.

"My wife has kidney issues herself," the pilot had explained to them in his folksy Texas drawl. "And I know how bad it can be. I'd be happy to be your 'mercy mission.'"

When they pulled up in the Humvee and Jake and Barbara emerged half dressed in fatigues, the pilot and his wife couldn't help but do a double take.

There was no time to explain though and so Barbara and Jake started to get her mom out of the Humvee and towards the plane as quickly as possible.

The pilot then asked, "Who's all going? I only got room for four."

"They're all together," Jake explained, pointing to Barbara, her mom, Olivia and Freddie, who had just popped out of the back of the Humvee. "They need to stay together. I'll stay behind."

"Are you sure?" Barbara asked Jake as the pilot started doing a quick calculation of the weight, bearing in mind the maximum load of the plane.

"Yes," Jake said adamantly. "You all need to stay together. I'll catch up to you later."

"Should be fine," the pilot drawled. "I didn't fuel her all the way up since this is a little jaunt."

"The little fella there," he said, pointing to Freddie. "Will have to sit between you two in the back seat. Gonna be tight though. We better hurry though, as the missus here doesn't look too well."

He hustled them all over to the plane and got them loaded up; Olivia, Freddie and Barbara in the back, then Barbara's mom in the copilot seat.

The pilot started the plane, went through his pre-flights checks and then gave a thumbs up to his wife and Jake who were standing back by the vehicles.

In just a few moments, the plane sped down the runway and soon was airborne. It banked to the northeast and all but disappeared into the night sky. The only trace of it was the green and red marker lights on the wings that blinked rhythmically.

As soon as it was gone, Jake moved to the back of the Humvee, opened the rear door and started transferring the boxes containing all of the Barbara's family's worldly possessions into the back of the couple's pickup truck.

"What are you doing," the pilot's wife asked in her own southern accent.

Jake didn't respond and continued transferring boxes. When the last one was loaded, he turned to her and said, "Please hold on to these for when they return; it's all they have."

"Why, sure."

"And tell them...tell them that I wish them luck and...and thanks for everything. Tell them they saved my life."

The woman was stunned and confused by the statement. But was even more surprised when Jake Sullivan, dishonorably discharged soldier and homeless vet, turned away, climbed into the Humvee and drove away, heading straight back into the darkness of California.

PART V:
THE RECKONING

CHAPTER ONE HUNDRED-SIXTY-TWO

CAL-OES
Mather, California
Sunday, 12:36 a.m.
+ 2 days, 22 hours, 1 minute

Although exhausted: physically, mentally, but mostly emotionally, Shanice Dixon never-the-less struggled like never before trying to get to sleep. It was as if her husband's statement was stubbornly echoing around in her head, refusing to leave.

...prisoner...prisoner...prisoner...

Finally, though, she drifted off, only to be awakened by a dream. Her nana was in it again. She appeared trapped and unable to escape from a situation that had befallen her. And again, she was trying desperately to tell her granddaughter something.

Shanice bolted awake, feeling compelled to try to make sense of the vision and her nana's message. She went to her nana's bible to tell her. She grabbed the book and it mysteriously fell open to Philippians 2:3.

"Let nothing be done through strife or vainglory; but in lowliness of mind let each esteem other better than themselves."

She read the psalm three times, then quickly got dressed and headed out to the floor of the SOC. All of the team members; logistics, planning, comms looked as exhausted as she was. They were still doing their jobs, for her, but mostly for the people of California. But for how long was the question. How long before they cracked?

She wondered about herself. Would she have a meltdown as well? But mostly she asked herself if she was really *doing her job*? Was she really serving the people of California and doing what was best for them?

Without hesitation, she approached the night shift head of logistics, Molly Jo Realy. Stephanie Holmes, the day shift supervisor had gone off to try to catch some sleep.

"Ms. Dixon," Realy exclaimed when she saw her. "What are you doing up? You should be sleeping."

"I couldn't sleep," Shanice explained, then switched gears. "Tell me Molly; who's your best number cruncher and analyst?"

"Morales," Realy answered without hesitation.

"Is he on now? I honestly can't keep the schedules straight," Shanice admitted.

"Yes, he is. Shall I get him?"

"Yes, please," Shanice Dixon said. "I have a favor to ask him."

CHAPTER ONE HUNDRED-SIXTY-THREE

CAL-OES
Mather, California
Sunday, 5:47 a.m.
+ 3 days, 3 hours, 12 minutes

The meeting took place in the main conference room. Besides Shanice, the logistics supervisor, Molly Jo Realy, her top analyst, Joe Morales, and Mark Barker from communications were in attendance and seated around the long conference table. The latter having dual degrees in both sociology and psychology.

Also seated in the room at the head of the table was Doyle, who despite having his own private suite and bathroom, still looked haggard. Just as most presidents visibly age over their term in office, Doyle had seemed to do the equivalent in just the past four days.

"Governor," Shanice began slowly. "First of all, we are doing our absolute best here and everyone is giving one hundred and ten percent."

Ever the savvy politician, Doyle's eyes narrowed slightly.

"Agreed", he said warily. "But that's not what you called me in here for, correct?"

"Correct," Shanice said. "I wanted to explain the ugly truth of what we are doing here."

"The 'ugly truth?'" Doyle repeated suspiciously.

"Yes," Shanice said. "Despite our best efforts, we are only at about fifteen percent of achieving our goal of getting back-up generators and keeping them fueled to maintain our water supply and sanitation—and we are quickly falling behind. Our communications have all but broken down, and we have a growing number of breakdowns, AWOLs, etc."

Doyle didn't respond but kept his eyes glued on Shanice. She took a deep breath and then continued.

"On top of that—or actually, because of it, our supply chains for food are lagging way behind. The stores are in shambles with no security to speak of, the refrigeration units are shuttered at distribution centers, and even if we could get fuel into enough trucks, we don't have enough drivers. The scale is just so vast."

"So, we need more fuel and generators is what you're saying?" Doyle offered.

"No sir," Shanice jumped in. "What we're saying is this; Even if—and it's a *huge IF*, we could get all of our distribution going again, then what?"

"What do you mean?" Doyle asked, genuinely perplexed. "We've done our job, haven't we; achieved our goal?"

"What I mean sir, is that all people are going to have, is food and water. Their children can't go to school and they can't go to work— and we won't be able to give them that. And they need that."

Sensing that she was quickly losing Doyle, Shanice gestured to Barker. "This is Mark Barker sir. He's from comms and he has dual degrees in sociology and physiology. Mr. Barker..."

Mark Barker cleared his throat and sat up a bit straighter. "Sir, people—humans, have an innate need to feel useful, and productive. It's a human condition of needing a sense of self-worth. They need the socialization they get from working, and that their children get from going to school. And if they don't have it, they flounder and it can lead to all sorts of issues."

Unmoved, Doyle argued right back. "Well, what about Covid?" He challenged. "We got through that and most people had to stay home."

"Correct sir, but at least they could work from home, and their children did on-line learning. And yes, we..." Barker made air quotes with his hands. "Got through it. But there were still numerous problems that came out of the Covid response and lockdowns—some of which still are with us today; domestic abuse, depression, a rise in suicides, drug overdoses—and that was with people being able to still feel somewhat productive and useful."

"And now they don't even have that, sir," Shanice added. "And we'll never be able to give them that until the electricity gets turned back on in a year, or even longer."

She turned to Morales. "This is Joe Morales from logistics sir. He's done some calculations of what it would take to try to get power into people's homes and businesses—*just to try,* to achieve some level of normalcy for them to work and so forth. Morales..."

"There are seven million single family homes in California governor," Morales recited. "And the average home would require a five-thousand-watt generator just to keep the lights and some of the appliances on. And that's not even including air conditioning units when the weather heats up."

Morales paused and took a deep breath before continuing. "Sir, there are not seven million generators in the entire world. It's more than have ever been produced."

"And that's just the homes," Molly Jo chimed in. "Single family homes, not including apartments."

"Correct," Morales agreed. "Even more difficult would be to try to get business and commerce on its feet again. California has over four million small businesses, each of which would probably require a ten-to-fifty-kilowatt generator minimum. It would be a hodgepodge of all sizes of generators. And even if there were that many in the world—which again; there are not, they would all have to be installed, tested, etc. Which would take an army of engineers and electricians not days, not months, but years to accomplish."

"And let's not even talk about trying to keep upwards of ten million generators fueled," Shanice added. "We can't even handle what we have on our plates now."

Doyle looked at each of them, ending his gaze on Shanice. He crossed his arms defiantly. "We're moving in the right direction," he said flatly.

"But it's a spit in the ocean sir," Shanice pleaded. "And people need more. Our country needs more. What are people going to do, just sit in their houses with their meager food and water and twiddle their thumbs for a year and a half?"

"Damn it! We're doing the best we can!" Doyle yelled. "People have to understand that!"

"I'm sorry sir, but it's not enough!" Shanice fired back, hearing her own voice rise, while still trying to remain respectful. "And it never will be!"

"What are you saying then?" Doyle snapped. He looked from person to person, pathetic expression to pathetic expression. "What is your solution to this problem? What are you all trying to tell me I should do?"

Shanice took a deep breath.

"Sir, we can't move the mountain to Mohamed, but we can move Mohamed to the mountain. Move him, them, forty million people to the mountain. We have to evacuate the state and relocate people."

"Evacuate!" Doyle screamed. "Is that what you're telling me I should do? To cut and run, to throw in the towel like some whipped puppy!"

He pounded his fist on the table so hard it made them all jump.

"I don't give up. I never have, and I *never* will!"

"We have to do it sir!" Shanice yelled, now nearly as loudly as him.

Governor Hunter Doyle III stood suddenly, so forcefully, his chair fell over behind him. He didn't bother to pick it up. His face was red, his eyes burning. He turned and headed for the door.

"No, we don't!" he muttered angrily with every step. "There has to be another way!"

"There is no other way!" Shanice yelled after him. "We are drowning sir, and we are dragging the people of California right down with us!"

Doyle wasn't having any of it. He grabbed the door knob, turned it and swung the door open so hard, it hit the wall with a loud bang.

Before he stepped through, he turned and looked back, glaring straight at Shanice, his eyes boring into her. He stabbed an accusatory finger directly at her.

"Maybe I made a mistake appointing you," he said matter of factly.

To the others he simply said, "Stay the course. I'm your governor and that's a God damned order!"

And then he was gone, the door left wide open behind him.

CHAPTER ONE HUNDRED-SIXTY-FOUR

CAL-OES
Mather, California
Sunday, 7:35 a.m.
+ 3 days, 5 hours, 0 minutes

The governor's aide had summoned Shanice to his private suite. Doyle had postponed the regular 7:00 am meeting until further notice.

She walked slowly up the staircase like a condemned person to the gallows, but with her head held high. Like any organization, word had already spread rapidly throughout the CAL-OES campus about the disastrous meeting with Doyle and especially what he had said to their leader, Shanice. With every step she took, Shanice Dixon felt the eyes and the pity of everyone in the room on her.

She didn't want their sympathy though, she just wanted to do her job. To do what was best for the state of California, and not for her own misplaced ego. The illusion about being able to magically save the day against impossible odds had cleared, and she had had a harsh reckoning with the reality of the situation. She had only wished that Doyle could see it himself.

The aide opened the door to the governor's suite, and Shanice walked a few steps into the room and stood there. Thankfully, no one else was present. Doyle's back was to her, his hands gripping a credenza. The aide departed, and quietly closed the door behind her.

After a few moments of tense silence, Shanice cleared her voice.

"I'll resign whenever you'd like me to governor," she said. "I have my letter of resignation already drafted on my computer. I'll give a complete turnover to whomever you appoint to replace me. Maybe they'll be a better fit than I was."

Doyle still didn't say anything, but his head began to shake.

Finally, he said, "You're not resigning."

Oh no, Shanice thought darkly. *He wasn't even going to let her resign; He was going to plunge the knife all the way in and fire her.*

"Sir I—," she started to say.

Doyle turned then, his eyes were moist and she wondered if it was the lack of sleep, or if he had been crying.

"You're not resigning because I need you, those people out there need you," he said, gesturing to the control center. Then he gestured more broadly. "But most of all; forty million residents of California need you. They need you to get them safely out of this state, so they can start their new lives."

"Oh, sir…" Shanice started to say, and felt her throat begin to tighten.

"I was wrong," Doyle said. "I was being stubborn and pigheaded. And well, prideful," he said, gesturing to a book he had opened on the credenza. It was a Bible.

Shanice looked from Doyle, to the Bible, and back to Doyle again.

"I…I didn't know you read the Bible sir," Shanice said.

"Not surprising," he said wryly. "Who in their right mind would accuse me of being pious with the foul mouth I have?"

"Roman Catholic by the way," he then added. "Not a big surprise, huh?"

"No sir," Shanice smiled. "Southern Baptist myself."

Then she pointed to the Doyle's Bible. "That's where I got my answer as well sir. Which verse for you?"

"Proverbs 11:2," Doyle said, then recited; *"Then pride cometh, then cometh shame: but with the lowly is wisdom."*

"Philippians 2:3," Shanice countered. *"Let nothing be done through strife or vainglory; but in lowliness of mind let each esteem other better than themselves."*

Doyle smiled. "You've got me beat."

Then he walked toward her and placed his hands gently on her shoulders.

"We will recover," he said. "The state will recover and eventually people will move back, and business will return. And when they do, they'll still be wildfires, and mudslides, and the occasional earthquake, and maybe—*hopefully,* not another pandemic."

They both shared a dark bit of laughter.

"And when they do return," he continued, "We're all going to need someone to manage them all, and that someone, is you Ms. Dixon."

Shanice Dixon stood for a long time looking into the eyes of the governor of the most populous state in the US. She might have even seen some tears in them, or maybe they were her own.

Finally, she started to break away and said simply, "Thank you Governor Doyle. I have to get to work now. And I won't let you, or anyone else in the state down."

"I know you won't," he said confidently.

PART VI:
EXODUS

For the next three and half months, the state of California, along with assistance from the federal government, other states, and private enterprise, began the Herculean task of evacuating and relocating the remaining population of the state. It was known as the CRP, or the California Relocation Plan.

Travel, charter, and school buses were brought in from all over the country and both commercial and military planes were rerouted to the states twenty-four commercial airports, which had been put back on line. General aviation airports, of which there were over two hundred, were also utilized as available. Amtrak increased scheduling of routes out of the state.

Communication about the evacuation utilized AM, FM and shortwave radio and PA systems broadcasting in each neighborhood. The airdropping of leaflets with instructions in fourteen different languages was also used, as well as skywriting.

Each evacuee was allowed two suitcases per person and pets were forbidden to travel with them. Because of this, the ASPCA began its own massive evacuation and relocation efforts for pets utilizing thousands of volunteers from around the country, although not every animal could be located or saved.

Based on familial relations or friends, evacuees were transported to hub cities and then put on other buses, trains, or aircraft to get them to their new locations. Every evacuee was given two bottles of water, and a box lunch. Adults and heads of households were also given a credit card with $1000 preloaded onto it.

Knowing that there would be those who would resist going along with the CRP, the state, led by Doyle, issued an ultimatum to the laggards;

"Either evacuate when you have the chance, or face the consequences. The door will close at some point, and the state will no longer work to keep the water running or the stores stocked with food. Take it or leave it."

In the end, over thirty million residents were evacuated from the Golden State, making it not only the largest evacuation in US history, but in the history of the world.

At least 3.5 million people from four states—Florida, Georgia, South Carolina, and North Carolina—were evacuated during Hurricane Floyd. At the time, it was the largest evacuation in U.S. history.

Source: https://www.scseagrant.org/floyd-follies-what-weve-learned/

Nearly 14 million people were evacuated because of massive flooding and landslides in north and central China in 1998.

Source: https://en.wikipedia.org/wiki/List_of_mass_evacuations

EPILOGUE

Eventually, Barbara Williams and her family relocated to Snyderville, Utah, just outside of Salt Lake City, and moved in with her sister's family. Barbara's mom—now recovered and back on her regular dialysis treatments, was thrilled; she was now able to see *both* of her daughters, as well as her newborn granddaughter on a regular basis.

Olivia was not happy with the move at first, but once she started back to school and made new friends, it was like she had never had a previous life in California. Freddie thought it was a great new adventure, but he also missed Jake.

It was cramped in the three-bedroom home for a few weeks, but then Barbara was able to find a new job as the assistant manager of the Salt Lake City Walmart and before long, they were moving out into a place of their own not far from her sister's. Her mom stayed on living with the sister and was busy playing babysitter to not only Freddie, but to her infant granddaughter as well.

After a several year hiatus, Barbara began dating again. She had a new and promising relationship with one of the sales reps she had met at Walmart.

After disappearing into the desert several months previously, Jake Sullivan was never heard from again.

It took some fancy lawyering and a vigorous charm offensive, but Alan Binder would only be given a suspended sentence and ordered to do community service for his actions in the air piracy of a private jet. After the story broke about his daring rescue of Marianne and risking his own life to save her, he was quickly deemed a hero in the court of public opinion. His rating on the IMDB 'star meter' rocketed to the top, and movie offers soon began pouring in.

After receiving an operation to repair her ruptured spleen and undergoing an extensive rehab, Marianne Corelli made a full recovery and was currently working as an assistant producer to Alan

Binder on "Rescue in the Darkness," a film he was producing, directing, and starring in. The film chronicled the dramatic story of Alan as he fearlessly and unselfishly worked to save Marianne's life in the midst of California's greatest disaster. Marianne wrote the script.

The remains of Walter Gronsky were consumed by various animals and insects and would not be found for decades. No one would bother trying to make a positive ID.

Discovering that she was pregnant, Shanice Dixon, took an indefinite leave of absence from her job at CAL-OES and relocated out of state, moving to Memphis, Tennessee to be close to her husband's mom. Her husband continued to work at his job as a CPA, while Shanice devoured and analyzed everything she could find on pregnancy, childbirth, and the rearing of children.

An ultrasound fifteen weeks in the pregnancy revealed that the couple was going to have twin girls. Shanice vowed that she would never test them against each other.

The Chinese party leaders watched with glee as the evacuation of California took place. They knew that the Americans were soft and could not endure hardships, even if it served the greater good. The cowardly imperialists did as they always did when they could no longer endure a tough situation; they would cut and run, just as they had done in Vietnam and Afghanistan.

The Chinese leadership also understood that the People's Republic would suffer economically in short term from the disruption of their biggest trading partner. But, as soon as the evacuees had resettled into their new locations, they would start craving all of the consumer goods and creature comforts they had left behind in California. And China would be there to resell them the same products all over again. It would be like a whole new market opening up.

The biggest prize of all however, would be all of the real estate that would soon become available. With no one paying the mortgages on homes, businesses, and prime land, the properties would quickly go into default. The United States, already crushed under the weight of the disaster, would have no choice but to allow the banks to sell it off at fire sale prices.

And ready to purchase it and gain a foothold on the west coast, would be the People's Republic. It was like taking an enemy's land without firing a shot.

To be continued ...

ABOUT THE AUTHOR

Christopher J. Lynch is a former California native and the author of numerous articles as well as the ONE EYED JACK novel series about a professional blackmailer. The debut novel in the series was a 2013 Shamus Award finalist and a 2014 Writer's Digest honorable mention for genre fiction. He also authored EDDIE: THE LIFE AND TIMES OF AMERICA'S PREEMINENT BAD BOY, the biography of Ken Osmond, the actor who played Eddie Haskell on the TV show, LEAVE IT TO BEAVER. The book is one of the highest rated celebrity biographies on Amazon.

Christopher enjoys helping other authors, and has given numerous free Self-Publishing Seminars, as well as taught creative writing classes at a maximum-security prison north of Los Angeles.

Besides writing, Christopher is a lover of adventure whether on bike or foot. He's ridden his bike in Alaska as well as across Cuba. He's also climbed Mount Kilimanjaro in Africa, Mount Whitney in California, and trekked to Everest Base Camp in Nepal. Not one to always keep his feet in the ground, he's flown an aerobatic biplane, as well as experienced weightlessness aboard the Zero-G plane, aka: the "Vomit Comet."

He considers his greatest accomplishment the training and leading a group of blind hikers to the summit of Mount Baldy, the third highest peak in Southern California and the highest in Los Angeles County. A documentary film of the epic journey is soon to be released. You can view of a trailer of it here: https://www.youtube.com/watch?v=5Qk3PtrRhZc

He lives with his wife, Charlotte, in Tennessee.

For more information, visit:
www.christopherjlynch.com

Made in the USA
Middletown, DE
11 February 2023

24566367R00262